Praise for Humphrey

The World According to Humphrey

'[A] charming, feel-good tale.' *Irish Times*

'A breezy, well-crafted first novel. Humphrey's matter-of-fact, table-level view of the world is alternately silly and profound and Birney captures his unique blend of innocence and earnestness from the start.' *Publisher's Weekly*

Friendship According to Humphrey

'An effective exploration of the joys and pains of making and keeping friends, which will strike a chord with many children.' *Daily Telegraph*

Trouble According to Humphrey

'Children fall for Humphrey, and you can't beat him for feelgood life lessons.' *Sunday Times*

Humphrey's Big-Big-Big Book of Stories

Betty G. Birney worked at Disneyland for many years, has written several children's television shows and is the author of over twenty-five books, including the bestselling *The World According to Humphrey*, which won the Richard and Judy Children's Book Club, *Friendship According to Humphrey*, *Trouble According to Humphrey*, *Surprises According to Humphrey* and *More Adventures According to Humphrey*. Her work has won many awards, including an Emmy and three Humanitas Prizes. She lives in America with her husband.

By the same author

The World According to Humphrey
Friendship According to Humphrey
Adventure According to Humphrey
(special publication for World Book Day 2008)
Trouble According to Humphrey
Surprises According to Humphrey
More Adventures According to Humphrey

The Princess and the Peabodys

Humphrey's Big-Big-Big Book of Stories

Betty G. Birney

faber and faber

This omnibus first published by
Faber and Faber Limited in 2009
Bloomsbury House, 74–77 Great Russell Street,
London, WC1B 3DA

Typeset by Faber and Faber
Printed in England by CPI Bookmarque,
Croydon, CR0 4TD

A CIP record for this book
is available from the British Library

ISBN 978–0–571–24131–6

2 4 6 8 10 9 7 5 3 1

Contents

The World According to Humphrey

To my husband, Frank,
who has been to Brazil, knows all the U.S. state capitals and can balance a broom on one finger.

Contents

1

The Return of Mrs Brisbane

Today was the worst day of my life. Ms Mac left Room 26 of Longfellow School. For good. And that's bad.

Even worse, Mrs Brisbane came back. Until today, I didn't even know there was a Mrs Brisbane. Lucky me. Now I want to know: what was Ms Mac thinking? She must have known that soon she'd be leaving without me. And that Mrs Brisbane would come back to Room 26 and I'd be stuck with her.

I still like – okay, *love* – Ms Mac more than any human or hamster on earth, but what was she thinking? 'You can learn a lot about yourself by taking care of another species,' she told me on the way home the day she got me. 'You'll teach those kids a thing or two.'

That's what she was thinking. I don't think she was thinking very clearly.

I'm never going to squeak to her again. Of course, I'll probably never see her again because she's GONE-GONE-GONE – but if she comes back, I'm not even going to look at her. (I know that last sentence doesn't make sense. It's hard to make sense when your heart is broken.)

On the other hand, until Ms Mac arrived, I was going nowhere down at Pet-O-Rama. My days were spent sitting around, looking at a load of furry things in cages just like mine. We were treated all right: regular meals, clean cages, music piped in all day.

Over the music, Carl, the shop assistant, would answer the phone: 'Open nine to nine, seven days a week. Corner of Fifth and Alder, next to the Dairy Maid.'

Back then, I feared I'd never see Fifth and Alder, much less the Dairy Maid. Sometimes I'd see human eyes and noses (not always as clean as they should be) poking up against the glass. Nothing ever came of it. The children were excited to see me, but the parents usually had other ideas.

'Oh, come and see the fishes, Cornelia. So colourful and so much easier to take care of than a hamster,' Mama might say. Or 'No, no, Norbert. They have the cutest little puppies over here. After all, a dog is a boy's best friend.'

So there we were: hamsters, gerbils, mice and

guinea pigs – not nearly as popular as the fish, cats or dogs. I suspected that I'd be spinning my wheel at Pet-O-Rama for ever.

But once Ms Mac carried me out of the door a short six weeks ago, my life changed FAST-FAST-FAST. I saw Fifth! I saw Alder! I saw the Dairy Maid with the statue of a cow in an apron outside!

I was dozing when she first came to Pet-O-Rama, as I do during the day, because hamsters are more active at night.

'Hello.' A warm voice awakened me. When I opened my eyes, I saw a mass of bouncy black curls. A big, happy smile. Huge dark eyes. She smelled of apples. It was love at first sight.

'Aren't you the bright-eyed one?' she asked.

'And might I return the compliment?' I replied. Of course, it came out 'Squeak-squeak-squeak', as usual. Ms Mac opened her purse with the big pink and blue flowers on it.

'I'll take him,' she told Carl. 'He's obviously the most intelligent and handsome hamster you have.' Carl grunted. Then Ms Mac picked out a respectable cage – okay, not the three-storey pagoda I'd had my eye on – but a nice cage.

And soon, amid squeals of encouragement from my friends in the Small Pet Department, from the teeniest white mouse to the lumbering chinchilla, I left Pet-O-Rama with high hopes.

We sped down the street in Ms Mac's bright yellow car! (She called it a Bug, but I could see it was really a car.) She carried my cage up the stairs to her flat! We ate apples! We watched TV! She let me run around outside my cage! She gave me my very own name: Humphrey. And she told me all about Room 26, where we'd be going the next morning.

'And since you are an intelligent hamster who is going to school, I have a present for you, Humphrey,' she said.

Then she gave me a tiny notebook and a tiny pencil. 'I got these for you at the doll shop,' she explained. She tucked them behind my mirror where no one could see them except me.

'Of course, it might be a while before you learn to read and write,' she continued. 'But you're smart and I know you'll catch on fast.'

Little did she know I could already make out some words from my long, boring days at Pet-O-Rama.

Words like *Chew Toys. Kibble. Pooper-Scoopers.*

Remember, a hamster is grown up at about five weeks old. So if I could learn all the skills I need for life in five weeks, how long could it possibly take to learn to read?

I'll tell you: a week. Yep, in a week I could read and even write a little with the tiny pencil.

In addition to schoolwork, I learned quite a bit about the other students in Room 26. Like Lower-Your-Voice-A.J. and Speak-Up-Sayeh and Wait-for-the-Bell-Garth and Golden-Miranda. (Even after I found out her name is really Miranda Golden, I thought of her as Golden-Miranda because of her long blond hair. After all, I am a Golden Hamster.)

Yes, life in Room 26 suited me well during the day. My cage had all the comforts a hamster could desire. I had bars on the window to protect me from my enemies. I had a little sleeping house in one corner where no one could see me or bother me. There was my wheel to spin on, of course, and a lovely pile of nesting material. My mirror came in handy to check my grooming (and to hide my notebook). In one corner I kept my food. The opposite corner was my bathroom area because hamsters like to keep their poo away from their food. (Who doesn't?) All my needs were taken care of in one convenient cage.

At night, I went home from school with Ms Mac and we watched TV or listened to music. Sometimes Ms Mac played her bongo drums. She made a tunnel on the floor so I could race and wiggle to my hamster heart's content.

Oh, the memories of those six weeks with Morgan McNamara. That's her real name, but she told her students to call her Ms Mac. That's how nice she is. Or was.

On the weekends, Ms Mac and I had all kinds of adventures. She put me in her shirt pocket (right over her heart!) and took me with her to the laundry room. She had friends over and they laughed and made a fuss over me. She even took me for a bike ride once. I can still feel the wind in my fur!

I didn't have an inkling – until this morning – of the unsqueakable thing she was about to do to me. On the way to work she said, 'Humphrey, I hate to tell you, but this is my last day in Room 26 and I'm going to miss you more than you'll ever know.'

What was she saying? I hung on to my wheel for dear life!

'You see, it's really Mrs Brisbane's class. But just before school started, her husband was in an accident, so I took over the class. Today, she's coming back for good.'

Good? I could see nothing good in what Ms Mac was saying.

'Besides, I want to see the world, Humphrey,' she told me.

Fine with me. I've thoroughly enjoyed all the world I've seen so far and would go to the ends of the earth with Ms Mac. But she wasn't finished yet.

'But I can't take you with me.'

All hopes dashed. Completely.

'Besides, the kids need you to teach them responsibility. Mrs Brisbane needs you, too.'

Unfortunately, she didn't tell Mrs Brisbane that.

Mrs Brisbane was already in Room 26 when we arrived. She smiled at Ms Mac and shook her hand. Then she frowned at me and said, 'Is that some kind of . . . *rodent*?'

Ms Mac gave her the speech about how much kids can learn from taking care of another species.

Mrs Brisbane looked horrified and said, '*I can't stand rodents!* Take *it* back!'

The 'it' she was talking about was me.

Ms Mac didn't bat an eyelash. She put my cage in its usual place next to the window and said the kids were already very attached to me. She attached Dr Harvey H. Hammer's *Guide to the Care and Feeding of Hamsters* to the cage, along with a chart to make sure I was fed and my cage was cleaned on time.

'The children know what to do. You won't have to do a thing,' Ms Mac said as Mrs Brisbane glared at me. Just then, my fellow-students came streaming into the room and within half an hour Ms Mac had said goodbye to everyone, including me.

'I'll never forget you, Humphrey,' she whispered.

'Don't you forget me, either.'

'Not likely. But I don't know if I can ever forgive you,' I squeaked.

And then she was gone. Without me.

Mrs Brisbane didn't even come close to my cage until recess. Then she walked over and said, 'Mister, you've got to go.'

But she doesn't know my secret: the latch on my cage door doesn't work. It never has. It's the lock-that-doesn't-lock.

So I've got news for Mrs Brisbane: if I've got to go, it will be when and where I decide to go. Not her. Meanwhile, I'm not turning my back on this woman. Not for a second. If I ever disappear and someone finds this notebook, just check out Mrs Brisbane. Please!

TIP ONE

Choose your new hamster's home very carefully and make sure it is secure. Hamsters are skilful 'escape artists' and once out of their cages they are very difficult to find.

Guide to the Care and Feeding of Hamsters

Dr Harvey H. Hammer

2

Night Life

For the rest of the day, I felt SAD-SAD-SAD.

'You look sad, Humphrey,' Golden-Miranda said when she was cleaning my cage right before lunch. According to the chart Ms Mac had left, it was her turn to take care of me, thank goodness. Miranda was the best cage-cleaner and never said, 'Yuck!'

She put on throwaway gloves, then cleaned my potty corner, changed my bedding, gave me fresh water and finally – oh, joy! – gave me fresh grain, some lettuce and mealworms.

'This will make you happy,' she said as she slipped me the special treat she'd brought from home: cauliflower. Naturally, Miranda had good taste. I promptly saved it in my cheek pouch until I could store it in my sleeping house. Hamsters like to stash food for the future.

After my cage was taken care of, I felt well enough to observe Mrs Brisbane more carefully.

Now, Ms Mac was tall, wore bright blouses, short skirts and high shoes. She wore bracelets that jingle-jangled. She spoke in a loud voice and waved her arms and walked all around the room when she taught. Mrs Brisbane, on the other hand, was short with short grey hair. She wore dark clothes and flat shoes and she didn't jingle-jangle at all. She spoke in a voice just loud enough to hear and sat at her desk or stood at the blackboard when she taught.

No wonder I was feeling drowsy after lunch. All that nice food and all that soft talking.

'Is that all this hamster does – sleep?' she asked at one point when she glanced over at my cage.

'Well, he's 'turnal,' replied Raise-Your-Hand-Heidi Hopper.

'Raise-Your-Hand-Heidi,' said Mrs Brisbane. 'What's "'turnal?"'

'You know. 'Turnal. He sleeps during the day,' said Heidi.

I was wide awake now. 'Nocturnal,' I squeaked. 'Hamsters are *nocturnal*.'

'Oh, you mean *nocturnal*,' said Mrs Brisbane, almost as if she had understood me. She turned and wrote the word on the board. 'Can anyone name another an animal that's nocturnal?'

'Owl,' said Heidi.

'Raise-Your-Hand-Heidi,' said Mrs Brisbane. 'But that is correct. An owl is nocturnal. Anyone else?'

A voice shouted out, 'My dad!'

Mrs Brisbane looked around. 'Who said that?'

'He did. A.J.' Garth Tugwell pointed at A.J.

Both boys sat at the table nearest to my cage.

'What about your dad?' Mrs Brisbane asked.

A.J. squirmed in his seat. 'Well, my mum always says my dad is nocturnal 'cause he stays up so late watching TV.'

Stop-Giggling-Gail and a few other students sniggered. Mrs Brisbane didn't crack a smile.

'Her use of the word is correct,' she said. 'Though, technically, humans are not nocturnal. Any others?'

Eventually, the class came up with more names of nocturnal animals, like bats and foxes and opossums, and Mrs Brisbane said that the class would be learning more about animal habits later in the year.

If she'd just look at me, she could learn a lot. But I noticed for the rest of the day that Mrs Brisbane stayed far away from my cage, as if I had a disease or something.

She read a mighty fine story to us in the afternoon, though. In fact, I couldn't get back to my nap afterwards. It was about a scary house and these scratching noises and . . . a ghost! THUMP-THUMP-THUMP, the ghost came down the hall! Oh, I had shivers and quivers.

I have to say, Mrs Brisbane knows how to read a story. Her voice changed and her eyes got wide and I forgot about her grey hair and her dark suit. To squeak the truth, my fur was on end! The story had a funny ending because it turned out the ghost wasn't a ghost at all. It was an owl!

At the end of the story, everybody laughed. Even Mrs Brisbane.

I was beginning to think that life with this new teacher wouldn't be so bad. But I changed my mind when the bell rang at the end of the day and all my classmates raced out of the room, leaving me alone with her.

She erased the blackboard and gathered up her papers. I could tell that we'd be going home soon. Suddenly, I began to worry. What if Mrs Brisbane lived in a scary house with spooky noises and a thumping ghost?

Or, even worse, what if Mrs Brisbane had a scary pet, like a dog?

My mind was racing as fast as I was spinning my wheel when she finally approached and looked down at me, frowning.

'Well, you're on your own now,' she said.

With that, she closed the blinds and walked

away. But I heard her mutter, 'Rodent,' under her breath.

She left the classroom and closed the door. She left me alone. All alone in Room 26.

I had never been alone before.

As the room slowly grew darker and quieter, I thought back to the happy times at Ms Mac's flat. There were always cheery lights on and music and telephone-talking and . . . Oh, dear, during the day I never noticed how the clock on the wall ticked off the seconds one by one very loudly.

TICK-TICK-TICK. I was feeling SICK-SICK-SICK.

I wondered if there were any owls around Room 26. Or ghosts.

I tried to pass the time by writing in my notebook about Pet-O-Rama and my days at Ms Mac's flat. Writing took my mind off my jittery nerves. But eventually, my writing paw began to ache and I had to stop my scratchings. If only I could roam free, as I had at Ms Mac's flat!

Then I remembered the lock-that-doesn't-lock.

It took only a few seconds to jiggle open the door. I skittered across the table. Then, grasping the top of the table leg tightly, I closed my eyes and slid to the ground.

Ah, freedom! I dashed along the shiny floor. I darted between the tables and chairs. I stopped to nibble a peanut underneath Stop-Giggling-Gail's chair. It tasted delicious and made the coolest crunching sound. I chewed and chomped and gnawed and nibbled. And when I stopped . . . I heard the sound.

THUMP-THUMP-THUMP.

Just like the story Mrs Brisbane had read to us.

THUMP-THUMP-THUMP.

Closer and closer down the hall, coming towards Room 26.

Then RATTLE-SCRATCH. RATTLE-SCRATCH.

THUMP-THUMP-THUMP.

Suddenly, I longed for the protective comfort of my cage. I dropped what was left of the peanut and scampered back. But when I reached the table, I thought a terrible thought. I had slid down the smooth, shiny leg, straight down. But how was I going to climb up again?

I flung myself against the table leg, grabbed on and pushed UP-UP-UP. But I had made only a little progress when I began to slide DOWN-DOWN-DOWN. I was right back where I'd started.

The rattling grew louder. The sounds weren't coming towards Room 26 any more. They were coming in Room 26.

Just then, I noticed a long cord running down from the blinds. Without hesitation, I leaped up and grabbed the cord and began swinging back and forth. My stomach churned and I wished I'd never touched that peanut. But with each swing, I got a little higher off the ground. As soon as I saw the edge of the table, I closed my eyes and dived towards it.

Whoosh! I slid across the table and scampered into the cage. As I pulled the door behind me, I was suddenly blinded by light.

The something had turned on the lights and was clomping across the floor. It was huge and heavy and coming right towards me.

Just then, my eyes adjusted to the light and I saw the thing. It was a man!

'Well, well, who have we here? A new student!' a voice boomed.

The man was smiling down at me. My, that was a lovely piece of fur across his upper lip. A nice black moustache. He bent down to peer in at me.

'I'm Aldo Amato. And who are you?'

'I'm Humphrey . . . and you scared me half to death!' I told him. But as always, all that came out was 'Squeak-squeak-squeak.'

Aldo squinted at the sign on my cage. 'Oh, you're Humphrey! Hope I didn't scare you half to death!' he said with a laugh. 'I've just come to clean the room. I come every night. But where have you been?'

He rolled up a big cart with a bucket and mops and brooms and all kinds of bottles and rags on it.

'Oh, that's right,' he replied, as if we were having a real conversation. 'Mrs Brisbane came back today. She's a good teacher, you know, Humphrey. Been teaching here a long time. Wish I'd had a good teacher like her. Say . . . do you like music, Humphrey?'

'SQUEAK-SQUEAK-SQUEAK.' I tried to tell him I love music almost as much as I love Ms Mac. Suddenly, a song came blasting out of the radio on his cart and he set to work: sweeping, mopping, moving desks, dusting. But Aldo Amato didn't just dust and mop. He spun and swayed. He hopped and leaped. He twisted and twirled.

'How do you like the floor show?' Aldo asked me as he grasped the mop like a dancer holding his partner. 'Get it? It's a floor show! 'Cause I'm cleaning the floor!'

Then Aldo roared the biggest roar of a laugh I'd ever heard. His big moustache shook so much, I thought it might fall off.

'You like that? I'll show you real talent, Humphrey!' Aldo Amato picked up his broom and very carefully stood it up with the tip balancing on one outstretched fingertip. It wiggled from side to side, but Aldo moved with the broom and managed to keep it balanced straight in the air for an amazingly long time. When he was finished, he bowed deeply and said, 'What do you think? I'm going to join the circus!' And he roared again.

Then Aldo wiped his forehead with a big bandanna and sat down at the table where A.J. usually sits. 'You know what, Humphrey? You're such good company, I think I'll take my dinner break with you. Do you mind?'

'PLEASE-PLEASE-PLEASE,' I squeaked.

Aldo pulled his chair right up to my cage.

'Hey, you're a handsome guy . . . like me. Here . . . a little bit of green won't hurt you, will it?' He tore off a piece of lettuce from his sandwich and pushed it through the bars. Of course, I hid it in my cheek pouch.

Aldo chuckled. 'Good for you, Humphrey! Always save something for a rainy day.'

The two of us shared a very pleasant meal as Aldo told me about how he used to a have a regular job where he worked during the day. But then his company closed down and he couldn't find a job for a long time. He couldn't even pay the rent when he was lucky enough to get hired here at Longfellow School. He was glad to get the job, but it's lonely working at night because his friends work during the day. They can never get together like they used to.

I tried to squeak to him about all the creatures, like me, that are also nocturnal and Aldo listened.

'I know you're trying to tell me something, Humphrey, but I can't tell what it is. Maybe you're just saying I'm not alone after all, huh?'

'Squeak.' He understood!

Aldo stood up and threw his rubbish into the plastic bag on his cart.

'Well, I've got a lot of other rooms to clean, my friend. But I'll be back tomorrow night. Maybe I'll take my dinner break with you again.'

Aldo pushed his cart towards the door and reached for the light switch.

'NO-NO-NO!' I squeaked, dreading the thought of being plunged into darkness again.

Aldo stopped. 'I hate to leave you in the dark. But if I don't turn off the lights, I could lose my job.'

He clomped back across the floor to the window. 'Tell you what. I'll leave the blinds open a little. There's a nice light right outside your window.'

After he turned off the lights and left, I chomped on the lettuce I'd saved and basked in the warm glow of the streetlight – and my new friendship with Aldo.

TIP TWO

Hamsters are not picky about their food and eat very little. Make sure to feed your pet a wide variety of tasty foods.

Guide to the Care and Feeding of Hamsters

Dr Harvey H. Hammer

3

The Two Faces of Mrs Brisbane

That week was BUSY-BUSY-BUSY, but I learned a lot. I learned all the capitals of the United States. (I didn't say I remembered them all, but I learned them all.)

I learned about how water changes from solid to liquid to gas.

I learned how to subtract fractions.

I learned something else. Something very weird. There are two Mrs Brisbanes.

And I thought one Mrs Brisbane was one too many.

The first Mrs Brisbane is a good teacher, just like Aldo said. She's better than Ms Mac was at getting A.J. to lower his voice. She's better at getting Heidi to raise her hand before she blurts something out loud.

Of course, nobody could get Speak-Up-Sayeh to

raise her hand or to blurt anything out loud. Sayeh is so quiet and gentle, she never gives an answer. If the teacher calls on her, she stares down at her desk without saying a word.

But when it's Sayeh's turn to clean my cage and feed me, she holds me in her hand so gently, I feel like I'm floating on a cloud. 'Hello, Humphrey,' she whispers. 'Your fur is so beautiful.' I always feel calmer when Sayeh holds me.

She's so nice, I wish Mrs Brisbane would leave her alone. Ms Mac hardly ever called on Sayeh once she realized how shy she was. But Mrs Brisbane calls on her all the time. She won't leave her alone.

'Sayeh, speak up, please. I know you know the answer,' she'd say while Sayeh stared at the top of her desk as if she were watching a TV show there. But I was shocked when Mrs Brisbane got annoyed with Sayeh – sweet, shy Sayeh – and said, 'You will stay in during break.'

Sayeh still stared down without moving a muscle. But a minute later, I saw something wet drop from Sayeh's eye to the tabletop.

I hated Mrs Brisbane.

Of course, I don't go out to break. In fact, I'm glad, since it's a great time to catch up on my sleep. So I was there when Mrs Brisbane talked to Sayeh. And I was all ready to squeak up on her behalf, if necessary.

Mrs Brisbane brought a stack of papers to the table and sat down across from Sayeh.

'Sayeh, you think I'm being mean to you, don't you?'

Sayeh slowly shook her head. I heartily nodded my head, but no one was looking at me.

'But I wouldn't call on you if I didn't know that you know the answers,' the teacher explained. 'Look at your essays and tests. You get a hundred per cent on everything: spelling, science, geography and arithmetic. Your vocabulary is excellent. But I have never heard you speak. Can you tell me why?'

I checked my notebook and I was quite impressed. I got only 85 per cent on the last vocabulary test. This girl is smart!

Sayeh still did not speak.

'Sayeh, I'm going to have to send a note home to your parents. Maybe they can help me work out what to do,' said Mrs Brisbane.

Sayeh looked up, very frightened. 'No, please,' she said.

Mrs Brisbane looked surprised. She reached over and patted Sayeh's arm. 'I won't send a note now . . . if you'll promise to try.'

Sayeh looked back down at the desk and nodded.

'I'll tell you what. I won't call on you if you promise that some time within the next week you'll raise your hand on your own and answer a question. Is that a deal?'

Sayeh nodded, very slowly this time.

'You have to say it,' Mrs Brisbane told her.

'Deal,' whispered Sayeh.

'Terrific!' said Mrs Brisbane, smiling. 'Now, how would you like to erase the board for me?'

Sayeh jumped up and hurried to the board. All the students in Room 26 like to erase the board, for some reason.

Mrs Brisbane was certainly hard to work out. She hadn't been mean to Sayeh at all. She just did what a teacher is supposed to do. I liked this Mrs Brisbane. I even liked the pink blouse she had on.

But at the end of the day when the students had gone, the second Mrs Brisbane came back. The really scary one.

She straightened up the room and came over to the window to close the blinds. I could only hope that Aldo would open them for me later.

She looked down and saw that the table around me was messy. The bag of shavings used for my bedding had torn and bits of litter were scattered all over the table. Garth had done the cleaning and left the lid off my treats box. The whole table looked untidy.

'Good grief,' said Mrs Brisbane in a very unhappy voice.

I decided to take a spin on my wheel. Usually,

that cheers up people. But not Mrs Brisbane.

She started to clean the table, getting paper towels and cleaning spray and muttering to herself the whole time.

'Not my job,' she grumbled. 'These children are not responsible. All I need is somebody else to take care of. Some . . . rodent!'

Nobody says *rodent* quite the way Mrs Brisbane does.

Then she looked down at me with angry eyes and said, 'You . . . are . . . a . . . trouble . . . maker. And somehow, I'm going to get rid of you!'

Then she grabbed her purse and her papers and stormed out of Room 26.

For once, I didn't mind being left alone. I didn't even mind the TICK-TICK-TICK of the clock.

I was just GLAD-GLAD-GLAD that the second Mrs Brisbane had gone.

I was worried about what she'd said, but I kept my mind occupied by practising my vocabulary words until the light was completely gone. (If Sayeh got 100 per cent correct, why couldn't I?)

Then I sat and waited.

Suddenly, bright lights blinded my eyes as the door swung open and a familiar voice roared, 'Never fear –Aldo's here!'

Aldo rolled his cart over to my cage and put his face right down next to mine.

'How's it going, Humphrey?' he asked.

I tried squeaking out my story, but Aldo didn't quite catch what I was saying.

'Whoa, pal! Something's got your tail in a tizzy! Well, this should cheer you up!' Aldo reached into a brown paper bag, pulled something out and dangled it in front of my cage.

'Something to gnaw on, little buddy,' he said, opening the door.

JOY-JOY-JOY! A tiny dog biscuit! One of Ms Mac's friends gave me one of those once. You can crunch on it for ever.

'Ha-ha! Suddenly, there's a smile on your face!' Aldo beamed with pride. 'Now I'll clean this room really fast so we can eat our dinner together.'

I never saw anybody move as fast as Aldo. He turned the music up full blast. Then he mopped and polished and swept and scrubbed, while I nibbled and gnawed on my biscuit.

When he was finished, Aldo pulled a chair up to my cage and took out his big sandwich.

'You know, Humphrey, some folks might think I'm crazy, talking to a hamster. But you're better company than a lot of people I know. Here . . . have a nice salad. It's good for you!'

He tore off a tiny piece of lettuce and pushed it

through the wires of my cage.

'Thank you,' I squeaked.

'You're welcome,' said Aldo.

'So, what were we talking about last night? Oh, yeah. Loneliness. You know, I have friends, Humphrey. But during the day, when I'd like to do something – go bowling or to a movie or something – they're at work. And when they want to do something, I'm at work. Of course, there's the weekend, but I usually see my family, you know. My brother and his family, my nieces and nephews – I've got a big family.'

Suddenly Aldo bopped the side of his head with the palm of his hand. 'Whoa, Humphrey. I never told you. My nephew . . . he's in your class. Richie Rinaldi. He sits over there.'

He pointed to the far side of the room. 'He always has the neatest desk in the class. He'd better or he'll hear from his uncle. Do you know him?'

'Of course,' I squeaked. Repeat-That-Please-Richie. One of the nicest boys in the class. But he mumbled a lot and usually had to repeat something two or three times to be understood.

Aldo crunched his bag and tossed it into his rubbish bag. 'Well, I'm out of here. You know, they've got a frog in Room 16, but he's not good company like you are. He sings, though.'

Sing! I'll sing for you, Aldo, I thought.

'SQUEAK-SQUEAK-SQUEAK!'

'Don't worry. I don't like him nearly as much as you, my friend,' Aldo said. He opened the blinds to let in the light.

Just as he was going out of the door, Aldo said, 'See you next week, Humphrey!'

Next week! A cold chill came over me. Tomorrow was Friday. When Ms Mac was in Room 26, she took me home for the weekend. But if Mrs Brisbane didn't take me home, I'd have two very long days and nights with no one – not even Aldo – to feed me or chat with me.

Even worse, what if Mrs Brisbane did take me to her house? What fate would await me there?

I had plenty to keep me busy for the rest of the night: worrying about Mrs Brisbane and how she planned to do away with me. Ms Mac . . . please come back!

TIP THREE

Hamsters enjoy a change in routine. Among their favourite activities are eating, grooming themselves, climbing, running, spinning, taking a nap and being petted.

Guide to the Care and Feeding of Hamsters

Dr Harvey H. Hammer

4
The Most Important Man in the World

Luckily, Friday went by smoothly. Sorry to say, Sayeh didn't raise her hand. But Heidi Hopper did – amazing! A.J. actually whispered. Richie cleaned my cage. I tried to imagine him with a big black moustache like his uncle Aldo.

Later, when Mrs Brisbane asked him to name the capital of Kentucky, Richie said, 'Hot dog.'

Everyone giggled, of course. Especially Stop-Giggling-Gail. Otherwise known as Gail Morgenstern.

'Repeat-That-Please-Richie,' said the teacher.

Richie realized he'd made a mistake, so he tried again. 'Frankfurter,' he said.

More giggles. Explosive giggles.

'Try again, Richie,' said Mrs Brisbane, who was on the verge of smiling herself.

'Uh . . . Frankfort!' he said proudly.

(That was the correct answer, by the way.)

So, you see, it wasn't exactly a bad day in Room 26. It's just that I was jittery, wondering what would happen to me when the bell rang. Would I be left alone . . . hungry, utterly forsaken for two whole days? Or would I be a captive in the haunted house of Mrs Brisbane?

At last, the bell rang and the students flew out of the door like a flock of homing pigeons in a movie Ms Mac showed us.

Just then, two classroom assistants stopped by. One was Heidi Hopper's mum and the other one was Art Patel's. (That's Pay-Attention-Art.) They came to talk to Mrs Brisbane about Halloween, which was less than two weeks away.

I didn't know what Halloween was, but it certainly sounded scary, especially when they talked about bringing bats and witches and, even worse, cats right into the classroom! SHIVER-QUIVER-SHAKE. What could they be thinking?

I was about ready to fling open my cage and escape when the door opened and in walked the headmaster, Mr Morales.

Mr Morales is the Most Important Person at Longfellow School. He runs the place and everyone respects him. You can tell. For one thing, Mr Morales always wears a tie. No one else in the whole school wears a tie. For another thing, when Mr Morales comes into the room, everyone stops what they're doing and waits to see what he has to say. And for a third thing, both Ms Mac and Mrs Brisbane sometimes threatened to send a misbehaving student to Mr Morales's office. As soon as the teacher mentioned the headmaster's name, the student would start acting very, very nice.

'Good afternoon, ladies,' said Mr Morales. He was wearing a light blue shirt and a tie that had tiny books all over it.

Everyone said, 'Hello.'

'Well, how's your first week back, Sue?' he asked.

'Sue' was apparently Mrs Brisbane, although I'd never thought of her having a first name before.

She said it was great to be back and what a wonderful class it was, which obviously pleased the mothers.

Then Mr Morales leaned over my cage and smiled. His tie dangled right over my head.

'I'll bet you're enjoying this furry little pupil,' he said with a grin.

I expected Mrs Brisbane to tell him what a trouble-making rodent I was. But instead, she forced a smile and said, 'Well, yes, but he's quite a bit of extra work.'

Mr Morales waved a finger at me. He didn't seem to hear what Mrs Brisbane said.

'I always wanted one of these fellows,' he said. 'But my papa wouldn't let me have one. He sure is cute.'

Mrs Brisbane cleared her throat. 'Yes, but I'm afraid he's a little distracting. I was going to see if Mr Kim in Room 12 wants him.'

I was shocked. Luckily, so were the classroom assistants. 'Oh, no! The children just love Humphrey,' said Mrs Patel.

'Heidi talks about him all the time. And it's a wonderful way to teach the kids responsibility,' Mrs Hopper said.

'Yes, but it's a little too much responsibility for me,' Mrs Brisbane sighed. 'At least I have a couple of days away from him this weekend.'

'You're not taking him home with you?' asked Mrs Patel.

Mrs Brisbane backed away from the cage. 'Oh, no. It's out of the question.'

'But Ms Mac always took him home,' said Mrs Hopper.

'He'll be fine. He has plenty of food,' Mrs Brisbane answered very, very firmly.

The classroom assistants were silent for a second. Mr Morales was still wiggling his finger at me.

Then Mrs Hopper spoke up. 'Why don't the kids take turns bringing Humphrey home for the weekend? They can sign up, we'll talk to their parents and give them instructions. It will be a great experience!'

'Some people might not want him,' said Mrs Brisbane.

Squeak for yourself, Mrs Brisbane!

'That's fine,' said Mrs Hopper. 'There'll be plenty who will.'

'I think it's great,' Mrs Patel agreed. 'I'd take him today, but we're going up to the lake for the weekend.'

'Oh, I'd take him, too,' said Mrs Hopper. 'But we're painting the house and the place is a mess. Next week for sure.'

'Yes, I could do it next week,' Mrs Patel agreed.

Mrs Brisbane smiled a fake smile. 'So who's going to take him this weekend?'

The classroom assistants looked at one another.

'I could make a few quick calls. Maybe the Rinaldis,' Mrs Patel suggested.

'CALL-CALL-CALL,' I squeaked.

Suddenly, Mr Morales stood up straight. 'I have a better idea,' he announced. 'I'll take Humphrey home for the weekend. My kids will love him. Then, starting next week, you can have the students take turns.'

The three women were almost as surprised as I was.

'Don't worry. He'll be in good hands,' Mr

Morales assured them.

Well, I suppose I would be. After all, I was going home with the Most Important Person at Longfellow School!

As he drove me to his house, Mr Morales told me how he'd always wanted a hamster when he was a kid. But his dad always said they didn't need another mouth to feed. 'I argued with him, Humphrey. I said, "Papa, I will feed him off my own plate." Then Papa said we'd have to buy the cage and stuff to put in it. I suppose he was right, Humphrey. We couldn't afford it.'

He smiled his big smile. 'But not any more. Now I'm the headmaster of my own school.'

I told you he was important.

His house was nice, but I didn't get to see much of it because as soon as we came in the door, two little whirlwinds tumbled into the room, shrieking and squealing.

'Quiet down, now. You'll frighten the little fellow,' Mr Morales told them. He got that right.

He introduced us. The little boy, who was about five, was named Willy. He kept poking his fingers through the wires of the cage. I was about to bite him – pure instinct – but then I remembered: this is the son of the Most Important Person at

Longfellow School. So I didn't.

The little girl, who was about seven, was named Brenda. She kept sticking her face up against the cage and squealing. I tried squeaking back at her, but I don't think she could hear me.

Mr Morales tried to quieten them down. He explained that I was a guest for the weekend and they had to treat me with respect.

They didn't listen.

A pretty lady rushed through the room, jingling her car keys. 'I'm late. I have a house to show.' She glanced in my direction. 'We'll talk about that later. *Adios*.'

Mr Morales wished her luck and she was gone. Then he carried me into the den with Willy and Brenda clinging to his legs and yelping.

My cage was swinging back and forth so much, I was getting airsick. Or cage-sick.

Mr Morales set my cage on a table in their living room.

'Now get back and listen to me,' he told his children. 'I'll tell you all about him.'

'Can we take him out?' screamed Willy.

'Can we put him in my room?' shouted Brenda. 'Can he sleep with me tonight?'

'We can't do anything until you settle down,' Mr Morales said.

Bravo, Mr Morales, I thought.

But still the children didn't listen. The Most Important Person at Longfellow School was not treated with respect in his own house.

Willy lurched forward and swung open the cage door.

'Oooh, there's *poo* in there!' he screamed.

'Where? Where?' shrieked Brenda.

Willy pointed to my potty corner, which I thought was unsqueakably rude of him.

'I want to hold him,' said Brenda, grabbing me.

She squeezed me so hard, I let out a squeal.

'Stop!' said Mr Morales. 'Put him back right now!'

She opened her hand and dropped me on to the floor of my cage. Luckily, I landed in a pile of soft bedding. Luckily, I didn't land in my poo.

I was a little dizzy, but I heard Mr Morales send Willy and Brenda to their rooms.

'I will not allow you to mistreat an animal. Upstairs. Doors shut. No playing until I say you can,' he said.

Suddenly, Mr Morales didn't look so important. He slumped down in the chair next to my cage and loosened his tie.

'Now you know my secret, Humphrey. At school, everybody listens to me. At home, nobody listens to me,' he said.

Mr Morales looked TIRED-TIRED-TIRED.

Above our heads came the sounds of thumping and bumping. It sounded as if the ceiling was about to fall in.

'They're bouncing on their beds, Humphrey. Not supposed to do that, either,' he said.

He slowly rose and went to the stairway in the hall. 'Willy! Brenda! Stop that now!' he yelled.

Surprisingly, the thumping and bumping stopped.

'They listened!' I squeaked when the headmaster sat down again. But the thumping and bumping began again in a minute.

'I wish I knew what to do,' he said. 'Some way to teach them a lesson.'

I nodded. A lesson is just what those children needed.

And I was just the hamster to teach them.

TIP FOUR

Never, ever squeeze, pinch or crush a hamster. If it runs away, squeals or mutters, leave the hamster alone.

Guide to the Care and Feeding of Hamsters

Dr Harvey H. Hammer

Plans Are Hatched

When Mr Morales went into the kitchen to get a glass of water, I carefully opened the lock-that-doesn't-lock and slipped out of my cage. I leaped over to the chair, then scampered down to the floor and hid in the corner, behind the long curtains.

Mr Morales returned and sat down again. The children were still thumping and bumping and were now screaming and screeching as well.

'Say, Humphrey, maybe you need some water, too,' he said and leaned towards my cage.

Mr Morales gasped when he saw that it was empty. 'Humphrey, where did you go? Oh, I should have known you'd escape! I'd run away from those kids if I could, too. But do me a favour, Humphrey. *Please come out!*'

In a panic, he darted around the room. 'The kids in Room 26 will hate me if I lose you!' he said.

I felt sorry for Mr Morales, so I scratched around a little.

'There you are!' he said, bending down to look at me. 'Now, let's get you back in your cage.'

Not quite yet, I thought. He reached down to pick me up and I scampered forward, just a few inches past his hand.

'Don't do this to me, Humphrey,' he said. 'Cooperate.'

But I wasn't doing anything *to* him. I was doing something *for* him.

'Work with me,' he said, but this time to himself. 'Maybe . . . hey, that's it!' He looked down at me. 'With your help, Humphrey.'

Mr Morales really swung into action then.

He raced upstairs. The thumping and bumping stopped. When he raced back downstairs, Willy and Brenda were with him.

'Close all the doors, Willy,' he said.

'But, Dad,' Willy whined.

'Close them,' his father repeated firmly. 'Now!' Willy closed all the doors.

'You two scared poor Humphrey with your screaming and poking and thumping. We may never see him again!' he told them.

Brenda burst into tears. 'Humphrey's dead!' she sobbed.

'No. Humphrey's too smart for that,' Mr

Morales told her. 'But he will run away if you two aren't nice to him.'

RIGHT-RIGHT-RIGHT. You have to be pretty smart to be a headmaster.

'Now, do you want to help me get Humphrey back?'

'YES!' the children shouted.

Mr Morales explained the plan. He said the only way they'd get me back in my cage was if they worked together. And they could work together only if they listened to him. Really listened.

They were listening now. And they kept listening, too. Because he told them the most important thing they could do was to be quiet.

So they were quiet.

'I'm pretty sure he's still in the room. Our job is to lure him back into his cage,' Mr Morales whispered.

He put my cage in the middle of the floor. Then he went to the kitchen and got a handful of sunflower seeds. Willy and Brenda helped him make a trail of seeds across the floor leading up to the cage.

'Good,' said Mr Morales. 'Now we have to be very, very quiet and wait for Humphrey to pick up the seeds. But if you say anything or even move, you might scare him.'

'We'll be quiet, Dad,' said Willy. Brenda agreed.

They all sat on the sofa.

'Do you think it will work?' Willy whispered.

'Of course,' Brenda answered. 'Dad's smart.'

Well, he's not the only one.

I waited for a while. After all, the Morales children needed all the practice staying quiet they could get. When Willy got restless, I started skittering along the floor.

'I hear him!' said Brenda.

'Shhh,' said Willy.

I waited a few more seconds, then scrambled out of the corner and grabbed the closest seed. I could hear loud gasps from the children, but I pretended not to notice. I scurried towards the second seed. This plan Mr Morales and I came up with was TASTY-TASTY-TASTY.

I could almost feel three pairs of eyes fixed on me, but I ignored them. I grabbed up the third and fourth seeds, hid them in my cheek pouch, then stopped right outside the open door of my cage.

Inside, Mr Morales had left a lovely pile of sunflower seeds.

It was nice to be free, but my cage was home, after all. Besides, until the day somebody fixes the lock-that-doesn't-lock, I can get out whenever I want.

The kids were still quiet, so I made a run for the cage. Mr Morales quickly closed the door and the children began to cheer.

‘We did it!’ said Brenda.

‘Dad’s the smartest man in the world!’ said Willy.

‘Hey, you kids helped. When we cooperate and work together, we make a pretty good team,’ Mr Morales told them.

‘°*Lo mejor!’* Willy agreed. ‘The best!’

Mr Morales squatted down and winked at me. ‘Of course, Humphrey helped, too.’

I’ll say.

The rest of the weekend with the Morales family was fine. Sometimes the kids started interrupting their dad or mum, but Mr Morales just reminded them that they could be polite if they tried.

Willy and Brenda tried.

Mrs Morales sold a house (it turns out that selling other people’s houses is her job), so they celebrated with pizza and ice-cream.

Brenda learned to hold me gently.

Willy even cleaned the poo out of my cage, which I appreciated.

Life is good, I thought as Mr Morales drove me back to school on Monday morning.

Then I remembered Mrs Brisbane. And how she’d said I was a troublemaker and she was going to get rid of me.

‘Humphrey, you are a true friend,’ said Mr

Morales as he carried my cage back into Room 26. 'I'll never forget what you did for me.'

As soon as class started on Monday, Heidi's mum came into the classroom and explained to everyone about taking me home on weekends.

'How many of you would be interested?' Mrs Hopper asked.

Every single hand in the classroom was raised.

Well, every hand except one: Mrs Brisbane's.

Still, it was a pretty good week.

I got 90 per cent on the vocabulary test. I'll bet Sayeh got 100 per cent. But she still didn't raise her hand, even though she'd promised.

And Aldo talked more and more every night. On Tuesday night, he leaned in close and asked, 'Humphrey, don't you ever wish you had a girl-friend?'

Like most hamsters, I'm pretty much of a loner, so I really hadn't thought about it before.

'Not sure,' I squeaked.

'I would like one,' said Aldo. 'A really nice girl-friend.'

I felt so sorry for Aldo, I squeaked extra loud when he performed his broom-balancing act for me.

I was still thinking about him on Wednesday. After everyone had left, while there was still light coming in the window, I meandered outside the cage to help myself to any mealworms that Heidi might have left behind when she fed me earlier in the day.

The table was covered with newspapers and while I nibbled, I browsed through the news. All of life was there on the pages of the newspaper. Births and deaths. Lost pets (SAD-SAD-SAD). Funny jokes. Good news and bad news.

Then there were the ads. My, there were so many shops. Not just Pet-O-Rama but Shoes-O-Rama and Food-O-Rama and Books Galore and Wide World of Tools!

And there were other ads, too. One in particular caught my eye that afternoon. It read:

WORK NIGHTS? LONELY? WANT TO MEET OTHERS WHO WORK NIGHTS?

THE MOONLIGHTERS CLUB

For people who work at night.
Meetings are held during the day on weekdays.
Hikes and outings to restaurants, parks, plays, movies and much more!

There was a name and a phone number at the end.

I could hardly believe it. This was exactly what Aldo needed! I could already see him, smiling and happy, going to parks and plays with the Moonlighters Club and having a girlfriend.

But how could I get Aldo to read this ad? He'd probably just throw it away. Still, if I cut it out and left it in a place where he couldn't miss it, well, maybe.

Hamsters can't use scissors, but we have nifty teeth. It took me a while to nibble the whole ad out neatly, but I did a pretty good job. Then I stood the clipping up against my cage. Aldo couldn't help but see it if he looked at me, which he always did.

That evening, I was more anxious than usual for Aldo to arrive. When he turned on the lights, I squeaked, 'Hello,' right away.

'Greetings to you, my little friend,' said Aldo as he pushed his cart into the room. 'You sound like you have something on your mind.'

'You bet,' I tried to tell him.

He ambled over to my cage and leaned down to look in. 'What's happening, Humphrey?' he asked.

I saw his eyes light on the scrap of newspaper.

'Hey, I can hardly see you.' He reached out and pushed aside the clipping.

'Read it!' I squeaked right out. Of course, he didn't understand.

He didn't even look at what the ad said. He just set it down next to the cage and leaned in closer.

I was squeaking a blue streak. 'Look at it now!'

'Calm down, Humphrey. I've got a treat for you,' said Aldo. He reached into his pocket and pulled out a tiny bit of carrot. 'Your pal Aldo would never forget you.'

My heart sank. You try to help a human and they don't even pay attention. But, as you know, I don't give up easily.

I squeaked happily while he balanced his broom on one finger, as usual. But my mind was on the Moonlighters Club and how to get Aldo there.

After he left, I scrambled out of my cage, picked up the newspaper clipping and tucked it inside my notebook. Then I hid the notebook behind my mirror. If I didn't, somebody mean (like Mrs Brisbane) might throw it away.

I was still wondering what to do with it the next day when Mrs Brisbane rolled in a trolley with a big machine on it.

'This is the overhead projector,' she told the class. 'I'm going to use it for some map work.'

When Mrs Brisbane turned on the machine, a bright light was projected on to the wall. Then she placed a paper map on the glass and suddenly that map showed up really big on the wall. She could write on it and draw on it and you could see everything she wrote.

A machine like this could come in very handy, I thought.

So when Mrs Brisbane turned off the machine and sent my classmates off to lunch, I thought about that machine.

When A.J. cleaned my cage and changed my water and bedding, I thought about that machine.

I thought about it so hard, I suddenly came up with a REALLY-REALLY-REALLY good plan. But it would be difficult to carry out and dangerous as well.

TIP FIVE

If a hamster manages to escape his cage, you can sometimes lure him back in with a trail of sunflower seeds.

Guide to the Care and Feeding of Hamsters

Dr Harvey H. Hammer

6 Moonlight Madness

I waited until the school was completely quiet. No students, no teachers, no Mr Morales.

Then I got busy because I had a lot of work to do. Big work for a small hamster.

First, I took the Moonlighters Club clipping out of my notebook. Holding it in my mouth, I opened the lock-that-doesn't-lock and scurried across the table.

Getting down off that table was still a problem. I grabbed hold of the leg and slid down, as I've done before. It makes me feel a little queasy in my tummy. But it would be worthwhile if I could get Aldo a girlfriend.

I hurried over to the big machine, which was very, very high off the ground. It seemed impossible for me to get up there, but I had it all planned out in my mind. Crawl up the waste-paper basket –

oooh, I didn't know it would sway like that! Leap over to the seat of Mrs Brisbane's chair. Whoa – slippery! Crawl up the rungs to the blackboard tray behind it. Along the blackboard tray to the bookcase. Then the hardest part: the dive from the bookcase to the overhead projector trolley. If you ever try it yourself, don't look down!

I was practically home free, but I still had to get up to the lit part. Still holding the newspaper clipping in my mouth, I grabbed on to a big screw sticking out of the side and hauled myself up. Then I reached up as high as I could and just barely managed to touch the top. Good thing I've got big muscles, because I was able to P-U-L-L myself up.

I was there! It was like climbing Mount McKinley, the tallest mountain peak in the United States! (Ask Mrs Brisbane.)

I quickly pushed the switch. I wished I had some sunglasses, because I was suddenly surrounded by blinding light. It was like being inside a light bulb.

I took the newspaper clipping out of my mouth and carefully laid it on the flat glass. Then I looked up at the wall and . . . NO-NO-NO! Up on the screen was a picture of a car and behind it there was jumbled up backward writing! I realized I must have laid the clipping on the glass upside down. I quickly turned it over and there it was: all the information about the Moonlighters Club right there on the wall with the outline of the car behind it.

Aldo would be coming soon, so I hurried back to the cage. It was faster getting back, because it was mostly downhill until the very end, when I had to swing my way up the cord to the blinds and back to the table.

I was panting pretty hard by the time I closed the cage door behind me. I didn't even have time to catch my breath before Aldo swung open the door.

'Whoa! Who left that on?' he exclaimed as he entered. 'That thing could overheat.'

He hurried over to the overhead projector.

'Look at the wall! Look up at the wall!' I squeaked, but the words only sounded like hamster peeps.

Aldo didn't waste a second. He flicked off the machine. All that work for nothing!

But then a funny thing happened. Aldo turned the machine back on and looked at the wall. 'What's this?' he muttered. 'Why did Mrs Brisbane have this up here? Hey, nice car!'

He squinted up at the screen. 'Look, Humphrey. The Moonlighters Club. For people who work at night, like me.'

And me, I thought. I was still quite exhausted from all that effort.

Aldo stared at the big ad on the wall for a while. Then he turned off the projector and went to work and never mentioned it again.

Yes, I was annoyed. I had failed, but at least I had tried, which was more than I can say for one of my classmates. Yes, Sayeh Nasiri. With my own furry ears, I had heard her promise Mrs Brisbane that she would raise her hand in class. But so far, she'd been as silent as a statue. Her week was almost up. Even though I'd scolded her the day she fed me, she paid no more attention to me than she had to her teacher. You should really listen to your teacher. Even Mrs Brisbane.

And you should always listen to your hamster.

I was worried about Aldo and about Sayeh. But I have to admit, my journey had been so tiring that – nocturnal or not – I slept soundly for the rest of the night. The next day began in a very surprising way.

'I have something to share with you all,' Mrs Brisbane announced. She held up a postcard with a picture of colourful parrots perched in lush green trees. 'A postcard from Ms McNamara.' (Mrs Brisbane would never call her Ms Mac.) 'It says: "Greetings to my favourite class in the world, Room 26! I am now working in a school here in

Brazil. This country is beautiful and friendly. I really enjoyed talking with the parrots in the rain forest. I miss you all, especially my pal Humphrey. Lots of love, Ms Mac."'

(Mrs Brisbane had to say Ms Mac since that's the way the card was signed.)

HAPPY-HAPPY-HAPPY! Not only did Ms Mac remember me, she missed me most of all. Oh, and I missed her most of all, too. Especially every time I looked at Mrs Brisbane and she glared back at me.

Mrs Brisbane showed us Brazil on the map and it's far away. I'd like to be that far away from Mrs Brisbane. My head was so filled with memories of Ms Mac that I got only 75 per cent on my vocabulary test.

After we marked the tests in class, Mrs Brisbane said, 'If you got one hundred per cent on the test, please raise your hand.'

That woke me up. What a clever way to get Sayeh to raise her hand. Because she always got 100 per cent.

A.J. raised his hand. Art raised his hand.

Sayeh just stared down at her desktop.

I was starting to get really angry with her.

When it was time for map work, Mrs Brisbane clicked on the overhead projector and there it was: the Moonlighters Club ad right on the wall. Mrs

Brisbane wrinkled her nose, picked up the paper and looked at both sides. Then she held it up to the light and I think maybe she noticed those tiny holes my teeth had made when I carried it over there.

Mrs Brisbane looked over at my cage and wrinkled her nose again. Then she crumpled the paper and threw it into the waste-paper basket.

She's smart, but she is also *mean*.

She's not the only one. While she went on with her map work, Wait-for-the-Bell-Garth Tugwell started making some *very rude* noises.

Mrs Brisbane didn't even turn round. When someone started giggling, she just said, 'Stop-Giggling-Gail.'

So Garth's rude noises got louder and even ruder. And a lot of other kids giggled along with Gail.

Suddenly, the teacher spun round to face them.

'Very well. The whole class will stay in during break for extra vocabulary words,' she announced.

Everybody groaned. 'It's Garth's fault,' said Heidi.

'Raise your hand,' Mrs Brisbane snapped back. 'You will all stay in during break. *Unless* the person making those noises wants to step forward and admit it.'

Nobody said a word, but everybody glared at Garth, including me.

‘Okay, I did it,’ he said.

‘Raise your hand,’ Heidi whispered loudly.

‘Very well, Garth. You, Heidi and Gail will stay in during break,’ the teacher said firmly.

Heidi and Gail protested until the bell rang, but all three of them stayed in during break. Instead of making them do extra vocabulary words, though, Mrs Brisbane let them rest their heads on their desks. *After* she had lectured them about their behaviour, of course.

All this commotion had made me a little hungry, and, for some reason, I hadn't been fed yet. So I decided to squeak up for myself.

Mrs Brisbane turned and pointed at me angrily. ‘I don't need any trouble out of you, either,’ she said.

Heidi raised her hand. ‘I don't think he's been fed today,’ she said.

Mrs Brisbane told Garth to feed me. Then she dismissed the girls and told them to go outside and play for the rest of break.

So she wasn't completely mean to them, anyway. She even trusted Garth to be alone in the room while she took some papers down to the office.

I'd always liked Wait-for-the-Bell-Garth, so I was surprised when he started grumbling at me as he filled the water bottle and put some fresh meal-worms in my cage.

'One of these days, you'll get in trouble, too,' he said. 'I'll see to that.'

'Huh?' I squeaked.

'Everybody hates me. Everybody loves you. You're just a rat in disguise.'

The words hurt me a lot. Why would Garth say that? I mean, yes, almost everybody does love me, but I don't make rude noises and get other people into trouble.

I was still pondering Garth's behaviour when my classmates returned to Room 26. Mrs Brisbane must have calmed down during the break, because she greeted them with a smile. 'I have a surprise for you,' she told the kids.

Surprises always get the class's attention. They think surprises are always good. However, I know that surprises can sometimes be bad, like the day Ms Mac left me for ever.

'We're going to pick who gets to take Humphrey home for the weekend,' she explained. 'Now, you all know whether your parents gave permission for you to bring him home. So, if you'd like Humphrey this weekend, raise your hand now.'

HEY-HEY-HEY. You should have seen all the hands that went up. I could hardly believe my eyes. Miranda and Heidi and A.J. and . . . Every single hand in the class, except Garth's. Even Sayeh Nasiri raised her hand.

Mrs Brisbane noticed.

'Sayeh, do you think it will be all right with your parents?' she asked.

Sayeh nodded her head.

'I can't hear you,' said Mrs Brisbane.

'Yes, ma'am,' said Sayeh.

It was strange to hear her voice in the classroom. Mrs Brisbane gave her a note to bring back from her family on Friday.

I napped for the rest of the afternoon, but whenever I woke up and glanced over at Sayeh's desk, I saw her doing something I'd never seen before.

Smiling.

TIP SIX

You can leave your hamster alone for a day or two. Otherwise, find a suitable caretaker, or, if possible, take your hamster with you. In its own cage, a hamster can be very portable.

Guide to the Care and Feeding of Hamsters

Dr Harvey H. Hammer

7

Sayeh Speaks Up

On Friday afternoon, Sayeh's father, Mr Nasiri, picked us up after school. He had a friendly smile and gentle eyes, but he was as quiet as his daughter.

Sayeh lived in a tall building, so Mr Nasiri carried my cage up one, two, three flights of stairs to their clean and quiet flat.

Mrs Nasiri opened the door for us. She spoke to her husband and daughter, but I couldn't exactly understand what they were saying.

'Hummy! Hummy!' a little voice called out.

Sayeh's little brother, Darek, toddled towards the door to greet me.

'Say *Humphrey*,' Sayeh gently corrected him.

'Rummy,' he said.

The Nasiris put my cage in the living room, right in the middle of a big table. Then they pulled up chairs so they could all sit and stare into my cage.

It seemed as if they were waiting for something to happen, so I decided to give them a show. First I spun on my wheel for a while. Then I climbed up the side of the cage and dived down into a pile of soft paper.

They were obviously impressed with my performance as they talked quietly. The funny thing is, I couldn't understand a word they were saying. No wonder Sayeh got 100 per cent on all her vocabulary tests. She and her family knew many more words than I did.

They finally went to the kitchen to eat dinner. Later, while the rest of the family watched television, Sayeh's mother quietly sat by my cage, watching me. She seemed NICE-NICE-NICE.

Eventually, it was bedtime for the Nasiris. But after the lights were out, Sayeh slipped out of her room and came back to my cage and whispered to me. I could understand her again.

'Now you know my secret, Humphrey,' she whispered. 'My family doesn't speak English. Well, my dad does a little, but he's shy about it. Mum hasn't learned any English at all. And Darek's too little.'

'I understand,' I squeaked.

'That's why I don't like to talk in class,' she explained. 'I don't talk like the other kids. I'm afraid they'll laugh at my accent. That happened to me when I was little.'

'But you don't sound different,' I frantically squeaked. 'I understand you just fine.'

Unfortunately, she didn't understand me. All she heard was 'Squeak-squeak-squeak.' I suppose maybe I have an accent, too.

'But I have an idea that maybe you could help me teach Mum English,' Sayeh continued.

'Glad to help out if I can,' I squeaked to her.

'You're a real friend,' Sayeh replied.

See? She understood me after all.

The next day, I dozed until late afternoon, when Sayeh led her mother back to my cage.

'Humphrey only understands English, Mama,' Sayeh said. 'Speak English. Say, "Humphrey."'

Sayeh's mum looked a little frightened, but she tried.

'Hum-freee,' she said.

'Rummy,' Darek cried as he raced into the room and climbed on to his mother's lap.

'Say, "Hello, Humphrey,"' Sayeh told her mother.

'Hel-lo, Hump-free,' Mrs Nasiri said.

I squeaked, 'Hello,' right back and she broke into a huge smile.

'Hello,' she said.

'Good job,' I said.

Well, things went swimmingly from then on. In a matter of hours, Sayeh's mum was saying, 'How do you do?' 'Nice to meet you.' 'Would you like some water?' (I did, thank you.)

Even when Sayeh and Darek left to go to the shops with their father, Mrs Nasiri kept on talking. I let her know I understood what she was saying by wiggling my whiskers and hanging by one paw from the top of my cage.

'Good boy, Humphrey,' she said.

Sayeh and her father were amazed at Mrs Nasiri's progress when they returned. The family spent the rest of the evening practising English.

First, Sayeh pretended to be a guest at the door. She went into the hall and knocked.

Her mother opened the door. 'Hello, Sayeh,' she said. 'Won't you come in?'

Then Darek went out and knocked. Mrs Nasiri opened the door and said, 'Hello, Darek. Won't you come in?'

He rushed in and toddled right over to the table, shouting, 'Humfy! Humfy!'

Next, Sayeh convinced her dad to practise English with her mum.

'What time it is?' asked Mrs Nasiri.

'What time is it?' Sayeh corrected her.

Mrs Nasiri got it right the second time.

Then Dad looked at his watch. 'Seven-fifteen,' he answered.

'Would you like some tea?' asked Mrs Nasiri.

'Yes, please. I would like some tea,' answered Mr Nasiri.

Guess what? They had a tea party right on my table. As a reward for all their hard work, I spun my wheel as fast as my legs would go, and they all cheered.

Later, after they'd gone to bed, Sayeh slipped out of her room to talk to me again.

'Thank you, Humphrey,' she whispered. 'My mum says she's ready to go to English classes now. But I wish you were the teacher.'

'So do I,' I squeaked, and I meant it.

There were more English lessons on Sunday, and Sayeh showed Darek how to clean out my cage. Suddenly, the boy began to giggle.

'Humphrey poop!' he yelled. His English was improving, too.

On Sunday night, Sayeh gathered her family together again.

'I want to teach you the American song,' she said. Then she opened her mouth and began to sing, 'Oh, say, can you see? By the dawn's early light.'

I stood up, just like we do in the classroom when 'The Star-Spangled Banner' is being sung. But I'd never heard it sung like that before. Sayeh had the most beautiful voice in the world! It was like a gentle breeze . . . No, like rippling waters . . . No, it was . . . well, it was beautiful.

If only our classmates in Room 26 could hear her!

Which gave me the start of another idea. But I didn't have time to think much at all. Because soon, the whole family was singing 'The Star-Spangled Banner', and I squeaked right along with them! Even on those high notes.

When we got back to school on Monday morning, though, I was a little disappointed. Mrs Brisbane asked Sayeh how things had gone over the week-end.

'Fine,' said Sayeh. And nothing more.

Like Ms Mac said, 'You can learn a lot about yourself by getting to know another species.' But, boy, sometimes it's a lot of work.

That Monday, I sat in my cage worrying about Sayeh for quite a while before I dozed off. When I woke up, I noticed that Room 26 had changed. The bulletin board was covered with brightly coloured leaves. The tops of the blackboards were lined with big paper witches, ghosts and skeletons. Hanging from the light fixtures were black crêpe-paper bats. Then I looked to my right and gasped. A horrible, huge orange face with an evil grin was staring directly at me. I jumped back, my heart pounding.

'Hey, Humphrey, don't you like old pumpkin head?' A.J. whispered to me from his seat near by.

'Look! Humphrey's scared of a little old jack-o'-lantern,' Garth said. 'Scaredy-cat. Scaredy-hamster.'

I stood up straight and looked as brave as I possibly could.

'Quiet, Garth and A.J.,' said Mrs Brisbane. Then she quickly returned to a maths question she was writing on the board.

Suddenly, I noticed a little movement in the centre of the room. A murmur. A change. I looked over and YES-YES-YES! Sayeh had her hand up. Everyone noticed it, except Mrs Brisbane, who had her back to the rest of us. 'Mrs Brisbane?' Heidi called out.

Without turning, the teacher said, 'Raise-Your-Hand-Heidi.'

Now Heidi had her hand raised as well as Sayeh.

'Well, what is it?' Mrs Brisbane turned to face the class and was obviously surprised by what she saw.

'Yes, Sayeh,' she said.

In a loud, clear voice, Sayeh said, 'May I move the pumpkin away from Humphrey's cage?'

Mrs Brisbane looked from Sayeh to the cage and back.

'Yes. I suppose it is a little close. Thank you, Sayeh.'

Sayeh rose and hurried to my table to push the

ugly old jack-o'-lantern away. She didn't say a word, but she winked at me and I knew what she meant.

'Heidi, did you want to say something?' Mrs Brisbane asked.

'Not any more,' she said.

Everything went back to normal until the bell rang for break. As my classmates all scattered and ran towards the door, Garth paused by my cage.

'Scaredy-cat,' he muttered. Then he moved the pumpkin right up against my cage again.

I puffed up my cheeks as big as I could get them. It was going to be a very long day.

TIP SEVEN

When hamsters feel intimidated, they often puff up their cheeks.

Guide to the Care and Feeding of Hamsters

Dr Harvey H. Hammer

8

Tricks and Treats

Hallow-Een. Or Hollowin'. Or Howloween.

I wasn't sure what it was, but I was pretty sure I didn't like it.

Especially on Monday night, after Mrs Brisbane turned out the lights. That's when those skeletons on the wall took on an eerie glow.

The bats hanging from the ceiling began to whirl and twirl.

And the smile on that ghastly orange pumpkin face looked more like a wicked smirk.

WEIRD-WEIRD-WEIRD.

So I was thrilled when Aldo flicked on the lights.

'Whoa. It looks like Halloween in here,' he exclaimed as he wheeled in his cleaning trolley. He strolled over to my cage as usual and bent down so we were face-to-face.

'So, are you going to wear a costume for Halloween? It's on Wednesday, you know. Halloween is when the ghosts and goblins come out to play,' he explained.

'Eeeek!' I squeaked.

'No, no, it's not scary. It's just fun. All the kids will wear costumes. Richie's going to be a werewolf. So what are you going to wear? A fur coat?' He laughed at his own joke, then began his cleaning routine, talking to me as he swept and dusted.

I started thinking about this costume thing. Ms Mac had a costume party once while I was staying with her. People dressed up like kings and pirates and ghosts, and Ms Mac dressed up like a clown with a sparkly pink wig and a funny face.

Nobody wore a fur coat.

I thought about this costume thing all night and the next day.

When Garth threw a piece of rolled-up paper in my cage, I wondered about the costumes.

When A.J. tripped on his way up to the blackboard and Gail didn't giggle, I wondered about the costumes.

Even when Mrs Brisbane called on Sayeh and she answered her, I wondered about the costumes.

And I came up with a plan of my own.

On Wednesday, Halloween arrived. But there were no costumes. I was extremely disappointed until Heidi blurted out, 'Mrs Brisbane, when are we going to have the party?'

'Raise-Your-Hand-Heidi,' the teacher told her.

Heidi obediently raised her hand and Mrs Brisbane called on her. This time, when Heidi asked her question, Mrs Brisbane said, 'We will have our lessons this morning. After lunch, you may put on your costumes and we'll start the party.'

I felt HAPPY-HAPPY-HAPPY and took a nice nap for the rest of the morning.

But I was wide awake after lunch. My classmates returned from the canteen, then scurried off to the cloakroom and the bathrooms and returned. But I hardly recognized them in their costumes.

Oh, they were wonderful! A dragon, two pirates, a princess, a ninja, two clowns, a ballerina, a bunny, a cat (thank goodness not a real one), a football player, a mad scientist, a skeleton, the Statue of Liberty, an angel and a devil!

Two parent volunteers came to help with the party. They were both dressed as witches. Still, Mrs Brisbane was the scariest of them all.

She didn't wear a costume – just a badge that had the words 'This IS my costume' printed on it.

She gathered everyone in a circle, pushing back

all the tables. Then she announced that the class would be having some treats. But in order to get them, they each had to do a trick: tell a joke, sing a song or perform a trick for the rest of the class.

Oh, I wish someone had told me. I had figured out the costume part, but what about this tricking for treats?

Art (the ninja) stood on his head. He stood on his head for so long that Mrs Brisbane finally had to thank him and tell him it was someone else's turn.

Gail (the ballerina) twirled around the room on her toes. Garth (football player) told a joke about a witch. Miranda (bunny) sang a funny song about your ears hanging low. It was all very entertaining, except for the fact that I was thinking about something else.

But Mrs Brisbane got my full attention when she called on Sayeh, who was dressed as the Statue of Liberty. She wore a flowing dress and had a crown on her head and a big cardboard torch in one hand. She stared down at the floor as she took her place in the centre of the circle.

'What trick will you do for us, Sayeh?' the teacher asked.

Sayeh still stared at the floor.

'Sing your song, Sayeh! Sing!' I squeaked out as loudly as I could. 'You can do it, Sayeh. Sing!'

Yes, I know all she could hear was 'Squeak-squeak-squeak,' but I did my best.

'I think Humphrey wants to hear from you,' said Mrs Brisbane in a surprisingly friendly voice.

Suddenly, without warning, Sayeh began to sing 'The Star-Spangled Banner' in her clear, sweet voice.

Everyone stood up right away, like you're supposed to when they sing the national anthem. Mrs Brisbane put her hand over her heart and the other kids did, too. Well, Pay-Attention-Art didn't until his mum came over and whispered in his ear.

I stood up, too, as proud as a hamster could possibly be.

When it was over, no one clapped or said a word. It seemed as if those sweet notes were still drifting around the room.

'That was lovely, Sayeh. Thank you for sharing your beautiful voice with us,' Mrs Brisbane said.

I wish she'd speak that way to me some day. Nice. Encouraging. Friendly.

Anyway, the tricks continued. And after A.J. told a few riddles, Mrs Brisbane looked around the circle and said, 'Did I miss anyone?'

This was the moment I'd been waiting for. No one had noticed, but the night before, I had sneaked one of Aldo's white dusting cloths into my sleeping hut. I had to act quickly. I pulled out the cloth and crawled under so it completely covered me. Then I stood up and began to shout like I'd never shouted before.

'Trick or squeak!' I cried. 'Trick or squeak!'

Miranda noticed first. 'Look!' she yelled. 'It's Humphrey!'

I wish I could have seen the faces of my classmates, but it was DARK-DARK-DARK under the cloth. I could hear them, though. First there were gasps, then giggles, then shouts of 'Look!' and 'Humphrey's a ghost!'

I continued to squeak my heart out until I heard Mrs Brisbane's firm footsteps coming towards my cage.

'Who did this?' she asked. 'Who put that on Humphrey?'

No one answered, of course. Not even me.

'He could suffocate under that,' she said.

'But he looks so cute,' Heidi called out.

Mrs Brisbane didn't answer. She just said, 'Will someone please uncover him?'

Golden-Miranda opened the cage door and whisked away the cloth. 'Humphrey, you are a riot,' she said.

Only a riot? Let's be honest here: I was a smash hit!

Then the two parent volunteers served up cupcakes with orange icing and cups of apple juice, and my classmates played games.

Just before the bell rang, Mrs Brisbane clapped her hands and made an announcement. 'Mrs Hopper and Mrs Patel and I have consulted with one another. We have decided to give the prize for Best Trick to Sayeh Nasiri.'

Everyone clapped and cheered as Mrs Brisbane handed Sayeh a blue ribbon. Sayeh looked over at me and smiled a beautiful smile.

Mrs Brisbane continued: 'And we have decided to award the prize for Best Costume to . . . Humphrey.'

She walked over to my cage and taped a big blue ribbon to it while my classmates cheered for me.

'Thank you,' I squeaked, but I'm not sure anyone could hear me over all the noise. 'Thank you all.'

The bell rang and the room was soon empty, except for Mrs Brisbane. As she gathered up her papers to take home, Mr Morales came in. He was dressed in a cap and gown like people wear when they are graduating.

'Happy Halloween, Sue. Did you have a good party?' he asked.

'Very,' she answered. 'Somehow your friend over there got hold of a ghost costume and won the prize.'

'See? I told you he'd add a lot to your classroom,' he said with a smile.

'He *has* livened things up,' said Mrs Brisbane.

JOY-JOY-JOY! I believed she was starting to like me. 'Just as long as he doesn't liven things up too much,' she added.

Poof. My hopes of winning over Mrs Brisbane's heart crashed to the ground.

Mr Morales said his kids kept asking about me and then he quickly left. Mrs Brisbane headed out of the door after him.

There I was, all alone in Room 26 with a bunch of half-torn bats and tattered skeletons hanging around me.

As I waited for Aldo to arrive, I sat in the darkening room and pondered my job as a classroom pet. Had I really accomplished anything? Mr Morales's children seemed to settle down when I was there. Sayeh's mother began to learn English. And Sayeh would probably never have sung in front of the class without my encouragement.

Still, Mrs Brisbane was not won over.

Neither was Garth Tugwell, although it seemed as if he had liked me well enough in the beginning. Now he always muttered things at me as he passed by my cage.

I noticed that he was the only one in class who didn't cheer when I won the award for Best Costume.

I was still worrying about Garth when the lights

temporarily blinded me as Aldo sailed into the classroom, yelling, 'Trick or treat!'

He was wearing his usual work shirt, dark pants and heavy shoes. But on his face he wore huge glasses with a bulbous nose attached. The centre of the glasses had giant eyeballs painted on with circles of red veins. His floppy moustache drooped out from under the nose.

'Great costume,' I squeaked.

'Hey, what's this?' Aldo rushed forward to examine my blue ribbon. 'Best Costume? For a fur coat? I'll have to ask Richie about that,' he said.

Aldo reached into his lunch box and pulled out a juicy slice of apple.

'I've got a special Halloween treat for you, Humphrey. 'Cause I'm very, very happy tonight,' he said.

I grabbed the apple and began nibbling as Aldo pulled his chair up close to my cage.

'You see, I went to the Moonlighters Club. You remember, the club in that ad I found on the projector?'

I squeaked an excited 'Yes.'

'And I met a really nice girl there, named Maria. She works all night at the bakery. So tomorrow, we're going out on a date. Lunch and a movie.' Aldo leaned back in his chair.

'She's a really nice girl. Pretty. Nice. Did I tell you she works in a bakery?'

Aldo rose and paced back and forth in front of my cage.

'You know what I can't work out? I can't work out how that ad got on that projector. Mrs Brisbane wouldn't show that to the class. And she wouldn't be interested herself. And it was weird how the projector was left on. Mrs Brisbane always leaves her room in shipshape condition.' He paused to rub his chin, then looked at me out of the corner of his eye.

'You know, if you weren't locked up in a cage, I'd think you had something to do with it,' he said. Then he laughed. 'Well, whoever it was, I owe them a big thank-you.'

'You're welcome,' I squeaked.

Too bad Aldo didn't understand me this time.

> TIP EIGHT
>
> Hamsters are most active during the evening.
>
> *Guide to the Care and Feeding of Hamsters*
>
> Dr Harvey H. Hammer

9
The Art of Self-Defence

Okay, I was having a great week, no doubt about it.

Not only did I get the blue ribbon on Wednesday, but on Thursday the class received a long letter from Ms Mac. She included a picture of her standing by a waterfall next to some very strange-looking creatures. They looked like hairy pigs or raccoony dogs.

'These are coatis,' Mrs Brisbane said, reading from the letter. 'Pronounced *ko-ahh-tees*.'

The coatis looked weird. Ms Mac looked gorgeous, especially with all the red, yellow and orange flowers surrounding her.

How I wished I could be there with her! Except maybe for the fact that those coatis might not be hamster-friendly.

At the end of her letter, Ms Mac wrote, 'So farewell to all my wonderful friends in Room 26, especially the small one with the big heart: Humphrey.'

SIGH-SIGH-SIGH.

Though the thought of Ms Mac made me happy, the weekend was coming up soon and I always felt a little nervous about where I'd be spending it.

When it was decided on Thursday that I was going home with Golden-Miranda – I mean Miranda Golden – I was so excited that I got only 83 per cent on my vocabulary test. (Sayeh got 100 per cent. I know, because this time when Mrs Brisbane asked who got 100 per cent, she raised her hand.)

I always thought that Miranda lived in a castle, because she reminded me of a fairy-tale princess in disguise. Wherever it was, it had to be wonderful if Miranda lived there.

Well, Miranda's home wasn't exactly a castle, but it was very tall. Miranda lived in a fourth-floor flat with her mum and her big dog, Clem. We had to take a lift to get there.

The flat was nice. The mum was nice. Clem was not nice.

Let me explain. Miranda has a small bedroom and her mum let me stay there, right on the desk. To welcome me, the two of them did a complete clean-out of my cage. 'I'll bet nobody's done this for a while,' said Miranda's mum, and she was right. Pretty soon, I felt like a brand-new hamster!

Suddenly, Clem bounded into the room, a big mass of yellow fur poking his huge nose right up against my cage. His wet nostrils were like two eyes staring in at me and he stuck out a giant tongue that came at me like a tidal wave. Luckily, the cage protected me.

'Mum!' Miranda yelled. 'Please get Clem out of here!'

Thank heavens Mum took Clem out for a walk in the park while Miranda showed me her room. She held pictures of her friends and family up to the cage so I could see. Her dad. Her stepmum. Her grandparents in Florida. Next, she introduced me to her goldfish, Fanny. She wasn't much of a conversationalist. I squeaked, 'Nice to meet you, Fanny,' and she said, 'Blub.'

I was thinking about how wonderful it would be to live with Miranda all the time when Clem returned from the park and galloped into the room.

'Clem, stay out!' Miranda shouted. But Clem just wagged his tail and barked.

Miranda closed the door so the dog had to stay outside, but we could still hear him whining and crying like a baby out in the hall.

Still, just being with Miranda made everything seem golden until her mum called her to go shopping. Miranda protested. Good girl! But Mum didn't want her to stay inside on such a nice day. She had no choice, unless she was rude to her mum, which Miranda never would be!

'I won't be gone long,' Miranda told me. 'And I'll make sure the door is shut tightly so Clem can't get in.'

Everything would be all right, I assured myself. After all, Miranda had said so. I was all set to get in a good daytime snooze.

But as soon as the door to the flat closed, Clem started whining outside the room. I could hear his big paws up on the door, trying to push it open. I was a little nervous, but Miranda had assured me I'd be all right. After all, she wouldn't be gone long.

Then I heard it, the slight turning of the door-knob as Clem flung himself repeatedly at the door. What a barbarian he was.

Suddenly, the door swung open and Clem burst in and ran straight to my cage.

I tried to distract him by spinning on my wheel. I can do that for hours, if necessary. I thought the spinning wheel might even hypnotize him, like in an old movie I'd seen with Ms Mac. (Ms Mac! Where was she when I needed her?)

But apparently all that spinning just excited Clem even more. He started barking at me, but I couldn't understand a word he said.

'Now cut that out!' I squeaked at him. That just seemed to make him more hot and bothered.

He plopped his front paws up on the desk and stuck his nose against the cage door, near the lock.

The lock-that-doesn't-lock.

'Easy now. Calm down,' I squeaked soothingly at the beast, but he kept poking his nose at the cage, showing me his huge tongue and the huge teeth around it.

(Let me just say that Clem could do with some breath mints.)

He poked the lock again and again. I knew if he jiggled it enough, the door would swing open and I'd be history. Poor Miranda would never know what had happened to me. She might even cry. I couldn't stand the thought of Miranda crying. I hopped back on my wheel and started spinning with all my might, hoping to buy some time.

Clem pulled back for a moment and stared at the wheel going round and round.

(Let me just say I'm glad that Clem is not well equipped in the brain department.)

Whew, I'm a good spinner, but I was getting worried about how long I could keep it up when Golden-Miranda rushed in. She never looked more beautiful to me than at that moment.

'Clem! Stop it!' she shouted in a very firm voice. 'Bad boy!'

Clem raced to her side, wagging his tail.

Miranda's mum dragged old Clem out of the room and closed the door behind her.

WHEW-WHEW-WHEW!

Miranda was very sorry. She opened the cage and reached in to pick me up. 'Poor Humphrey,' she said, hugging me. She set me on her desk and stroked me gently with one finger. 'I'm so sorry, Humphrey. So sorry.'

Ohhhhh. I don't know what felt better: the petting or Miranda's soothing words.

Miranda felt so terrible about what had happened, she let me play on her desk. She lined up books all along the edges so I wouldn't fall off. Then she let me wander around and see the sights.

A desktop is a very interesting place, in case you've never explored one. Miranda's desktop had a big cup with hearts all over it. The cup was filled with pencils. Ah, pencils smell so sweet. She had a round, silvery container full of paper clips and a square, purple container full of rubber bands. She had lots of paper in a pink box. And she had a great big fat dictionary. I could really use one of those. I wonder if they make doll-sized dictionaries you can hide behind a hamster's mirror?

Miranda giggled as she watched me check things out. When I tried to climb into the paper-clip box, she stopped me with her finger.

'No, no, Humphrey. Those would hurt you.'

She did the same thing when I tried to roll in the rubber-band box.

'No, Humphrey. Rubber bands can be very dangerous,' she told me.

Well, I suppose I knew *that*. Hadn't Garth shot a rubber band at A.J. last week and almost got sent to Headmaster Morales's office? Hadn't A.J. held his arm and said, 'Ow,' when the rubber band hit him?

Anyway, I really enjoyed my time on the desk, until I heard Clem barking. Then I made a beeline for home. 'Oh, Humphrey, I won't let Clem hurt you. Honest,' Miranda assured me as she gently helped me back in my cage.

I believed her. I really did.

But when it was bedtime and Miranda's mum came into the room to say goodnight, she said some words that sent a chill up my spine:

'Don't forget, we're going to the Nicholsons' house tomorrow night.'

Miranda protested. 'I hate to leave Humphrey. Clem gives him such a hard time.'

'We'll lock the door this time, honey. He'll be okay,' her mum said. 'And tonight, Clem will be in my room.'

After her mother left, Miranda assured me that

Clem loves to sleep in Mum's room. 'But if anything happens and you get scared, just give me a squeak,' she told me.

'Don't worry, I will!' I assured her.

I didn't sleep that night. For one thing, the stars on Miranda's ceiling glow in the dark and they're so beautiful, I couldn't take my eyes off them.

For another thing . . . well, I am nocturnal.

But mainly I didn't sleep because I was worried about Clem.

After my experience that afternoon, I believed that no lock could hold him back. And how could a little hamster fight back? What weapon would I have against a big, hairy, bad-breathed, small-brained creature?

What weapon, indeed! I had an idea.

Clem hadn't made a peep for hours, so I took a chance and quietly opened the lock-that-doesn't-lock and dashed across the desktop to pick my weapon, just in case of another encounter with Clem. Then I scampered back to the cage with it and quietly closed the door.

I hid my weapon behind my mirror, next to the notebook, where no one could find it. Then I managed to get forty winks or so of sleep around sunrise.

Miranda and her mum kept Clem out of my sight all day, until it was time for them to go to their party.

'I'm still worried,' said Miranda,

'I'm locking your door with a key on the outside,' her mum said. 'I'm locking Clem in my room. And Humphrey's cage is closed tightly. Right?'

Miranda checked it. Everybody always checks it. It always seems locked from the outside. It even makes a clicking sound. But from the inside, believe me, it's a piece of cake to open.

Miranda seemed satisfied with the arrangement, but I wasn't. So I remained on high alert all that afternoon and evening. And here's what happened.

After Miranda and her mum left, Clem barked for a while.

Then I heard jiggling and joggling for about an hour.

Next, I heard big hairy feet padding down the hall towards Miranda's room. Towards *my* room.

I sucked in my breath and waited. Yes, I knew Miranda's mom had locked the door with a key. But Clem didn't seem to let little things like that stand in his way.

The doorknob squeaked and rattled. It twisted and turned. Nothing happened. But that didn't seem to bother Clem the barbarian.

He jiggled-rattled-and-twisted it some more. When he got tired of that, he threw his whole body at the door. And then, very slowly, the door opened.

Clem actually seemed surprised, but I wasn't. I had spent the last two hours carefully preparing for this moment.

But my heart was still going THUMP-THUMP-THUMP very loudly. Even Fanny the fish seemed nervous.

Clem trotted right up to my cage and stuck his big wet nose up against it.

'Stay away! Keep your distance!' I squeaked. 'I'm warning you.'

Clem wasn't discouraged one bit.

'Woof!' he barked, sending a foul cloud of doggy breath my way.

I didn't even flinch.

He barked a few more times and then began poking his big nose against the cage door. I wondered if he knew the lock was broken.

The time had arrived to put my plan into action. I was in grave danger and I had no choice. I would have only one chance at Clem because I had only one weapon: a rubber band. It had taken me a long time to get it hooked around the edge of my food dish. Now I carefully pulled it back as far as I could, aiming directly at those big doggy nostrils.

‘You asked for it, beast!’ I squeaked.

Then I let loose. The rubber band snapped and sailed through the air, hitting Clem squarely on the nose.

He yelped like a baby and raced out of the room as if he’d seen a ghost. Too bad I didn’t still have my ghost costume. That would have been a nice touch.

I suppose Clem wasn’t quite as stupid as I had thought, because he never even tried to come back in the room again.

Of course, Miranda and her mum were really puzzled when they came home and found both bedrooms unlocked and Clem cowering under the living-room sofa.

‘I don’t get it,’ said Miranda. ‘Humphrey looks just fine. Maybe it was a burglar.’

But Miranda’s mum checked the cupboards and drawers, and nothing was missing. ‘Now, that’s a mystery,’ she said after she’d searched the whole flat.

Miranda stared at me, shaking her head. ‘If only Humphrey could talk,’ she said.

‘But I can if you’d just listen,’ I told her.

‘I bet you’d have a lot to tell us,’ Miranda continued, not understanding my squeaks.

Yes, I do, I thought. Enough to fill a book.

TIP NINE

Hamsters do not enjoy contact with other animals. A cat or dog may eat a hamster or at least do it bodily harm.

Guide to the Care and Feeding of Hamsters

Dr Harvey H. Hammer

Garth Versus A.J.

'If you have dogs or cats, you have to be very careful not to let them get near Humphrey,' Miranda warned the rest of the class when we returned to Room 26.

'You can say that again,' I squeaked. But she didn't.

I still considered Golden-Miranda to be a special friend and I had a very clean cage to show for my weekend, as well as a new respect for rubber bands. But I also decided that even though Miranda is practically a perfect person, I was not in a hurry to stay with her again.

A.J. raised his hand and Mrs Brisbane called on him.

'May I have Humphrey this weekend? We don't have a dog or a cat,' he bellowed.

'Lower-Your-Voice-A.J. I'll let you know on

Thursday. There may be other students who want Humphrey as well.'

At least half the hands in the classroom went up as kids started shouting, 'Me, me!' I was quite flattered. But for some reason, the whole subject seemed to make Garth angry.

Within minutes, he shot a rubber band at A.J.

'Ouch!' A.J. complained loudly. When he told the teacher what had happened, Garth denied it.

'Humphrey did it,' he said.

Gail giggled. Mrs Brisbane did not. 'I don't believe a hamster can shoot a rubber band,' she said sternly. A lot she knows!

The next day, Garth stuck out his foot and tripped Art as he went to sharpen his pencil.

'I didn't do it! He's just clumsy,' Garth protested when Mrs Brisbane angrily scolded him.

That same day, Garth pushed Gail during morning break. He spent afternoon break inside.

'Garth Tugwell, you're halfway to Headmaster Morales's office right now.' Mrs Brisbane sounded really angry.

Garth just shrugged his shoulders.

On Wednesday, Garth sneaked back into the room while Mrs Brisbane went to the office during break, and he headed straight for my cage. The two of us were all alone in the room.

'Hello, rat. Why don't you just run away? Then

nobody will take you home at the weekend,' he said. He opened my cage door and grabbed me. 'You'd like your freedom, wouldn't you, rat?'

He set me on the floor. My heart was pounding. THUMP-THUMP-THUMP!

'Go on, rat. Skedaddle.' He gave me a little push with his hand.

I scampered under the table. I wanted to say something, but for the first time ever, I was scared squeakless. 'Have fun,' he said, and in an instant he was gone.

I was pretty confused. For one thing, I didn't want to run away. I was perfectly happy staying in Room 26 and having adventures at the weekend.

Where would I go? What would I do?

There was no time to waste. I scampered over to the cord that hung down from the blinds and grabbed on to it. Then I started the old swinging routine, back and forth, swinging a little higher each time until I reached the tabletop. Back-forth-back-forth-back-forth . . . leap! There wasn't time to think about my queasy stomach as I raced into my cage, slamming the door shut behind me.

Just then, Mrs Brisbane returned. I darted into my sleeping house so she wouldn't see how hard I was breathing.

I saw her look at the window, puzzled. She walked over to it and stared at the blind cord, which was still swinging. She reached out and stopped it with her hand. Then she shook her head and walked away.

When morning break was over and my classmates filed back into the class, Garth looked over at my cage, half smiling. But that smile quickly disappeared when he saw that the door was closed. He leaped out of his seat and looked in my cage.

'Howdy,' I squeaked at him.

'Garth, please return to your seat,' Mrs Brisbane told him.

'But Humphrey!' he protested.

'Well, what is it?' Mrs Brisbane was getting irritated.

'He's in his cage!' he said.

A few of my classmates giggled, but not Mrs Brisbane.

'In case you haven't noticed, he's always in his cage, Garth,' she said. 'Now get back to your seat.'

Garth did what she said, but for the rest of the day I noticed him staring over at me.

On Thursday, Mrs Brisbane announced that I would be spending the weekend at A.J.'s house.

'Yes!' shouted A.J., delighted at the news.

A few seconds later, a series of rubber bands hit A.J. on his neck, shoulder and head.

'Cool it, Garth!' yelled A.J., jumping out of his chair. 'Man, I'm tired of these rubber bands.'

Garth acted innocent. 'I don't know where they came from. They could have come from anywhere.'

'Garth did it,' Heidi said. 'I saw him.'

Mrs Brisbane didn't remind Heidi to raise her hand. But she did tell Garth to stay in during afternoon break.

'Not fair,' Garth muttered under his breath.

When the bell rang for break, Garth stayed in his seat. Mrs Brisbane closed the door when all the other students had left and walked to his desk. Normally, I would have been napping at this time, but I was wide awake and wondering what that boy had to say.

'Garth. You've been acting strangely lately. You never got into trouble at all until two weeks ago. Now you are shooting rubber bands at people and disturbing the entire class. Can you tell me why?'

Garth slowly shook his head.

'Your marks are slipping, too. Has something changed in your life?'

Garth slowly shook his head again.

'How about at home? Is anything wrong?'

Garth didn't shake his head. He didn't move a muscle.

'Should I talk to your parents about your behaviour, Garth?'

Garth's face went very red. 'No,' he said with a choking sound.

Mrs Brisbane moved closer and put her hand on Garth's shoulder. 'Tell me what's wrong.'

'My . . . mum's . . . sick,' he said. 'Really sick.' Tears ran down his cheeks. I was feeling a little teary-eyed myself.

'How sick?' Mrs Brisbane asked.

'She lost all this weight and she was in and out of the hospital and now she's just tired all the time and . . .' Garth didn't try to finish his sentence. He wiped away the tears with the tissue Mrs Brisbane handed him. 'That's why I can't take Humphrey home. My dad says we can't let anything bother Mum. Well, my little brother bothers her and we let him in the house.'

Mrs Brisbane smiled slightly. 'Humphrey is a big responsibility, Garth. That's why I don't take him home. My husband has been sick, too. Did you know that?'

Garth shook his head. 'No.'

'So I know what it's like. Listen, I'll make a few calls tonight. Maybe we can find a way for you to spend some time with Humphrey,' she said.

'But he hates me,' I squeaked.

'I'd like to,' said Garth.

Huh? I was confused.

'But you have to promise me that you won't disrupt the class any more,' Mrs Brisbane told him. 'Is that a deal?'

Garth nodded. 'Deal.'

As you know, I'm very good at coming up with plans to solve human problems. Very, very good. But try as I might, I couldn't imagine what Mrs Brisbane's plan to get Garth to spend time with me could be.

I was still trying to work it out when Aldo arrived that night.

'Humphrey, my man!' he yelled when he opened the door.

I almost fell off my wheel.

'You are the most handsome, intelligent hamster in the world! And I am the luckiest man in the world! Because I am dating the most beautiful woman in the world!'

Aldo swept his way towards my cage, then lowered his voice. 'Uh, but don't tell anybody I said so. Not yet. After all, Maria and I have been out only three times. But, oh, what times we've had!'

He pulled up a chair and sat very close to me.

'And it's all thanks to the Moonlighters Club. And that clipping over there . . .' He pointed towards the spot where the overhead projector had once stood. 'And you! I know you had something to do with it. I just can't figure out what. Anyway, don't tell anybody, but some day, I'm going to marry Maria. And when I do, I want you to be best man. Or best hamster, I suppose. I really mean it.

If you were a guy, I'd buy you a burger.'

He reached in his pocket and pulled out a little piece of foil. 'Instead, I got you this.' He unwrapped a piece of carrot and put it in my cage.

'Thank you, Aldo,' I squeaked. 'I wish you lots of happiness.'

'I knew you'd be happy for me, Humphrey.' Aldo smiled and then jumped up. 'Whooo! I've got so much energy, I can clean this room in half the time. I could climb a mountain and not even get tired! I could conquer the world!' He leaned forward and grinned through his glorious moustache. 'Ain't love grand?'

'If you say so,' I replied.

I'd never seen anyone so happy before. The only thing that would make me that happy would be if Ms Mac came back.

She's not coming back.

And I'm still stuck with Mrs Brisbane. And she's stuck with me.

I wonder what she meant when she said she doesn't take me home because her husband's sick. Did she mean she *would* take me home if her husband wasn't sick?

I thought about it all night and came up with this answer: NO-NO-NO.

She doesn't take me home because she doesn't like me.

Maybe I'm lucky after all.

TIP TEN
Hamsters are incredible acrobats and climbers. They seem to defy the laws of gravity.

Guide to the Care and Feeding of Hamsters
Dr Harvey H. Hammer

11

TV or Not TV

Wow! Friday was a great adventure because A.J. took me on the school bus. It was noisy and smelly and very, very bumpy, and just about everyone on the bus wanted to get a good look at me, including the driver, Ms Victoria.

It was exciting – almost too exciting because A.J. couldn't hold my cage steady and I was slipping and sliding and bouncing until I was quite dizzy.

'Sorry, Humphrey. I'm trying to hold still,' A.J. told me as someone bumped his elbow and sent me sprawling on the floor of my cage.

'It's all right,' I squeaked weakly.

The bus let us off close to A.J.'s house. It was a two-storey old house with a big porch. As soon as I entered, I got a warm welcome from A.J.'s mum, his younger brother Ty, his little sister DeeLee, and his baby brother Beau.

'Anthony James, introduce us to your little friend,' his mum said, greeting us.

Anthony James? Everybody at school called A.J. by his initials or just 'Aje'.

'This is Humphrey,' he answered.

'Hello, Humphrey,' said Mrs Thomas. 'So how was your day, Anthony?'

'Lousy. Garth kept shooting rubber bands at me. He won't leave me alone.'

'But you two used to be friends,' his mother said.

'Used to be,' said A.J. 'Until he turned into a JERK.'

Mum patted her son on the shoulder. 'Well, you've got the whole weekend to get over it. Now take Humphrey into the den and get him settled.'

Mrs Brisbane called him Lower-Your-Voice-A.J. because A.J. always talked extra loud in class. I soon noticed that everybody at A.J.'s house talked extra loud. They had to, because in the background the TV was always blaring.

Now, every house I've been in so far has had a TV. Even Ms Mac had a TV, and I enjoyed some of the shows I saw with her.

There's one channel that has nothing but the most frightening shows about wild animals attacking one another. I mean *wild*, like tigers and bears and hippopotamuses. (I hope *that*'s not in our vocabulary test in the near future.) Those shows make me appreciate the protection of a nice cage. As long as the lock doesn't quite lock.

There's another channel that only has people in funny-looking clothes dancing and singing in very strange places. It makes me glad that I have a fur coat and don't have to work out what to wear every day.

Mostly, I like the cartoon shows. Sometimes they have mice and rabbits and other interesting rodents, although I've never seen a hamster show. Yet.

Anyway, the difference at the Thomases' house is that the television is on *all the time*. There's a TV on a table across from a big, comfy couch and a big, comfy chair and someone's almost always sitting there watching. I know because they put my cage down on the floor next to the couch. I had a very good view of the TV.

I couldn't always hear the TV, though, because A.J.'s mother had a radio in the kitchen, which was blaring most of the time while she cooked or did crossword puzzles or talked on the phone. No matter what she did, the radio was always on.

When A.J.'s dad came home from work, he plopped down on the couch and watched TV while he played with the baby. Then A.J. and Ty plugged in some video games and played while Dad watched. DeeLee listened to the radio with her mum and danced around the kitchen.

When it was time for dinner, the whole family took plates and sat in the den so they could watch TV while they ate.

Then they watched TV some more. They made popcorn and kept watching.

Finally, the kids went to bed. The baby first, then DeeLee and later Ty and A.J.

After they were all in their rooms, Mr and Mrs Thomas kept watching TV and ate some ice-cream.

Later, Mrs Thomas yawned loudly. 'I've had it, Charlie. I'm going to bed and I suggest you do, too,' she said.

But Mr Thomas just kept on watching. Or at least he kept on sitting there until he fell asleep on the couch. I ended up watching the rest of the wrestling match without him. Unfortunately, the wrestler I was rooting for, Thor of Glore, lost. Finally, Mr Thomas woke up, yawned, flicked off the TV and went upstairs to bed. Peace at last.

But the quiet lasted only about ten minutes. Soon Mum brought Beau downstairs and gave him a bottle while she watched TV. When Beau finally fell asleep, Mrs Thomas yawned and flicked off the TV. Blessed relief.

Five minutes later, Mr Thomas returned. 'Sorry, hamster. Can't sleep,' he mumbled to me as he flicked on the remote. He watched and watched and then dozed off again. But the TV stayed on, leaving me no choice but to watch a string of commercials for car waxes, weight-reduction programmes, exercise machines and 'Red-Hot Harmonica Classics'.

The combination of being nocturnal and being bombarded with sight and sound kept me wide awake.

At the crack of dawn, DeeLee tiptoed into the room, dragging her doll by its hair, and switched to a cartoon show about princesses.

She watched another show about cats and dogs. (Scary!) Then Mr Thomas woke up and wanted to check some sports scores. Mrs Thomas handed him the baby and his bottle and soon the older boys switched over to video games and their parents watched them play.

It was LOUD-LOUD-LOUD. But none of the Thomases seemed to notice.

'What do you want for breakfast?' Mum shouted.

'What?' Dad shouted louder.

'WHAT DO YOU WANT FOR BREAK-FAST?' Mum yelled.

'TOASTED WAFFLES!' Dad yelled louder.

'I CAN'T HEAR THE TV!' Ty hollered, turning up the volume.

'DO YOU WANT JUICE?' Mum screamed.

'CAN'T HEAR YOU!' Dad responded.

And so it went on. With each new question, the sound on the TV would be turned up higher and higher until it was positively deafening.

Then Mum switched on her radio.

The Thomases were a perfectly nice family, but I could tell it was going to be a very long and noisy weekend unless I came up with a plan.

So, I spun on my wheel for a while to help me think. And I thought and thought and thought some more. And then it came: the big idea. I probably would have come up with it sooner if I could have heard myself think!

Around noon, the Thomases were all watching the football game on TV. Or rather, Mr Thomas was watching the football game on TV while A.J. and Ty shouted questions at him. Mrs Thomas was in the kitchen listening to the radio and talking on the phone. DeeLee played peekaboo with the baby in the cosy chair.

No one was watching me, so I carefully opened the lock-that-doesn't-lock on my cage and made a quick exit.

Naturally, no one could hear me skittering across the floor as I made my way around the outside of the room, over to the space behind the TV cabinet. Then, with great effort, I managed to pull out the plug: one of the most difficult feats of my life.

The TV went silent. Beautifully, blissfully, silently silent. So silent, I was afraid to move. I waited behind the cabinet, frozen.

The Thomases stared at the TV screen as the picture slowly went dark.

'Ty, did you hit that remote?' Mr Thomas asked.

'Naw. It's under the table.'

'Anthony, go and turn that thing on again,' Mr Thomas said. A.J. jumped up and hit the power button on the TV. Nothing happened.

'It's broken!' he exclaimed.

Mrs Thomas rushed in from the kitchen. 'What happened?'

Mr Thomas explained that the TV had gone off and they discussed how old it was (five years), whether it had a guarantee (no one knew) and if Mr Thomas could fix it (he couldn't).

'Everything was fine and it went off – just like that. I guess we'd better take it in to get fixed,' Mr Thomas said.

'How long will it take?' DeeLee asked in a whiny voice.

'I don't know,' her dad replied.

'How much will it cost?' Mrs Thomas asked.

'Oh, yeah,' her husband said. 'I forgot. We're a little low on funds right now.'

The baby began to cry. I thought the rest of the family might start crying, too.

'Well, I get paid next Friday,' Dad said.

A.J. jumped up and waved his hands. 'That's a whole week away!'

'I'm going to Grandma's house. Her TV works,' said Ty.

'Me, too,' DeeLee chimed in.

'Grandma's got her bridge club over there tonight,' Mum said.

'I know,' said Dad. 'Let's go to a movie.'

'Do you know how much it costs to go to a movie?' Mum asked. 'Besides, we can't take the baby.'

'Oh.'

They whined and bickered for quite a while. They got so loud, I managed to scamper back to my cage, unnoticed. Then I suppose I dozed off. Remember, I had hardly had a wink of sleep since I'd arrived. The bickering was a nice, soothing background after all that racket.

I was only half asleep when the squabbling changed.

'But there's nothing to do,' DeeLee whined.

Her father chuckled. 'Nothing to do! Girl, my brothers and I used to spend weekends at my grandma's house and she never had a TV. Wouldn't allow it!'

'What did you do?' A.J. asked.

'Oh, we were busy every minute,' he recalled. 'We played cards and board games and word games. And we dug in her garden and played tag.' He chuckled again. 'A lot of times we just sat on the porch and talked. My grandma . . . she could *talk*.'

'What'd you talk about?' Ty wondered.

'Oh, she'd tell us stories about her growing up. About ghosts and funny things, like the time her uncle was walking in his sleep and went to church in his pyjamas.'

Mrs Thomas gasped. 'Oh, go on now, Charlie.'

'I'm just telling you what she told us. He woke up in the middle of the service, looked down and there he was, in his blue-and-white striped pyjamas.'

I let out a squeak of surprise and the kids all giggled.

Then Mrs Thomas told a story about a girl in her class who came to school in her slippers by accident one day. 'Yes, the fuzzy kind,' she explained with a big smile.

They talked and talked and Dad got out some cards and they played a game called Crazy Eights and another one called Pig where they put their fingers on their noses and laughed like hyenas. When Beau fussed, they took turns jiggling him on their knees.

After a while, Mrs Thomas gasped. 'For goodness' sake! It's an hour past your bedtimes.'

The children all groaned and asked if they could play cards tomorrow, but in a few minutes all the Thomases had gone to bed and it was QUIET-QUIET-QUIET for the first time since I'd arrived.

TIP ELEVEN

Be careful. If set free, hamsters are experts at disappearing in a room.

Guide to the Care and Feeding of Hamsters

Dr Harvey H. Hammer

12

Peace Breaks Out

Early in the morning, Ty, DeeLee and A.J. raced downstairs and played Crazy Eights. Later, they ran outside and kicked a football around the yard.

The Thomases were having breakfast with Beau when the phone rang. Mr Thomas talked for a few minutes, mostly saying, 'Uh-huh, that's fine.' When he hung up, he told Mrs Thomas, 'We're going to have a visitor. But don't tell Anthony James.'

Oooh, a mystery. I like mysteries because they're fun to solve. Then again, I don't like mysteries because I don't like not knowing what's going on. So I waited and waited.

A few hours later, the doorbell rang.

The visitor turned out to be Garth Tugwell and his father! 'I really appreciate this,' Mr Tugwell told the Thomases. 'It was Mrs Brisbane's idea. Since Garth can't have Humphrey at our house right now, she suggested that he could help A.J. take care of him over here.'

Sounds like Mrs Brisbane. As if I'm any trouble to take care of.

But Garth had been crying because he couldn't have me. So maybe – *maybe* – she was trying to be nice.

After Mr Tugwell left, Mr Thomas called in A.J.

A.J. ran into the room and practically backed out again when he saw Garth.

'We have a guest,' said Mr Thomas. 'Shake hands, Anthony. Garth is here to help you take care of Humphrey.'

A.J. and Garth reluctantly shook hands.

'How come?' asked A.J.

Garth shrugged his shoulders. 'Mrs Brisbane said to.'

'Well, come on. We'll clean his cage and get it over with,' said A.J.

The boys didn't talk much while they cleaned my cage. But they started giggling when they cleaned up my potty corner. (I don't know why that makes everybody giggle.)

After they stopped giggling, they started talking and kidding around. They decided to let me out of the cage, so they took a set of old building blocks from DeeLee's room and built me a huge maze. Oh, I love mazes!

When we were all tired of that game, A.J. offered to teach Garth to play Crazy Eights and then Ty and DeeLee joined them in a game of Go Fish.

Nobody mentioned the TV.

Nobody shot any rubber bands.

Later in the afternoon, the kids were all outside playing football. I was fast asleep until Mrs Thomas came into the den with a broom and started sweeping. A minute later, Mr Thomas entered.

'What are you doing, hon?'

'What does it look like? I'm sweeping. You know, all the snacking we do in here makes a real mess on the floor,' she said.

'Beau's asleep?' her husband asked.

'Uh-huh.'

Mr Thomas walked over to his wife and took the broom away from her. 'Then you sit down and rest for a while, hon. I'll sweep. Go on, don't argue.'

Mrs Thomas smiled and thanked him and sat down on the couch. Mr Thomas swept all around the outside of the room.

Even behind the TV. Uh-oh.

When he got there, he stopped sweeping and leaned down.

'Well, I'll be,' he muttered.

'What's wrong?' asked Mrs Thomas.

'The TV is unplugged,' he said. 'It's unplugged!' He came out from behind the TV, plug in hand and a very puzzled look on his face. 'But it couldn't have just come unplugged while we were sitting there watching. I mean, a plug doesn't just fall out,' he said.

'Plug it in. See if it works,' his wife told him.

Well, you guessed it. The TV came on as bright and loud as ever.

'I don't get it,' Mr Thomas muttered. 'But at least we don't have to pay to get it fixed.'

Mrs Thomas stared at the screen for a few seconds, then glanced out of the window at the kids playing happily outside.

'Charlie, what do you say we keep it unplugged for a couple more days?' she asked. 'We just won't tell the kids.'

Mr Thomas grinned. Then he bent down and unplugged the TV. 'Couldn't hurt,' he said.

He put down the broom and sat on the couch near his wife and the two of them just sat there in the den, giggling like – well, like Stop-Giggling-Gail!

Suddenly, Mr Thomas looked over at me.

'You don't mind a little peace and quiet, do you, Humphrey?'

'NO-NO-NO!' I squeaked. And I promptly fell asleep.

Things were a lot better when A.J., Garth and I returned to Room 26. No rubber bands flew through the air. Garth didn't trip anybody or make fun of anybody. That meant Gail didn't get in trouble for giggling. Heidi didn't get in trouble for speaking out without raising her hand because she wasn't trying to tell Mrs Brisbane what Garth had done.

But the best change was with Sayeh, who *did* raise her hand. Every single day.

One day, she raised her hand to volunteer to stay in during break to clean the blackboard. Miranda raised her hand, too. Mrs Brisbane chose them both.

'Girls, I think I can trust you to stay here while I take this report down to the headmaster's office,' Mrs Brisbane told them.

Of course she could trust them.

Once the girls were alone, they began to talk.

'I really liked your singing,' Miranda told Sayeh.

'Thanks.'

'My mum and I are going to a musical version of *Cinderella* over at the college this weekend,' Miranda continued. 'We have an extra ticket. Would you like to come with us? My mum will pick you up.'

Sayeh quickly turned to face Miranda. 'Oh, yes. I have not been to a play before.'

Miranda grinned. 'Good! I'll have my mum call your mum.'

Suddenly, Sayeh's face fell. 'Oh, better not. She's so busy. Ummm. Give me your number and I'll have my father call your mother.' Sayeh watched Miranda's reaction carefully. So did I.

'Cool.'

That was it. Miranda jotted down her number. Sayeh looked greatly relieved.

I knew that Miranda's mother didn't care how well Sayeh's mother spoke English. Maybe now Sayeh would figure that out, too.

Another great thing that happened was that Mrs Brisbane started reading a book out loud to the class.

Sometimes, I doze right through these sessions. But this time, she picked out a really good book. When she announced that it was about a mouse, Gail giggled.

'What did she say?' Art whispered to Richie.

'Pay-Attention-Art,' Mrs Brisbane said. 'It's about a mouse.'

Several of the boys groaned.

'Baby stuff,' one of them muttered.

'We'll see,' Mrs Brisbane told them. She started to read and, oh, what a tale it was! All about mice no bigger than I am who were great warriors. I was longing to put on some armour myself by the time she stopped reading.

'Continued tomorrow,' she announced as she stuck a bookmark in place and closed the book.

Tomorrow! That woman truly has a mean streak. She's proved it again and again. I would have sneaked out of my cage at night to finish the book, but she's so mean, she stuck it in her desk drawer – the one she locks with a key. Grrrr!

The weekend came around quickly, though, and I went home with Richie.

I'm still not quite sure how many people actually live at the Rinaldis' house because there were always so many people coming and going: aunts, uncles, cousins, grandparents, neighbours. One meal seemed to flow right into the next and Richie's mum was *very generous* with treats. I'll tell you one thing: you could never be lonely or hungry at the Rinaldis' house.

On Sunday afternoon, guess who showed up? Remember Richie's uncle? That's right: Aldo Amato! This time, my buddy Aldo was not lonely because he brought along his girlfriend, Maria, to meet the family. She was a very nice lady who wore her long hair piled up high on her head. She was dressed in bright red from head to toe: red earrings, red sweater, red skirt and red shoes. I think red is a very happy colour. I think Maria is a very happy person, especially when she's with Aldo.

All the Rinaldis made a big fuss over Maria and praised the bread and cake she'd brought from the bakery where she worked.

After all the commotion of their arrival died down, I heard Aldo tell Maria, 'Now there's someone really important I want you to meet.'

And he introduced her to ME-ME-ME!

'Believe it or not, Humphrey is one of my best friends,' he told her. 'And he was the very first friend I told about you.'

'Then I am honoured to meet you, Humphrey,' Maria said, smiling down at me.

'The pleasure is all mine!' I squeaked.

'See? He likes you,' said Aldo.

And indeed, I did.

The world seemed like a pretty nice place for a handsome young hamster like me, I can tell you. I was sitting on top of the world when I returned to Room 26 on Monday. But I just about toppled off when Mrs Brisbane made an alarming announcement.

'Class, as you know, this will be a short week, due to Thanksgiving,' she said. 'And that means Humphrey will need a home for four days instead of two. Now, who wants to volunteer?'

You won't believe what I'm going to say. *Not one*

hand went up. I actually fell off my wheel.

Mrs Brisbane was surprised, too. 'No one?' she asked. 'Heidi, didn't you want to take Humphrey home?'

'Oh, yes. But we're going to my grandma's house for Thanksgiving,' she explained.

'Art, didn't you ask for Humphrey last week?' Mrs Brisbane asked.

'Yes, but we're having all my relatives for Thanksgiving and Mum says it wouldn't be a good time,' Art explained.

And so it went on. Every single classmate had big plans for Thanksgiving. Plans that didn't include having an extra hamster around.

I was WORRIED-WORRIED-WORRIED. I didn't want to spend four days alone in Room 26.

I worried all day Monday. I worried all day Tuesday. I worried even more all day Wednesday.

At the end of the day, Headmaster Morales stopped by to give Mrs Brisbane an envelope. I think it was her pay-cheque, because she was especially glad to see him.

'I have a huge favour to ask,' she said.

'Sure, Sue. What is it?' asked Headmaster Morales. He was wearing a tie with little turkeys all over it.

'Could you possibly take Humphrey for the weekend?'

I had my paws crossed that he'd say yes. But Headmaster Morales didn't even smile.

'Oh, Sue, I'd love to, but we're going out of town for the holiday,' he told her. 'Another time, I'd love to.'

Another time wouldn't matter. I needed a place to go now.

After the headmaster left, Mrs Brisbane sighed and began gathering up her papers.

Then she turned to me.

'Well, Humphrey, it looks like you're going home with me for Thanksgiving,' she said grimly.

My fate was sealed. I was going to the home of the woman who had once vowed to get rid of me – for four whole days! And, frankly, I was worried I'd never come back!

TIP TWELVE

If you must leave your hamster with a caretaker, make sure that it is someone you know and trust.

Guide to the Care and Feeding of Hamsters

Dr Harvey H. Hammer

13

Thanks but No Thanks

Since Mrs Brisbane didn't say a word to me for most of the drive home, I had time to reflect on the last few months. I had not had a bad experience with any of the families I had visited. In fact, they had all been gracious and welcoming (except Miranda's dog, Clem, but I knew how to handle him). In return, I'd lent them a helping paw here and there. After all, you can learn a lot about yourself by getting to know another species.

I was overdue for trouble. And I was likely to get it at Brisbane's House of Horrors. That's how I pictured her home: decorated with skeletons and bats and eerie jack-o'-lanterns all year long. I was shivering at the picture I had in mind when Mrs Brisbane finally spoke.

'Humphrey, I need you like I need a hole in the head,' she complained.

'THE SAME TO YOU!' I squeaked back rudely, knowing she wouldn't understand.

'I don't know what Bert's going to say about you. But whatever it is, it won't be pleasant. Nothing he says is, lately,' she continued.

Bert? Who's Bert? Then I realized it must be her husband. The one who's sick. Well, I was certainly not looking forward to meeting him after what I'd just heard.

'It won't be much of a Thanksgiving,' she said. 'We don't have much to be thankful for this year. But I'll try.'

'Good for you,' I squeaked.

She almost smiled. 'Thanks for the support.'

The Brisbane house was yellow with white shutters and lots of big trees. Rust-coloured leaves covered the front yard.

'And on top of everything else, I have to rake!' Mrs Brisbane said through gritted teeth.

Inside, the house was surprisingly cosy. Not a skeleton or bat in sight. Lots of pretty pictures on the walls and some big yellow flowers in a vase on the table.

'Bert? I'm home,' Mrs Brisbane called out.

A few seconds later, an old man rolled into the room in a wheelchair. His grey hair was uncombed and stuck out in places it shouldn't. His chin was covered with grey stubble and he wore very wrinkled tan pyjamas.

His expression was so sour; he looked as if he'd just drunk a glass of vinegar.

Mrs Brisbane set my cage on the low coffee-table. 'We have a guest for the weekend.'

I could tell she was trying hard to sound cheerful.

'His name is Humphrey.'

Mr Brisbane sneered. 'This is unacceptable! For the little pay you get, that school can't force you to spend your weekend baby-sitting a rat!'

I bit my tongue to keep from saying something unsqueakably bad.

'They're not forcing me,' argued Mrs Brisbane. 'It's just that no one else could do it. Let's not make a mountain out of a molehill.'

Pardon me, but I resented being called a mole-hill almost as much as being called a rat.

Mrs Brisbane quickly changed the subject. 'I thought you were going to get dressed today.'

'Why should I? I'm not going to see anybody,' Bert Brisbane growled. 'Except you and the rat.'

Mrs Brisbane got up and walked out of the room without saying another word.

Boy, nobody in Room 26 could get away with talking to Mrs Brisbane like that. I wished I could send her husband to Headmaster Morales's office right now.

Everything was really quiet around the house for

a while. Mrs Brisbane changed her clothes (to jeans!) and moved my cage on to a card table in the corner of the living room. Then she sat down and read the *Guide to the Care and Feeding of Hamsters* and the chart my classmates kept on me.

'Looks like your friends have been taking good care of you,' she said.

'VERY-VERY-VERY GOOD,' I squeaked.

She fed me and gave me clean water and then she and Mr Brisbane ate dinner in another room while they watched TV. They went to bed early.

I'll bet they didn't say two words to each other. Even Ms Mac talked more at home than they did, and she lived alone.

The next morning, Mrs Brisbane was up very early and soon the house smelled yum-yummy. I thought maybe I would like this Thanksgiving thing after all. At least the good-smelling and eating parts.

What I didn't like about Thanksgiving was Mr Brisbane. While Mrs Brisbane was clattering pots and clinking pans and making things smell good, he sat in his wheelchair in the living room and frowned. No, I know a better vocabulary word: scowled.

After a while, he called into the kitchen. 'Sue, why don't you stop all the cooking and just sit down for a minute?'

Mrs Brisbane popped her head through the door and said it wouldn't be Thanksgiving without turkey and all the trimmings. Then Mr Brisbane said he didn't have anything to be thankful for. Mrs Brisbane went back in the kitchen and banged around some pots and pans again.

That sour expression on the old man's face was starting to get to me, so I decided to take a little spin on my wheel. I really got that thing going at high speed. I was going so fast, I couldn't even see whether Mr Brisbane was smiling or frowning.

Finally, Mrs Brisbane came into the room to sit down.

'Would you look at that, Sue?' her husband asked.

'He does that all the time,' she said.

'Just spinning his wheels like me. Stuck in a cage and going nowhere.' Mr Brisbane's voice was so grim, I stopped spinning.

Whew. I was a little dizzy.

'You're wrong, Bert,' said Mrs Brisbane. 'Humphrey's not stuck; he goes everywhere. Every weekend, he goes to a new house. He eats different foods. He gets out of the cage and runs through mazes. He runs and jumps and climbs. You're the one spinning your wheels and going nowhere. You're stuck in a cage, but it's a cage you made!'

Well. You could have knocked me over with a feather when I heard Mrs Brisbane talk that way.

Mr Brisbane was surprised, too.

'Do you think I wanted that car to hit me? Do you think that was my choice?' he asked.

'Of course not, Bert. I'm so grateful you lived through it. That's the point. You're alive, but you certainly don't act like it.'

With that, Mrs Brisbane got up and went back into the kitchen. Meanwhile, Mr Brisbane scowled and frowned and glared . . . at me!

Finally, Mrs Brisbane put the food on the dining-room table. I watched them eating their dinner from my vantage point on the table in the living room. They ate, but they didn't say much.

'The food is delicious,' Mr Brisbane finally said.

That's the nicest thing I'd heard him say so far.

'Thank you,' Mrs Brisbane replied.

There was silence for a while. Then Mr Brisbane said, 'Just think, last year after Thanksgiving dinner, Jason and I played football in the backyard. Now I'm stuck here and Jason is in Tokyo.'

'Let's call him, Bert,' his wife suggested.

'It's too early there,' he said. 'We'll have to call later.' Football. Jason. Tokyo. You can learn a lot if you stop spinning and start listening.

I listened late that night when they called Jason, who turned out to be their grown-up son who was working in Tokyo, which is FAR-FAR-FAR away, even farther than Brazil, according to the maps in Room 26.

Wow, there were more Mrs Brisbanes than I'd ever dreamed possible. One was mean to me. One was nice to students. One was a wife. Another was a mother. One was a cook. One wore dark suits. Another wore jeans.

But which one was the *real* Mrs Brisbane?

That night, as they headed out of the living room and towards the bedroom, I heard Mrs Brisbane, the wife, say, 'I know you think I was being hard on you, Bert. But it really is time for you to think about what you're going to do with the rest of your life.'

Mr Brisbane didn't answer.

TIP THIRTEEN

Remember, hamsters are very, very curious.

Guide to the Care and Feeding of Hamsters

Dr Harvey H. Hammer

14
Hide-and-Go-Squeak

Apparently, the day after Thanksgiving, humans do two things: eat leftovers from the day before and go shopping.

Mr Brisbane didn't go shopping, of course. But Mrs Brisbane left early in the morning, after telling Mr Brisbane that there were plenty of leftovers for him in the refrigerator.

So there I was: stuck with old sourpuss. And all he did was sit in his wheelchair, looking unhappy.

I'd much rather have been hanging out with Headmaster Morales or chatting with Sayeh's family. I could have been tricking Miranda's dog, playing cards with A.J.'s family or watching Aldo balance a broom on his finger. But no, I was watching a sad and grouchy old man act sad and grouchy.

I could have just settled in for my nap, but I remembered what Mrs Brisbane had said. This man had to get out of his cage. 'Out of your cage!' I squeaked out loud without realizing it.

'Quiet, you little rat,' Mr Brisbane growled at me. Then he wheeled over to the front window and stared out.

Okay. If he wasn't going to get out of his cage, then I'd get out of mine. Because I had a new plan.

Mr Brisbane didn't notice me open the lock-that-doesn't-lock. He didn't see me scamper out of the cage, across the table and on to the couch. He wasn't aware that I leaped down to the floor. He didn't even think about me until I stood in the middle of the living room and said, 'CATCH ME IF YOU CAN!'

I know he only heard me squeaking, but I definitely got his attention. He was as surprised as could be to see me there.

'How did you get out? And how am I ever going to get you back in?' He rolled towards me. 'Come on, whatever-your-name-is. Let's get back in the cage.'

I let him get just close enough to reach me. He bent forward, cupping his hands. But just as he reached out to grab me, I dashed over to the opposite side of the room.

'You little rat,' he said. 'You can't outsmart me.'

He rolled over to the cupboard and took a baseball cap off a hook. Again, he approached and I let him get almost within arm's reach. This time, he raised the baseball cap and said, 'Okay, fella. Let's play ball.'

'We'll see about that,' I squeaked as I bustled off to the living room.

We quickly established the rules of the contest: 1) I would stay out in the open, in places he could reach in his wheelchair; 2) he would use his cap to capture me.

If he could.

Once he reached the dining room, I rushed into the den.

'Oh. Think you're clever? We'll see who's clever,' he challenged.

From the den, I scuttled over to the hallway. By now, Mr Brisbane's cheeks were pink and he was almost smiling. 'You're smart, but you won't win this one!'

This time, I let him get that cap within a whisker of capturing me, just to keep the game interesting. Then I scurried back to the living room. But before he followed me, Mr Brisbane slammed the bathroom, bedroom and guest-room doors. Aha! He was limiting my range of possibilities. Pretty cunning.

In the living room, I decided to make a bold move. I hid under the couch. Then I let Mr Brisbane stew for five minutes.

'Come here, Humphrey. You'll have to come out sooner or later,' he called. And I thought he didn't know my name.

He shook the curtains and pushed the chairs to see if he could rouse me.

Too bad he didn't think of using sunflower seeds like Mr Morales did. Yum!

I finally got kind of bored, so I made a dash for the dining room. Mr Brisbane followed and this time I let him scoop me up in the cap.

'I win!' he shouted triumphantly. He was beaming with pride as he stared down at me. 'But you were a worthy opponent.'

He put me back in my cage and I scrambled into my sleeping house. I have to admit, the game had made me a little drowsy.

I don't think it was very long before Mrs Brisbane returned, carrying several shopping bags full of packages.

'What happened, Bert?' she asked when she saw her husband.

'Nothing,' he said.

'But your face is all rosy. You look different. And you're wearing a baseball cap,' she said.

'Sit down, Sue,' he answered. 'I'll tell you all about it.'

He told her every detail of our match, chuckling and swinging his cap back and forth.

'I guess there are some things I can still do,' he said. 'Now, how about a game of gin rummy?'

Mrs Brisbane was almost speechless. 'Okay,' she said, starting to get up.

Mr Brisbane waved her away with his cap. 'I'll get the cards. You just sit.'

As he wheeled into the den, Mrs Brisbane turned to me and quietly said, 'Thank you, Humphrey.'

Mr Brisbane didn't frown for the rest of the day and evening, except when Mrs Brisbane beat him at cards. The next morning, which was Saturday, she couldn't even find her husband.

'Where could he be?' she asked me. 'He hasn't left the house in months!'

A minute later, he came into the house from the garage, his lap full of boards and bricks and things.

'I've got an idea for our friend Humphrey,' he said.

Mr and Mrs Brisbane spent most of the rest of the day building an obstacle course on the coffee-table in the den. They lined up boards along the side (so I couldn't stray too far) and then they set up things for me to climb over and duck under, like bricks with holes to hide in and big cardboard tubes, and Mr Brisbane constructed a series of ramps for me to climb. Oh, we had a wonderful day. Mr Brisbane got out a stopwatch to time me on my runs and they made bets on how long it would take me to get from start to finish. Mrs Brisbane even added a few treats to the maze: bits of apple and biscuit. I had FUN-FUN-FUN. The Brisbanes did, too. I could tell.

On Sunday afternoon, the Brisbanes invited their neighbours over to watch me run through my maze. Mr and Mrs Robinson brought along their five-year-old twins.

'Glad to see you looking so chipper,' Mr Robinson told Mr Brisbane.

'I think he's finally feeling better,' Mrs Brisbane whispered to Mrs Robinson.

Mr Brisbane looked a little vinegary again on Monday morning, though. 'Why can't we keep him here, Sue?' he asked.

'The children would never forgive me,' she told him. 'He's really their hamster. But . . .' She grinned. 'There's a two-week Christmas holiday coming up soon. I think Humphrey had better spend it here.'

Could I believe my cute, furry ears? She liked me so much, she actually wanted me to come back? This was a whole new Mrs Brisbane. One who liked me.

By the time Mrs Brisbane and I returned to Room 26, I was pretty tired. But it was a good tired and I knew I could rest after my weekend during morning break.

TIP FOURTEEN
Hamsters should be let out of their cages to run in a closed environment for an hour or two at a time.

Guide to the Care and Feeding of Hamsters

Dr Harvey H. Hammer

Happy Hamsterday

In December, things in Room 26 really began to change. For one thing, it got cold outside and a little chilly by my window. In the early morning, frost pictures would appear on the glass. One picture looked like a big snowflake. Another looked like a lion. Scary.

Still, it was nice and cosy in my sleeping house.

More snowflakes appeared. Not real ones, but cut-out paper snowflakes, bordering all the blackboards. And there were snowmen made of fluffy cotton and pictures of candles and packages and sleighs.

The holidays were almost here: Christmas and Hanukkah and Kwanzaa! There were songs to be sung and presents to be wrapped and a big two-week holiday to come!

The weekend after Thanksgiving, I went home

with Pay-Attention-Art. He paid a lot of attention to me.

But sometimes – not every night – during the week, Mrs Brisbane would take me home to see Mr Brisbane and he'd put up his obstacle course and we'd laugh and squeak and have a wonderful time.

The next weekend I stayed at Gail Morgenstern's house. Friday night was really nice because she convinced her mum to let me watch while she lit the menorah for the family. And the food was yummy.

I was glad that Mrs Brisbane didn't take me home every night. For one thing, if I ran through the obstacle course every night, I'd probably waste away to nothing. For another thing, I wouldn't have been able to see Aldo.

Aldo could now balance the broom on his head. Yep, he'd put the tip of the broomstick on top of his head and keep it up there a while. He'd have to bob and weave to keep it balanced and he made funny faces, too.

But one night during the week, Aldo pulled his chair up close to my cage and said, 'Humphrey, old pal, I've got something to discuss.'

This sounded serious, so I put on my most serious, problem-solving face.

'I'm thinking of getting Maria a ring for Christmas. You know, like an engagement ring.

With something shiny in it. I know, we haven't known each other very long. And we wouldn't have to get married right away. On the other hand, I'm no spring chicken and I'd like to settle down and raise a couple of kids and maybe a couple of hamsters, too, you know?'

'I understand,' I squeaked softly.

'So what do you think?' Aldo fixed his big brown eyes on me. 'Should I ask her to marry me?'

I stood up on my hind legs and screeched, 'DO IT! DO IT! DO IT!'

Then he stood up and shouted, 'You're right! I will! I'd be crazy not to!'

He raced out of the room so fast, he forgot his cleaning trolley, but when he returned for it, he yelled, 'Thanks!'

Sometimes – most times – it pays to squeak up.

The third weekend after Thanksgiving I spent at Heidi Hopper's house and watched her family put up their Christmas tree. It was the most beautiful thing I'd ever seen, second only to the little tree Heidi put in my cage. It was made of my favourite treat: broccoli!

And then it was almost Christmas holidays.

Suddenly, it seemed as if we didn't have quite as much work to do in class. Everybody was planning the party for the last day of school.

One day, Garth (who never used to wait for the

bell) stayed after school to ask Mrs Brisbane a question.

'May I please take Humphrey home with me over the holidays?' he asked.

Mrs Brisbane looked as surprised as I was. 'Well, Garth, I thought that was a problem.'

Garth smiled broadly. 'My mum is much better now and Dad says it's okay to bring Humphrey home.'

Mrs Brisbane smiled back. 'That is wonderful news. But I think two weeks might be a little much. How about the first weekend in January?'

Garth nodded, but he looked disappointed.

'Tell you what, why don't you have your parents bring you by our house to see Humphrey over the holidays? You can watch him run through his obstacle course.'

Garth didn't look disappointed any more.

On the last day of school, everybody was very dressed up. I had on my fur coat as usual. Mrs Brisbane wore a red-and-green striped sweater and a green skirt. She also wore a Santa Claus hat.

This was an entirely new Mrs Brisbane. The dressing-up Mrs Brisbane.

'Class, I have an important announcement. We're having a surprise visitor this morning, before our party. So there'll be no vocabulary test today.'

After the cheers died down, Mrs Brisbane went out in the hall and waved. A minute later, you'll never guess who entered the classroom. Mr Bert Brisbane!

He was wearing a Santa Claus hat, too. He looked a lot better now. No grey stubble or wrinkled pyjamas. On his lap, he had a large box. Mrs Brisbane introduced him to the class and they all applauded. Then he told them that his surprise was actually for ME-ME-ME!

First, he pulled out something like my cage – only bigger.

'This is my gift to Humphrey. This extension attaches to his cage and makes it bigger. Now you're all going to help me build Humphrey his Christmas present: his very own playground.'

The kids squealed and giggled and clapped, and I couldn't hold back a big squeal of my own. I could keep my homey cage with its lock-that-doesn't-lock, but I'd also have my own park to play in!

Mr Brisbane gathered my classmates around the big table and explained his plans. Mrs Brisbane unloaded the pieces. First there was a seesaw, then a tree branch to swing from, a big jungle gym and two ladders: one to climb and one to walk across like a bridge. MY-MY-MY!

Sayeh held me while the other kids worked on my cage. She patted me gently and murmured comforting words. Meanwhile, Mr Brisbane patiently instructed the children as they arranged the pieces. He even made sure everyone got a turn.

Then Mr Morales dropped by to see how things were going. He was wearing a tie that had little Christmas lights that really lit up!

He and Mrs Brisbane stood behind the children, watching as my playground took shape.

'Looks like Bert should be a teacher, too,' the headmaster told Mrs Brisbane.

'He already is,' I heard Mrs Brisbane respond. 'He just started teaching arts and crafts to seniors and kids at the Community Centre.'

'So he's made a new start,' said the headmaster.

'Thanks to Humphrey.'

I believe those words were the best present I could ever have.

'Guess what I got my kids for Christmas,' the headmaster said. 'A hamster. Maybe it's a present for me, as well. I think my papa will enjoy it, too.'

When Sayeh put me back in my cage, everyone watched as I raced to my new playground, climbed the jungle gym, made a leap to the tree branch and jumped over to the seesaw. Now I could have play-time whenever I wanted. Whoopee!

Just then, two parent volunteers arrived with cupcakes and juice. While they passed around the food, Sayeh and Miranda slipped quietly out of the room.

A little while later, Mrs Brisbane announced that she had another surprise: gifts for the class. The door opened and in came Miranda and Sayeh, wearing red dresses trimmed in white fur (not real fur like mine) and white fur hats. They each had a basket filled with small presents and they danced around the room singing a song about the wonders of winter while they handed out the gifts. When the kids opened their packages, they each found a keyring with a small furry toy hamster attached. The hamsters came in all colours: red, green, purple, gold, silver. Nice.

The classroom assistants presented Mrs Brisbane with a gift – a pair of red earrings, which she put on right away. I already thought it was a perfect day. But it wasn't really totally perfect until Mr Morales peeked out into the hall and announced that he had a big surprise.

I wasn't sure we could stand many more surprises.

And then she walked in. The biggest surprise I could imagine.

Ms Mac was back!

She was wearing a long flowered skirt and a

bright red blouse, and she had a butterfly in her hair. (Not a real one, of course.) She also had a huge canvas bag with her.

'Remember me?' she asked with a huge smile.

My classmates were thrilled and they all rushed to her side.

I was so surprised, I was positively squeakless.

Mrs Brisbane made everyone sit down again and asked Ms Mac (of course, she insisted on calling her Ms McNamara) about her travels.

Ms Mac told us about the rain forest and teaching in a school in Brazil. Then she opened her big bag and took out a stack of holiday cards. Her Brazilian students had made a card for each child in Room 26!

While my classmates were sharing their cards with one another, Ms Mac came over to see me at last.

'Well, I can see by your cage that you've done very well for yourself,' she said with a smile. 'And I thought you'd be pining away for me.'

'I HAVE BEEN!' I squeaked.

She reached into her big bag. 'And I have a present for you. But don't tell anybody.'

She pulled out a brand-new tiny notebook with blank pages – lots of them. And a new tiny pencil with a very sharp point. 'I thought you might need this.' Then she tucked it behind my mirror.

Ms Mac stared at me a little longer, then softly said, 'I've seen a lot of creatures in a lot of places in the last few months, but you're still the handsomest and smartest of all.'

YES-YES-YES!

'And don't worry. I'll be back to see you again.' She was still the same wonderful Ms Mac. I'd follow her to the ends of the earth, I thought. Or at least to Brazil.

But then, it hit me. As much as I love her and she loves me, Ms Mac doesn't need me. Not as much as the Brisbanes and my classmates and their families do. Maybe that's what Ms Mac was thinking when she left me in Room 26. This is where I belong.

All too soon, the bell rang. School was over for the day. School was over for the rest of the year. My head was reeling from all the surprises and excitement as we headed out to the car.

In the car park, Aldo raced over to greet us and wish us merry Christmas. He had come to pick up Richie.

'I hope you have a very happy Christmas, too,' Mrs Brisbane told Aldo.

Aldo grinned until his huge moustache shook like Santa's tummy. 'I'm sure I will. You see, I just got engaged! I'm going to get married!'

'Yahoo!' I squeaked with delight.

Aldo leaned towards me. 'Thanks, my friend.'

That night at the Brisbanes' house there was one more surprise. The doorbell rang and a very tall and good-looking young man appeared. He was wearing a Santa Claus hat, but he wasn't Santa.

He was Jason, the Brisbanes' son. He'd come all the way from Tokyo to surprise his parents. They were so happy to see him, they both cried, just a little.

I almost cried, too.

Soon, the house was filled with friends and neighbours and Mrs Brisbane played the piano while everyone sang carols and drank hot cider.

I nibbled on raw apple and squeaked along.

Later that night, when the house was quiet, I thought about all I'd done in the months since I had left Pet-O-Rama. I didn't know anything about the world then, but I've certainly learned a lot. I can read and write and I know all the capitals of the United States. Just ask me one!

I learned you should never turn your back on a dog. And that it's a good idea to turn off the TV once in a while.

I found out that kids have problems and so do teachers and headmasters. But sometimes all people need is a little encouragement.

Most of all, I learned that one small hamster really can make a big difference.

I decided to write down some of the things I've learned from my adventures, but there was just one more line left in my first notebook. So I thought and thought and then I scribbled down exactly what I was feeling deep in my hamster heart:

JOY-JOY-JOY to the WHOLE WIDE WORLD!
(And that includes YOU!)
Humphrey

Humphrey's *Guide to the Care and Feeding of Humans*

1 Like hamsters, humans come in many, many sizes, shapes, colours, talents and tempers. If you judge them by looks alone, you'll miss out on knowing some wonderful people.
2 Humans like to be entertained. And it doesn't take much to entertain them. Just squeak or swing or spin. They'll love it!
3 Humans are pretty entertaining themselves. They can sing, dance, tell jokes and balance brooms.
4 All humans REALLY-REALLY-REALLY need someone to listen to their problems. Preferably someone small and furry.
5 Even really *important* humans (like headmasters) have problems and need help.

6 Rubber bands hurt. Do *not* shoot rubber bands at one another. *Unless* it's absolutely the only weapon you have against a creature much bigger than you.

7 Humans are not very good at working out technical things, like how to fix a broken lock.

8 Humans have unlimited access to all kinds of yummy foods, so be nice to them!

9 If you are nice to humans, they will be nice to you. So nice, they might even build you a playground.

10 Humans have good memories. Even if they go far away to teach in another country, they will not forget you. And, believe me, you won't forget them, either!

Most importantly, remember: you can learn a lot about yourself by getting to know another species. Even humans.

Friendship According to Humphrey

To Jane Birney de Leeuw, sister and friend, and to Humphrey's BEST-BEST-BEST friend and editor, Susan Kochan

Contents

1
Strange Change

BUMP-BUMP-BUMP!

Mrs Brisbane and I were heading back to Longfellow School after the long winter holiday. But there were a lot more bumps in the road since the last time I rode in her small blue estate car.

'Now, Humphrey,' Mrs Brisbane said. She was interrupted by another BUMP! 'Don't be surprised.' BUMP! 'If there are a few changes.' BUMP! 'In Room 26.' BUMP!

My stomach felt slightly queasy as I hung on tightly to my ladder, so I had a hard time understanding what she was telling me. What did she mean by 'changes'?

'While you were at home with Bert.' BUMP! 'I came back to school to get things ready.'

I was at home with her husband Bert a lot over the holidays, and as much as I like him, I was worn out from running mazes a couple of times a day. Mr Brisbane loves to watch me run mazes. At least back in school, I could catch forty winks once in a while. And since I am a classroom hamster, I belong in the classroom.

My stomach calmed down a bit as Mrs Brisbane pulled her car into a parking space.

'Now, what about these changes?' I asked, but it came out as 'Squeak-squeak-squeak,' as usual.

'It's good to shake things up once in a while, Humphrey,' Mrs Brisbane assured me as she opened the car door. 'You'll see.'

I was already shaken up from the bumpy ride. Then a blast of icy wind made me shiver and I couldn't see a thing because Mrs Brisbane had thrown a woollen scarf over my cage. I didn't mind, as long as I was on the way back to my classroom, where I'd see all my friends again. Just thinking about them gave me a warm feeling. Or maybe it was the heat from the school boiler as we walked in the front door.

'Hi, Sue! Are we on for today?' a familiar voice called out. I couldn't see Miss Loomis, but I recognized her voice. Miss Loomis taught a class down the corridor. She was also Mrs Brisbane's friend.

'Sure, Angie. How about after morning break?'

'See you then,' said Miss Loomis.

Finally, Mrs Brisbane put my cage down in

Room 26 and removed the scarf. When she did, I was in for a shock. Something unsqueakable had happened to my classroom! For one thing, the tables faced the wrong direction. They used to point towards the front of the room. Now they were sideways.

Instead of being arranged in neat rows like before, the tables were clumped together in groups. Mrs Brisbane's desk had moved to the corner of the room. Pictures of people I'd never seen before replaced the happy snowmen who had covered the notice board in December.

I was so dizzy from all the changes, I didn't notice the room filling up until Lower-Your-Voice-A.J. yelled, 'Hiya, Humphrey!' as he came out of the cloakroom.

Soon my other friends stopped by to say hello.

'Did you have a good holiday?' asked Miranda Golden. Miranda is an almost perfect human. That's why I think of her as Golden Miranda.

'My mother sends you her greetings,' Speak-Up-Sayeh said in her sweet, soft voice.

'Hey, Humphrey-Dumpty,' Garth shouted. That made Gail snigger, but I didn't mind. She laughed at everything.

At that moment, the bell rang. 'Class, look for your names and please take your seats now,' Mrs Brisbane said.

There was a lot of thumping and bumping as my classmates located their new seats. Now I had a better view of some of the students who used to sit on the opposite side of the room, like Don't-Complain-Mandy Payne, Sit-Still-Seth Stevenson and I-Heard-That-Kirk Chen. Maybe it is good to shake things up once in a while.

Then I noticed something odd. There was a stranger in Room 26, sitting near Sayeh, Gail and Kirk.

'Mrs Brisbane, she doesn't belong here!' I squeaked out loud. 'She's in the wrong room!'

Maybe Mrs Brisbane didn't hear me.

'Class, as you can see, we're making some changes this year. And one of our changes is our brand-new pupil,' the teacher announced. 'Come here, Tabitha.'

The new girl seemed SCARED-SCARED-SCARED as she got up and stood next to Mrs Brisbane. 'This is Tabitha Clark and I want you all to welcome her. Tabitha, why don't you tell us something about yourself?' The new girl looked down and shook her head. Mrs Brisbane quickly turned back to the class. 'We'll do that later. Now, who would like to be in charge of showing Tabitha around today?'

'Me!' a voice called out. Of course, it was Raise-Your-Hand-Heidi Hopper, who always forgets to raise her hand.

‘Hands, please, Heidi. I think Mandy had her hand up first. Mandy, you will be Tabitha’s buddy. I expect each of you to introduce yourself to Tabitha and include her in your activities.’ She turned to the girl. ‘I know you’ll make a lot of good friends in Room 26. You may sit down now.’

The girl kept staring at the floor as she returned to her seat. She looked as if she needed a friend. I was so busy watching her, I only half listened to what Mrs Brisbane was saying. Was she really talking about ‘poultry’?

‘After all, this is Longfellow School,’ she said. ‘And as I hope you know, Henry Wadsworth Longfellow was a famous American poet.’

Poetry! Nothing to do with chickens or turkeys, thank goodness. I have to admit, I’m a little scared of things with feathers, ever since my early days at Pet-O-Rama. I still have nightmares about the day a large green parrot escaped and flung himself at my cage, screeching, ‘Yum, yum! Time to eat! Bawk!’ He was still shrieking as Carl, the shop assistant, carried him away.

That unpleasant memory was interrupted when someone blurted, ‘I’m a poet and I don’t know it. My feet show it – they’re *long fellows*.’

‘I-Heard-That-Kirk,’ said Mrs Brisbane. ‘Now, as I was saying, much of this term will be spent reading and writing poetry.’

The groans were loud. I guess some people are afraid of poetry, even without feathers.

Seth squirmed in his seat and pretended to pound his head on the table. 'Poetry,' he moaned.

'Sit-Still-Seth,' said Mrs Brisbane.

Sitting still wasn't easy for Seth. Now that he was practically right in front of me, I could see him wiggling and jiggling in his chair, which made Gail Morgenstern laugh.

'Stop-Giggling-Gail!' Mrs Brisbane warned.

Gail stopped giggling and started hiccuping.

'Please, go and get a drink of water,' Mrs Brisbane told her. She turned to the new girl. 'Tabitha, please put that toy away.'

Everybody stared at Tabitha, including me. She was cradling a scruffy teddy bear in her arms. The grey bear had cotton coming out of his ears and wore washed-out blue overalls with a button missing. Even his smile seemed a little faded.

'Now, please,' said Mrs Brisbane.

It was quiet in the room, thank goodness. I'm afraid that if Gail had been there, we would have heard peals of laughter and heaps of hiccups!

Tabitha slid the shabby bear under her table without a word.

Just about then, Mr Morales, the headmaster, marched through the door.

'Sorry for interrupting, Mrs Brisbane. I just

want to personally welcome you all back to school!'

The headmaster looked spiffy, with a tie that had little pencils all over it. He always wore a tie because he was the Most Important Person at Longfellow School.

'Thank you, Mr Morales,' said Mrs Brisbane. 'We have a new student, Tabitha Clark, and a whole new set-up for our class, as you can see.'

'Welcome, Tabitha,' said the headmaster. 'I'm sure you'll love it here in Room 26. I'm glad to see that our friend Humphrey is back as well.'

He walked all the way across the classroom to my cage.

'GLAD TO SEE YOU!' I squeaked in my loudest squeak.

'Hi, old pal,' he greeted me. He turned back to the rest of the class. 'You can all learn a lot from Humphrey. And I wish you a very successful term.'

After he left, I turned my attention back to Tabitha. She was still staring straight down. I couldn't see her face clearly, but it was almost as red as her copper-coloured hair. I guess I watched her for a long time, because suddenly the bell rang for break.

'Come on, Tabitha, let's get our coats,' Mandy said. Tabitha slipped the teddy bear into her pocket and followed Mandy to the cloakroom.

As soon as the students were gone, Miss Loomis

bustled into the room. Two pink dots of excitement coloured her cheeks and her curls bounced in all directions.

'Are you ready? Should we do it?' she asked Mrs Brisbane excitedly.

'Why not?' my teacher answered. 'I'll make room for him now.'

They walked over to the table in front of the window where my cage sits.

'Yes, he'll fit right here,' said Miss Loomis, pointing to a spot near my house.

Mrs Brisbane slid some of my supplies down to the end of the table. 'Now, you're sure he's not a lot of trouble?'

'Oh, no. Not nearly as much trouble as a hamster,' Miss Loomis answered.

WHAT-WHAT-WHAT? Not nearly as much trouble as a hamster! Since when have I caused any trouble in Room 26? Since when did I not totally dedicate myself to helping my classmates and teacher? Surprisingly, Mrs Brisbane didn't correct her. I was about to squeak up for myself when the bell rang again and Miss Loomis scurried out of the room.

I wondered who wasn't as much trouble as I am. 'He,' Miss Loomis had said.

He who? Curiosity made my whiskers twitch and my paws tingle.

My fur was practically standing on end as the tables filled up. I saw Tabitha slip her bear out of her pocket. Heidi saw it too, and rolled her eyes at Gail, who almost giggled but managed to stop herself.

'Now, class, I told you there were some changes in our room this year,' Mrs Brisbane announced. 'Another of the changes is a brand-new classroom pet. I think he'll add a lot to Room 26.'

New classroom pet? Why did she want a new classroom pet when she already had a wonderful, terrific – OK, perfect – classroom pet, namely me? Was I being replaced?

Miss Loomis entered, carrying a large glass tank. I couldn't see what it was because my classmates were standing up, craning their necks, *ooh*-ing and *aah*-ing and chattering away.

'It's a frog!' shouted Heidi.

Miss Loomis put the glass box right next to my cage. Now I could see some water, rocks, and something green and REALLY-REALLY-REALLY lumpy.

'Meet our new frog,' said Mrs Brisbane. 'Miss Loomis will tell you about him.'

'Well, boys and girls, as you may know, we have a frog in our classroom. His name is George and he's a bullfrog. Before the holidays, one of our students brought in this frog to keep George company. We named him Og the Frog. Unfortunately, George didn't like Og. And being a bullfrog, George let us know he didn't like Og by making a lot of noise. That upset Og, I guess, because he would leap and splash all day long while George was croaking.'

My classmates laughed, but I didn't. On the one paw, I could see why George didn't want another frog to compete with. On the other paw, croaking at Og wasn't a very friendly way to act.

'With all the noise, we were having trouble getting any work done at all,' Miss Loomis continued. 'So I asked Mrs Brisbane if your class would like to have Og, and she said yes. He's a very quiet frog. Do you like him?'

My friends all yelled, 'YES!' Everyone except Tabitha, who was secretly petting her little bear.

Somebody went 'Ribbit-ribbit' in a funny croaking voice. It wasn't the frog.

'I-Heard-That-Kirk. That's quite enough. Og can provide the sound effects from now on. I think he'll make a nice friend for Humphrey,' Mrs Brisbane said.

A friend for me? At least he wasn't my replacement – whew! But I was already friends with every single person in Room 26, so she really didn't need to find me another one. Still, I didn't want to act unfriendly, the way George had.

After Miss Loomis left, Mrs Brisbane let the students have a closer look at Og.

Seth tapped at the glass.

'Don't do that, Seth,' the teacher warned him. 'You'll frighten him.'

'He doesn't seem frightened of anything,' Miranda observed.

'I think he's smiling,' added Kirk. 'That must mean he's *hoppy*.'

For once, Gail didn't giggle, which seemed to bother Kirk. 'Get it? Hoppy? Happy?' he tried to explain.

Gail rolled her eyes and groaned, which didn't make Kirk hoppy at all.

Mrs Brisbane called to the new girl. 'Come and see Og, Tabitha.'

Tabitha stared down at her table and shook her head.

'Come on, Tabitha!' Mandy sounded impatient.

Again, Tabitha shook her head.

'She hasn't wanted to do anything all day!' Mandy grumbled.

'Mandy –,' Mrs Brisbane warned her.

'Is he really a frog?' Richie stared hard at Og, who stared right back. 'Don't frogs live in water?'

'Some do,' said Mrs Brisbane. 'And some frogs live in trees. Og is a common green frog. He likes to live near the water, but not in it. That's why he has a tank that's half land and half water.'

A common green frog didn't sound very interesting, but Og had certainly attracted the attention of my classmates.

'Can I take care of Og?' A.J. asked loudly.

'Lower-Your-Voice-A.J.,' said Mrs Brisbane. 'We will all take care of him.'

Once the students had returned to their seats, Mrs Brisbane held up a book on the care of frogs. 'We'll have to study this,' she explained. 'Taking care of Og will be quite different from caring for Humphrey. After all, Humphrey is a warm-blooded mammal. Og is a cold-blooded amphibian.'

Amphibian! That's nothing like a mammal. The very word made my warm blood run cold! I hoped that she would never ever put that word in a spelling test.

Mrs Brisbane looked through the book. 'Aha,' she said. 'It says that the common green frog is a medium-sized frog with a calm nature. It makes a distinctive twanging sound.'

'BOING!'

I almost fell off my ladder. What on earth could that noise be?

Then I heard another sound: the laughter of my classmates.

'That certainly is a distinctive twanging sound,' said Mrs Brisbane, looking puzzled.

'BOING!' This time the noise was clearly coming from the frog. What kind of a way is that to talk?

Aren't frogs supposed to say 'ribbit'?

Mrs Brisbane turned towards Og's glass box. 'Thank you for the demonstration, Og.'

Then I heard: 'Boing-boing-boing!' It didn't come from the frog this time.

'I-Heard-That-Kirk Chen,' said the teacher. She continued to talk on and on about amphibians and their life cycle.

'What does he eat?' Heidi called out.

'Hands, please, Heidi,' said Mrs Brisbane wearily. 'Mostly insects. Miss Loomis gave me a container of crickets.'

'Cool!' said Kirk.

Everybody else in the class groaned. 'Ewwwww!'

When I finished gagging, I squeaked, 'LIVE insects?' Not that anyone was listening to me. Especially not Og, who calmly sat there doing absolutely nothing.

At the end of the day, as the students gathered up their books and coats and filed past our table, at least half of them said, 'Bye, Og,' or 'Catch you later, Oggy.'

Not one of my classmates said goodbye to me. I suppose they all forgot.

Mandy stayed for a minute after class. 'Mrs Brisbane, you told me to be friendly to that new girl, but she isn't very friendly back.'

'Don't-Complain-Mandy,' said the teacher. 'It's not easy to be the new kid in the classroom. Put yourself in her shoes. Give her some time. After all, we've got the whole term ahead of us.'

A whole term ahead of us – and I had to spend it with a frog?

Mrs Brisbane had shaken things up all right. And I felt queasy all over again.

> **The better part of one's life consists of his friendships.**
>
> Abraham Lincoln, sixteenth president of the United States

2

Upset Pet

I'd had bad days before. The worst day was when Ms Mac left. She was the supply teacher who found me at Pet-O-Rama and brought me to Room 26. She almost broke my heart by moving to Brazil, which is so far away.

I'd also overcome problems before. Like getting Mrs Brisbane and her husband Bert to go from not liking me to liking me a WHOLE-WHOLE-WHOLE lot.

But I'd never had a problem like this: how to make friends with a frog. Back in my early days at Pet-O-Rama, I'd met guinea pigs, mice, rats, gerbils and chinchillas in the Small Pet Department. If there were frogs around, they must have been over with the fish and other less interesting pets.

After school was over, Mrs Brisbane gathered up her coat, gloves and books, walked over to Og and me and said, 'Well, fellows, you're on your own tonight. Have fun!'

And with that she left.

I recalled the first night I was alone in Room 26. As it slowly got dark outside, I slowly got scared inside. I would have liked a friend to talk to that night. Maybe Og felt the same way. Like Tabitha, Og was new to the class, and I thought I should try and make friends with him. Mrs Brisbane had said it's not easy to be new. You should always listen to your teacher.

'Don't worry, Og,' I squeaked to him. 'They'll all be back tomorrow. And Aldo will be here later.'

I waited for an answer. All I heard was silence. I knew he probably couldn't understand me. Still, I'd learned to understand what humans said, and for the most part, they seemed to understand me when I chose to squeak up. Surely I could do as well with a frog. I decided to try again.

'CAN YOU HEAR ME?' I squeaked as loudly as possible.

Either he couldn't hear me or he was just plain rude. I couldn't see him all that well from my cage, what with my wheel, ladders, tree branches, sleeping house and mirror. Since I knew Aldo wouldn't come in to clean the room for hours, I decided to introduce myself. As an experienced (and well-loved) classroom pet, I could share my wealth of knowledge about the timetable, the students and the studies in Room 26. Og could come to me for advice whenever he wanted.

After all, you can learn a lot by taking care of another species, as Ms Mac told me. Surely that included frogs.

I easily opened the door to my cage. It has a lock-that-doesn't-lock. However, I'm the only one who knows about it. To humans, it looks like it's tightly latched, but trust me, it's not.

'I'm coming over, Og,' I announced.

Again, there was no response. I scampered over to meet my new roommate anyway.

The glass tank had a big dish of water on one side and pebbles and plants on the other. There was a screen on the top. Sitting under a large green plant was a large green lump.

I tiptoed over close to the glass and peered in.

The lump was even uglier than I first thought. At least compared with me. After all, I am a Golden Hamster with soft fur, dark, inquisitive eyes and a little pink nose. Intelligent humans such as Miranda Golden and Sayeh Nasiri have told me I am cute.

This Og thing, on the other hand, was a sickening shade of green with bulging eyes and not a bit of fur on him. Even worse, he had a huge mouth – as wide as his whole body – that curved up at the ends as if he were grinning. He didn't look happy, just creepy. I tried not to shudder.

'Allow me to introduce myself. I am your neighbour Humphrey,' I squeaked as politely as possible.

No answer. Maybe he couldn't hear me. After all, he didn't have cute rounded ears like me. He didn't seem to have ears at all. But at least he could see I was acting in a friendly manner.

'OG?' Stepping closer, I squeaked a bit louder this time. 'Even though we don't know each other, I'm happy to extend the paw of friendship –'

Then, with no warning at all, Og lunged right at me and let out a very loud 'Boing!'

I must have leaped a foot backwards! Og couldn't get through the glass, but goodness, he startled me!

'I was only trying to be friendly,' I told him, backing towards my cage.

'Boing!' He sounded like a broken guitar string.

I sneaked a peek at him. Was that grin a leer? Or a sneer?

My heart was still pounding as I darted back into my cage and slammed the door behind me. Some friend Og was, scaring me like that!

I tried to put myself in his shoes, like Mrs Brisbane said, but he didn't wear any. Neither did I, for that matter.

I grabbed the tiny notebook and pencil from behind my mirror. Ms Mac gave them to me. No one in Room 26 knew about them. No one knew I could read and write. Writing helps me sort out my thoughts. And I had a lot of thoughts rolling around my brain that night – not all of them nice.

I scribbled away for several hours and Og was pretty quiet, except for some annoying splashing. Goodness, I can manage to groom myself and get a drink of water without making that much noise!

Suddenly the room filled with blazing light and I heard a familiar CLANG-CLANG-CLANG. It was the Longfellow School caretaker, Aldo Amato.

'Be of good cheer 'cos Aldo's here!' a voice announced.

'Aldo! My friend!' I squeaked as I jumped on my wheel and began spinning happily.

Aldo parked his cleaning trolley near the door and clomped over to my cage.

'Happy New Year, Humphrey! You're looking handsome and healthy,' he told me.

Aldo is a true friend!

'And you the same,' I squeaked back.

'Who's your buddy?' Aldo glanced at Og. 'Hey, I know you. The frog from down the corridor. What are you doing here?'

'You don't want to know!' I squeaked.

Aldo turned back to me. 'Calm down, pal, I

brought you something.' He reached into his pocket and unwrapped the most beautiful tiny tomato I've ever seen. I could have cried.

'Thanks, Aldo,' I squeaked as I tucked the treat in my cheek pouch.

'You're welcome, Humphrey.' Aldo looked over at Og again. 'Sorry, I don't know what frogs eat.'

'You don't want to know that either!' I assured him.

Aldo grabbed a paper bag and pulled a chair up close to me. 'May I join you for supper?' he asked.

He didn't need to ask. We'd shared many happy evenings while he ate his supper. I took a deep breath. Aldo gave off a pleasant smell of chalk dust and pine spray. He smelled the way I imagined a forest smells. Somewhere, WAY-WAY-WAY back in time, wild hamsters must have lived in forests, down in sweet, earthy piles of rotting leaves and fallen pine cones. Yeah, Aldo smelled like home!

'Mind if we have a little talk?' he asked.

Of course I didn't. I'd been trying to get old lumpy to talk all evening.

'I've got something to tell you, Humph. Remember how I gave my girlfriend Maria an engagement ring for Christmas? Well, I've got bigger news. On New Year's Day she and I ran off and got married!' He held up his left hand. A gold ring glittered on one finger.

'I hope you'll be HAPPY-HAPPY-HAPPY!' I squeaked with delight.

'Thanks, pal. I know I told you that you'd be at my wedding, but we decided to get hitched quietly. You understand?' he asked.

Naturally I squeaked, 'Yes.' After all, I'd helped them get together in the first place. And when I met Maria, she was as nice as Aldo.

'Yeah, I'm an old married man now. Really happy. But I've started thinking, Humphrey. I like this job, but it doesn't pay a whole lot.' Aldo paused to chew a bite of his sandwich. 'I'd like to have kids and a house and maybe raise a couple of hamsters of my own.'

Fine with me, as long as he didn't raise any frogs.

'I'd really love to have my evenings free to spend with my family. Pal, I've got to find a way to get a better job,' Aldo continued.

'You can do it!' I squeaked.

Aldo was quieter than usual as he finished his supper. I spun on my wheel to entertain him, but he was lost in thought. Finally, he folded up his bag.

'Guess I'm not good company tonight, Humphrey. I bet that frog makes better conversation than I do.'

'Fat chance,' I squeaked.

After Aldo had cleaned the room and left, I did some thinking. Personally, I believed that Aldo was already as fine a human as I've ever seen. I'd miss him if he worked somewhere else. But he was my friend, so if he wanted a better job, I wanted to help him.

I started jotting down ideas in my notebook and lost track of time. Later, I heard splashing. I'd almost forgotten about you know who next door.

'Hey, what's shaking, Og?' I called out to him. Maybe he'd thought about his behaviour and wanted to apologize for his bad manners.

There was no reply, just splish-splash-splish. Personally, the idea of being covered in water is disgusting to me. I prefer to groom myself the time-honoured way: using the tongue, teeth, paws and toenails. I thoroughly clean myself every day. The students in Room 26 love to watch me. At least they did before goggle-eyes came along.

Still, if I had to share a table with him, I thought I might TRY-TRY-TRY again to be friendly. 'Having a nice bath?' I asked.

There was no answer. Not even another splash. But there was another sound: the crickets. So they were alive after all!

Og *would* have to eat noisy food. My Nutri-Nibbles and Mighty Mealworms didn't make a sound until I crunched down on them. But the crickets – who I actually felt sorry for – made a funny singing noise: 'Chirrup, chirrup!' Apparently, they were nocturnal like me.

It was going to be a long night, with noisy crickets and a silent frog. I hopped on to my wheel and tried to spin my irritation away.

It didn't work.

> The only way to have a friend is to be one.
>
> Ralph Waldo Emerson, American poet and essayist

3
Sad-Mad-Bad

I'll tell you how the whole week went: TERRIBLE-TERRIBLE-TERRIBLE! It must have been National Frog Appreciation Week, because frogs were all we talked about in Room 26.

First, Mrs Brisbane taught everybody how to take care of Og. The students gathered around as she put on rubber gloves, picked up the container of insects and sprinkled a few into Og's tank. She didn't seem too happy about the crickets, which turned out to be quite large and ugly. The way they leaped around the tank, no wonder Og went 'Boing!'

'Did you see his tongue?' A.J. bellowed. 'It must be a foot long!'

'Oooh, he ate one!' Heidi squealed.

'Gross!' said Seth as Og's tongue grabbed the rest of the crickets.

‘I want to pet him,’ said Mandy. Before anyone could stop her, she slid the top off the tank, reached down and picked up the big lump of frog.

‘No, Mandy!’ said Mrs Brisbane. But it was too late.

‘He peed on me!’ Mandy shrieked, dropping Og back into his tank. Not that I blamed her. What unsqueakably bad manners! Is that any way for a classroom pet to act?

Seth jumped back, shaking his hands. ‘Oooh!’

Gail giggled, of course, as did everyone else.

‘Wash your hands with plenty of soap and hot water,’ Mrs Brisbane told Mandy. To the rest of the class, she said, ‘That’s what frogs do when they’re frightened. We must all be gentle with poor Og. If you have to touch him, you must wear gloves. Pick him up by the shoulder blades and never squeeze his stomach or you’ll hurt him.’

She ordered my classmates back to their seats (not including Mandy, who was washing her hands). Then we had to learn more frog facts. They don’t start out as cute, furry little babies like hamsters. NO-NO-NO! They start out as funny little tadpoles, and end up as big, lumpy frogs with bulgy eyes.

For some strange reason, everyone was fascinated with frogs, except Tabitha and me. She paid more attention to her teddy bear than to anything else in class.

I overheard Mandy complain to the other girls that Tabitha wasn't very friendly. 'I tried to get her to play at break, but she wasn't interested in anything besides that old bear. She's a big baby.'

Sayeh murmured, 'Maybe she's shy.' I was pleased that Sayeh had learned to speak up. But the other girls decided Tabitha was just unfriendly.

Like someone else who was new to Room 26.

After so much frog talk, Mrs Brisbane moved on to the subject of poetry.

First, we read a scary poem about a tiger. We also read a poem about a bee, followed by a silly poem about a purple cow. Some poems rhyme and some don't. But there are a lot of rhyming words, like 'moon' and 'June', and 'cat' and 'rat'. (Funny that those last two words rhyme, isn't it?)

At night, while Og stared into space, I made lists of rhyming words in my notebook. Better than trying to talk to him, as he continued to give me the silent treatment.

Jumpy, bumpy, grumpy, lumpy. Funny that those words rhyme too!

After a few days spent reading poems, Mrs Brisbane said it was time for us to write our own poems. There were louder groans than on the first time she mentioned poetry. Mrs Brisbane held up her hand, which meant everybody had to be quiet.

'All this is in preparation for Valentine's Day, when our class will present a Poetry Festival for all the parents. Each of you will recite a poem you wrote or one you like.' There were no groans now. In fact, some of the students looked excited. Even Pay-Attention-Art Patel was paying attention.

Mrs Brisbane explained that our assignment was to write a poem about an animal, at least six lines long, with words that rhymed.

Mandy raised her hand and the teacher asked her to speak. 'My name rhymes with "candy cane",' Mandy proudly announced.

Mrs Brisbane smiled. 'That's right: "Mandy Payne" rhymes with "candy cane". Does anyone else have a rhyming name?'

'"Richie" rhymes with "itchy"!' A.J. blurted out.

'What?' asked Repeat-It-Please-Richie.

Words were flying through my brain. Humphrey-pumphrey-dumphrey-lumphrey.

'"Gail" rhymes with "hail"!' Heidi forgot to raise her hand again.

'And "fail",' Kirk muttered.

'I-Heard-That-Kirk Chen,' said Mrs Brisbane.

'Well, "Kirk" rhymes with "jerk",' said Heidi, who was always ready to defend her best friend Gail.

'Please, no more,' Mrs Brisbane said firmly. '"Kirk" also rhymes with "work". So let's get back to work.'

I never saw my classmates work so hard before. Richie chewed on his pencil, Seth jiggled his leg, Heidi erased more than she wrote, Kirk scratched his head and Miranda wrote and wrote and wrote. Then she stopped writing and raised her hand.

'Mrs Brisbane, can you think of anything that rhymes with "hamster"?' she asked.

'Let's throw that one out to the class,' said the teacher. 'Anyone?'

Leave it to Golden Miranda to ask such a good question. It got everybody thinking, because the room was so quiet you could have heard a pencil drop. Two pencils did drop, in fact.

'How about "gangster"?' a voice called out.

'Raise-Your-Hand-Heidi.' Mrs Brisbane walked to the blackboard. 'How about that, class? Does "HAMster" rhyme with "GANGster"?'

She wrote the words on the blackboard and repeated them. 'Hear that? They don't have quite the same sound, do they?'

Well, I should hope not! Gangsters are bad guys and I am definitely a good guy.

'Maybe you'd better find another word to rhyme,' the teacher instructed.

'Try "Humphrey"!' I squeaked in encouragement. There had to be something that rhymed.

'Try "frog"!' shouted A.J.

'Lower-Your-Voice-A.J.,' Mrs Brisbane reminded him.

'And raise your hand,' added Heidi.

Mrs Brisbane shook her head, then began to write words on the board as my classmates shouted them out. Dog, fog, log, slog, clog and more.

Nothing rhymed with 'hamster', but everything rhymed with 'frog'. How depressing! I wondered how many words rhyme with 'sad'? Like 'mad' and 'bad'.

After break, it was Miranda's turn to clean my cage. She always does an extra-good job of cleaning my potty corner and changing my water and bedding. And she always has a special treat for me, like a piece of cauliflower. Yum.

'Sorry, Humphrey, I tried to write a poem about you,' she told me. 'I think I'm going to have to write about Clem instead.'

Clem was Miranda's dog, the one who tried to eat me when I stayed at her house. How Golden Miranda could put up with Clem was beyond me.

That night, I wrote my very first poem ever. I asked Og if he wanted to hear it. His silence wasn't too encouraging, but I decided to read it anyway.

When Ms Mac left me for Brazil,
She made me SAD-SAD-SAD.
When Clem the dog was mean to me,
I felt real MAD-MAD-MAD.
Now Og's moved in and he has got me
Feeling BAD-BAD-BAD.
In fact, this is the worst week
I ever HAD-HAD-HAD!

I waited to hear Og applaud or at least give me a grudging 'Boing'. I heard only silence. When I glanced over at my neighbour, he was grinning from ear to ear. Or he would have been if he had ears. Somehow, his smile didn't cheer me up at all.

I felt better the following day, though, because it was Friday. That meant I would get a little break from Room 26 and the green and grumpy lump. Every weekend a different student took me home, and I'd had many wonderful adventures with my classmates and their families. I'd even gone home with Mr Morales the headmaster!

This week, I was going home with Wait-For-The-Bell-Garth Tugwell. He'd wanted to take me home for a long time.

'Can I take Og home, too?' asked Garth.

'I think Og can stay here,' Mrs Brisbane

answered. 'Frogs don't need to eat every day, except when they're young.'

Funny, I didn't feel quite so sad-mad-bad any more.

'Can't your mum pick us up?' A.J. asked Garth after school.

I couldn't see him, but I could hear him as we waited outside for the bus. I had a blanket over my cage because it was cold outside. I didn't mind, though, as long as I was FAR-FAR-FAR away from Og. (Who hadn't even tried to say 'goodbye' to me.)

'My dad said not to bother her. She's been ill,' said Garth. 'Couldn't your mum pick us up?'

'I wish.' A.J. sighed. 'She has to pick up my sister from kindergarten and put the baby down for a nap.'

'Did you tell your parents about Bean?' asked Garth.

At least I thought he said 'Bean'. Things sounded a little muffled under the blanket.

'Nah,' said A.J. 'Last time I said somebody was picking on me, my dad signed me up for boxing lessons. I hated people punching me. It was worse than being picked on.'

I tried to sort out what A.J. meant about getting picked on. By a bean? By a boxing bean? I didn't have time to figure it out before the bus arrived.

'Here goes,' said Garth, lifting my cage. 'Let's stick together, no matter what.'

'OK. Be sure to sit in front by Miss Victoria,' whispered A.J. 'That's the safest.'

By the shuffling and scuffling sounds, I could tell that we were on the bus. Luckily, a corner of the blanket slipped down and I could see Miss Victoria, the bus driver, glancing over her shoulder.

'Keep moving, guys,' she said in a firm voice. 'Whoa, ladies, one of you has to go. Can't have three in a seat.' Three first-year girls were huddled together in the seat right behind the bus driver. 'We're not moving until one of you goes. You move, Beth.'

The girl on the end timidly got up and started down the aisle, nervously looking back at her friends.

'Keep going, folks,' Miss Victoria snapped.

Suddenly – BOOM! The girl named Beth fell down flat on the floor right in front of us. Her books slid around the floor in all directions.

The bus was quiet as Beth lay there, until somebody said, 'Hey, clumsy, you dropped something!' That was followed by a nasty snigger.

'You tripped her,' said A.J. in a voice not quite as loud as usual.

'Says you, A.J.! What do those letters stand for anyway? Awful Jerk?'

I crawled over to the side of the cage to see who was speaking. He was BIG-BIG-BIG for a kid. He had spiky hair and a scowl on his face.

As Garth and A.J. bent over to help Beth pick up her books, Miss Victoria called to the back of the bus.

'Garth and A.J., if you don't sit down so I can get moving, I'm going to report you two.'

'Yeah, Garth Bugwart, sit down,' the big kid sneered.

'I'm going to tell,' Beth said softly.

'Don't!' A.J. whispered back. 'Bean will only get worse.'

So this was the scary Bean they were talking about!

Beth slid into a seat with all her books. Just as A.J. stepped forward, Bean stuck his leg into the aisle. So that's how he had tripped her! After A.J. managed to step over it, Garth and I (in my cage) were standing right next to Mr Nasty.

'What's in the cage, Bugface? Your lunch?' He snorted a few times, but no one else on the bus laughed. 'Or is that your girlfriend?'

That did it! I was fighting mad. Somebody had to squeak up to this fellow. 'For your information, I am a male Golden Hamster. And you are one MEAN BEAN!'

'Anybody got a mousetrap?' Bean snarled.

'Why aren't you guys in your seats?' Miss Victoria yelled from the front of the bus. 'I'm reporting you, Garth and A.J.!'

Garth slid into a seat next to A.J. I was about to give Miss Victoria a piece of my mind when the bus lurched forward and I had to hold on to my cage for dear life. I was sorry I'd eaten those Nutri-Nibbles just before we left.

All week, I'd been looking forward to going home with Garth. Now I wasn't sure I'd ever make it there!

> Friendship is one mind in two bodies.
>
> Mencius, Chinese philosopher

Mean Bean

A.J.'s stop was before Garth's. 'Come on over tomorrow,' Garth told his friend. As soon as A.J. left, Garth moved up to the front of the bus to get away from Bean.

'What part of "sit down" don't you understand, Garth?' Miss Victoria sounded pretty irritated.

'Sorry. The cage wouldn't fit on the seat,' he said.

'What on earth is in there, anyway?'

Before Garth could answer, the bus stopped in front of his house. He pulled the blanket down around my cage and hurried down the steps.

Mrs Tugwell was waiting in the doorway of the house. She had wavy brown hair like her son. She had glasses and freckles like her son too. She helped him set my cage up on the living-room table. Garth's little brother Andy raced into the room. He had wavy brown hair, glasses and freckles too. 'Mine!' he shouted.

'Nope. He's mine. At least for the weekend,' said Garth.

'Tell Andy about Humphrey,' Garth's mum said.

'He's a hamster. And you have to be nice to him,' Garth explained.

He got that right!

'I like ham,' said Andy, rubbing his stomach. 'Yum-yum!'

I hopped on to my wheel to show Andy that a hamster wasn't anything like a ham.

'Wheee! Ham go round!' said Andy.

Garth's mother brought in a plate of peanut butter and crackers. Ooh, that smelled good!

'How was school?' she asked.

'OK,' said Garth. 'But Mum, could you say something to Bean's mum? He's mean to everybody on the bus.'

'Martin Bean?' Garth's mum sounded surprised. 'Why, he's always polite when I see him.'

'Well, he's not polite any other time,' Garth explained. 'He tripped a girl on the bus and called everybody names.'

'That doesn't sound like Martin. What did the bus driver do?'

'Nothing,' Garth answered.

'Well, I think she should be the one to work

things out,' said Mrs Tugwell.

'But you're friends with Mrs Bean!'

'I probably won't be if I complain about her son. Maybe if you were friendlier to him, he'd act nicer.'

'Mum . . .' Garth moaned.

'It's worth a try,' his mum suggested.

I had to squeak up. 'He's the Meanest Bean I've ever seen!'

'Goodness, what's the matter with Humphrey?' asked Mrs Tugwell.

'Maybe he doesn't like Marty either,' Garth muttered. He's one smart fellow.

Shortly after Mr Tugwell came home, Natalie arrived. She was the babysitter, but I didn't see any babies around for her to sit on. Garth wasn't a baby, Andy wasn't a baby and certainly I was no baby.

Natalie had black hair and wore a black shirt, black trousers and black shoes. She had glasses with black frames. Her lips were bright red.

'Order a pizza,' said Garth's dad, handing Natalie some money. 'I got some videos for the guys.'

'OK,' said Natalie. 'Mind if I do some home-work?'

'As long as you get the boys into bed at nine,' Mrs Tugwell agreed.

Natalie glanced at my cage. 'What about the rat?'

I felt quite discouraged. I'd already been called a mouse and a ham that day.

'He's a hammer!' Andy yelled.

'Oh, a hamster. How cute,' said Natalie, leaning in towards my cage. 'Hi there, big boy.'

Whew! After a miserable week and a rough ride home, I suddenly felt a whole lot better.

Later, the boys ate pizza and watched videos while Natalie read from a big thick book.

'What's that?' asked Andy, leaning over her shoulder. 'How come it doesn't have any pictures?'

'College books don't have pictures.'

Andy wrinkled his nose. 'What's college?'

Natalie sighed. 'After you go to secondary school and pass your exams, if you want a good job like a doctor or a lawyer or a teacher, you have to go to college.'

'I know that,' Garth piped up. 'City College is right down the street. Mum took classes there last year.'

'That's where I go,' said Natalie. 'I'm studying psychology.' The way she said it, that big word sounded like 'sigh-coll-eh-gee'. But the word on her book was spelled 'Psychology'. I wrote it down in my notebook later. (I hope that word is never in a spelling test!)

'In psychology, you find out what's inside people's heads.' The babysitter reached for Andy's head.

'Ooey-gooey brains,' said Garth.

'Don't go into my head!' screamed Andy, leaping off the sofa.

Natalie laughed. 'Not like that. Psychology teaches you how people think. Do you know what I'm thinking?'

Andy shook his head.

'I'm thinking it's time for bed,' Natalie said. 'Nine o'clock.'

The boys both groaned. 'Not yet,' Garth protested.

Andy folded his arms. 'You can't make me!' he said firmly.

Surprisingly, Natalie sat back and smiled. 'I suppose you're right. I can't make you.'

Andy's eyes practically bugged out of his head. 'Huh?'

'Why don't you put on another video? We can stay up till your parents get back,' the babysitter continued. 'It'll be fun!'

'Yes!' Garth exclaimed as he and his brother gleefully high-fived each other.

But I was a little confused. Hadn't Mrs Tugwell told her to get the boys into bed at nine? I was sure that Natalie had lost her mind.

Garth settled back on the sofa, but after a minute his smile disappeared. 'When do you think Mum and Dad will be back?'

Natalie shrugged her shoulders. 'They didn't say.'

'Won't they be upset if we're still up?'

'I suppose we'll find out, won't we?' Natalie answered with a mischievous grin.

Andy looked worried. 'They'll be cross if we're not in bed.'

'So?' said Natalie. 'We still have time to watch more TV.'

Garth stood up and yawned loudly. 'I'm kind of tired.'

'Me too,' said Andy, stretching his arms.

Natalie smiled. 'Well, if you really think so, OK. You two get ready for bed and I'll be up in a minute.'

As the brothers raced upstairs, Natalie chuckled to herself, then leaned in towards my cage.

'And that, Humphrey Hamster, is what is called "reverse psychology". You get people to do what you want by telling them to do the opposite.'

Reverse psychology. (Remember, it's pronounced sigh-coll-er-gee.) So that's how people's minds work. Just tell them to do the opposite of what you want them to do.

You can really learn a lot at college.

You can learn a lot from a good babysitter too.

The next afternoon, A.J. came over to Garth's house to play. Mrs Tugwell took Andy out to buy new shoes. Mr Tugwell was paying bills in the kitchen. The boys were alone with me in the living room.

'Humphrey needs some exercise,' said A.J. 'Let's take him out.'

'OK. You can watch him while I clean his cage.'

A.J. gently took me out while Garth put on gloves and began to clean my cage. Both boys chuckled when Garth got to my potty corner – everyone does – but he did a good job of cleaning it. While he worked, they talked.

'Any chance your dad can drive us on Monday morning?' asked Garth.

A.J. shook his head as he gently petted me. 'He has to leave for work really early. How about your dad?'

Garth shook his head. 'He always talks about how he had to walk to school and how lucky I am to ride on a bus.'

'I know,' A.J. sighed and put me down on the table.

'Watch it!' said Garth. He set up a row of big tall books all around the edge of the table. 'We don't want Humphrey to get away.'

'Maybe he'll be sick on Monday,' Garth suggested.

'Are you kidding? He's the healthiest guy at school. Man, if he wasn't so big, I'd really give it to him,' said A.J., making a fist.

'Me too,' Garth agreed.

It wasn't hard to work out that they were talking about big mean Marty Bean.

'I don't know why Miss Victoria always takes his side,' Garth said after a while.

'He knows how not to get caught.'

The boys were silent again until Garth said, 'Miranda was getting a drink at the fountain at break, and he came up and pushed her out of the way.'

The thought of someone pushing Golden Miranda, an almost perfect human, really ruffled my fur.

'Did she tell?' asked A.J.

'Yeah. He said he didn't do it,' Garth explained. 'Said he wasn't anywhere near her. He said Kirk did it. Kirk almost got into trouble, so Miranda said it was all a mistake to get Kirk off the hook.'

'Kirk the Jerk. That's what Bean calls him,' said Garth. 'He's got a name for everybody. That's why he doesn't have any friends.'

He stepped back and pulled off his rubber gloves. 'I think that's one clean cage.'

'Great,' I squeaked. 'But what are we going to do about Bean?'

'Bean's a pretty funny name,' A.J. said with a chuckle. 'Bean brain.'

'Bean breath,' said Garth.

The boys started laughing.

'Bean bag!'

'Bean jeans!'

'Green Bean!'

'Mean Bean! Hey – that rhymes! Mean green Bean!'

Mrs Brisbane would be proud to hear them rhyming! I liked hearing them laugh. However, I was worried. Bean had said something about a mousetrap. The mere mention of those contraptions makes me shiver and quiver. And I didn't want to see anybody get tripped or pushed again.

'Ready to go back in, Humphrey-Dumpty?' asked Garth.

'YES!' I squeaked, which for some reason made the boys howl with laughter again.

Once I was back in the cage, the boys went up to play in Garth's room. That gave me time to think. Here were Garth and A.J., really good friends. They were nice to each other and stuck together. Marty Bean wasn't friendly to anybody and he didn't have any friends.

All my classmates liked Og, but when I offered to be his friend, he leaped at me in a very rude way. The business of friendship is not as easy as it sounds, I figured, just before dozing off for a long afternoon nap.

It was nice at Garth's house that weekend. The announcer on TV said it was COLD-COLD-COLD outside, so the Tugwells stayed inside. The family popped popcorn – did that smell good! And they watched TV and snuggled on the sofa. As happy as I should have been, I worried about Monday's bus ride. What I needed was a Plan. And maybe a little psychology.

'Are you sure the little fellow won't catch cold?' asked Mrs Tugwell when Garth was ready to leave for school on Monday.

'He's got a fur coat. And I'll cover him,' Garth assured her. I was plunged into total darkness as he threw a blanket over the cage.

'Bye, Ham!' shouted Andy.

'Bye, Andy!' I squeaked back. After all, a 'ham' isn't the worst thing that a person can call you.

Soon, I heard the squeal of the bus's brakes as it stopped in front of the Tugwells' house.

'All aboard!' I heard Miss Victoria say. 'Find a seat.'

'This cage is too big. Can't I sit up here?' asked Garth.

'Do you see any empty seats up here?' the bus driver replied. 'Get moving and keep moving.'

I was already queasy just thinking about Bean. As Garth walked towards the back of the bus, looking for an empty seat, my cage swayed back and forth like a ship on a rough sea, which didn't help my stomach at all. Once we sat down, the bus started rolling. At the next corner, it abruptly stopped and I slid across the floor of my cage. Ouch!

'All aboard!' I heard Miss Victoria say. 'Find a seat, A.J.'

A.J. walked back to our seat. 'Move over,' he told Garth.

'I have to sit on the aisle,' Garth replied. 'The cage won't fit in the seat.'

A.J. crawled over Garth so that he was close to the window. As he did, he bent down and whispered, 'Told you he'd be here. He's always here.'

As the bus lurched forward, my cage wobbled enough for the blanket to part, so I could see a little. And what I saw was most unpleasant: Marty Bean sitting right next to us.

'Hey, Garth, is that your face or did somebody throw up on you?' I could see the smirk on his face as he leaned in close, mere inches from my cage.

'Is that a cage, Bugwart, or is it your handbag?' Bean asked. He hooted at his own joke even though it wasn't funny.

It may have been cold outside, but I was getting pretty hot. Og might be unfriendly, but this Bean was even worse. I hadn't thought of Og all weekend. Now it came back to me: the green skin, the repulsive grin, and the way he had leaped up and scared me. I had taken it from the frog, but I wasn't going to take it from this big bully.

This was the time to act!

I quickly opened the lock-that-doesn't-lock and took a deep breath before leaping on to Martin Bean's leg. 'Stop being mean, Bean!' I yelled at the top of my voice. It may have sounded like squeaking to him, but I made my point.

'Eeek!' Marty shouted. 'It's on me! A mouse!' He threw his hands up in the air and screamed as I ran in circles on his leg. 'Help me, somebody! Help!'

The faces around me were a blur and I was getting dizzy. As Marty continued to scream, the other kids began to laugh, softly at first, then louder and louder.

'He's only a little hamster,' I heard Garth say as he scooped me up in his hands. 'He wouldn't hurt a flea.'

I like being called a 'he' a lot more than being called an 'it'.

'It tried to bite me!' Marty exclaimed. Everybody on the bus, including Beth and her first-year friends, laughed.

'What is going on back there, Martin?' Miss Victoria called out as she slammed on the brakes.

'They – they threw a big rat on me!' He was almost in tears. 'A giant rat!'

'I think you'd better come up and sit behind me,' the bus driver said. 'Now!' She made the girls in the seat behind her move as Marty shuffled to the front of the bus.

Garth put me back in my cage.

'Thanks, Humphrey,' he whispered. 'I don't know how you got out, but I'm really glad you did.'

'Always happy to help out a pal,' I squeaked.

The rest of the ride was uneventful. When Miss Victoria stopped the bus in front of Longfellow School, she made an announcement. 'This was the quietest ride we've ever had. From now on, Martin Bean, I'm assigning you the front seat. Permanently.'

Marty didn't argue. He was in too much of a hurry to get off the bus. He could probably hear all the rest of the bus passengers – including me – shouting, 'Hooray!'

> No enemy can match a friend.
>
> Jonathan Swift, Irish author

5

Rhyme Time

I felt pretty proud of myself after the bus ride. Once I was back in Room 26, I looked over at my pop-eyed neighbour.

'Morning, Og,' I squeaked to him, hoping that after the long, lonely weekend he might be in a friendlier frame of mind. He responded to my greeting with dead silence and a grim grin. Or maybe he couldn't see me, because there was a huge piece of paper taped to the front of his glass box.

And something about that note must have been pretty funny, because all my classmates were laughing. Hard.

'All right, what's so funny?' asked Mrs Brisbane.

'Og!' said Gail. She was giggling so hard I was afraid she'd get the hiccups again.

Mrs Brisbane ripped the paper off the tank and

read it. 'Help! I'm a prince who's been turned into a frog. Kiss me quick!'

Somebody made loud smacking sounds, which made everyone laugh even louder. Mrs Brisbane looked up from the paper. 'I-Heard-That-Kirk. Are you volunteering to kiss Og?'

It was a pretty disgusting thought to me, but everyone else laughed.

'I think it has to be a girl,' said Kirk.

Mrs Brisbane folded up the paper. 'Thank you for our joke of the day. You can Stop-Giggling-Gail. Now, let's all calm down and get to work. I'm anxious to hear the poems you've written, but let's get our spelling test out of the way first. Please take out a pencil and a piece of paper.'

Whoops! I'd done a lot of thinking over the weekend. Something I hadn't thought about was our spelling test. Mrs Brisbane and my classmates don't know that I usually slip into my sleeping house with my notebook and pencil and take the tests, too. I still hadn't got 100 per cent, like Sayeh. I hoped I would some day.

This would not be the day.

I did all right with 'market', 'jewel' and 'pound'. But 'accommodate'? Did Mrs Brisbane really think anyone except Sayeh would get that right? It looks like they threw in some extra letters left over from another word!

Next, it was time for the poems. 'Kirk, you seem to want to be the centre of attention this morning. You can go first.'

Kirk jumped up and said, 'I've got to write mine on the board.'

Mrs Brisbane told him to go ahead. When he was finished, he read it aloud.

'It's called 'Frog'. Here goes:

Funny
Ribbits
Oily
Green.

That's a **frog**.
Take away the **f**unny **r**ibbits
You've got **Og**?!'

Mrs Brisbane smiled and nodded her head. 'Well done, Kirk. Very clever. What do you think, class?'

'Does that say "oily"?' asked Repeat-It-Please-Richie. 'Frogs aren't oily.'

Kirk wrinkled his nose. 'Well, he looks oily, even if he isn't. Besides, I need an O word to spell "frog".'

Mrs Brisbane asked the class to help Kirk out with another O word. I decided to squeak up.

'Obnoxious! Offensive!' I yelled. I almost said, 'Unfriendly,' but it doesn't begin with an O.

No one seemed to hear me. Sometimes I wish I had a big booming voice like A.J.'s.

'"Honest"?' asked Seth, jumping up out of his seat.

'Sit-Still-Seth. That's a good guess, but "honest" starts with a silent H.' Mrs Brisbane wrote the word on the board. Silent H – not fair! I'll have to watch out for that one.

'How about "odd"?' suggested Art.

'What do you think, class? Do some people think frogs are odd?'

Some students nodded their heads. Nobody nodded harder than me.

'What do you think?' the teacher asked Kirk.

'Maybe "oddball" fits him better,' Kirk said, smiling. Everybody seemed to like the answer and I was not about to disagree.

I glanced over at Og to see what he thought. 'Boing,' he twanged. Everybody laughed, even Mrs Brisbane.

'Oh, Og, you are so funny,' she said.

Oddball, yes. Funny, no. In my humble opinion.

Heidi waved her hand in the air. 'Og doesn't say "ribbit". He goes "boing".'

'R is for "boing"? Heidi, that makes "roing".' Kirk looked very pleased with himself.

Heidi frowned. 'That's not what I meant.'

'That's enough on that one, Kirk. Why don't you

work on it a little more?' said Mrs Brisbane. She called for another volunteer. This time Heidi actually remembered to raise her hand. When the teacher called on her, she stood up and read her poem.

I met a little frog
And said, 'How do you do?
My name is Hopper.
Is that your name too?'
He croaked, 'My name is Leaper.
That's what I do all day.'
But when I tried to pick him up,
Leaper ran away.

'Nicely done, Heidi,' said Mrs Brisbane. 'Good rhyming. It's a good idea to use your own name. Anyone else?'

No hands were raised this time.

'How about you, Tabitha?' asked the teacher. 'What did you write?'

Tabitha looked SCARED-SCARED-SCARED.

Mrs Brisbane put on her friendliest smile. 'Don't be afraid. We won't bite, will we, class?'

Most of the kids smiled and shook their heads. Kirk growled like a lion, just to be funny, but I couldn't tell if Tabitha noticed.

Slowly, she stood up and picked up her paper. In a soft voice, she read her poem like it was one sentence, really fast, like this:

'People-think-bears-are-mean-but-they've-never-seen-Smiley. He-doesn't-growl-or-make-you-sad-he-wouldn't-ever-be-bad-Smiley. I-don't-care-what-people-say-he-helps-me-get-through-the-day-Smiley.'

Tabitha quickly sat down and stared at her table.

'Thank you, Tabitha. That's a lovely poem about a bear. And I liked the rhymes,' said Mrs Brisbane.

I saw Tabitha reach into her pocket and pat her teddy bear.

I also saw Mandy look over at Heidi and roll her eyes. I could even read her lips as she mouthed the word 'baby'.

'Any volunteers?' asked the teacher. 'Garth?' Garth stood up to read his poem.

Roses are red,
Frogs are cool,
Now we've got one
Here at school.

He folded up his paper. 'That's it.'

Mrs Brisbane reminded Garth that the poems were supposed to have at least six lines and that his poem had four.

Personally, I was in shock.

'Frogs are *cool*'? What kind of a poem is that? After I helped him and A.J. with Mean Bean, Garth wrote 'Frogs are cool'?

We didn't have time for any more poems

because the bell rang for break and my classmates raced to get their coats and gloves.

Tabitha took her time, waiting to see that no one was watching, and secretly stashed her bear in her pocket. Sayeh stayed behind too, and approached her.

'I liked your poem. Is Smiley your bear's name?' she asked.

Tabitha nodded, but she didn't say anything. She didn't know how shy Sayeh was or how hard it was for her to come up and talk like that. But I knew.

'He's nice,' said Sayeh. 'Are you coming out to break?'

Tabitha nodded again. Sayeh waited, but when Tabitha didn't budge, she said, 'See you outside,' and hurried to the cloakroom with her head down, looking embarrassed.

I've got to admit, Speak-Up-Sayeh is a favourite friend of mine. To see Tabitha treat her that way made me MAD-MAD-MAD. She was about as friendly as a frog!

The new girl waited until everyone else had left the room before rising to get her coat.

Later, after the students left for the day, Miss Loomis came into Room 26, all bundled up in her coat, hat and gloves.

'Hi, Sue. I'm ready when you are.' She walked over to Og's cage. 'How's your star pupil doing?'

'Fine. He and Humphrey seem to get along all right. At least they don't disturb each other,' said Mrs Brisbane.

Don't disturb each other? I was pretty disturbed when Og leaped at me!

Mrs Brisbane put on her coat. 'Let's stop for coffee to warm us up on the way home.'

'Sounds great,' Miss Loomis answered. 'I can't thank you enough for giving me a lift.'

'What are friends for?' asked Mrs Brisbane.

After they left, I felt as gloomy as the sky looked. Spinning my wheel warmed my fur up, but it didn't make me feel any warmer inside. What are friends for? For fun and talking and helping and sharing. Right?

'Hey, Og!' I called out, peering through the bars of my cage at his glass house. 'I hope you've been paying attention here in Room 26.'

I waited a few seconds to allow him to answer, which he didn't, of course. 'I hope you've seen what good friends the kids are. I mean, like Garth and A.J., the way they stick together. And Heidi and Gail, the way they like to giggle. Sayeh and Miranda are pals. Art and Richie, too. Wouldn't it be nice to have fun friends like them?'

I didn't actually expect an answer, of course, but this time I did get something: splashing. Splish-splash-splish. At least I knew Og was alive. Maybe he was even listening. I kept going. 'Even if we can't actually talk to each other, we could – I don't know – have jumping contests.' Suddenly, I had all kinds of ideas. 'We could sing together. Or make funny faces at each other. Maybe you could teach me how to go "boing".'

'Boing!'

I almost fainted. Was he answering me?

'Boing,' I said, though I didn't sound much like a frog. 'Boing to you, Og!'

'Boing-boing!' said Og.

'Yeah . . . boing!' I replied. My heart was thumping quite loudly. Were we actually having a conversation? 'Uh . . . so what else is new?' I continued.

I waited, but there was no answer. 'Og?' I called out. 'Og, answer me!'

Silence. This was one frustrating frog. I tried again, but there were no more boings. Not even a splash. The room was silent as a tomb. That's about as quiet as it can get.

Somehow, it felt even worse to think that Og tried to talk to me and gave up. Still, Sayeh had learned a brand-new language when she came to this country. Maybe Og and I could learn to understand each other. I returned to my wheel and started spinning as fast as I could. I spun until it was almost dark.

At last, the door swung open and the lights came on.

'I have arrived!' Aldo announced, waving his broom. 'No applause, please.'

'HELLO-HELLO-HELLO!' I shouted. I was never so glad to see anybody in my life.

Aldo hurried towards my cage, rubbing his arms.

'Hey, it's cold in here. They turn the heat down at night to save money, but it's freezing outside. And it's almost freezing in here,' said Aldo. He glanced at Og's cage. 'Hey, Og, how's the world treating you?'

When Og didn't answer him, Aldo turned back to me. 'He's the strong, silent type, I suppose. Say, Humph, old pal, I've been thinking. About that idea of getting a better job, you know? Maria thinks I should go back to school.'

I tried to imagine Aldo sitting at a little table all day with Miranda, Richie and Seth. I didn't think his legs would fit.

'I could go to college during the day and still work here at night.'

College! I hoped they had bigger chairs there.

Aldo pulled up a chair so we were practically whisker to whisker. 'See, I went to college for a year. When my dad died, I quit because I needed to make money. I thought I'd go back, but I never did.'

'It's never too late,' I squeaked.

Aldo shook his head. 'I'm not a kid any more.' He reached into his pocket. 'Maria got me this application for City College, but I don't know.'

City College! That's where Natalie the babysitter went! She said that's where people go to become doctors and lawyers and teachers. That's where people go to study things like psychology and get good jobs.

'GO-GO-GO!' I said, hopping up and down.

'Maria thinks I'm clever enough,' said Aldo. 'I just don't know if I can handle all that studying.' He sighed and rose from his chair.

'Guess I'd better get this room cleaned or I won't have a job at all.' Aldo tucked the application back into his pocket. 'First, I'm going to go and turn up the heat.'

Good old Aldo. He was a thoughtful fellow. And a smart fellow, too. I hoped his wife could talk him into going back to school.

I wasn't sure I could do it all by myself. And I was pretty sure Og wouldn't be any help at all.

> One of the most beautiful qualities of true friendship is to understand and to be understood.
>
> Seneca, Roman playwright

6

Crabby Abby

The next morning, Kirk hurried from the cloakroom and stuck a big piece of paper on my cage. It almost blocked my view of Og, which was not a bad thing.

Once the other students had settled in their seats, they started giggling and pointing, led by Gail, of course. Mrs Brisbane looked puzzled until she glanced over at my cage. The sign read: HELP! I'M BEING HELD PRISONER IN ROOM 26!

'And who is responsible for this, as if I didn't know?' she asked.

Kirk rose and took a bow as everyone applauded. I joined in, though I was the only one who knew I could never be a prisoner with my lock-that-doesn't-lock.

'Let's all sit down now,' said Mrs Brisbane. 'And get back to poetry.'

Somebody made a very, very rude noise and Mrs Brisbane did not like that one little bit. 'I-Heard-That-Kirk. And I don't ever want to hear it again.'

During the rest of the week, we heard a lot more animal poems. Most of them were about frogs. One was about a dog (Miranda's). Sayeh wrote about a beautiful bird called a dove. ('Dove' rhymes with 'love.')

Nobody wrote about hamsters.

Aldo didn't mention City College again. And Tabitha still didn't talk to anybody except Smiley.

I was looking forward to a change of scenery by the end of the week. A relaxing getaway to one of my classmates' cosy homes. One with plenty of heat and no frogs.

On Friday, Mrs Brisbane said, 'I can't remember – who asked me about taking Humphrey home this weekend?' Miranda's hand shot up.

'Yes, Miranda. I got the note from your father. That will be fine.'

I let out a little 'Eek!' I don't think anyone heard me. Everyone knows that I have a special place in my hamster heart for Miranda. After all, her name is Golden and I am a Golden Hamster. We both have lovely golden hair.

But I have a terrible fear of her dog Clem. I barely escaped a terrible fate the last time I went home with her, but could I do it again?

Then it hit me. 'Wait a second! Did you say "father"?' I squeaked. Because when I went home with Miranda before, there was only her mum. And the dog, of course. And Fanny the fish.

Mrs Brisbane chuckled. 'I think Humphrey approves.'

I puzzled over this all afternoon. Sure enough, at the end of the day, a tall man called Mr Golden arrived to pick up his daughter. At least I wouldn't be riding on the bus with Marty Bean – that was a break! Miranda, thoughtful as ever, threw a warm blanket over my cage. As they carried me out, Mrs Brisbane picked up Og's cage.

'I thought you said Og stayed here at weekends,' said Miranda.

Mrs Brisbane chuckled. 'It's a surprise for my husband. He always enjoys Humphrey, so I thought he'd get a kick out of having Og for the weekend.'

I felt COLD-COLD-COLD and we were still inside! I thought the Brisbanes were my best friends of all. Were they ready to replace me with a frog?

Once we were in the car, I didn't have time to worry about the Brisbanes. I was too worried about facing Clem again. I could practically see his sloppy tongue and drippy nose and smell that bad breath waiting for me up in Miranda's flat.

What a shock it was when the car pulled up in front of a house, not a block of flats. 'Here we are, Humphrey,' Miranda announced. 'You've seen my mum's place, but this weekend we're staying at my dad's place.'

A nice lady Miranda called 'Amy' met us at the door.

'Hi, honey,' said Mr Golden, kissing Amy on the cheek. 'Meet Humphrey the hamster.'

'Cute,' Amy replied. 'I think he should stay in the girls' room.'

'What about the living room?' asked Miranda. 'Or the dining-room table?'

'I think he'd get in the way,' Mr Golden said. 'Let's go to your room.'

Miranda's room in the flat had a bed, a desk, a fish tank and stars on the ceiling. Her room in this house had two beds, a dresser, a desk and no stars. Everything in this room was pink, from the walls to the bedspreads to the carpet on the floor. A girl about Miranda's age was sprawled across one bed, reading a magazine.

'What's THAT?' she asked in an unpleasant voice.

'Humphrey. He's our class hamster,' Miranda explained.

'Well, he's not staying in my room,' the girl stated firmly.

'It's Miranda's room too, Abby,' Amy said as she came through the door behind us. 'Put Humphrey on the desk.'

Miranda thoughtfully opened my cage to straighten out my ladder and my water bottle, which had slid around during the drive.

'Mum, I have to do homework on that desk,' said Abby, sitting up.

Huh? Amy was Abby's mum and she was married to Miranda's dad? Things were quite confusing.

'OK, we'll put his cage on the floor,' said Amy.

I heard a baby crying in another room. 'I've got to see what Ben wants,' she said. Mr Golden followed her and Abby got up to close the door.

'He stays on your side of the room,' Abby told Miranda. 'And don't forget, no crossing the line.'

Abby took her foot and dragged it in a straight line across the middle of the pink carpet. 'No crossing the line. Ever.'

Miranda sighed. 'I know. You tell me every time I'm here.'

'Sometimes you forget. And don't touch anything of mine.'

'I never do,' Miranda countered.

'You used my hair slide last time,' said Abby.

'It was a mistake! It looks exactly like mine!'

Good for Miranda for standing up for herself! 'I didn't complain when you borrowed my book without asking.'

Abby plopped back on to the bed again and thumbed through her magazine. 'Just don't cross the line,' she muttered.

I hopped on my wheel for a spin. Sometimes it cheers people up to watch me spinning. Abby was not one of those people. She glared at me. 'Don't tell me it makes a noise,' she said nastily. 'Can't you stop it?'

'Humphrey is not an "it". He's a "he",' said Miranda. I love that girl! 'You could read in the living room,' she suggested.

'I was here first.' Abby suddenly slammed down her magazine and stood up. 'OK, anything to get away from you.'

After she left, Miranda leaned down close to my cage. 'I was hoping she'd like you, Humphrey. She certainly doesn't like me. It's not my fault my dad married her mum. It's not my fault she has to share her room with me every other weekend.' She sighed. 'I've tried to be friends with her, but it's no use. She's a wicked stepsister, like in Cinderella.'

Miranda looked SAD-SAD-SAD, so I leaped up on my ladder and hung from it by one paw to cheer her up.

She smiled, so I leaped on to my tree and began

swinging from branch to branch, like that Tarzan guy I saw on TV. That made Miranda laugh.

Abby returned with a sour expression on her face. I must have looked that way the day somebody in Room 26 (I'm still trying to work out who) slipped me a slice of lemon.

'Mum wants us to help make supper. She's got to feed the baby.'

She disappeared as quickly as she had appeared.

'See you, Humphrey,' Miranda whispered. 'And remember, don't cross the line!'

After she had left, I squinted my eyes, but I couldn't see a line anywhere. All I could see was a sea of pink. So much pink, I felt a little ill.

Later that night, while Miranda took her bath, I was alone with Abby. I decided to try and be friendly.

'Nice room you've got,' I squeaked politely.

Abby turned towards me and frowned. 'Were you squeaking at me?' She shook her head. 'This is the last straw. First, I have a room all to myself. Then Mum marries *him* and pretty soon I have a stepsister taking half my room and a new baby brother crying all the time and nobody knows I exist! I'm supposed to be happy about the whole thing when it wasn't my idea. And now they've moved in a guinea pig!'

That wasn't a huge insult, because guinea pigs are cute and furry like me, only not quite as cute. Anyway, I could see Abby's point. I wasn't happy about Og moving into Room 26 and it certainly wasn't my idea! The difference was, Miranda is actually nice. And Og is, well, Og.

Miranda returned and the two girls settled into their respective beds.

'Night, Humphrey,' Miranda said to me.

Neither girl said a word to the other.

I had a long night ahead of me, and since I'm nocturnal and do most of my sleeping during the day, I had a lot of time to think.

What Abby had told me helped me to understand why she was so crabby with Miranda. If only I'd studied psychology like Natalie, maybe I could get inside her head and work out how to make her like Miranda as much as I did.

* * *

The next morning, Miranda cleaned my cage while Abby lounged on the bed, writing in her diary.

'What are you doing anyway?' she asked Miranda.

'Taking out the old bedding, putting in new. Changing the water, stuff like that.'

Abby slammed her diary shut. 'It doesn't – you know – go to the toilet in there, does it?'

'Well, of course.'

Abby leaped off her bed and pointed to the door. 'That's the most disgusting thing I've ever heard. Get it out of my room right now!'

(I've worked out a lot about humans, but I still don't know why my little potty corner is always such a big deal to them. I'm really quite tidy.)

Miranda didn't budge. 'He's on my side of the room.'

I was all for Miranda. On the other paw, I could see that Abby had been through a lot of changes in a short time. It's not easy getting a new roommate. I learned that the hard way! I also knew what a good friend Miranda can be. Friends help friends, so I figured it was time I did something about it.

I had a Plan. A Plan using reverse psychology. Since Miranda had no luck in getting Abby to like her, my Plan would make them *not* like each other even more. (If that was possible.)

OK, it didn't make a lot of sense, but when Natalie used reverse psychology, it worked REALLY-REALLY-REALLY well.

I had the chance to set my Plan in motion a short time later when Mr Golden announced that the whole family was going to a museum.

'Do we *all* have to go?' asked Abby.

'Yes, all of us. We're a family, you know,' said her mum.

Abby wrinkled her nose. 'Even the baby?'

'We'll bring the buggy,' said Miranda's dad. 'He'll like it.'

Despite her grumbling, Abby joined the rest of the family and I soon had the whole house to myself. My Plan would take speed, strength, courage and lots of time. It would be well worth it . . . IF it worked.

Once I was sure they were gone, I opened the lock-that-doesn't-lock and hurried over to Abby's bed. I had been studying it all morning and thought that if I grabbed hold, I could climb the bedspread, paw over paw, like a rope. I was huffing and puffing by the time I reached the top, but I made it! Sitting on top of the bedspread was the purple-and-pink-striped pen Abby used to write in her diary. I gave it a big push and it rolled off the bed and on to the floor.

After that, I scrambled over to Abby's dressing table. There, I found her pink bracelet with ABBY spelled out in purple and white beads. I pushed that on to the floor too.

The next part of my mission was fun. I grabbed the edge of the bedspread and slid DOWN-DOWN-DOWN really fast!

I was far from finished. Next I climbed all the way up Miranda's bedspread to get to her gold ring with the pink stone, which I pushed on to the floor, along with a red loopy thing she sometimes used to pull back her hair. (You don't expect a boy hamster to know what it's called!)

I was halfway to my goal, and the hardest part of my Plan was yet to come.

All morning, I'd had my eye on a big ball of string on the desk. A long piece of the string hung down almost to the floor. I grabbed it and pulled as hard as I could. More and more string unrolled and fell to the floor. I chewed it off and set to work.

Looping the string around the pen and the bracelet, then holding the string in my teeth, I climbed up Miranda's bedspread again. Whew! Mrs Brisbane says exercise is good for you, but that was work! Once I was on the bed, I tugged on the string, pulling up the pen and the bracelet. (Believe me, for a small hamster, those two items are very heavy!) I carefully laid them both on Miranda's pillow where she couldn't miss them.

As tired as I was, there was no time to rest. I slid down to the floor, looped the string around Miranda's ring and the hair holder and pulled them up on to Abby's bed, laying them on her pillow.

(I'm happy to say those two items were not as heavy as the others.)

When the girls came back, Miranda would find Abby's belongings on her own pillow. Abby would find Miranda's things on her own pillow.

I scurried back to my cosy cage and closed the door behind me. I wanted to be safe when the fireworks began!

> **Little friends may prove to be great friends.**
>
> **Aesop, writer of fables**

7

Fright Night

Abby entered first, plopped down on her bed as usual and sighed a big sigh.

'THAT was fun,' she said. 'Especially when the baby threw up in the restaurant.' I don't think she was actually talking to me, but I listened anyway.

A second later, Miranda came in. 'Hi, Humphrey. Did you miss me?' she asked, bending down close to my cage.

'Of course!' I squeaked.

'I suppose you understand what it's saying,' Abby said sourly.

'Sort of,' said Miranda. 'I think he's trying to tell me he missed me.'

Bingo!

I watched Abby closely as she reached for her diary and pen. 'Where's my pen?' she asked. She looked at her pillow. 'What's this stuff doing here?'

Miranda pointed at Abby's bed. 'Hey, that's my hair scrunchie!'

So that's what the hair thing is called!

'And my ring!' Miranda jumped up, crossed over the imaginary line and grabbed her things. 'You took them!'

Abby spotted something on Miranda's pillow. 'There's my pen! You took it! And my name bracelet!' She snatched her items and glared at Miranda. 'You're always taking my things.'

'You took my things! I didn't touch yours,' Miranda insisted. I had never heard her sound that angry before.

Abby's face turned red. 'Why would I take your dinky ring and your stupid scrunchie? I have my own ring and my own scrunchie!'

'Why would I take your stupid pen and a bracelet with your name on it? And why would I put them on my pillow where you can see them?' asked Miranda.

'Just to be mean?'

'I'm not mean!' said Miranda. 'Anyway, isn't it weird that my things were on your pillow and your things were on my pillow?'

Abby thought for a moment. 'Like somebody planned it.'

'Like somebody wanted us to notice,' agreed Miranda.

Suddenly, they were actually talking instead of arguing. I crossed my paws. This had to work!

Abby sat back down on her bed. 'Who would do that? My mum wouldn't. Or your dad.'

Miranda collapsed on to her bed. 'Well, the baby didn't do it.' She started to giggle.

'Maybe Humphrey did it,' said Abby, and she started to giggle.

I chuckled too.

'Those things didn't fly from bed to bed,' said Miranda. 'Somebody put them there on purpose.'

'Or some*thing*,' said Abby. 'Like a . . . a ghost!'

Miranda turned pale. 'You don't have ghosts here, do you?'

'No,' said Abby, shaking her head. 'At least I don't think we do.'

'There are no such things as ghosts,' insisted sensible Miranda. She sounded like she was trying to convince herself.

'NO-NO-NO, there aren't any ghosts, except in stories,' I squeaked. I think I was trying to convince myself.

'I know,' said Abby. She opened her diary and tore out a page. 'I'll write down every possibility of who could have done this. Number one: Miranda.'

'I didn't!' Miranda protested.

'I'm just writing down all the possibilities. Miranda, me, my mum, your dad, Ben, Humphrey.

They're the only ones in the house – right? Unless there was a burglar.'

The fur on my back stood straight up. Burglars are scary things!

'Burglars break windows and steal things,' Miranda pointed out. 'The doors were locked, the windows were locked and nothing was stolen.'

'I'm writing all this down. Burglar. Ghost.' Abby quietly stared at the paper for a moment. 'Would you swear you didn't do it?'

'Of course,' said Miranda.

'And I'd swear I didn't do it. Hey, wait a second! Maybe it was Humphrey!' Abby jumped up and walked over to my cage. She bent down and checked the door. 'Nope. It couldn't be him because his door is locked.'

Thank goodness that old lock-that-doesn't-lock fools them every time!

'The only thing on the list that makes sense is a ghost,' she announced.

'But it doesn't make sense,' said Miranda.

'I know,' Abby agreed.

The girls actually agreed on something. This was progress! They'd gone from not liking each other to being REALLY-REALLY-REALLY mad, to talking things over.

After a while, the girls left the room to have supper. This time, they left together. When they came back much later, they were still together.

'Dad said it didn't make sense,' Miranda was saying.

'And Mum agreed,' Abby replied. 'What now?'

The girls flopped down on their respective beds. 'I know,' said Abby. 'Let's stay up all night.'

'Why?'

'To see if any ghosts show up.'

I felt a chill creep down my spine. I knew I was the one who moved their things around. And I knew I wasn't a ghost. But I still got a shiver thinking something SCARY-SCARY-SCARY just might show up.

'Lights out, ladies.' Mr Golden stood at the door later that night, smiling. 'Hope you have sweet dreams. You too, Humphrey.'

'Thanks!' I squeaked back.

'Everybody all tucked in?' Amy appeared at the door, holding baby Ben.

'Yes, Mum.' Abby snuggled down in her bed and pulled up the covers.

'Good night,' said Miranda, pulling up her blanket as well.

The lights went out and it was DARK-DARK-DARK in the room, except for the night-light in the wall, which gave off a pink glow.

The girls were quiet for a few minutes. Then

Abby whispered, 'Are you awake?'

'Yes,' Miranda whispered back.

'Know any scary stories?' asked Abby.

I certainly knew a few. Like about the time Clem the dog almost ate me. Or the time Aldo first came into the room at night and I thought he was a ghost.

Miranda thought for a minute and said, 'I remember one from camp.'

'Tell it,' said Abby. 'But not too loud.'

Miranda – sweet Golden Miranda – told a fur-raising tale about a hitchhiker who turned out to be a ghost. The way she told it was scarier than facing Clem!

'That was a good one,' said Abby. 'I know one too.'

Her story was even worse. It was about a group of kids who dared each other to go into a graveyard at night. One girl went in, saw a horrible face and died of fright. Recalling Og's gruesome grin, I felt faint after that story!

'Abby?' Miranda whispered. 'Maybe we shouldn't tell any more scary stories. I'm feeling kind of weird.'

'Me too,' said Abby. 'Let's be quiet.'

It was quiet all right. Maybe a little too quiet for a nocturnal fellow like me. Without thinking, I hopped on to my wheel for some exercise. I suppose that wheel needs oil, because it went *SCREEEECH*!

When the wheel screeched, both girls screamed, 'EEEEEE!' By the little pink light, I could see them leap from their beds and wrap their arms around each other.

The door abruptly swung open and the big light came on.

'EEEEEE!' the girls screamed again.

'It's just me,' said Mr Golden, rushing in. 'What's going on?'

He must have been as surprised as I was to see Miranda and Abby hugging one another for dear life.

'There was this terrible noise!' said Abby.

'Horrible,' said Miranda.

That was my cue to hop back on to the wheel. *SCREEEECH*!

All eyes were on me.

'You mean that noise?' said Miranda's dad, pointing at my cage.

'That's the one,' I squeaked.

Both girls started giggling.

'It was Humphrey,' said Miranda.

'I thought it was a ghost,' said Abby.

Mr Golden laughed too. 'I think that ghost is pretty harmless,' he said. 'Now, do you think you two – or you three – can get some sleep?'

They agreed and he tucked the girls into their beds.

'It's good to hear you two laughing, but no more screaming, OK?' he said as he turned out the light.

The girls were quiet for a while longer and I stayed away from the wheel. I heard Abby whisper,

'Miranda, could you sleep over here with me, just for tonight?'

'I was going to ask you the same thing,' said Miranda.

Miranda crawled into bed with Abby.

'Did you ever hear the story about the ghost in the attic?' Abby whispered.

'Tell it,' said Miranda.

And she did. I couldn't have slept that night, even if I wasn't nocturnal.

On Sunday morning, neither girl mentioned how the ring and the bracelet, the pen and the hair scrunchie all got moved. Neither girl mentioned an imaginary line either. They did their homework at the desk, braided each other's hair and made a maze for me to run.

And when they said goodbye on Monday morning, Miranda said, 'See you in two weeks.'

Abby said, 'Great!'

> All things are in common among friends.
>
> Diogenes, Greek philosopher

Ill Will

I returned to school with a great sense of accomplishment.

But once I remembered where Og had spent the last two days, it was hard to concentrate on geography or maths. I couldn't help imagining all the fun Og must have had with the Brisbanes. I glanced over at my neighbour in his glass tank. With that horrible grin on his face, he looked like a Hallowe'en lantern. (Scary.)

It was VERY-VERY-VERY cold outside, which meant that the heat inside was turned way, way up. Whew! That must be fine for a cold-blooded amphibian, but I was wishing I could take off my fur coat. Then the warm air woke up the crickets, who started singing. And there was a SQUEAK-SQUEAK-SQUEAK that was not coming from me, but from Seth as he wriggled in his chair. It sounded like 'Jingle Bells': Squeak-squeak-squeak . . . squeak-squeak-squeak . . . squeak-squeak-SQUEAK-squeak-squeak! The squeaking made Gail giggle noisily, which made Mrs Brisbane loudly shush her. I was looking forward to some peace and quiet during break (knowing Og wouldn't want to chat). But when the time came, Mrs Brisbane announced that the class would stay inside. She brought out all kinds of interesting things to play with. I must admit, I wished I could get out of my cage and play along with the rest of the class.

Art and Richie built a tall tower out of tiny bricks, while Kirk and Seth worked on a jigsaw puzzle. A.J. and Garth played a game where you slapped down cards. Heidi and Gail played another kind of game, moving little plastic men around a board. Mandy, Sayeh and Miranda came over to ask Tabitha to play with them. She didn't even look up. She just shook her head.

'I don't know why we even try to be friends with her,' Mandy whispered to the other girls.

Sayeh just sighed sadly. I knew how she felt.

'Og, can you hear me?' I squeaked. 'I have something to ask you.' I figured even though I couldn't understand him, maybe he could understand me.

'See how much fun it is to play with your friends?' I asked. It probably sounded like

'Squeak-squeak-squeak,' but he could at least have responded with a 'Boing!'

I decided to squeak up louder this time. I couldn't even hear myself because of all the yelling.

Yelling?

I looked around to see who was making all that noise. It wasn't Lower-Your-Voice-A.J. or Repeat-It-Please-Richie. It was Gail. She had stopped giggling and started shouting. The person she was shouting at was her best friend Heidi.

'You cheated! I saw you!' she yelled.

'I didn't,' Heidi said. 'I wouldn't cheat.'

'You must have. You always win. I'm never playing with you again, cheat,' Gail shouted.

Mrs Brisbane quickly moved towards them. 'Girls, please!'

'I didn't cheat,' insisted Heidi. 'I'm not a cheat.'

Gail put her fingers in her ears. 'Did too, cheat, cheat, cheat!'

Everyone else in the class stopped playing and stared at the two girls. Mrs Brisbane was right between them now. 'Girls, please calm down and be quiet.'

Heidi and Gail were quiet, but they glared at each other angrily.

'Tell me what happened, Gail. Calmly.'

Gail wiped away some tears. 'She was supposed to move her man five spaces and she moved it six spaces. That gave her a bonus jump and she won. She cheated!'

'Did not!' Heidi shouted. 'I only went five!'

The teacher held up both hands. 'Stop. I want you two to cool off before we talk about it. You're such good friends, let's work this out.'

'She's not my friend any more!' said Gail. She was crying harder.

'Thank goodness!' Heidi shot back. 'Because I can't stand you! Crybaby!'

'Cheat!'

Mrs Brisbane shook her head. 'Heidi, you go over there by Humphrey and Og,' she said firmly. 'Gail, you go and sit at my desk. Try and settle down.'

The girls did as they were told. I think they were glad to get away from each other. Soon, Heidi was leaning up against the table where Og and I have our homes.

'Crybaby,' she whispered so softly that only we could hear her.

It was hard for me to believe that Heidi would cheat her best friend. It was hard for me to believe that Gail would lie about Heidi. I thought friends always got along, no matter what.

'First, all she does is giggle. Now all she does is cry,' Heidi muttered.

At Mrs Brisbane's desk, Gail glared over at Heidi and wiped away a few more tears.

When break was almost over, Mrs Brisbane took the two girls out into the corridor to discuss the argument. They came back in and quietly returned to their seats. But as soon as Mrs Brisbane turned her back, I saw them stick their tongues out at each other. Maybe friendship wasn't all it was cracked up to be.

It was snowing by afternoon break, so Mrs Brisbane divided the class into four teams. Each team had questions to answer. They had to decide as a group what the answer should be. Mrs Brisbane kept score.

She wisely put Heidi and Gail on different teams so they wouldn't argue or make faces. Both their teams lost.

The winning team had Miranda, Kirk, Seth and Tabitha on it. And, to my surprise, the reason they won was Tabitha!

Mrs Brisbane asked each team questions about all kinds of things: flowers, books, poetry, sport, animals (but not hamsters, I'm sorry to say) and countries. Nobody knew much about flowers. Everybody knew a lot about animals. Sayeh was the best at answering questions about countries. (Would you believe, there's a country with a capital called Tegucigalpa? I had to write that one down.)

But Tabitha was the best at answering questions about sport. She knew soccer teams, volleyball rules and golf champions. The boys all seemed amazed. As the quiz went on, there seemed to be more and more questions about sport. Maybe that was an accident, but when Mrs Brisbane is involved, things don't usually happen by chance.

By the end of break, Tabitha's team had scored forty points. They would have scored even higher if Kirk hadn't said that the Gettysburg Address was the number on the Gettysburg family home. (Even I know it was a speech written by a very famous American president.) He got a laugh and lost two points, but it didn't matter. The next closest team only had twenty-eight points.

'We won!' yelled Seth, the team captain. 'Way to go!' He high-fived Tabitha, Miranda and Kirk.

'Three cheers for Tabitha!' said Miranda.

'Hip hip hooray! Hip hip hooray! Hip hip hooray!' I squeaked, jumping up and down for joy.

Nobody called her a baby. Even Tabitha looked happy.

Unfortunately, Heidi and Gail didn't seem cheered up at all. In fact, while all the attention was focused on Tabitha, I saw Gail mouth 'cheat' to Heidi.

Heidi stuck her tongue out at Gail.

It was enough to make a grown hamster cry. A less sensible hamster than me, of course.

'Og, you may not understand me, but if you could, you'd want Heidi and Gail to be friends again. Right?' I asked my neighbour once everyone had gone home for the day. I didn't expect him to understand me. I was just thinking out loud.

I was amazed to get an answer: 'BOING!'

Og jumped straight up and down, up and down, over and over again. I didn't know if he had sat on a needle or eaten something that didn't agree with him.

'Og! Are you all right?'

'BOING-BOING!' he said. 'BOING!'

I jumped up and looked over at him. I was pretty sure he was agreeing with me!

'So what are we going to do?' I asked him. 'How can we help them?'

As abruptly as he had begun, Og stopped bouncing and boinging and sat as still as a rock, as usual. I was discouraged, and puzzled too. Either he didn't have any ideas or he'd given up on trying to get me to understand him. I felt we both had failed.

Finally, I spoke again. 'They sure were good friends.'

Og stayed silent the rest of the night.

Hours later, when Aldo arrived, I was still trying to work out what google-eyes had been trying to tell me. This was a most peculiar frog.

'Good evening, gentlemen. Mind if I join the party?' said Aldo as he flicked on the lights and rolled his cleaning trolley into Room 26.

'Without you, there is no party,' I told him.

'Speaking of parties, Richie is having a big party for his birthday soon.' Repeat-It-Please-Richie Rinaldi happened to be Aldo's nephew. 'It's going to be a very big deal.'

Since I had never been to one, any birthday party sounded special to me.

'They're having entertainment, like a show or something. Hey, you guys want to see my latest trick?' asked Aldo, grabbing his broom.

The caretaker had already proved his talents to me by balancing his broom on the tip of one finger for a LONG-LONG-LONG time. Once, he balanced it on top of his head.

This time, he threw his head back and balanced the tip of the broom on his chin for an equally long period of time. When the broom finally wobbled too far, Aldo caught it and took a deep bow.

'Bravo, Aldo!' I squeaked as loudly as I could.

'Thank you, Humph.' He glanced at Og. 'What's the matter, Froggy? You don't like tricks?'

'It's not you,' I said softly. 'It's him.'

Aldo grabbed his bag and pulled a chair close to my cage. 'Aw, it's just a silly trick. I'm not good at anything useful.'

'Not true!' I argued.

Aldo took a sandwich out of his bag and began chewing on it.

'No, Humph, I've been thinking about it a lot. Because of this.' He pulled a piece of paper out of his pocket.

'This is the application for City College. If I want to go there, I have to fill it in. So I wrote my name, address, all that. When I got to the part that asked what I want to study, I got stuck,' he explained. 'I'm practically middle-aged and I still don't know what I want to be when I grow up.' Aldo put down his sandwich and stared at the application.

'I'm not sure what I'm good at. I thought of being a teacher, but I don't know. Would the kids like me? Am I clever enough to be a really good teacher?'

'Yes! Be a teacher! Please!' I insisted. For once, Aldo didn't seem to hear me.

'Besides, they want a letter of recommendation from somebody important. Somebody who believes I can succeed,' said Aldo.

'I'll do it!' I assured him, but he wasn't paying attention.

'I'm just not sure.' He tossed his bag back on to the trolley. 'Don't think I forgot you, pal,' he told me as he dropped a small piece of carrot into my cage.

'Thanks a heap!' I squeaked.

'You're welcome,' Aldo replied.

At least *he* understood most of what I said. One thing I understood: it was time for me to take action!

Never injure a friend, even in jest.

Cicero, Roman writer and orator

9 Mrs Brisbane Explains

After the caretaker left, I noticed something odd beside my cage. Aldo was usually good at picking up things that didn't belong in the classroom. However, this night he had left something behind: his City College application. I opened the good old lock-that-doesn't-lock and slipped out of my cage.

'Don't worry, Oggy old boy. I won't bother you if you won't bother me,' I assured him. Maybe I was reassuring myself he wouldn't leap at me again.

The application was a big piece of paper that folded up. Half of it was stuck under my cage, and it was hard to read what Aldo had written. If you're a small hamster, human handwriting looks HUGE-HUGE-HUGE. The only light I had to read by was from the streetlamp outside the window. I squinted my eyes and I could read: AREA

OF STUDY. On the line next to it, Aldo had written 'Teaching' and scratched it out.

On the line marked RECOMMENDATION, he hadn't written anything.

I was tempted to get out my little pencil and write a nice recommendation myself. But a big college probably wouldn't care about the opinion of a small hamster, even a classroom hamster who could read and write. No, Aldo needed help from someone a lot bigger and more important than me.

I knew who that person was. I just hoped she would help.

I pulled the application out farther and neatly left it right between my cage and Og's.

'No splashing over here, Og,' I warned my neighbour. 'We want to keep this application in good shape.'

He didn't splash all night long. Who knows, maybe Og understood me after all, even without ears.

I could hardly wait for Mrs Brisbane to arrive the following morning. When she finally turned up, it took her a long time to take off her coat and gloves and arrange her desk. At last, she strolled – slowly – over to my cage.

'Morning, Humphrey,' she said with a smile.

'You're lucky you don't have to go out in this freezing cold weather. You can stay right here in your cosy cage.'

Stay in my cage? If she only knew!

She turned to Og. 'Morning, Og. As you've heard in class, amphibians are cold-blooded, which means we've got to keep you warm.'

She smiled at Og and turned away.

'Wait! Stop!' I shouted, jumping up and down. 'Look at the paper!'

She turned back and laughed. 'What's the matter, Humphrey? Are you jealous of Og?' She leaned closer. 'You know you're my favourite hamster. And you mustn't let jealousy, that old green-eyed monster, get the better of you.'

Eeek – a monster? I was about to dive into my sleeping house for protection, but then I remembered that jealousy is when you envy somebody else. Jealousy wasn't a real monster, just a giant bad feeling. Was that why I felt bad when everybody else paid attention to Og? I wasn't sure. After all, my eyes are brown, not green. I was trying to sort it all out when Mrs Brisbane turned to walk away.

I'd forgotten something REALLY-REALLY-REALLY important!

'The application!' I shouted. I knew all she'd hear was squeaking, but I had to try.

Mrs Brisbane came back to the cage. 'For goodness' sake, calm down, Humphrey.'

I didn't calm down. I started squeaking and jumping, jumping and squeaking, because I couldn't think of anything else to do . . . except open the cage door and hand her the application.

I couldn't do that because she'd find out about the lock-that-doesn't-lock.

'What's this?' Mrs Brisbane picked up the application – phew! – and started to read! 'Aldo must have left this here by mistake. I'll put it in his letterbox.'

She folded it up without finishing it.

'Tell her, Og! Help me . . . help Aldo!' I was shrieking more than squeaking now, and to my amazement, Og let out a rather large 'BOING!' which I really appreciated.

'What's the matter with you two? It's an application. It's private.'

'BOING! BOING!'

'SQUEAK-SQUEAK-SQUEAK!'

Working together, we kept up the noise-making and Mrs Brisbane looked confused. She opened the application and started reading – thank goodness, because I was getting quite hoarse.

'Well, well. Aldo is applying to go back to college. That's a good idea. And he wants to study . . .' She stopped and stared a bit longer. 'He wrote in

"Teaching" but crossed it out again. I wonder why?'

'Ask him!' I shouted with the last bit of my voice.

'I'd better give Aldo a ring,' said Mrs Brisbane.

'Hi, Mrs Brisbane!' a loud voice yelled. It was Lower-Your-Voice-A.J.

Mrs Brisbane greeted him and folded up the application. She took it to her desk and didn't look at it again all day.

There was nothing to do now but keep my paws firmly crossed, which I did.

Some time in the afternoon, I must have dozed off, but I was awakened by a now familiar noise: 'Chirrup!' That was the sound of a cricket. This time, it was coming from the middle of the room.

'Mrs Brisbane?' a voice called out.

'Chirrup!'

Our teacher turned away from the board, where she was writing out a maths problem. 'Yes, Kirk?'

'I think a cricket has got loose.' Kirk pointed to the floor near his table.

'Well, pick it up, please,' Mrs Brisbane said.

'Chirrup! Chirrup!'

Kirk bent down and cupped his hands, touching the floor. 'I've got it!'

'Good. Now please put it back where it belongs.'

Kirk lifted his hands and sat upright in his chair.

'I don't know, Mrs Brisbane. I think it might get away.'

Everyone was watching as Kirk stood up and started walking towards the cabinet where the crickets were kept. As he passed by Heidi, he suddenly opened his hands up right over her head. 'Oops! Dropped it. Sorry, Heidi.'

Heidi leaped up and started jumping around the room, shaking her head and running her hands through her hair. 'Help! Get it off me. Get it off!' she screamed.

Everyone was laughing. Everyone except Mrs Brisbane.

'Kirk Chen, you find that cricket,' she said in a very stern tone of voice. 'Now!'

Kirk grinned. 'Aw, there was no cricket. I was making that noise.'

Heidi stopped jumping around and glared at him.

'Hear it? Chirrup. Chirrup.' Kirk really sounded like a cricket. 'Boy, that Heidi Hopper sure can hop!' he added.

Gail giggled until Heidi shot her a very angry look, then quickly covered her mouth to stop herself.

Mrs Brisbane slowly walked towards Kirk. 'You, my friend, are in trouble. Big trouble,' she said. 'You will stay in during break and we'll have a little talk.'

As Kirk returned to his seat, the room was very quiet. Except for a loud 'Chirrup!'

Without even turning to look at him, Mrs Brisbane said, 'I-Heard-That-Kirk Chen.'

*

I wouldn't have wanted to be Kirk when it was time for break. Once the other students had cleared out, Mrs Brisbane marched over to him. Boy, was he in trouble! So I was surprised at the first thing she said.

'I have a confession to make. I think you're a funny guy, Kirk. You make me laugh a lot. Some day, you might star in a funny movie, and I promise you, I'll be the first one in the queue to buy a ticket.'

Kirk looked as confused as I felt.

'But –' Uh-oh, here came the clincher. 'There's a time to be funny and a way to be funny that's appropriate. And there's a time to be funny and a way to be funny that is not. It's time for you to learn the difference.'

I waited for a 'Chirrup', or at least an argument, but Kirk remained silent.

'Why did you pretend to drop a cricket on Heidi's head?' Mrs Brisbane asked.

Kirk shrugged his shoulders. 'Because it was funny?'

'Do you think Heidi thought it was funny?'

Kirk shook his head.

'I think you did it to get attention. And if that's the case, it worked.' I'm not sure, but I think Mrs Brisbane smiled. 'Now, why do you like to get attention?'

Kirk shrugged again.

'So people will like you?' the teacher asked.

'Maybe.'

'Then I have good news for you. You don't have to play pranks any more. People already like you. You're one of the most popular students I have.'

I'm not sure, but I think Kirk smiled a little too.

'So the next time you think of doing something funny, I want you to think about two things. First: is it really funny? Or is it hurtful to someone? Second: are you just doing it to get attention? Can you work on that?'

'Yes, ma'am,' said Kirk.

'Because if you continue to act like you acted today, I'm afraid you're going to be doing a solo comedy act in the headmaster's office. And he may not think you're funny at all.'

I think Mr Morales has a good sense of humour. But I also think that Mrs Brisbane is good at working out what's going on in people's heads. I bet she studied psychology in college.

Kirk was quiet for the rest of the day. So were Og and the crickets.

After my classmates went home, Mrs Brisbane hung around longer than usual. I soon learned why. Aldo came to Room 26 to see her.

'Mrs Brisbane, thanks for your call,' he said.

'And I thank you for coming in early to talk,' she said.

They looked funny sitting in those little student chairs.

'I hope you'll forgive me for reading this application you left behind. It was none of my business,' she explained.

Maybe not, but I'd made sure it was her business, with a little help from Og.

'When I saw that you had written in "Teaching" and then crossed it out, I thought perhaps you'd like to talk.'

'Yes, I would,' said Aldo. He was strangely quiet, and I suppose he was nervous, because he kept tugging at his collar. 'I was thinking I'd like to be a teacher, but I'm kind of . . . afraid.'

Mrs Brisbane listened while Aldo explained his fears about not being clever enough or interesting enough to be a good teacher.

'Everybody feels that way,' she said with a warm smile. 'What makes you think you would like to teach?'

Was I surprised to hear Aldo talk about how much he liked books, science, history, maths, learning . . .

how much he liked children! (He didn't mention hamsters, but I knew how he felt about me.)

When he had finished, Mrs Brisbane laughed out loud. 'You'd better become a teacher or I'll be angry with you. You sound like a born teacher!'

'How can I know for sure?' Aldo asked.

'Would you like to try it out?' Mrs Brisbane asked.

'Try out . . . teaching?'

'Yes. We'll pick a day for you to come in and teach a subject to the class. You can choose any subject. See how it feels to be in front of a classroom. See how the students react to you.'

Aldo rose and began to pace up and down. 'That's a wonderful offer. I don't know. Sounds good. Maybe.'

'Please think about it, talk it over with your wife and let me know,' Mrs Brisbane suggested. 'But you'll have to do it soon. This application is due in a week.'

'I will, I will,' said Aldo. 'If I could be half the teacher you are, I'd be happy.'

Mrs Brisbane laughed. 'Thank you, Aldo. But even after all these years, I still have my bad days.'

Aldo shook her hand about ten times before leaving.

Mrs Brisbane gathered together her things, and when she was ready to leave for the day, she turned to Og and me. 'Hope you're satisfied, guys,' she said.

I don't know about Og, but believe me, I was HAPPY-HAPPY-HAPPY.

I wasn't surprised that Mrs Brisbane helped Aldo. It happened just the way I planned it. But the next day, I had a big surprise I never could have planned.

My classmates were all hurrying out of Room 26, heading for the canteen. Usually, Sit-Still-Seth would have raced out of the room. But on this day, he hung behind the others.

'Coming?' Kirk asked impatiently.

'Meet you there,' said Seth.

Seth was the only student left in the room except for Tabitha, who was trying to stuff Smiley into her pocket as Seth approached.

I couldn't imagine what he was doing. Tabitha had given the girls the cold shoulder when they tried to be friends. And Seth is a boy. Everybody knows boys and girls can't be friends. At least, that's what I heard Art and Richie say.

'How'd you know all that sport stuff the other day?' he asked her.

Tabitha shrugged her shoulders. 'I don't know. I just like sport. And I remember things I hear about sport.'

'Me too,' answered Seth. 'What sports do you like best?'

Tabitha thought about it. 'Basketball and baseball. Football. Tennis.'

'Me too,' Seth agreed.

Mrs Brisbane was in the doorway. 'Are you two coming?'

'Right away,' said Seth. But he turned back to Tabitha. 'Listen, I've got to ask. Why do you keep that stupid bear with you? Aren't you too old for that?' he asked.

Tabitha shrugged again.

'When I was little, back in first year, I had a truck I used to bring to school with me. I couldn't stand to be without it,' Seth told her.

'Do you still have it?' asked Tabitha.

'It's in my wardrobe. Sometimes I take it out, but I don't bring it to school any more.'

Mrs Brisbane waited at the door. Now she didn't seem to be in such a hurry to get to lunch.

'My mum gave me Smiley,' Tabitha explained. 'My real mum. I haven't seen her for four years.'

'Oh,' said Seth. 'I get it.'

'You two are going to miss lunch,' Mrs Brisbane reminded them.

'OK.' Seth rushed out of the door, but Tabitha stayed in her seat. Mrs Brisbane came towards her.

'Tabitha, I know you've been moved around a

lot. Your foster mother told me you've been with five families in four years. But she also told me that she wants you to stay with her for ever.'

Tabitha stroked Smiley's fur. 'They all say that. It just never works out.'

Mrs Brisbane sat in the chair next to Tabitha so they were eye to eye. 'I don't mind having Smiley in class. But I think you'd make more friends if you left him at home. He'd be waiting for you there. You can make new friends without giving up the old ones. Don't you know that little song?'

Now Mrs Brisbane has surprised me many times, but I almost fell off my ladder when she started to sing.

> Make new friends, but keep the old,
> One is silver and the other's gold.

What a beautiful song! And Mrs Brisbane had a nice voice too. We were all quiet afterwards until Tabitha asked, 'What's the good of making friends if you're not going to stay?'

'A person can have many friends in her life. Even if you move on, a friend can be for ever. At least in your memory.'

Oooh, I felt a little pang somewhere close to my heart. Ms Mac was the teacher who brought me to Room 26. Although she had to move on without me, she was a for ever friend who would always be in my memory. Ms Mac was pure gold.

'Listen to her! She's right!' I squeaked.

Mrs Brisbane smiled. 'Sounds like Humphrey wants to be your friend too. How would you like to take him home with you this weekend?'

'I'd have to ask my mum. My foster mum.'

'I'll ring her right now, while you get some lunch,' said the teacher.

I have to admit, Mrs Brisbane is the BEST-BEST-BEST teacher in the world and also a golden friend. Even if she did let Og into the classroom and made us study frogs.

> To like and dislike the same things, that is indeed true friendship.
>
> Sallust, Roman politician and historian

10 Test Distress

As Aldo swept the floor later that night, he talked and talked.

'Maria thinks I should take Mrs Brisbane up on her offer. I don't know, Humph. Can you imagine me as a teacher?'

'YES-YES-YES!' I squeaked.

'I mean, what could I teach those kids? What do I know?'

Aldo spent many an evening talking to me while we ate our suppers. Believe me, he knew a lot! But I'd never seen him act like this before. He muttered while he mopped the floor. He mumbled while he dusted. He argued with himself while he sat down to eat his sandwich.

'Science? Maths? History? Which would be best?' he asked.

'Anything except frogs,' I squeaked, and to my

surprise, Og responded with a 'Boing!'

'I bet they've learned a lot from you, Humphrey. You've probably taught these kids more than I ever could.'

I was too modest to answer 'Yes.'

Aldo dug down into his bag and pulled out a piece of broccoli. 'Here's something for you, buddy.' He held it up and examined it. 'Funny, it looks small to me, but to you, I bet it looks like a great big tree!'

What it looked like was delicious. 'Thanks,' I squeaked.

Aldo leaned in closer and stared at me. 'I guess everything looks different to you, pal.' He held up his finger. 'I just see a finger, but I'll bet you see every little line and swirl in the skin.'

I wasn't quite sure what Aldo was getting at, but I squeaked in support.

Aldo took a long sip of coffee from his thermos. 'Of course, no two people see things exactly the same, either. And the more you look, the more . . .'

He suddenly jumped up. 'This might be it, Humphrey. I mean, it's interesting, it's different. Like a microscope. Yeah!'

I had no idea what he was talking about, so I munched thoughtfully on the broccoli. (Why some humans don't like it is a mystery to me.)

Aldo wheeled out his cleaning trolley. 'You

always give me the best ideas, Humph! See you later!'

He disappeared, but then quickly popped his head back into the doorway.

'You too, Og. Don't want to leave out my fine froggy friend!'

So, Og was Aldo's friend . . . but still not mine.

I suppose the grumpy lump next door didn't know or care, because all I heard from him was splashing.

•ö•

Tabitha's foster mum said yes. I'd be spending the weekend at her house. But I figured I wouldn't get much attention from Tabitha since all she cared about was Smiley the bear.

There were SO many problems in Room 26. Garth and A.J. were still worried about Marty Bean. Heidi and Gail were still MAD-MAD-MAD. Miranda and Abby were friends now, but would they stay that way without me around to help? I spent so much time thinking about these problems, I forgot the other problems in Room 26.

Maths problems.

I had been dreaming (the sleeping kind and the day kind) during maths for most of the week. When Mrs Brisbane started revising for a big maths test coming up, I had no idea what she was talking about!

I wasn't alone. Mrs Brisbane gave the class a surprise quiz and guess what? Half of us failed!

'It's not fair!' Mandy complained, while everybody else moaned and groaned. Our teacher was not pleased.

'All right, class. The quiz won't count towards your marks. But the rest of the school year builds on these concepts. You've got to master these problems,' she explained. 'I've prepared a study guide for the test next week. I want you to complete this over the weekend.'

You should have heard the moans and groans then!

'I'm sorry, class. This is important to me and to you,' Mrs Brisbane insisted as she handed out the papers. 'Put your name on your guide and bring it back – completed – on Monday.'

'I flunked. How about you?' Seth whispered to Tabitha.

'Almost,' she whispered back.

'It's time for break,' Mrs Brisbane said. 'Put your study guides in your backpacks now so you won't forget them.'

Papers rustled as my classmates tucked away their study guides.

The second hand on the big clock circled around. TICK-TICK-TICK. Those study guides made me think up a Plan, but I wasn't sure I'd have the time to pull it off.

Once the bell rang, the students rushed to get their coats and raced out of the door. Mrs Brisbane gathered up some papers from her desk and hurried out of the door too. Sometimes she spent break in the staffroom. Luckily, this was one of those days.

There was no time to waste, so I flung open my cage door. 'Og, don't you tell a soul what I'm about to do!' I told my neighbour.

It's not easy to get from my cage to the classroom floor, but I'd mastered a technique. First, I slid down the smooth table leg. It wasn't difficult, but it was a bit too fast for comfort. The way back was more challenging. I couldn't slide back up the leg, so I'd grab on to the cord from the blinds and swing myself back up. It was a dangerous undertaking that was always scary. But I had to take the chance because I had important work to do.

Once I hit the ground, I scampered over to Seth's chair. His backpack was on the floor. Happily, he'd left his study guide sticking out of the pocket. I had to use my paws and teeth to pull it out and drag it over to Tabitha's table.

Getting the paper into the pocket of her backpack – which was my goal – was a challenge. Her backpack was hanging from her chair. The pocket I wanted was at least a foot off the ground – awfully high for a small hamster.

By chance, there was a long cord dangling down from the pocket zipper. Holding the paper firmly in my teeth, I grabbed on and tried to pull myself up with all my might.

'BOING!' Og was trying to tell me something, but what?

Just then, the bell rang. It seemed much louder than usual. So that's what he was trying to tell me! He was trying to warn me that I was in serious danger of being caught outside my cage. I was also in danger of being trampled on by large feet. At least they were large compared with me!

I dropped the study guide and scurried as fast as I could towards the table. With no time to waste, I grabbed the cord and began swinging back and forth, higher and higher.

'BOING-BOING!' croaked Og.

'I know, I know!' I squeaked back. My stomach did flipflops as I saw the edge of the table. I took a deep breath and leaped on to the tabletop.

Mrs Brisbane opened the door and I could hear the thunder of feet as my friends rushed to the cloakroom. I sprinted across the table. Please don't let them see me. PLEASE-PLEASE-PLEASE, I thought as I darted into my cage, pulled the door behind me and collapsed on to a pile of wood shavings.

I held my breath, waiting to hear if I'd been

caught in the act. I heard Mrs Brisbane's footsteps approach.

'Why is the cord swinging like that?' she wondered out loud. 'That's odd.'

Og began splashing like I'd never heard him splash before. 'BOING!' he croaked. 'BOING!'

'Calm down, Og,' said Mrs Brisbane. 'Are you hungry or something?' She told Art to feed him some of his beloved insects.

Og had made Mrs Brisbane switch her attention to him, so that she'd forget about the cord. For the first time, I was pretty sure that the frog was talking to me – even helping me. Maybe he was friendlier than I'd thought. He'd helped me get back safely, thank goodness, although my mission had failed.

Once my heartbeat had returned to normal, I squeaked a big 'Thanks' to Og and looked over at Tabitha's table. Seth's study guide was still lying on the floor near her backpack.

Mrs Brisbane talked about something called 'helping verbs' for the rest of the afternoon. When it was almost time for the bell to ring, Mrs Brisbane reminded the class about their maths study guides.

'Tabitha, I believe yours is on the floor. Put it in your backpack, please.'

'Yes!' I squeaked out loud. This was too good to be true! The bell rang. Seth grabbed his backpack and headed to the cloakroom.

Tabitha didn't bother to look at the paper. She just stuffed it into her backpack pocket. Hooray! She also put Smiley into her bag as the other students streamed out of the classroom.

Soon, Tabitha's mum – her foster mum – arrived to pick us up for the weekend.

When I glanced over at Og, he looked a little gloomy, despite that stupid grin plastered on his face. Maybe he wished he could go home with our classmates at the weekends too. Maybe Og was jealous of me. I had a bad feeling just thinking about that old green-eyed monster again.

Suddenly I felt SAD-SAD-SAD about leaving Og alone for the whole weekend.

> **A friend is what the heart needs all the time.**
>
> Henry Van Dyke, American clergyman, educator and writer

11
Study Buddies

Tabitha's mum looked like the usual kind of mum, even though Tabitha said she wasn't her real one. Tabitha called her Carol.

'I've been looking forward to this all day,' said Carol, with a smile that showed she meant it. I liked her enthusiasm. 'You'll have to show me how to take care of Humphrey. I've never had a hamster before.'

'It's a doddle!' I squeaked.

'I think Humphrey's trying to tell us something,' Carol said. Smart lady!

Once we were home, Carol put my cage on the table and made some hot chocolate. 'How was your day?' she asked.

Tabitha shrugged her shoulders. 'Just like any other day.'

If she only knew!

She opened her backpack and pulled out some papers. 'I've got maths homework.'

Carol examined the paper. 'Honey, this isn't yours. It belongs to somebody named Seth Stevenson.'

Tabitha grabbed the study guide. 'We must have switched.' She rummaged around in her backpack and pulled out another study guide. 'Hang on. This one's mine.' She showed Carol the study guide with her name on it.

'Is this important?' asked Carol.

'Very,' said Tabitha.

'VERY-VERY-VERY.' I couldn't help squeaking up.

'Seth will need this. We'd better try to ring him,' Carol said.

It looked as if things were working out according to my Plan, but you can never be sure with humans.

Seth and his mum arrived the next morning.

'Thank you for ringing,' said Mrs Stevenson. 'Seth was in a panic when he couldn't find his homework.'

'It took me a while to get your number. I finally called Mrs Brisbane,' Carol explained.

'I'm sorry we never met before. I didn't even know there was a new girl in the class,' Seth's mum said.

Seth and his mother – whose name is June, I found out – took off their coats, and Carol made hot chocolate again.

'I'm so happy to meet somebody from Tabitha's class,' said Carol.

'Did Tabitha get invited to Richie's birthday party?' June asked.

Carol shook her head.

'I'll ring his mum. She invited everyone in the class, but I'll bet she didn't know about Tabitha either. I'm sorry no one called to welcome you. We'd love to have you at the parent-teacher meetings.'

Carol poured out the steaming chocolate. 'I'd like that. I'm kind of new to the mother business.'

'Looks like you're off to a good start,' said June. The two mothers moved into the living room, while Seth and Tabitha sat by my cage. Smiley the bear lay on the table.

'Hey, Humphrey,' Seth greeted me.

I spun on my wheel to show him I was happy to see him.

'If Richie invites you to his party, will you go?' he asked Tabitha.

'I don't know,' she said. 'Maybe.'

Seth rubbed his nose. 'Well, if you do, could you leave Smiley at home?'

Tabitha looked surprised. 'Why?'

Seth sighed. 'Well, I know you're not weird, but

the other kids think you are because of the bear. If you'd leave him at home, they'd know you're – you know – normal, like them. Then they'd like you.'

Tabitha thought it over. 'Are you going to be there?'

'Sure. Richie says he's planned a cool surprise!'

Tabitha frowned. 'I don't like surprises.'

'This will be a good surprise. A great surprise,' said Seth.

Tabitha didn't answer right away. 'OK. If you'll be there, I'll come. And I'll leave Smiley at home.'

Seth looked relieved. 'Great.'

They watched me spin on my wheel and talked about the maths test. After a while, Tabitha said, 'The basketball game's on. Want to watch it?'

The two of them raced out of the room and I didn't see them again for the rest of the afternoon. June went home, but Seth stayed and she picked him up later. I didn't care because I wasn't worried any more.

Tabitha left Smiley on the table next to my cage. He seemed to be smiling even more than usual.

It looked as if a nice, shiny, silver friendship had begun.

I felt warm inside all weekend, especially when Seth rang Tabitha on Sunday night to ask her some questions about maths.

But it was COLD-COLD-COLD on Monday. Shivering, quivering cold.

It was even chillier if you were standing near Heidi and Gail. Even when she wasn't around Heidi, Gail hardly ever giggled any more.

Then came Tuesday, the day of the big maths test. It was probably the quietest day of the year, as my classmates were very serious about this test. Kirk groaned a few times during the test. Seth got up three times to sharpen his pencil. Everyone seemed glad when it was over. Especially me.

Aldo was unusually quiet that night too. Instead of talking to me while he ate, he spent a lot of time writing in a big notebook. Sometimes he'd stop to stare at me, then go back to writing.

It started to snow on Thursday. When the students got to class, they were all bundled up in heavy hats and scarves and they all had red noses. (A few of those noses were runny, I'm sorry to say.)

After class began, Mrs Brisbane rubbed her hands together as if they were still cold. 'I have finished marking your maths tests,' she announced. 'Every single mark went up. Most of them a lot. I know how hard you all worked and I'm proud of you. Now we can get back to preparing for the Poetry Festival.'

When she handed the tests back, there were sighs of relief this time and not one groan.

'Now I have a big surprise for you. Today we're going to have a guest teacher.'

'Is that like a supply teacher?' asked Heidi. Of course, Mrs Brisbane reminded her to raise her hand.

'No. He's coming in to teach one class. And many of you already know him. It's Aldo Amato.'

'You mean my uncle Aldo?' asked Richie.

'Yes, your uncle – Mr Amato,' said Mrs Brisbane.

And there he was at the door. Aldo had become Mr Amato. He wore a white shirt, a red waistcoat, dark trousers and a tartan tie. He looked almost as spiffy as Headmaster Morales, and his cleaning trolley was nowhere in sight.

'Come on in,' Mrs Brisbane said.

'Thank you, Mrs Misbane . . . Mrs Bisbrain . . . Mrs Brisbane,' Aldo stammered. It might have been cold outside, but Aldo was sweating. I was pretty nervous myself.

He turned to the students and said, 'Hello everybody. I spend a lot of time in this classroom when you're not here, so it's nice to see real people sitting in these chairs for once. A good-looking group, I must say.'

A few students chuckled, and Aldo relaxed a little.

'I was talking to my pal Humphrey the other night and I started thinking about what the world looks like from his point of view. I mean, here he is, a small animal in a room full of much larger animals. Namely – you!'

When everybody laughed, Aldo looked a lot more relaxed.

'Anyway, Humphrey gave me a great idea for something we can all try together today.'

Who, me? Gosh!

Aldo held up a pencil. 'Can anybody tell me what this is?'

'A pencil!' answered Heidi.

'Oops. Hands, please,' said Aldo.

Heidi's hand shot up.

'Yes, ma'am', said Aldo.

I was impressed. Mrs Brisbane never called anybody 'ma'am'.

'It's a pencil,' said Heidi.

'Really? What do you think?' Aldo pointed at Pay-Attention-Art, who was staring up at the ceiling.

'Who, me? What?'

Aldo walked towards Art, holding the pencil up. 'I ask you, sir, what does this look like?'

Mrs Brisbane never called anybody 'sir' either.

'A pencil?' answered Art.

Aldo stared at the pencil for a second. 'I think you're right. But what does it look like to Humphrey?' Aldo asked.

To tell you the truth, I thought it looked like a pencil, but that clearly wasn't the answer Aldo wanted.

He approached my cage and held the pencil up right in front of me, very close. 'What do you think Humphrey sees?'

The class was quiet for a few seconds before hands began going up. Even Heidi remembered to raise her hand.

Aldo picked Kirk this time.

'He probably sees a big strip of yellow,' he said.

'I think you're right. What do you think?' Aldo pointed to Sayeh.

'Maybe something grainy. Like a yellow tree trunk,' she answered.

'Yeah. If you look closely, you can see the texture.' Aldo turned to me. 'Right, Humph?'

'Whatever you say, Aldo,' I squeaked.

That sent Gail giggling until she caught Heidi's eye. Heidi made a face at her and Gail turned serious.

'So today we're going to look at the world from a Humphrey's-eye point of view. Ready to start?'

My classmates all smiled and nodded. Aldo opened a briefcase – I'd never seen that before – and took out an envelope full of tiny squares that were open in the middle, like picture frames.

'These little squares will help us look at things more closely.'

Aldo must have spent a lot of time cutting out those one-inch squares. He handed one to each student. Next, he took out all kinds of things from his briefcase and spread them on Mrs Brisbane's desk. Coloured leaves, pieces of lettuce, tomato and broccoli, lemon peel, onion skin, heavy paper, a purple feather, pieces of bread – many interesting and yummy things!

'I want you to draw what you see with your coloured pencils or crayons and answer a few questions,' said Aldo. 'OK, you can start exploring now.'

Soon my friends were wandering around the room, examining things through their square inch. They were so BUSY-BUSY-BUSY, no one seemed to notice that Mr Morales had slipped into the room. He and Mrs Brisbane both watched Aldo. They were nodding and smiling.

The kids were smiling too.

'Ooh, you should see this!' A.J. yelled as he viewed his glove through the square.

I was the only one who noticed that Sayeh went over to Tabitha and asked her if she could borrow Smiley and study his fur.

'He's not here,' Tabitha answered. 'He's at home.'

You could have knocked me over with a purple feather!

While my friends looked at the world from a different point of view, I looked at Og. How did he see the world? His goofy eyes pointed in two different directions. Perhaps I looked like two hamsters. Or a much bigger hamster than I am. Maybe that's why he leaped at me the first night. It would take more than looking through a little square for me to figure out Og.

After a while, Aldo asked the kids to return to their seats.

'What did you see?' he asked them.

They couldn't wait to share their discoveries. A.J. said his gloves had a million little squares where the lines of yarn crisscrossed. Art's green leaf had a lot of yellow in it and although it seemed smooth, when you saw it up close it was covered with wrinkles. Og's green skin had black dots in it. According to Mandy, my beautiful golden fur was actually brown and white as well as yellow!

'And what did you learn?' asked Aldo.

Gail raised her hand. 'That things look different when you look at them more closely.'

Aldo smiled broadly. 'Good! You learned to observe.' He wrote the word on the board. 'And observation is what scientists do. Sometimes they use microscopes or telescopes to get a closer look. The more you observe, the more you learn. Today, you took a first step towards being a scientist.'

Wow, I never knew I was in a classroom full of scientists!

The bell rang for break. As they hurried to get their coats, my classmates thanked Aldo one by one. Finally no one was left except Aldo, Mrs

Brisbane and Mr Morales the headmaster.

'Excellent job,' said Mrs Brisbane. 'I wish you'd come back and get them excited over maths.'

'Now are you going to send in that application?' asked the headmaster.

Aldo nodded. 'I'm going to do it.'

'I'd like to add something to that application. A letter of recommendation,' said Mrs Brisbane.

I thought Aldo would faint. 'Would you?'

'I'd be proud to write one too,' said Mr Morales.

'I can't thank you enough,' said Aldo.

'Do me one favour,' added the headmaster. 'When you graduate and are ready to start teaching, you come to Longfellow School first.'

Aldo shook his hand. 'I wouldn't go anywhere else,' he said.

Whew! That was a relief. I was SAD-SAD-SAD when Ms Mac left for Brazil. I'd be even sadder if Aldo left too.

Tell me your friends and
I'll tell you who you are.

Assyrian proverb

12
Party Hearty

That week, there was plenty of chatter about Richie's forthcoming birthday. All that excitement gave me a wiggle in my whiskers and a pounding in my heart. What was this big surprise Richie talked about all the time?

On Friday, Mrs Brisbane announced that Richie would be taking me home for the weekend.

'Yeah! Humphrey's coming to the party too,' A.J. yelled.

I'd never been to a party outside Room 26 before. Overjoyed, I jumped on my wheel and spun as fast as I could.

'BOING!' Og croaked.

Oops! I realized that Og had not been invited to the party.

'What about Og?' asked Richie. 'Can he come too?'

Mrs Brisbane shook her head. 'I think you have all you can handle. Besides, I'm taking Og home with me. My husband is working on a surprise for him.'

'Eeek!' I squeaked. It just slipped out. Mr Brisbane, whom I hadn't even seen since Christmas, was working on a surprise for the frog? I could feel that green-eyed monster inside me again. I was jealous of a large lump with a ghastly grin and I wasn't proud of myself.

Richie was hopping from one foot to another, like a frog, by the time his mum came to pick us up after school. 'We're going to party hearty, Humphrey!' he shouted.

'Try to relax, Richie,' Mrs Rinaldi told him as we got into the car. 'If we're going to have this party, you'll have to calm down.'

The Rinaldi house was in quite an uproar that night. First of all, there were so many aunts, uncles, grandmas and grandpas there, I wasn't sure which was which.

Everyone was hustling around, moving chairs and putting up decorations in the basement, or bustling around the kitchen, cooking. As busy as they were, they all managed to stop and say, 'Hi, Humphrey.' Or, 'Isn't he a cutie?'

Uncle Aldo and his wife Maria came round to help. When Aldo announced he was starting college again, his relatives slapped him on the back and said, 'Way to go!' They were as HAPPY-HAPPY-HAPPY about it as I was!

•o•

On Saturday morning, there was even more commotion as Richie's family hurried up and down the stairs, preparing for the party. Aldo and Maria came back to help. Early in the afternoon, Aldo put on a top hat and picked up my cage.

'OK, Humph. Time for us to party on!'

He carried my cage downstairs to the basement.

What sights I saw there! The ceiling was covered with balloons of every colour. Along the walls were brightly coloured booths made out of big cardboard boxes. A circle of chairs surrounded a large platform. Happy circus music was playing and I could smell popcorn and lemonade.

Aldo put my cage on a big table and said, 'Welcome to Richie Rinaldi's Crazy Carnival! Step right up, one and all!'

Soon my friends from Room 26 made their way down the stairs. Gail and Heidi (not together, of course), Kirk, Garth, Mandy, Sayeh, A.J. and Art, Miranda, Seth and Tabitha.

As soon as Sayeh saw Tabitha arrive, she hurried

over to greet her. 'Oh, I'm glad you came!' she said.

Then, down the stairs came Marty. Marty? I blinked hard and looked again. Sure enough, Martin Bean, the guy who's REALLY MEAN, was right there in Richie's basement!

'My mum made me invite him,' I heard Richie tell Garth. 'He's in my Sunday-school class.'

There's school on Sunday too? You learn something new every day.

The kids all put brightly wrapped presents on a table. Most of them said hello to me. Then Aldo said, 'Step right up and play the most amazing games on earth!'

Each of the booths along the wall featured a different activity. Richie's dad had a booth where the kids tossed rings at empty lemonade bottles. If three rings landed over the bottles, you got a pink ticket.

Cousin Mark's booth featured a game where you threw a small basketball through a hoop. You got a pink ticket for each basket made.

In Grandpa Rinaldi's booth, you had to knock little bowling pins down with a ball. If you knocked them all down, you got a pink ticket.

Closest to me was Maria's booth. She had a flowered scarf on her head and a big glass ball in front of her. 'Come and hear Madame Maria tell your fortune,' she called to the crowd.

Madame Maria told Mandy that, in the future, she would eat 'much popcorn'. (I think she already had.) Then Maria told Kirk that, in the future, he would have a lot of fun. Kirk always does!

There was so much noise in Richie's basement, I was tempted to go into my sleeping house for some peace and quiet. But I didn't want to miss any of the fun.

Then – uh-oh – I noticed someone not having fun. Heidi Hopper was on her way to the basketball booth when Big Mean Bean stood in front of her, blocking her way. She moved to the right to go around him. Marty moved to the right and blocked her.

'What's your hurry?' he asked in a nasty voice.

Heidi moved to the left to go around him. Marty moved to the left and blocked her.

'Say the magic word,' said Marty.

'Please,' Heidi said in a soft voice.

'Can't hear you!'

'Please!' Heidi spoke much louder now.

Marty sneered. 'That's not the magic word. Guess again.'

Once more, Heidi tried to go around him and he stopped her. She was almost in tears. This was unsqueakable behaviour!

'Let her go!' I yelled. Not that anyone could hear a small hamster over all the hubbub.

Suddenly Gail appeared out of nowhere. 'Stop it,

Marty!' she said, and she pushed him out of the way. She grabbed Heidi's hand and pulled her towards the fortune-telling booth. 'Come on, Heidi.'

Marty stood there with his mouth wide open. I could hardly believe what I'd seen myself. First of all, I thought Gail was angry at Heidi. Second of all, no younger kid had ever dared to push Marty before. Especially not a girl. Gail's a lot stronger than she looks.

'Yoohoo, ladies! Fortunes told! Let Madame Maria tell you what your future will bring!'

Heidi and Gail looked at one another.

'Step this way,' Maria called to them.

The two girls scurried over to her booth and sat down as Maria stared into the glass ball.

'You will be best friends for ever,' Maria predicted. Hooray! Heidi and Gail looked happy with their fortunes. As they walked away, I heard Gail say, 'I'm sorry I said you were a cheat. I was wrong.'

'I'm sorry I called you a crybaby,' said Heidi.

They didn't seem to know what else to say, until Mandy raced up and asked if they'd tried the ring-toss yet. The three of them hurried off to the booth. Those old, gold friends, Heidi and Gail, were back together at last.

Meanwhile, Marty seemed puzzled by the whole incident. He stood motionless, watching the other partygoers pairing off and having fun together. I guess Aldo was watching, because he marched over to him and said, 'If you need something to do, I could use some help giving out prizes.'

Marty didn't answer.

'Or would you rather be with your friends? You do have friends, don't you, Marty?'

Marty stood like a statue, staring at Aldo.

'You know, Marty, if you stopped pushing everybody around, people might start liking you. So why don't you come over and do something nice, like handing out prizes?'

Aldo didn't wait for an answer. He put his hand on Marty's shoulder and marched him to the prize booth.

Meanwhile, Richie and Seth cheered on Tabitha as she got three baskets in a row. Smiley the bear was nowhere in sight.

After Miranda and Sayeh had each earned a handful of pink tickets, they headed for the prize booth. But when they saw Marty there, they stopped in their tracks.

'I'm not going over there if he's there,' said Miranda. 'He'd probably steal my tickets.'

A.J. and Art were already at the prize booth, trying to choose from the assortment of little puzzles, paddles with balls attached and funny cardboard glasses with eyeballs painted on them. Aldo and Marty stood behind the prize table.

'Hurry up and take something,' Marty said in a gruff voice. He tried to stuff the glasses into A.J.'s hand. 'Move it along.'

Aldo nudged Marty. 'Give them a chance to decide what they want, Marty,' he suggested. 'How about a train whistle?' he asked, holding up a big wooden whistle in the shape of a train.

'Maybe,' said A.J.

'Paddleball is always good,' said Art. 'I'll take that.'

'Good choice,' Marty mumbled.

'I'll take the whistle,' A.J. decided. 'Thanks.'

'You're welcome.' It sounded strange to hear Mean Martin Bean say those words.

Kirk rushed to the prize booth with a handful of tickets.

'Well, if it isn't Kirk the Jer–' Marty stopped himself before he finished.

'Kirk the Basketball King!' said Aldo. 'Pick a prize.'

Kirk had enough tickets to get a flower with a bulb attached that could squirt water.

'Good choice,' said Marty. His voice sounded different. I suppose he wasn't used to saying nice things.

At last, Sayeh and Miranda, who had been watching Marty, finally came forward, clutching their prize tickets.

'Ladies, come and get your prizes,' said Aldo. 'Marty will help you. He likes to help. Right, Marty?'

'Here are some key chains,' Marty told the girls as they nervously stepped forward. 'Or maybe you'd like this noughts-and-crosses game.'

Miranda and Sayeh were obviously surprised that Marty was acting like a human being is supposed to act, but they handed over their tickets.

'Thanks, Marty,' said Miranda, taking the key chain.

Aldo grinned. So did Marty.

Everybody was having such a good time, I was tempted to open the lock-that-doesn't-lock and join the fun.

While I was thinking it over, Aldo blew a whistle and asked everybody to come to the 'centre ring' for the big show.

As I watched my classmates rush for their chairs, I realized that I had an excellent hamster's-eye view of the centre of the ring. There was no need to plan an escape after all.

Once everyone settled down, Aldo took centre stage and waved his top hat dramatically. 'Ladiezzzz and gentlemen, get ready to be dazzled by the one, the only, the Amazing Magic Mitch!'

Amazing Magic Mitch turned out to be a tall, skinny man also wearing a top hat. His long blond hair touched his shoulders. He had on an oversized black jacket with a red-and-white-striped T-shirt and wore huge red-rimmed glasses.

Aldo applauded and the rest of the audience joined in. Magic Mitch carried a table in one hand and a suitcase in the other. He put the suitcase on the table and pulled out a large black wand.

Now I understood. Amazing Magic Mitch was a magician! I'd heard about magic shows, but I'd never seen one before. My whiskers started to quiver as the act began.

He talked the whole time he performed his act. TALK-TALK-TALK! First, he started out with a card trick. He brought A.J. out of the audience and asked him to pick a card, memorize it and return it to the pack. The magician mixed up the cards and asked A.J. to pick another card. The card A.J. selected this time happened to be the EXACT card he had picked the first time!

'Think it's a trick pack?' asked the magician.

'Yes,' A.J. answered.

So Magic Mitch called Tabitha out of the audience. He asked her and A.J. to check the pack of cards to see that everything was normal. It was! Then Tabitha had to pick a card and memorize it. Mitch shuffled the cards all around again. When Tabitha picked another card from the pack – you won't believe it – it was the exact same card she had picked before!

Everybody applauded, except me. This fellow seemed a little too crafty for me. I decided to keep a close eye on him.

Magic Mitch asked if he could borrow a coin from somebody. Marty volunteered one he had in his pocket. Imagine, a grown-up taking a coin from a kid!

Mitch rolled the coin up into a handkerchief and it disappeared completely, right before our eyes. He shook out the handkerchief, but the coin was gone! Marty gasped. Somebody should have warned Magic Mitch not to make Mean Bean angry.

The magician leaned over and asked, 'What's that in your ear?' He reached out to touch Marty's ear and produced a coin: the same one Marty had given him!

Now, I ask you, how can a coin disappear into thin air and then turn up in somebody's ear? This guy was CHEATING-CHEATING-CHEATING!

Next, Magic Mitch had the nerve to ask if the birthday boy had had any paper money for his birthday. Richie came up and gave the magician a brand-new banknote. You won't believe what Magic Mitch did with that note. He folded it all up, took out a pair of scissors and cut it into small pieces! That's the rudest thing I've ever seen. Even Og wouldn't do something like that. Richie's eyes were practically popping out of his head as Magic Mitch took the pieces of the note, put them in his fist and waved a magic wand. Nothing happened.

'I forgot to say the magic words!' he exclaimed. 'Eeny, meeny, miny, moe, you will see the money grow!' This time, when he opened his hand, the banknote was back, all in one piece again.

Thank goodness, or I think Richie would have been pretty angry!

Magic Mitch asked Sayeh and Mandy to help him with a trick where he cut up a rope, did some hocus-pocus and returned it in one piece.

And Art helped him make a glass of water disappear under a handkerchief. I mean a whole glass of water!

I would not invite this man to my house for supper, I can tell you.

Everybody seemed to like the show, though. They gasped and clapped at everything he did.

Finally, he announced the Big Moment! 'Ladies and gentlemen, at this point in the show, I usually make a rabbit appear out of my hat. But today, my rabbit is on strike. So I'm going to borrow your class hamster for this amazing trick.'

It took me a few seconds to realize that the class hamster was – gulp – me! Richie came over to my cage and gently picked me up, cupping me in his hands.

'Don't be scared, Humphrey. It's only a trick,' he whispered.

I knew that, but I didn't want to be cut up in pieces or disappear into thin air. No wonder the rabbit went on strike.

'Since Humphrey is already here, I can't pull him out of my hat. So instead, I will make him disappear into my hat!'

Magic Mitch first held his hat upside down and let anyone who wanted to come up and inspect it. Everybody agreed it appeared to be an ordinary hat.

Mitch took me from Richie and put me in the hat. It was DARK-DARK-DARK inside and I have to admit, I don't like dark places.

As he dropped me down, he pulled something with his finger and I fell into a secret compartment at the top of the hat. A false bottom came down over my head. I was trapped in a dark, scary place.

I could hear Magic Mitch's muffled voice saying, 'Abracadabra, Humphrey dear. I will make you disappear!'

Whoa! The magician turned the hat all the way over. Now I was lying on my back, feeling a little seasick.

'Humphrey! Where are you?' Magic Mitch called out.

He shook the hat to show that it was empty. Except it wasn't.

'Oooh,' I squeaked weakly as I bounced up and down, trapped in this stuffy cave.

I guess nobody heard me, not even Magic Mitch.

I could hear the sounds of kids gasping and shuffling around in their seats.

'Where's Humphrey?' I heard A.J. ask.

'Beats me,' said Magic Mitch. He turned the hat around and put it on his head. 'Want to see another trick?'

'Bring back Humphrey!' Richie said, in a voice as loud as A.J.'s.

'Humphrey who?' asked the magician. He started to do another trick. I couldn't see what he was doing, since I was completely in the dark.

Well, if Magic Mitch wasn't going to do anything about getting me out of that hat, I was going to do something for myself.

When I squinted my eyes, I could see a pinpoint of light above me. If I could see light, there must be an opening there. I crouched in the little space and reached up with my paws. I pushed. And I scratched. And I pushed some more. I may be small, but I'm strong for a hamster.

I could hear Magic Mitch repeating, 'Now you see it, now you don't. Which shell has the pea under it?'

'Bring back Humphrey!' more voices shouted, but Mitch ignored them.

Now I could see a lot more light. The top of the hat was opening from all my pushing. There was a space barely big enough for me to squeeze through. I pushed myself up with all my might and popped right out of the top of the hat! I could see my friends from Room 26, Richie's relatives, and also Marty Bean all staring up at me!

Magic Mitch kept going even though nobody paid any attention to him.

There was giggling, pointing, nudging and nodding. The giggling turned to chuckling, chortling, laughing and howling!

'Now you see it . . . now you don't.' Mitch sounded confused. 'Everyone? Are you paying attention?'

I could hear my name being whispered around.

I stood up very tall as everyone stared at me. 'Greetings, one and all!' I squeaked as loudly as I could.

This produced shrieks of laughter. I took a bow.

The audience began to shout my name. They stamped their feet and clapped their hands as they chanted, 'Hum-phrey! Hum-phrey! Hum-phrey!'

'OK.' The magician sounded quite annoyed. 'I'll bring him back!'

He took his hat off and there I was, eyeball to eyeball with Magic Mitch. He looked very pale. 'What are you doing? You've ruined my whole show!'

‘It’s my show now,’ I squeaked to him.

‘Next time, I’m bringing the rabbit,’ he said glumly.

Nobody else heard him because all my friends continued to clap, stamp and cheer.

Aldo quickly entered the ring and said, ‘Let’s have a big round of applause for the Amazing Magic Mitch!’

Mitch waved his magic hat – which now had a hole in the top – and hurried away from Richie’s basement as fast as he could.

The crowd kept applauding and cheering. I knew they were cheering for me.

A friend is a present you give yourself.

Robert Louis Stevenson, Scottish novelist and poet

13

Show Business, Snow Business

My classmates were still talking about the party on Monday. Even Mrs Brisbane chuckled when Richie told the whole story of my triumphant re-appearance.

But there was something else to talk about: Og's surprise.

Bert Brisbane had built Og a genuine swimming pool! Instead of a large bowl of water, a whole section of the glass box was now water, while the rest of it was built up all around with lush green plants.

It was a terrific surprise and I felt just a tiny pang of green-eyed jealousy. Then I noticed that Og's grin looked more like a real smile this time. I guess we'd both had good weekends after all.

After everyone had admired the swimming pool, Mrs Brisbane got down to business. 'The Poetry Festival is less than two weeks away. We've got to finalize our selections, memorize the poems, finish the artwork and make our Valentine's Day letterboxes.'

From that moment on, there was a mad flurry of activity. Some students retreated to the cloakroom to memorize their poems. Others drew pictures for the notice board while another group made Valentine letterboxes using glue, glitter, paint, crayons, buttons, lace and stickers.

Don't worry – Mrs Brisbane didn't forget to teach us maths, science, geography, social studies and spelling. (Believe me, she'd never do that.) But in between, my classmates worked like crazy on poetry and Valentines. Our classroom assistants, Mrs Hopper and Mrs Patel, came in to help for two days.

At night, it was just Og and me in Room 26. I wondered what he had done at the Brisbanes' house over the weekend as I watched him swimming and diving in his new pool. He could make a lot more noise splashing around in it. Each night, I got a little more annoyed, until one night I realized why. Here we were, side by side, but I still felt lonely. We had communicated a little and he'd helped me once, but I still wasn't sure if we were friends.

It was time to find out. I opened the lock-that-doesn't-lock. Gathering up my courage, I walked over to his glass house and said, 'Hello, Og.'

Abruptly, Og turned towards me. I must admit, my hamster heart skipped a beat. Was he going to leap at me again?

'Look, maybe I haven't been much of a pal to you, Og. Maybe I was even a little jealous. But I'd like to try again.'

This time, instead of leaping, he dived into the water with a gigantic SPLASH! The water splashed up to the top of the box, through the screen, on to my nice dry fur! And if there's one thing hamsters hate, it's wet fur. My usually fluffy golden coat was drippy, droopy and dull. If Og was looking for attention, he was about to get it.

'Thanks for nothing, Og,' I squeaked. 'I just want you to know that I have a million friends, so I don't really care if you're my friend or not. So if you're thinking you should be my pal, just forget it!'

Og just stared at me with that same old smile.

'And remember that time you leaped at me?' I continued. 'You didn't even scare me.'

Not wanting to press my luck, I scampered back into my cage. I'd finally told him off, but I didn't feel better. Not one bit.

Thursday was the gloomiest day I'd ever seen outside. But inside Room 26, the students were far from gloomy. Heidi and Gail were best friends again. Tabitha was friendly with Seth, Sayeh, Miranda – everybody! The poems were coming along as well.

No one, except me, seemed to notice that it was GREY-GREY-GREY outside. In the afternoon, it began to snow. I hopped on to my wheel and watched giant circles of lace float to the ground.

That sounded so good, I wrote it in my notebook: 'Giant circles of lace.' Those words might turn into a poem some day.

The snow continued falling after school came out. It was pretty with all those lacy circles tumbling down from the sky. After a while, the lacy circles turned into a thick blanket of white.

It was so quiet, you could have heard a frog burp. Not that Og ever did. He was as silent as the snowflakes.

I knew something was terribly wrong when Aldo didn't turn up to clean that night. There were no cars in the car park and just one car parked on the street. It looked more like a giant snowball than a car.

I counted the hours until morning would arrive. The snow continued falling until it reached the top of the wheels on the parked car. The carpet of snow was beautiful, but the silence made my fur stand up on end. I missed A.J.'s loud voice, Mandy's complaints and Gail's giggles.

When the bell rang for the start of school on Friday, a funny thing happened: nobody turned up. Not Mrs Brisbane, not Garth, not Miranda, nobody. There were no cars in the car park, no buses pulling in.

The snow showed no sign of stopping. I was snowed in with Og the Frog!

> A life without a friend is a life without sun.
>
> French proverb

Oh No, More Snow!

It was eerie to hear the bell ring for morning break, lunch and afternoon break when there was no one at school except Og and me.

Staring out at all that snow gave me a chill. The temperature was dropping inside as well. What was it that Aldo had said about turning down the heat at night to save money? I felt even chillier as I realized there was no one around to turn the heat up again.

Luckily, I had my fur coat, my sleeping house and a nice pile of wood shavings I could crawl into to keep warm. I wondered how Og was doing with nothing more than four glass walls, some greenery and an unheated swimming pool.

I dozed for much of the day and nibbled on the stash of food I keep hidden in my sleeping nest. We hamsters are clever about saving up food in case of emergency. But my food dish was empty and my water was getting low.

Between naps, I gazed out of the window. There were still no cars on the street. In fact, I couldn't tell where the street ended and the pavement began. Everything was a solid sheet of white.

Og was quiet most of the time and the crickets were silent too. I was BORED-BORED-BORED all alone in the classroom. I even missed maths class! Finally, I hopped on to my wheel for some lively exercise. That warmed me up, but it also made me hungry. When I checked my stash of food, the only thing left was a limp tomato stalk!

The bell signalling the end of school finally rang. I wondered what my classmates were doing. A.J. was probably watching TV with his family. Garth and Andy would be playing video games. I figured Miranda was cuddling up with Clem. (Didn't his bad breath bother her?) Sayeh was no doubt helping her mum care for her younger brother. And Mrs Brisbane was probably bustling around her warm, toasty kitchen while Mr Brisbane built a birdbox.

They were all warm, all cosy and all well-fed! They were definitely not worrying about me. Or Og.

I wasn't helping myself by thinking of these things. I decided to work on my poem. What rhymes with 'gloom'? Doom!

I slipped my notebook and pencil out of their hiding place behind my mirror and burrowed down into my pile of wood shavings to keep warm.

I promptly fell asleep. It was night-time when I woke up.

'Hey, Og, do you think Aldo will come tonight?' I asked my neighbour.

Og didn't answer. Aldo didn't come. The snow kept falling.

Around midnight, I heard a funny whirring sound and looked out of the window. A huge machine, much bigger than a car, crept down the street like a giant yellow snail with an orange light spinning around on top. It rolled along slowly, then disappeared.

Three hours later, it returned from the opposite direction and disappeared again.

'Did you see that, Og?' I squeaked loudly.

He was definitely ignoring me, and I didn't blame him. I'd said terrible things to him, things he probably understood. Guilt made me feel even colder.

'Og, I didn't mean it when I said I didn't care if you were my friend,' I called out from my cage. 'I'll forgive you for splashing me if you'll forgive me for saying those things. OK?'

'Boing?' I think he meant 'OK,' but there was something odd about the way Og sounded. Maybe he was hungry, like me. Then I recalled that he didn't need to eat as often as I do. Frogs have all the luck.

The next morning, the snow stopped falling. But the ground was covered and there were still no cars or people to be seen, except for that parked snowball – I mean car.

Even if it hadn't snowed, nobody would have come to school, because it was Saturday. One week ago today, I was starring in Magic Mitch's show. Now I was alone (almost), COLD-COLD-COLD, hungry and forgotten.

All my life, some human had brought me food and water and cleaned my cage. I'd been well cared for. I'd never had to fend for myself. But I was a clever and capable hamster. It was time for me to take care of myself like my wild hamster ancestors, the ones who lived in the forests with piles of leaves and pine cones. And all the fruits and nuts they could collect.

Hunger must have clouded my brain because it hadn't occurred to me until that moment that all my hamster food was right there on the table. Yummy things like hay, mealworms, grains and vitamin drops. All I had to do was help myself!

I opened the lock-that-doesn't-lock and stumbled out of my cage.

'Og, are you OK?' I called out.

'Boing,' he replied weakly. It had been a while since he'd eaten too. And I remembered Mrs Brisbane talking about how important it was for frogs to have fresh water.

'I'm going to get some food,' I explained. 'Maybe I can find some mealworms for you. I don't think I can get into the cricket cabinet.' Lucky for the crickets.

'Boing.' Og sounded even weaker this time. And he didn't look as green as usual. For a frog, that's not good.

I rushed across the top of the table, slightly faint from hunger. And there they were: a great big bag of Nutri-Nibbles, a taller bag of Hamster Hay and a giant jar of Mighty Mealworms. Yum! Of course, getting from the table to the top of those containers was a big problem for a small hamster. If I climbed up the bag of Nutri-Nibbles, for example, I would be in serious danger of falling into the bag and getting trapped there. Even though I love Nutri-Nibbles, I didn't want to spend my last minutes on earth being crushed by them.

No, the only sensible approach was brute force. I decided to take a run at the bag and knock it over. The treats would tumble out and I could eat to my heart's content.

I took a deep breath and ran at the bag, yelling 'Charge!'

It didn't quite work out according to my plan. I hit the bag with all my might and it tipped a little. Unfortunately, then the bag tipped back the other way and crashed down on top of me!

I wasn't crushed, but I was trapped underneath the bag of treats. There was a little air space around me and I could see a glimmer of light. I could breathe too. I just couldn't get out.

What I could do was yell. 'Help! I'm trapped!' I squeaked, although the bag muffled the sound.

I'm not sure why I was yelling. 'Help me, please!' probably sounded like 'SQUEAK-SQUEAK-SQUEAK!'

I squeaked anyway, and waited.

What was that I heard? 'Boing, boing, boing! BOING, BOING, BOING!! *BOING, BOING, BOING*!!!' Followed by a large crash!

I couldn't imagine how Og thought that all that noise would help me. Then I heard a new sound: bop-bop-bop. Soon, Og was grinning at me through the slit of light.

That crazy old lump of a frog had managed to hop all the way out of his house, and he'd come to save me! He started leaping at the bag, each time hitting it harder and harder. The bag shifted and the space around me started to open up as I crawled towards him.

Og kept bashing the bag, screaming, 'Screee!

Screee!' This was a whole new Og and a whole new sound.

The space got bigger and bigger and I crawled along until I could reach out and grab Og. Although I was weak from hunger and all that effort, I managed to grab on to Og's back just as the bag shifted again, flattening out. I was GLAD-GLAD-GLAD I wasn't underneath it any more.

'Screee!' Og repeated. I pulled myself up on to Og's back and he hopped away from the bag.

What a thrill! I was rocking and rolling on his back, like a cowboy riding a bucking bronco! 'Yee-haw!' I yelled. 'Go, Og! Go, Frog!'

'Screee!' he yelled.

All of a sudden, the lights came on and I heard footsteps.

'Oh no! Look at that, they're out of their cages.' It was Mrs Brisbane. 'They knocked the food over. They must be starving, poor things!'

'Smart little critters,' said Mr Morales, chuckling. '*Muy inteligente.*'

I hardly recognized those two, bundled up in heavy coats and woolly hats with huge scarves almost covering their faces.

'How on earth did they get out?' Mrs Brisbane wondered.

'Maybe somebody didn't lock Humphrey's cage tightly,' said the headmaster. 'And I suppose the frog hopped out of his tank. Look, he pushed the lid off.'

So I have a lock-that-doesn't-lock and Og has a top-that-he-can-pop!

'Never fear, Aldo's here!' another voice yelled out.

A bundled-up Aldo hurried into the room. 'Are they OK? The snowplough didn't clean our street until half an hour ago. I was going to walk over here, but the radio said it was too dangerous to go out.'

'I know,' said Mrs Brisbane. 'Bert and I have been worried sick. If I'd known the storm was coming, I would have taken them home with me. And everybody's rung me. All the parents, Angie Loomis – everybody.'

Mrs Brisbane put me back into my cage and gave me a handful of Nutri-Nibbles. Mr Morales put Og back into his box and fed him some icky crickets (gag!). Aldo went to get us both fresh water.

'It's too cold in here for Og,' Mr Morales said. 'He pulled through all right, but I'm going to buy him a heater.'

More footsteps clomped across the floor. 'We came as soon as we got shovelled out!' said Miranda as she, Amy and Abby arrived.

'The girls have been worried all day,' said Amy.

We hadn't been forgotten after all. Heidi's mum, Garth's dad and Sayeh and her dad turned up too, every one of them worried about Og and me.

I wanted to thank them, but it's not polite to talk with your mouth full.

They all asked to take us home for the rest of the weekend, but Mrs Brisbane was quite firm. 'I'm going to be selfish this time. I'm taking them home with me. My husband would never forgive me if I didn't.'

Mr Morales told everyone to be VERY-VERY-VERY careful on the drive back home. He and Aldo helped Mrs Brisbane prepare our houses for the trip.

Finally, my tummy felt full. 'Og?' I squeaked. 'Thank you, my friend! Does this mean you forgive me?'

'Boing!' he answered. Which was an extremely nice thing for a frog to say.

> Real friendship is shown in times of trouble; prosperity is full of friends.
>
> Ralph Waldo Emerson, American poet and essayist

15 Poetry Festivity

Bert Brisbane was waiting at the door for us. 'Hurry on in. It's freezing!' he said.

Mr Morales helped Mrs Brisbane carry in our houses and all the bags of food and bedding. 'Who knows how long they'll have to stay?' he said.

Mrs Brisbane went to make a pot of tea, and soon Mr Brisbane was cleaning Og's tank. Mr Morales may be the Most Important Person at Longfellow School, but the headmaster rolled up his sleeves and cleaned out my cage. He didn't even complain about what was in my potty corner. (He did wear gloves and washed his hands afterwards.)

'This is a good lesson for all of us,' said Mrs Brisbane as she brought in a tray of steaming cups of tea, a plate of biscuits and some yummy pieces of broccoli and lettuce for me. 'If you decide to have a pet, you have to take total responsibility.'

Mr Morales munched on a biscuit. 'I think they took responsibility for themselves. How on earth did such small creatures knock down that big bag?'

'I was wondering about that too,' said Mrs Brisbane. 'I think it was teamwork.'

'A frog and a hamster? Never heard of such a thing,' said Bert. 'I really wish I'd seen those two.' He smiled and shook his head. 'I always knew that Humphrey was sharp as a needle, but now we know there's a lot going on in Og's head too.'

'Boing!' Og croaked, and he lunged at the side of his glass box.

Mrs Brisbane chuckled. 'He's feeling better. Looks like he wants to play a game of leapfrog.'

Leapfrog is a *game*? Had I been wrong about Og since that very first night? Instead of trying to scare me, he wanted to play?

Like Mr Brisbane, I wasn't sure what went on in Og's head, but he had some good ideas, like rescuing me. He even had another sound he could make. Nobody knew it but me, and that made me feel kind of special. Like a friend.

The sun came out that afternoon and so did the snowploughs. While the gardens were still covered with snow, the streets were clear and cars travelled freely again.

Across the street from the Brisbanes, two children built a snowman. Inside the Brisbane house, I was more than happy to run mazes and play hide-and-squeak with Bert for old time's sake. Og watched from his glass house, but said very little.

By Monday, the roads had improved enough for everyone to go back to school. Thank goodness, because the Poetry Festival was coming up on Friday and there was still a lot of work to do.

Some of the students had worked on memorizing their poems or writing them out at home over the long weekend. Most had not.

Garth Tugwell had changed poems three times. On Monday, he changed again. Mrs Brisbane sent him to the cloakroom to memorize his new selection.

Mrs Brisbane surprised Kirk by asking for his help. 'You've been a lot better lately about knowing when to be funny and when to be quiet,' she said. 'Now I need your help. We don't want this Poetry Festival to be too serious. We want it to be fun. Would you introduce the poems for us?'

Kirk's whole face lit up. 'Sure!'

'Be sure to make it funny,' she told him.

By the end of the day on Tuesday, the notice board was covered with illustrated poems the students had copied out. Along the edge of the board were cut-out pictures of famous poets, from Longfellow to a man named Shakespeare and a lady named Emily Dickinson.

Late in the day on Wednesday, my classmates finished their Valentine letterboxes. What they did with ordinary cardboard boxes was excellent! Some of them were covered with red hearts, glitter and pieces of lace. Others were covered with buttons and lots of paint. Garth's had a big dinosaur on the side. Miranda's letterbox had cut-out pictures of her family pasted on: her mum, dad, Abby, Amy, baby Ben and (yes) Clem. Tabitha's letterbox had pictures of basketballs, footballs and soccer balls glued across the outside.

Then – SURPRISE – Mandy presented Og with a green box with pictures of frogs and insects all over it. And A.J. gave me a box covered in golden, furry-looking material. (It wasn't real fur. I checked.)

As nice as that was, I felt SAD-SAD-SAD because no matter how many Valentines I received, there was no way I could make Valentines for everyone in the class. How could I let them know how much I valued their friendship?

I was still feeling low when Aldo arrived on Wednesday night. He was in an unusually good mood.

'It's a beautiful evening, gentlemen. And I have

good news to share with you!' he announced as he wheeled in his trolley.

'I could use some good news, Aldo!' I squeaked back.

'Boing!' added Og.

Aldo pulled up a chair next to my cage. Instead of taking out his sandwich (or a treat for me), he pulled out a piece of paper.

'Behold my first mark from college. A test in psychology.' (I wondered if he was in the same class as Natalie the babysitter.)

'My mark, as you can plainly see . . .' Aldo held the paper up to my cage. 'Is an A! Can you believe it, my friends?'

'Three cheers for Aldo!' I squeaked as I hopped on to my wheel for a joyful spin.

'I haven't shown this to Maria yet. I'm saving it for her Valentine's present. Along with some flowers and sweets, of course. I think this mark will be her favourite gift.' Aldo leaned back and smiled with satisfaction.

Og dived into his pool with a huge splash. I think a little water got on Aldo, but he didn't seem to mind.

'Splash away, Og my friend,' Aldo said. 'It makes a happy sound.'

Og splashed because he was happy? All I'd thought about the splashing was that it was irritating!

Aldo was grinning from ear to ear, almost like a frog. 'You see before you a happy man. There's nothing better in the world than to have someone to share good news – and even bad news – with. You see, Maria is my wife, but she's also my best friend.'

I stopped spinning because I felt a little dizzy. I'd learned a bit about friendship this year by watching my classmates in Room 26. There were friends who got really angry but made up afterwards. There were friends who stuck together through thick and thin. There were friends who reached out to you even when you didn't think you needed a friend.

There were friends who would actually rescue you when you were in trouble. There were new friends, old friends, silver and gold friends.

Later that night, I was SORRY-SORRY-SORRY I'd ever doubted Og was my friend. I hadn't understood that sometimes a frog feels jealous and sometimes he feels splash-happy. But he had come through for me when I needed help. So how do you say thank you to a frog?

I decided to write a poem. Not just a 'roses are red, frogs are green' poem, but a poem that said what I really felt.

I pulled out my notebook and started to write.

The next day was spent rehearsing for the Poetry Festival and straightening up the room. (Boy, those kids' tables can get pretty messy.) I didn't pay much attention. I was hunkered down in my sleeping house, writing my hamster heart out.

Friday was Valentine's Day and everyone was excited. In the morning, the students 'posted' their Valentine cards in a big box on Mrs Brisbane's desk. During break, the teacher sorted out the cards and delivered them, humming happily as she dropped them into the boxes.

After break, the students opened their cards. There was a lot of giggling and even some crunching, since Mrs Brisbane had also dropped sugar hearts into all the letterboxes.

Out of the blue, A.J. shouted, 'Hey, hold on!' That got everyone's attention. 'I got a card from Martin Bean!'

Seth groaned loudly.

'No, listen. He says he's sorry,' A.J. explained.

'I got one too!' said Garth.

Miranda and Heidi had also got 'I'm sorry' cards from Marty.

'But he's so mean,' Mandy blurted.

'People can change,' said Mrs Brisbane. 'I think it must have been quite difficult for Martin to write those cards, and he gave them to me to deliver. Maybe it's time to give him a second chance.'

Whew, giving Mean Bean a second chance wouldn't be easy. Yet I recalled that once he got started, he was actually pretty nice when he handed out prizes at the birthday party. Maybe Aldo's talk with him had done some good. No wonder he got that A in psychology.

'I'll give him a second chance!' I exclaimed. Of course, it came out 'Squeak-squeak-squeak.'

'I haven't forgotten you, Humphrey,' said Mrs Brisbane. She came over to help Og and me with our letterboxes. We received cards from all the students in class. Each one was special, but the one I remember the most was from Miranda.

> Though 'hamster' doesn't have a rhyme,
> I love you, Humphrey, all the time.

She'd worked out how to write a poem with the word 'hamster' in it after all!

I had one more card in my letterbox than Og. It was from Brazil! Yes, Ms Mac had remembered me with a teeny little card that said, 'Humphrey, you will always be a special friend. Love, Ms Mac.'

She'd sent a letter to the whole class as well, with greetings from her pupils in Brazil.

Wonderful as it was to receive those cards, I kept one eye on the clock all morning, because I had a special mission to accomplish during lunch.

A hamster's work is never done.

The bell finally rang and the students left, which was good. But Mrs Brisbane stayed behind, which was bad. She busily rearranged all the chairs into a big half-circle. She picked scraps of paper off the floor and straightened a few tables. Wasn't this woman going to eat?

At last, she glanced up at the clock, picked up her lunch bag and hurried out of the room. I didn't have much time, so I tore a page out of my notebook, jiggled the lock-that-doesn't-lock, flung open the door and slid down the leg of the table.

Og started boinging in alarm, but I didn't have time to explain.

I raced across the floor as fast as my legs would carry me, straight to Mrs Brisbane's desk. When I got there, I gasped with surprise. My plan was to climb up her chair and take a giant leap on to the desk. It was dangerous and risky, but sometimes you have to be bold! However, the teacher had ruined everything by moving her chair FAR-FAR-FAR away from her desk, into the circle of other chairs.

Even worse, her desk didn't have legs to climb up. It was a solid block of wood.

My Big Plan was completely spoiled!

The clock ticked away. My only option was to put the piece of paper on the floor near her desk and scramble back on to the table. I grabbed the cord from the blinds and began to swing back and forth until I got up to the top of the table. I took the final leap and scurried back to my cage, pulling the door shut behind me.

'Boing-boing-boing!' croaked Og.

'You'll understand soon,' I told him. 'I hope.'

After lunch, Mrs Brisbane returned to the classroom, followed by her other students. The classroom assistants arrived with juice and biscuits. Next, the other parents entered. Everyone was so busy saying hello and admiring the decorations that I lost track of Mrs Brisbane.

I could hear her, though. 'Ladies and gentlemen, if you could take your seats, we're ready for the Poetry Festival to begin.' She talked about what we'd been studying and all the hard work we'd put in. Then she turned the celebration over to Kirk Chen.

Kirk was in good form. He introduced each student with a short poem. The rhymes were funny, but they didn't hurt anybody's feelings. For instance, when it was Heidi's turn, Kirk said, 'Here's something fun by Heidi Hopper. When it comes to poems, you can't top her!'

He introduced Tabitha by saying, 'Tabitha's new, but boy, can she rhyme. We hope she stays a long, long time.'

And for A.J.'s poem he said, 'A.J.'s poem makes him proud, so don't be surprised if he speaks real loud.'

(A.J. did, too.)

I was PROUD-PROUD-PROUD of my classmates as one by one they stood in front of the room and recited their poems. Heidi recited the frog poem she wrote. Instead of her Smiley poem, Tabitha performed a funny poem about a baseball player named Casey. Sayeh recited the dove poem. Pay-Attention-Art lost his place in his poem, but he started over again and did fine. If anybody forgot a word, Mrs Brisbane whispered it and nobody seemed to notice.

The parents clapped heartily for each and every poem. I did too!

Then my heart sank as Mrs Brisbane said, 'That concludes this year's Poetry Festival. I hope you'll all stay for refreshments.'

My Plan had failed utterly! I glanced over at Og. He was still smiling, but he didn't know what I had planned.

But Mrs Brisbane kept talking. 'I have one more poem I'd like to share. I found this scrap of paper on the floor as you arrived. I think it expresses the feelings the children in this room have for each other. It's very tiny and a little hard to read, but I'll try.'

A friend doesn't have to be a work of art,
Just have a heart.

A friend doesn't need to have fur or hair
To care.

A friend doesn't have a thing to do
But like you.

A friend doesn't need to say a word
To be heard.

It's not so hard to be a friend
In the end.

The room was silent until Heidi's mum started the applause and everyone joined in.

'There's a scratchy kind of scribbling at the bottom. I can't make out the name,' said Mrs Brisbane. 'Would the pupil who wrote this like to stand up and identify himself or herself?'

I was standing up all right. And I squeaked at the top of my voice, 'I wrote it! I wrote it for Og! It's my Valentine to him!'

'Sounds like Humphrey knows who wrote it,' Mr Golden joked, and everybody laughed. Everybody except Og.

'Boing-boing!' he shouted, hopping up and

down. At last, I'd got through to him. And now I knew exactly what he was saying.

'You're welcome, Og,' I replied. 'You're welcome, you grinning, green, lumpy, bumpy, hairless, goggle-eyed, cricket-eating friend. You're entirely welcome.'

Later that night, I looked over at Og as he dived into his swimming pool with a giant splash! He looked the same as ever, yet everything was different. What had seemed like a sneery leer was really a friendly grin. The splashing that once annoyed me made me feel good, because I knew Og was HAPPY-HAPPY-HAPPY. And a lunge that once scared me just meant Og wanted to play a game.

Sometimes humans are hard to understand, especially when they act mean, like Marty Bean, or get crabby, like Abby. But with patience (and a little psychology), you can usually figure them out.

It's the same with frogs. And even hamsters.

I'd made a few mistakes, but I'd managed to keep my old friends in Room 26 and make a new one too.

Suddenly, my heart went 'BOING!' as I thought about my shiny-silver new friend.

My friend Og.

Of what shall a man be proud, if he is not proud of his friends?

Robert Louis Stevenson, Scottish novelist and poet

Humphrey's Guide to the Care and Feeding of Friends

1. If you act like a jerk and tease people, you won't have any friends. Guaranteed.
2. If you do the opposite, and are nice to people, you'll have friends. It might take a while, but you'll have friends.
3. If you act like a jerk to your friends and they get angry, but you're REALLY-REALLY-REALLY sorry and let your friends know it, they will probably forgive you.
4. People don't always think so, but boys and girls can be friends.
5. Sometimes you may want to be friends with somebody, but that person (or frog) doesn't want to be friends back. That seems SAD-SAD-SAD, but it's not, because there are other people out there

waiting to be friends with you. You just have to look for them. Keep looking – don't give up!

6 A friend is someone you like to be with and you don't even have to talk. Or squeak.

7 Friendship has its own language. Even if you don't understand the words your friend says, you can understand the meaning.

8 You might not know somebody's your friend until he has a problem and you realize you care.

p.s. Tegucigalpa is the capital of Honduras, a country in Central America. Look it up on the map!

Trouble According to Humphrey

To my son,
Walshe Hinson Birney,
who is as big-hearted
and clever as Humphrey –
but a lot taller!

Special thanks to
Dr Christina Swindall,
Judy Brady and the
Studio City Animal Hospital,
Studio City, California;
and to Stephanie Kelly
of Slidell, Louisiana.

Contents

1

Before the Trouble

'Welcome to our brand-new town!'

Mrs Brisbane's voice woke me from my cosy afternoon doze. Was I dreaming when I heard her mention a new town? Had we moved while I was having my afternoon nap?

Staying awake is a constant problem for a classroom hamster like me. After all, hamsters are nocturnal, which means we're sleepier in the daytime than at night. I always try hard to keep up with my fellow students in Room 26. However, I'd spent the long holiday weekend at Kirk Chen's house. His whole family is funny like he is. It was hard to get much sleeping done there since I was laughing all the time.

But with Mrs Brisbane's announcement, I was suddenly wide awake. I looked around and saw that I was in the same old Room 26 in my same old cage on the table next to the window. Og the Frog's same old glass house sat next to mine.

Around me were the usual tables and the familiar students like Speak-up-Sayeh, Lower-Your-Voice-A.J. and Wait-For-The-Bell-Garth. The same teacher, Mrs Brisbane, stood in front of the class.

I guess I wasn't the only one who was confused. 'What new town?' Heidi Hopper asked.

'Please Raise-Your-Hand-Heidi,' Mrs Brisbane said. 'Since we are studying how communities work, I thought it was time to create our own community of Room Twenty-Sixville.'

Whew! I was relieved because I love our classroom right where it is and I wasn't in the mood to move.

'BOING!' said Og in his twangy voice. I guess he was relieved, too.

'We've been studying what makes a community – right?' asked Mrs Brisbane.

YES-YES-YES, I'd learned a lot about communities recently. First, I learned that there are two Ms in the word. I'm trying to remember that in case it shows up in a spelling test in the future. I'd learned that a community isn't just a place on a map, it's also made up of the people who live there. (I'm sure Mrs Brisbane meant to include animals, too, but forgot to mention us.)

I'd also learned that everyone's job helps the

community in some way or another. There are police officers and firefighters to protect us and people who sell books or clothes or even sell wonderful pets like me! After all, I came from Pet-O-Rama, a shop in our community. There are people who grow and sell food and people who keep the streets clean and people who keep the classrooms clean, like Aldo, our caretaker. There are also doctors who people go to when they are ill and dentists who help people keep their teeth healthy.

Then there's the biggest job of all: teacher. Teachers like Mrs Brisbane help us learn about things we wouldn't know otherwise, such as the life cycle of a frog (though I still can't picture Og as a tadpole), writing poems and adding and subtracting big numbers. Sometimes my paw gets tired from writing down really long problems in the tiny notebook I keep hidden behind my mirror, but I keep writing anyway because it's important.

My mind wandered while Mrs Brisbane continued to talk about all we'd learned until I realized – oh no! – I wasn't listening at all! If I kept daydreaming, I'd end up like Pay-Attention-Art-Patel, who only paid attention in class about half the time and whose recent marks, I'm sorry to say, were dreadful. Not at all like Speak-Up-Sayeh, the quiet girl who always pays attention and gets the best marks in the class (better than mine, I have to admit).

There I was again, my mind wandering to Art's problems instead of listening to Mrs Brisbane. I hopped up on my ladder and vowed to listen to every word she said.

'It's one thing to talk about a community and another thing to be part of one,' the teacher was saying. 'So that's why I decided to create our own community here. We'll lay out our town right in this classroom and everyone will have a job.'

Garth's hand shot up. 'Will we get paid?'

'Not in money. You will get points for doing your jobs correctly and extra points for doing your job especially well.'

Another hand went up. Mrs Brisbane called on Don't-Complain-Mandy-Payne. 'I don't like the name Room Twenty-Sixville,' she said.

I don't think Mandy realizes how much she complains.

Mrs Brisbane smiled. 'Do you have a better name?'

Mandy scratched the tip of her nose. 'Brisbaneville?'

'I don't want to name it after me,' said the teacher. 'Besides, there already is a famous town named Brisbane. It's in Australia and they pronounce it "Brisbin".'

'Maybe we should call it Boringville,' a low voice muttered.

'I-Heard-That-Kirk,' Mrs Brisbane said. 'It was a rude thing to say. Do you really think school is boring?'

'Sorry. I was making a joke.' I believed him because Kirk is such a big joker. He's also a quick thinker. 'Og looks pretty bored,' he said.

All heads – including mine – turned to gaze at Og, who sat completely motionless on his rock, staring into space without even blinking.

'Og is a frog,' Mrs Brisbane said. 'He always looks that way.'

I'm never completely sure what Og thinks, but *I* don't think Room 26 is a boring place at all. I decided to squeak up on the subject, so I leaped up and grabbed onto a leafy tree branch our teacher's husband, Mr Brisbane, had put in my cage. He was always adding new and interesting things to my home, like my ladders and a large cage extension.

Mrs Brisbane turned towards me. 'Humphrey certainly doesn't seem bored.'

I loudly squeaked 'NO-NO-NO,' and jumped to another branch.

'Let's call it Humphreyville!' That was definitely A.J.'s loud voice and this time he forgot to raise his hand, too.

'Humphreyville!' Voices burst out from around

the room, along with chuckles and giggles.

'Humphreyville?' Mrs Brisbane thought it over. Unfortunately, it was hard to think because Gail had gone into one of her giggling fits.

'Stop-Giggling-Gail,' said the teacher. 'Please. Now what do the rest of you think? Miranda?'

Miranda Golden – or Golden-Miranda as I like to think of her – didn't hesitate a bit. 'I love the name!'

'Sayeh, what do you think?' For once, quiet Speak-Up-Sayeh didn't have any trouble speaking up. 'Yes, it sounds like a real place.'

'What is it again?' Pay-Attention-Art asked.

'Humphreyville,' Sayeh told him.

'I never heard of a town named after a hamster,' said Art.

Well, I may be a hamster but I'm no ordinary hamster. I am an exceptionally cute golden hamster (I've been told) who happens to know how to read and write. Not that anyone knows about that except me. Or the fact that my cage has a lock-that-doesn't-lock so I can come and go as I please when no one's looking.

'Humphreyville,' Art repeated. 'Sounds pretty good.'

I saw lots of heads nodding and heard murmuring around the class that sounded as if people were agreeing.

Imagine – a whole town named after me! I leaped onto my wheel and began spinning with joy.

'Why don't we take a vote?' asked Mrs Brisbane. 'All those in favour of naming our community "Humphreyville", raise your hands.'

While I was spinning, I could see hands going up. Even Heidi remembered to raise her hand. Every hand was raised except one: Tabitha's. I stopped spinning.

Tabitha was the new girl in our class and I thought she liked me. I'd even helped her make friends with Seth, although she didn't actually know it. I have some sneaky, squeaky ways of making things like that happen.

'Tabitha, do you have another suggestion for a name?' Mrs Brisbane asked.

'No,' said Tabitha. 'I like Humphreyville. I'm just afraid Og will be jealous.'

Jealous! I hadn't thought about that, even though when Mrs Brisbane brought Og in as a second classroom pet, I'd been jealous of him. It's embarrassing to admit it, but it's true.

'That's something to think about, isn't it? After all, if we named our community "Tabithaville", the other students might be jealous,' the teacher agreed.

'Yeah, and it's hard to say,' Heidi blurted out.

'Heidi, you simply must remember to raise your

hand!' Mrs Brisbane had helped a lot of students to change their bad habits. Somehow, she'd never been able to get Heidi to remember to raise her hand.

'Now, class, why don't we let Og decide?' The teacher walked over to the frog's glass house. 'Og, do you vote for Humphreyville?'

I wasn't expecting much, because I'd learned that Og, being a frog, has an unusual way of expressing himself. His 'BOINGS' are nothing like the energetic squeaks of a hamster or the giggles and shouts of the kids. In fact, sometimes Og doesn't communicate at all. Still, he and I had learned to be friends. So I wouldn't have been surprised if he just continued to sit motionless, as usual.

But that's not what he did at all! Instead, he started leaping up and down on his rock, splashing water up onto Mrs Brisbane's chin. 'BOING-BOING-BOING!' he twanged as only Og can do.

The students laughed uproariously. Even Mrs Brisbane chuckled as she wiped the water off. 'Thank you for your vote, Og. Now let's try again. All in favour of naming our new community "Humphreyville", raise your hands.'

This time every hand went up, including Tabitha's. Whew! She liked me after all. Og stopped leaping and splashing and sat quietly on his rock again.

Mrs Brisbane looked pleased. 'Welcome, class, to the town of Humphreyville!' She wrote the name on the board in great big letters. 'And to keep track of the progress of our town, we'll be starting a daily newspaper. I think *The Humphreyville Herald* would be a good name, don't you?'

My friends all agreed!

My heart hopped around in my chest like a happy frog. Had any hamster ever been honoured like this before? Probably not. I decided right then and there that I would try to remain as humble as possible and do whatever I could to make Humphreyville the BEST-BEST-BEST town in the world!

I jumped on my wheel and spun for a while until I realized that Mrs Brisbane was still talking. 'There's a whole lot more to building a community than finding a name.'

I stopped spinning and started listening.

'What's the first thing you need when you move to a new place?'

I knew what I'd need: a cage. There was no point in my raising my paw since I never get called on, but a lot of other hands went up. Mrs Brisbane called on Repeat-It-Please-Richie. 'A car,' he said. 'Or a truck to carry all the stuff you're moving.'

'What if you didn't own anything at all?' asked

the teacher. 'What would you need first?'

'Bargainmart!' Richie said. Everybody laughed. I figured Bargainmart must be some kind of shop, like Pet-O-Rama.

'I think you're jumping ahead. Tabitha, did you have your hand up?'

Tabitha nodded. 'You'd need a place to live. A house.'

'Or a tent!' Heidi blurted out.

'Very good,' said Mrs Brisbane, ignoring Heidi's outburst. 'Something like a house. Your first assignment is to design a place that represents where you would live in the town. You can draw a picture or make a model out of clay or build it out of cardboard. Be creative and think about what kind of home you'd like for yourself in Humphreyville.'

The bell rang. 'We'll have maths after break and then we'll get to work on your homes.'

Break is a time when my classmates all go out and play. It must be fun because my friends usually come back laughing and joking. At this time of year – late February – they also come back with rosy cheeks and red noses.

I always stay inside and try to get some exercise, climbing my ladder or spinning on my wheel. I must admit, sometimes I go into my sleeping hut for a nice nap because remember, I am nocturnal.

On this day, when Mrs Brisbane wasn't paying

attention, I sneaked my notebook into my sleeping hut and thought about what kind of house I'd build. I loved my cage, but sometimes I'd think about the fancy houses they sold at Pet-O-Rama. One was a Chinese pagoda and one was like a TALL-TALL-TALL castle. Ms Mac, the supply teacher and superb human being who first brought me from the pet shop to Room 26 of Longfellow School, couldn't afford one of those, which was okay with me. Anything Ms Mac did was fine with me. Yet, it was fun to think about my perfect house.

After all, if you have a whole town named after you, you should have a nice place to live!

NEW TOWN IN ROOM 26 TO BE NAMED AFTER CLASSROOM HAMSTER

Houses will be going up in Humphreyville within a week, teacher predicts.

The Humphreyville Herald

2

The Problem with Paul

Humphreyville wasn't the only thing new in Room 26 that Monday. Once everyone was seated after break, Mrs Brisbane opened the door and in walked a small boy I'd never seen before. He stood very straight and held his chin high. 'Welcome, Paul,' the teacher said.

All of my classmates turned to stare at the boy, who stared right back at them. I craned my neck to get a look him. All I could tell was that this Paul looked VERY-VERY-VERY serious.

'Class, some of you might know Paul Fletcher from Mrs Loomis's class. He's going to be coming into our class for maths every day from now on.'

'He's a year behind us!' That was Heidi Hopper, of course.

Gail started to giggle but stopped herself, although I'm pretty sure Paul noticed. His chin sagged for a second.

'Heidi, please. Paul is an excellent maths student and Mr Morales asked if he could sit in on our class. I expect you to treat him like any other classmate and be as helpful as possible. Some of you probably already know Paul, don't you?'

Mrs Brisbane waited. Very slowly, Art raised his hand.

'He lives across the street from me.' Art kept doodling on a piece of paper. He was a great doodler. If I doodled as much as he did, I'd fill up my whole notebook in a day. Unlike Seth, who had a hard time sitting still, Art sat quietly but his pencil was always moving.

'Let's pull up a chair next to you. Here, Paul.' Paul sat, though he and Art didn't look at each another. 'Why don't we go around the room and introduce ourselves?'

One by one, my classmates said their names. Gail giggled when she told hers. Richie mumbled and Mrs Brisbane had to say, 'Repeat-It-Please-Richie.' A.J. said his name extra loud and Sayeh said, 'I am Sayeh Nasiri. Welcome, Paul.' That was nice.

When they were finished, I squeaked out, 'And I am Humphrey!'

Mrs Brisbane laughed and said, 'I think Humphrey wants to make sure you meet him, too. And Og, our frog, of course.'

Og silently stared out of his glass house. Sometimes I wish he was a little friendlier.

Mrs Brisbane quickly launched into the maths class with a difficult problem for us to work out. Everybody went to work except me. I was too busy watching Paul writing like crazy. Mrs Brisbane walked around the room to see how each student was working out the problem.

'Good, Heidi. Make sure those numbers line up,' she said. 'That's perfect, Sayeh.' She told A.J. and Tabitha to try again.

When she saw Paul's answer, she smiled and said, 'Excellent, Paul.'

When she saw Art's answer, she stopping smiling and said, 'Needs work, Art. Try going back to that first step and starting again.'

I watched the two boys as the teacher did more explaining.

Art hadn't done well with his problem and he looked unhappy.

Paul had done REALLY-REALLY-REALLY well with his problem but he looked unhappy, too!

At the end of all her explaining, Mrs Brisbane told us that we'd have a test the next week and handed out a study sheet.

'Eeek!' I squeaked. I didn't mean to – I just realized that I'd been paying so much attention to Art and Paul that I hadn't listened to the teacher at all.

You should always listen to your teacher.

'Any questions?' she asked.

Paul raised his hand and she called on him. 'What is Humphreyville?' he asked.

'It's our town we're creating for Social Studies.'

'Oh,' said Paul.

'Well, if there are no other questions, you may go, Paul. We'll see you tomorrow!' Mrs Brisbane used her especially cheery voice.

Paul didn't waste any time before grabbing his exercise book and hurrying out of Room 26.

I liked Paul but I wasn't sure that he liked us back.

By the next day, Humphreyville was taking shape. My fellow students had already begun to build their homes. Oh, there were so many different kinds! A.J. made a house out of blocks. He didn't care if somebody knocked it over because he could build it up again. Garth made a log cabin. Seth's 'house' was a spaceship – cool! Golden-Miranda drew a picture of a purple castle (she deserves a castle). Heidi, true to her word, made a blue tent with pink and yellow polka dots.

Sayeh built a tall block of flats. She said since Humphreyville would be such a popular place, we would need a lot of places for people to live.

Mandy's house was very tall and narrow. She explained that each floor was for a different member of her family. Unfortunately, it kept tipping over.

The house that got by far the most attention was Art's. He used small plastic bricks and metal springs and sprockets and things-I-don't-know-the-names-of to build a house that had a big slide coming out of the attic, inner rooms that revolved like a merry-go-round and train tracks that went right through the middle.

'I believe Art's house will put Humphreyville on the map,' Mrs Brisbane said. I think that for this project he got the first A he's had all year. I definitely gave him an A.

When Paul came into class for maths, he sat next to Art, although they ignored each other completely. It sounds strange, but Paul looked even smaller when he walked out of Room 26 than when he walked in.

On Wednesday evening, I scribbled in my notebook, working on the drawing of my house. It got dark early. Luckily, I could sketch by the light of the street lamp outside the window. Of course, the sound of the crickets (Og's special treats) going CHIRRUP-CHIRRUP sometimes made it hard to concentrate.

Suddenly, I was blinded by bright lights. 'Surprise, surprise! Aldo has arrived!' My eyes adjusted to the light and there was our friendly caretaker, Aldo Amato, bowing from the waist. I quickly slipped my notebook behind my mirror.

'Greetings, Aldo,' I shouted. I knew it came out SQUEAK-SQUEAK-SQUEAK, but Aldo always seemed to understand me.

'Hello, Humphrey! Howdy-do, Og!' Aldo pulled his cleaning trolley into the room, took out his broom and started sweeping. He stopped as soon as he had started. '*Mamma mia*, what's all this?' he asked, looking around at the room.

'HUMPHREYVILLE,' I squeaked loudly.

'BOING!' shouted Og.

I could see how surprised Aldo was and with good reason. Since the night before, the whole room had changed. Tables with all the students' homes lined the back of the room and the rows between the tables had big signs on them with street names. My classmates had argued over – I mean *discussed* – what each street should be named. When Mrs Brisbane suggested First Street, Second Street and so forth, the students didn't like that idea. Then she'd suggested naming the streets after presidents, but my friends weren't interested in that, either.

'We want something that stands for us,' Garth said. 'Names that are things we like.'

Now the growing town of Humphreyville had Soccer Street and Basketball Avenue, Video Game Way and Break Lane as well as Pizza Place and Taco Boulevard.

Aldo's big black moustache bounced heartily as he laughed and looked around. 'Welcome to Humphreyville,' a sign announced in big bright letters. The table where Og and I live had some grassy material on it with a sign that read: 'Og the Frog Nature Reserve'.

I was glad they named something after Og, so he wouldn't be jealous. Jealousy feels BAD-BAD-BAD.

Aldo started sweeping again. 'I'm lucky I get to clean Mrs Brisbane's room every night because I learn so much about being a teacher!' He had just returned to college so that he could teach in school, which was an excellent idea.

'Humphreyville!' he repeated with a chuckle. 'Looks like the perfect place to live!'

Aldo went about his work in his usual quick and efficient way, then pulled a chair up near my cage and took out his lunch bag. He always took his supper break with Og and me and talked about his life. He talked about his wife Maria, who worked at the bakery and had a beautiful smile. Lately, he talked a lot about college.

'Whew, Humphrey, I knew that studying wouldn't

be easy, but it's getting harder all the time,' he said. 'I'm lucky Maria is an understanding woman because I hardly have any free time. I haven't even been bowling for weeks.'

Although I wasn't completely sure what 'bowling' was, I knew it was something Aldo enjoyed. He chewed his sandwich thoughtfully for a moment. 'Still, it will be worth it. I can be a teacher and work with kids and maybe have a house like one of these,' he said, waving towards the back tables. 'Like the one with the train tracks going through it.'

He reached into his sandwich and pulled out a piece of lettuce. 'Here's to your health, Humphrey.' He pushed the lettuce into my cage.

I squeaked a heartfelt 'thanks'.

'Sorry I don't have something for you, Og my man,' he told my neighbour. 'You're a lot pickier than Humphrey.'

Picky? The frog eats *crickets*! Yech. Not nearly as appealing as the mealworms I enjoy.

Aldo hurried out of the door with his squeaky trolley. Although I was sorry my friend didn't have time to go bowling, I was glad he was going to be a teacher, like Mrs Brisbane. I could hardly believe that when I first met Mrs Brisbane I didn't think she was a very nice person. In fact, I thought she was out to get me. Now, she's one of my favourite humans – and I have a lot of favourite humans!

During the next few days, my classmates worked hard at building up Humphreyville. Every day, Paul came in for the maths class. Though he sat next to Art, his neighbour never even looked at him. Every day, Paul left the classroom in a big hurry.

On Friday afternoon, it was time for Mrs Brisbane to announce which student would be taking me home for the weekend. It was always an exciting moment for my classmates but an even more exciting moment for me. My whiskers wiggled wildly as I waited to find out where I'd be staying.

'Pick me,' said Mandy, frantically waving her arm. 'You've never let me take Humphrey home.'

She was right. I'd been home with many of my friends – some of them even twice – but I'd never gone home with Mandy.

'You haven't brought back the permission slip I sent home with you,' said Mrs Brisbane.

Mandy let out a huge sigh, then said, 'My parents have been busy.'

'Well, tell them I'm waiting for their signatures. Now, I believe Seth is scheduled to take Humphrey home this weekend.'

Sit-Still-Seth-Stevenson was so excited, he jiggled his chair until it actually tipped over. Luckily, he wasn't hurt.

'Try to stay calm,' said Mrs Brisbane.

'I WILL-WILL-WILL.' I covered my mouth with my paws when I realized that she had been talking to Seth. I made a mistake. After all, I'm only human. I mean . . . only a hamster (which is a very good thing).

NO HOUSING SHORTAGE IN HUMPHREYVILLE!

Building boom keeps Room 26 students hopping. Population swells as Paul Fletcher joins maths class.

The Humphreyville Herald

3

The Situation with the Stevensons

The reason I used to think Seth's full name was Sit-Still-Seth was because he always wriggles in his chair and Mrs Brisbane always reminds him to sit still. He really does try but he has so much energy, he just has to move. I suppose that's why he loves sport a lot, both playing it and watching it, along with our other sport fan in Room 26, Tabitha.

As much as I like Seth, I was hoping his whole family didn't fidget and squirm as much as he did. I always have my wheel to work off my excess energy. Too bad Seth doesn't have one, too.

On Friday, Seth's mum June drove us home without so much as a twitch. She did tell her son to stop bouncing up and down on the seat, which I appreciated, as car rides always make me queasy even without Seth's jiggling and joggling.

'Thanks for picking me up, Mum,' Seth said. 'I

thought Grandma would do it.'

'I was afraid she'd have trouble with the cage. The shop wasn't busy and Carolyn covered for me. I'll do the same for her next week.' She laughed. 'I'll be glad when your sister can drive you.'

Seth bounced a little higher. 'I won't!' he exclaimed.

Once we were home and I was placed in the living room on a big table, I saw the other members of Seth's family. His sister was a teenager named Lucinda, and Grandma was an older lady I later worked out was June's mum and Seth's and Lucinda's grandmother.

'Want to meet Humphrey?' Seth asked his sister.

She turned up her nose. 'Hamsters are for children,' she said and walked away. 'I'm going to write in my journal now so please don't disturb me.'

'Don't worry, I won't!' I squeaked at her. Hamsters are for children! Try telling that to Mr Morales or Aldo or even Mrs Brisbane.

The older woman slowly approached the cage and leaned over to get a closer look at me – but not too close.

'Don't worry, Grandma. He won't hurt you,' said Seth.

'Is it clean?' she asked.

'Probably cleaner than I am,' Seth joked.

Grandma didn't crack a smile. 'I'm afraid that

might be all too true,' she said. She backed away from my cage and left the room.

'You'd better give him some fresh water,' Seth's mum suggested. 'And some food?'

At least Seth's mum didn't call me an 'it', which I always appreciate.

Once I was settled in, Seth started playing video games. He didn't merely sit and play video games. He bounced and bobbed, he shook and shimmied, he rattled and rocked. I was feeling kind of woozy, so I crawled into my sleeping hut for a nice doze. I woke up when Seth's mum announced that supper was ready. Luckily, the living room had a big wide opening right into the kitchen, which is where the family sat down to eat.

Suppers at my classmates' houses are always fascinating to me – there are yummy smells and interesting things to hear, all about one person's day at work and another person's day at school. Some people were loud while they ate, like Lower-Your-Voice-A.J. and his family. Some people were quiet, like Tabitha and her foster mum.

Seth's family didn't talk much but when they did, it was always about one subject: Seth.

'Can't you sit still?' asked Lucinda, in a superior tone of voice I didn't care for.

'I am sitting still,' said Seth.

'You are not! You bumped the table. See, my

water spilled,' his sister replied.

'Do try and be calm, honey,' Seth's mum said.

'In my day –' Grandma began, then started again in a much more dramatic voice. 'In *my* day, boys and girls had to sit still at the table without saying a word. That was what we called manners. Are you listening?'

'Yes, ma'am,' said Seth, sounding quite miserable.

Everything was quiet for a while except for the clinking and clanking of knives and forks (I don't know why humans need those when they have a perfectly good set of paws, like I do). Then Lucinda exclaimed, 'He's doing it again!'

'What?' said Seth.

'You know what. Shaking your legs.'

'Sorry, *Cindy*,' he said.

'My name is Lucinda!' she answered icily.

'You used to like to be called Cindy.'

'Well, I don't now.'

Seth and his family were silent for a while until Lucinda clanked her fork loudly and said, 'Oh, really! If you bump that table leg once more I'll . . .'

'It was an accident,' said Seth.

'Kids, please.' Seth's mum sounded tired.

'In my day,' Grandma began again. 'In *my* day, children were not allowed to argue at the table.'

'I'll bet Seth can't stay still for one minute,' said Lucinda in a nasty voice.

'I'll bet you can't stay still for two minutes,' said Seth.

'June, you should not allow your children to gamble,' Grandma grumbled. 'In *my* day –'

'Mother, you're not helping,' said June, which was true.

'My mother wouldn't allow us to make bets.'

This conversation was getting on my nerves so I hopped onto my wheel to try and relax. Unfortunately, my wheel always makes an annoying SCREECH!

'What on earth is that creature doing?' asked Grandma.

'He's on his exercise wheel. It's good for him,' Seth replied.

Grandma sniffed loudly. 'I guess nobody around here can sit still except me.'

'Well, *I* certainly can,' Lucinda objected.

'You move as much as anybody,' said Seth. 'Look, you just blinked!'

'Blinking doesn't count! It's banging the table like you do that counts.' Somebody – maybe Lucinda – banged a hand on the table. I could tell because the dishes rattled.

Someone else – I'm guessing it was Seth – banged a hand on the table, too.

'That's enough!' Seth's mum sounded as if she was about to explode. 'Night after night, all you do is bicker about who's sitting still and who's not and who's right and who's wrong! Well, I've had enough. We're going to leave the table and go into the living room and settle this once and for all.'

'For goodness' sake! And let my supper get cold?' Grandma asked in a sad little voice.

'It's a salad. It's supposed to be cold,' said June. I'd heard irritated mums before and she sounded as if she'd really had enough.

She marched into the living room and surprisingly Lucinda, Seth and Grandma followed.

'Now, just sit down on the sofa,' she said firmly.

'In my day, children – even adult children – didn't address their parents in that tone of voice,' said Grandma.

'You don't have to be in this contest, Mother. You can go and finish your salad. This is between Seth and Lucinda.'

Grandma slowly moved back towards the kitchen, then hesitated. 'What contest?'

'The Sitting-Still Contest to see who can sit the longest without moving.'

'What does the winner get?' asked Lucinda.

June thought for a few seconds. 'A pair of tickets for the winner and a friend to the pictures tomorrow. I'll also provide popcorn money and transport.'

'I could take my friend Adele,' said Grandma.

'I'm in.' She planted herself on the sofa right between Lucinda and Seth.

'Can we take anyone we want?' asked Lucinda.

'You may take anyone who is old enough to go to the cinema and behave.' Boy, Seth's mum really meant business.

I'd been so caught up in this whole fascinating discussion, I didn't realize I was spinning on my wheel. June twirled around and pointed an accusing finger at me.

'You have to sit still, too, Humphrey.'

I stopped cold and tumbled off my wheel. There's a trick to getting off a spinning object which I temporarily forgot.

'Is Humphrey in the contest?' asked Seth.

'I suppose he can't go to the pictures. But if Humphrey stays still longer than anyone, he gets a nice big chunk of whatever he likes.'

'Apples!' I squeaked.

Seth looked thoughtful. 'He likes fruit,' he said. Smart guy!

June sounded a bit calmer. 'Let's all relax for a minute and take a few deep breaths.'

'Mum, can we move Humphrey's cage closer? I'm going to concentrate on him. As long as I stare at him, I think I can do it,' said Seth.

'Any objections?' asked June.

'I don't care, as long as I don't have to touch it,'

said Lucinda. 'Besides, hamsters never stop moving. Look at it.'

I realized that she was right. We hamsters do tend to be as jumpy as Seth. Even if we're standing still, our whiskers are wiggling or our noses are twitching. However, if my keeping still could help Seth . . . well, he was a classmate and in Room 26 we stick together.

Seth's mum pushed my table closer to the sofa and checked her watch. 'I have a second hand on my watch. In thirty seconds, I'll say "Start". At that point, you must stop all movement. You'll be eliminated as soon as you move.'

'Who gets to be the judge?' asked Grandma.

'I do,' said June in a voice that no one would want to argue with. No one did – least of all me!

'Can we blink?' asked Lucinda.

'Yes, you can blink and you can breathe. That's it.'

June's watch was very quiet but I could almost feel it TICK-TICK-TICKing away the seconds, the way the clock in Room 26 does when everyone goes home and it's awfully quiet.

I was pretty worried because I was looking straight ahead at Seth and he was tapping his fingers on the table. Lucinda seemed quite determined, with her arms folded tightly against her body. Grandma sat up very straight (I bet people 'in her day' always did).

'Ten, nine, eight, seven, six, five, four, three, two – freeze!' said June.

I froze. The Sitting-Still-Contest had begun!

Oh dear, oh dear. If you don't have whiskers, you have no idea how difficult it is to keep them from moving. I stared straight ahead at Seth, who was as motionless as Og is when he sits on his rock. In fact, I tried to pretend I *was* a frog, which is not an easy thing for a hamster to do.

'You can do it . . . you can do it . . .' I sent out my thoughts to Seth. Even though he probably couldn't hear my thoughts, I figured that as long as I could stay still, maybe he could, too. My tail felt like twitching and my nose was itching and I'd never gone so long without moving. Seth stared at me and I stared back.

After a while, Grandma's chin dropped and her head bobbed up and down. Grandma had moved and she didn't even know it because she was asleep! She began to snore softly.

'One down,' said June, keeping her gaze fixed firmly on Lucinda, Seth and me.

No one else had made a move yet and neither did I, although seeing Grandma asleep like that not only made me want to wiggle, it made me want to giggle.

Seth was as frozen as a statue and I was proud of him. However, Lucinda looked like she was made of solid steel.

TICK-TICK-TICK. That imaginary clock sounded loud in my brain. Amazingly, Seth still hadn't moved a muscle. I tried to keep my gaze firmly on him, though once in a while I glanced at Lucinda. I was beginning to believe the girl had turned to stone. Suddenly, I saw her blink. Okay, blinking was okay but this was like a double blink. Like a wink. Followed by another and another. Pretty soon she was blinking both eyes, hard.

'Aha,' I thought. 'She's trying to throw me off. Because she thinks that if she throws me off, I'll throw Seth off.' Which would be a shame, because even if Seth lost, he had already sat still longer than ever before.

Then it happened. Lucinda's head twitched and the blinking got even faster until she jumped up off the sofa, holding her eye with one hand. 'My contact lens! I've got something in my eye!' she wailed and raced out of the room.

'Two down,' said June, sounding less edgy than before. 'I think you're the winner, Seth.'

Even then, Seth didn't blink an eye. He stared straight at me. At *me*! Now I got it – Seth was determined to stay still longer than I did.

I wanted to squeak with joy because Seth had done so well. But there was the matter of this little itch right next to my nose. It was a little itch that grew into a bigger, more irritating itch that grew into an UNBEARABLE TICKLING ITCH. At last, I reached up to scratch it.

'Three down,' said June. 'Seth, you *are* the winner!'

Seth leaped up from the sofa and jumped up and down making Vs with his fingers. 'I won! Tell Lucinda! I won!'

Grandma's head jerked up as she awoke with a start. 'Whatizzit?' she asked groggily. 'Did I win?'

'No, mother. You moved first when you fell asleep.'

'Perfectly ridiculous. I was just resting my eyes.'

'Seth won!' June gave her son a hug. 'Now we know you can control yourself if you put your mind to it.'

'I suppose,' said Seth. He looked worried. I bet he was wondering if he was going to have to sit like a statue for ever.

'Not all the time, of course,' said June. I do believe parents can sometimes read their children's minds. 'Just when you need to, like during a test.'

Seth sighed. 'I'll try harder, I promise. Mum, can I call Tabitha and ask if she can come and see that football film tomorrow?' asked Seth.

'I'll call her mother after supper,' said June.

Lucinda wandered in, rubbing her eye. 'Stupid contact lens. I don't suppose we can have a rematch?'

'Any time you want,' said Seth, confidently.

'*I'll* have a rematch,' said Grandma.

'No rematches,' June stated firmly. 'Now, what do you say we order some pizza to go with that salad?'

'They didn't have pizza in your day, Grandma, did they?' Lucinda asked.

'Pizza! In my day, we *invented* pizza! Pepperoni and onions for me, hold the peppers.'

I was glad they weren't arguing any more, but I worried about those extra peppers (they're far too spicy for me).

The next day, as promised, June took Seth and Tabitha to see the football film at the shopping centre (a place I've never been to) and took Lucinda shopping. Grandma stayed at home. That made me a teensy bit nervous, because I had a feeling that in her day, people didn't have hamsters. Or if they did, they did something worse with them than put them in a cage!

For a while, she ignored me and watched a couple of programmes on television where grown-ups sat around and argued with each other. Whew! I'm glad Mrs Brisbane doesn't let the kids in Room 26 argue all the time. I guess even Grandma got tired of those shows because she turned the TV off and came over to my cage.

'Let's get a good look at you, young man.' She pulled her glasses out of her pocket and leaned in to examine me.

'Well, you're just a little bit of a fellow, aren't you? Not good for much, I suppose.'

Me – Humphrey the hamster – not good for much! I decided to show Grandma a thing or two. I scurried up my ladder, leaped onto a tree branch and hung there from one paw. It was a trick that had never failed to please humans. So far, Grandma wasn't anything like the other humans I'd met. I swung myself up to my bridge ladder, dashed across it and dived onto my wheel. WHOA-WHOA-WHOA – I almost lost my balance but I managed to get the wheel going without falling over.

'Why, aren't you Mr Show-Off?' said Grandma. 'Quite the daredevil.'

Then she did something surprising. She chuckled.

Since I was on a roll, I hopped off my wheel, grabbed onto my ladder and hung on with both paws, swinging my body back and forth.

'Ha-ha! Reminds me of a song we sang as kids.' Amazingly, Grandma began to sing.

He floats through the air with the greatest of ease,
The daring young man on the flying trapeze . . .
His actions are da-da,

Da-da-da-da-dee,
And my heart he has stolen away!

It was an excellent song. She had a pretty good voice, too, even if she couldn't remember all the words. I liked being the daring young hamster on the flying trapeze.

'I'd almost forgotten that old song. I'll tell you, Humphrey – that's your name, isn't it?'

'Of course!' I squeaked.

'My name is Dot Larrabee. Humphrey, when I was young we used to sing all the time. Now kids just listen to music. In my day, we made our own.'

I dropped down from my 'trapeze' and listened.

'And for fun we'd go to the roller rink.' Dot's eyes lit up as she talked. 'There used to be a roller-skating rink where the shopping centre is now. Next door was an amusement park with a ferris wheel and a merry-go-round. You could go on a couple of rides, maybe have some cotton candy or a snow cone. Once I saw a dancing bear there. A man would play the accordion and the bear would really dance! Now all there is to do is spend money on clothes. Who cares about clothes?'

'I don't!' I was squeaking the truth. I was perfectly happy with my fur coat.

'I've seen a lot of changes in my day,' said Dot. 'But nobody wants to hear about my life.'

'I do!' I squeaked and I meant it.

She smiled again. 'You're a lively fellow. I like you, kiddo. I really do.'

And I REALLY-REALLY-REALLY liked Dot.

'We lived in a yellow house with white trim, down on Alder Street. It was a small house with a nice big garden with trees to climb and places to play hide-and-seek. It was near the Dairy Maid, only back then, it was a little corner shop.'

Alder Street! Dairy Maid! That was right where I came from, next door to Pet-O-Rama!

'They tore all that down, that street of pretty houses. Put in a pet shop and a music shop or something. Right where I used to play when I was a girl.'

They tore down her house to build Pet-O-Rama! I was learning a lot, because I'd imagined Pet-O-Rama had always been there at the corner of Fifth and Alder. My mind was a million miles away when I heard a door slam, followed by the stomping and clomping of feet.

'Mother?' June called out.

'I'm in here with Humphrey,' said Dot.

June, Seth and Lucinda came into the living room, all bundled up in coats, hats and scarves.

'You were probably wise to stay home,' said

June. 'It's started to sleet!'

I wasn't exactly sure what sleet was but it sounded COLD-COLD-COLD.

'Of course it is,' said Dot. 'Anybody with a lick of sense would expect it. Today's the first of March. And you know what they always say: March comes in like a lion and goes out like a lamb. Hardly ever fails. Why, in my day, we had three feet of snow on the first of March one year. I must have been ten. Or maybe eleven.'

Seth and Lucinda rolled their eyes, as if to say, 'There she goes again.'

But when I looked at Dot, I saw a young girl gazing out of the window of a yellow house with white trim, watching the snowflakes fluttering down, thinking about a dancing bear.

Later that night, I was feeling especially nocturnal, so I decided to perform my daring-young-hamster-on-the-flying-trapeze routine for Seth. I leaped up, grabbed onto my bridge ladder and swung across it.

'If you were a human, you could be in the Olympic gymnastics team,' said Seth and it sounded like a very good thing.

'I wish Dad could see you,' he continued. 'He lives in Arizona where it's warm all the time. He teaches high-school basketball. I spend the whole summer there and boy, it's hot. I don't suppose Mrs Brisbane would let you stay for the whole summer.' He seemed disappointed and I guess I was, too. I knew that the capital of Arizona is Phoenix – whew, that's not easy to spell – but I wanted to know what it would be like to live in a place where it was warm all the time.

I glanced out of the window, and not only was it *not* warm, tiny pieces of ice were falling outside. Sleet!

On Sunday, I saw an amazing sight: the trees outside the window were covered in ice, which glittered like diamonds when the sun came out in the afternoon. Dot stood at the window admiring the display. 'Yessir, March came in like a lion so you know she'll go out like a lamb. Days like this when I was a kid, we'd go skating over on Dobbs's Pond. Don't kids do that any more, June?'

June joined her mother at the window. 'They paved that over and built houses there years ago, Mother.'

'Fools! What do you bet they get water in the cellars when it rains? You can't stop nature.'

June called to Seth. 'Did you see these trees? They're really beautiful.'

Seth was watching a basketball game on TV. 'I

saw them,' he said, but I knew he hadn't taken his eyes off the screen for the whole game.

June went into the kitchen but Grandma stayed at the window, watching the sun shine through the icy branches.

'On a day like this, I'd be out skating on Dobbs's Pond.' Dot sounded wistful.

If I had a choice, I'd be out there skating with her.

FREEZING RAIN AND SNOW KEEP STUDENTS INSIDE OVER THE WEEK-END!

Humphrey stays warm at Seth Stevenson's house.

The Humphreyville Herald

4
The Great Cage Catastrophe

The sun melted all the ice that Sunday afternoon. On Monday, it was cold and windy. 'March comes in like a lion,' Dot had said and she sure was right. I shivered in my cage, despite the heavy blanket that Seth put over it before he and his mum took me out to the car. Being chilly is one thing but a lion can be big trouble. Was trouble blowing its way towards Room 26? (The answer is YES-YES-YES. I just didn't know it yet.)

It was warm and cosy back in the classroom. I tried to tell Og about my weekend at Seth's house but Mrs Brisbane had to 'shush' me. During the spelling test, I was so busy watching Seth that I didn't concentrate as hard as I should have. Seth did a lot less fidgeting than usual, and I noticed that when he started jiggling in his seat, he'd glance over at me for a second and settle down. Good job!

I marked my test and was shocked to see that I'd only got 79 per cent. Sayeh, as usual, got a hundred per cent. I'm not sure what mark Seth got but he was smiling. Whatever mark Art got, it must not have been good, because (a) he wasn't smiling and (b) the teacher asked him to stay in during break. *Everybody* knew what that meant.

Then, we had a surprise visit from Mr Morales, the head teacher. He's the Most Important Person at Longfellow School and a personal friend of mine, ever since I spent a weekend at his house. Mr Morales always wears a special tie. Today his tie had colourful little houses all over it.

'I hope you don't mind me dropping in on Humphreyville,' he said. 'I've heard so much about it, I had to see it for myself.' He strolled past the tables, admiring the houses and the street signs and ended up near my cage. 'I can't think of a better name than the one you've picked.'

'THANKS-THANKS-THANKS!' I squeaked. As usual it came out 'SQUEAK-SQUEAK-SQUEAK,' and everybody laughed.

'You're just in time for the next phase of our town-building,' said Mrs Brisbane. 'Today, we're all going to get jobs.'

I heard gasps and murmurs around the room, and my mind was whirling. Mrs Brisbane already had a job: being our teacher. I had a job: being the classroom pet to help students learn about other species. As Ms Mac said when she first brought me to Room 26, 'You can learn a lot about yourself by taking care of another species,' and it was true. Now I shared the job with Og. But I sometimes wondered whether there was anything new for my friends to learn now that I'd been in class for a while.

My mind was spinning a bit too fast and I missed some of what Mrs Brisbane was saying. Something about people in a community contributing by doing specific jobs. She'd already started writing names of jobs on the blackboard as students called them out:

TEACHER
POLICE OFFICER
FIREFIGHTER

'That's what I want to do,' Garth said, aiming an imaginary fire hose at A.J. and making loud squirting sounds.

'Garth –' Mrs Brisbane used her warning voice and kept on writing.

DOCTOR
NURSE
DENTIST

'Who needs a dentist?' joked Kirk, folding his lips over his teeth so that he looked completely toothless. Gail giggled but Mrs Brisbane ignored them both and kept going.

SHOPKEEPER
FARMER
BUILDER

'You left out one job,' said Mr Morales. 'Head teacher. And I'd better get back to my job before Mrs Brisbane gives me a new one!'

Everyone laughed as he left and the list-making continued.

When things quietened down, the teacher made her own suggestions. 'I think we're forgetting a few other important jobs in a town. People to keep the electricity going and run grocery shops and petrol stations.'

'Car washes,' said Seth.

'Car dealers!' added A.J. 'You can't wash your car until you buy one.'

All these interesting jobs had my head whirling. I dashed into my sleeping hut and quickly wrote the list down in my secret notebook. I'm grateful that Ms Mac gave me the little notebook and pencil when she first brought me to Room 26, before I met Mrs Brisbane. After Ms Mac moved to Brazil, she came back to visit and brought me a brand-new notebook (although I worry about what I'll do when I fill this one up, so I write extra-extra small).

Finally, Mrs Brisbane said, 'I think we have a good list here. Now, I'm going to assign jobs for Humphreyville.'

The room was in an uproar as students called out the jobs they wanted.

'I'll be a firefighter!' said Garth.

Mandy frowned. 'I don't want to clean the dirty old streets. Or wash dishes.'

Mrs Brisbane smiled. 'These aren't exactly the kind of jobs we're going to have in Humphreyville. These will be classroom jobs, based on the real jobs in a community.' She walked over to the map, which was pulled down. 'Here's the list I've made.' She rolled the map UP-UP-UP and behind it on the blackboard was a chart with a whole list of jobs I'd never even heard of before.

'Are you paying attention, Og?' I squeaked to my neighbour. 'We're going to have new jobs!'

There was such a loud buzz in the room, Mrs Brisbane had to say 'Shush,' then 'Class!' and then 'Quiet now!' before everyone calmed down.

'Listen carefully, please,' she said. 'The jobs will rotate on a weekly basis. So whatever your job is the first week, you'll have a different job next week. If you don't get the job you want the first time, you'll have another chance at it. You'll be marked on a points system. You'll get ten points for doing a good job. I will add extra points for doing an especially good job and subtract points if you don't do a good job. Understand?'

Heads nodded 'yes' around the room and a few hands shot up. Mrs Brisbane called on Mandy.

'If we like our jobs, why can't we keep them?' Mandy asked in her whiniest voice.

'Because I think you'll learn more by switching around.'

Mrs Brisbane turned and began filling in names next to the jobs listed.

Pencil Patrol – Heidi Hopper
Paper Monitor – A.J. Thomas
Door Monitor – Kirk Chen
Blackboard Eraser – Gail Morgenstern
Energy Monitor – Art Patel
Line Monitor – Sayeh Nasiri
Plant Technician – Richie Rinaldi
Table Inspector – Mandy Payne
Animal Keeper – Miranda Golden
Teacher Assistant – Seth Stevenson
Homework Monitor – Tabitha Clark

Name after name, job after job, each one sounding more interesting than the next! Imagine erasing the blackboard at the end of every day. Or being Mrs Brisbane's actual assistant!

I was especially thrilled that Golden-Miranda was going to be in charge of Og and me because she takes such good care of us.

But not everyone was happy. Hands were raised. Kirk thought that being the door monitor sounded boring. Heidi wanted to know what a pencil patrol person did. When she heard she had to make sure the students had sharp pencils when they needed them, she didn't complain.

Mandy, on the other hand, did complain when she found out the table monitor was supposed to make sure everybody's work space was neat. 'I don't want to clean up somebody else's mess.' Mrs Brisbane explained that she didn't have to clean up the mess. She just had to give a student a written notice stating that their work space needs straightening. If someone's table didn't get straightened, she was to report that student to Mrs Brisbane.

'It's an important job,' the teacher explained. Mandy seemed satisfied.

'Any more questions?' Mrs Brisbane asked.

Art slowly raised his hand. 'What's that energy monitor job?'

'At break, lunch and the end of school, you make sure the lights are turned off to save electricity. When everybody comes back, you turn the lights on.'

'That sounds easier than being a table monitor,' Mandy argued.

'Don't worry,' the teacher replied. 'You'll all switch jobs at the end of the week. Okay, we'll start this afternoon.'

When it was time for break, my friends put on their coats and rushed outside. Pay-Attention-Art stayed behind as Mrs Brisbane had requested. Once my classmates had cleared out, she went over and sat down next to him. In her hand was Art's spelling test.

'Art, about this F –'

My heart pounded. Art got an F! F as in failure! F as in flunking! F as in family-being-really-cross if you bring home one of those on your report card!

'Art, I know maths can be a problem for you, but you've always done better with your spelling. What happened?'

Art stared down at the table and shrugged his shoulders. 'I messed up.'

'Did you study?'

'I forgot.'

F as in Forgot to study!

'You've been forgetting a lot lately. What's on your mind?'

Art shrugged his shoulders again. 'I don't know.

I just think about stuff I like.'

Mrs Brisbane examined the elaborate house that Art had built, the one with the train tracks going through it. 'Stuff like building this house?'

'Yeah. I like building things.'

'And you're good at it. Look, I know you can do better than this. If I let you retake the test tomorrow, will you study for it tonight? Otherwise, I'll have to let your parents know about this F.'

Art perked right up. 'I'll study tonight. I promise!'

Mrs Brisbane pushed back her chair and stood up. 'Don't disappoint me, Art. Tonight, what are you going to do?'

'Study!' He sounded convincing to me.

'Good,' the teacher said with a smile. 'Now why don't you get your coat and go on out to break?'

Art didn't waste any time before grabbing his coat and dashing out of the room. After he left, Mrs Brisbane stopped smiling. 'I hope you do study, Art,' she said softly.

After school, I stared at the job list I'd written down. Good thing I had, too, since Gail was such an excellent blackboard eraser that Mrs Brisbane had to stop her before she erased the list of jobs. On the other hand, Art had not exactly been a great energy monitor. He left the lights on at the end of the day. I wished he'd pay more attention.

Usually, I would have been glad the lights were on, so I could study my notebook. But I had something else on my mind. I turned to my neighbour.

'Og? Can you hear me?'

I heard the faintest splashing of water. At least I knew he was listening.

'I've been thinking about this job thing,' I squeaked.

The splashing got louder. My small hamster voice couldn't be heard over the noise so I opened my cage's lock-that-doesn't-lock. It looks like it's locked when a human closes my door, but I can easily open it from the inside. No one knows about it except Og, thank goodness! I couldn't have helped my friends and had so many adventures without that good old lock.

I scampered over to Og's house. 'Our friends have helping kinds of jobs like taking care of us. Even if we can't erase the blackboard or turn off the lights, there must be something useful we can do.'

'BOING!' Og jumped up alarmingly high.

'Mrs Brisbane didn't even think of us. So we're going to have to find jobs of our own. Real jobs, like turning off the lights.'

'BOING-BOING!' Og jumped up even higher.

'Good! You want a job, too. Is that what you're saying?'

'BOING-BOING-BOING!' My froggy friend was quite frantic, which was certainly unusual for him.

I didn't realize that he was actually trying to warn me until Aldo hurried into the room, pulling his trolley. 'What are the lights doing on? A waste of energy,' he grumbled.

My heart was thumping so loudly, Aldo could probably hear it. I couldn't let anyone discover the secret about my lock! I madly dashed back to my cage and almost made it, too, but it's hard to stay ahead of Aldo.

'Hey, buddy, hold on there!'

His big hand reached down and picked me up. 'What are you doing out of your cage? This classroom could be a dangerous place for a small fellow like you. Somebody could have squashed you or something.'

He gently placed me back in my cage and closed the door, checking to see that the lock was firmly locked. 'It seems okay,' he said. 'But just to be safe, I'll give you some extra protection.' He searched around until he found a large paperclip, which he straightened out. Then he bent it around the door of my cage.

'EEK!' I squeaked. I was *really* locked in now.

Aldo stroked his moustache thoughtfully. 'Somebody must have left your door open. I wonder who took care of you today?'

He thought for a minute, then took out a piece of paper and sat down to write a note to Mrs Brisbane. 'I'd better tell her that whoever's supposed to take care of you didn't do a very good job.'

I swallowed hard. Golden-Miranda had the job of animal keeper and no one took better care of pets than her (even if she personally owned a scary dog named Clem).

'NO-NO-NO!!' I squeaked, trying to make Aldo understand that he was making a big mistake. 'Not Miranda!'

For once, Aldo didn't get it. 'I know, pal. It must have been pretty scary being out of the cage like that. Mrs Brisbane will take care of it.' He folded the note and put it on her desk.

My stomach was bumpy and jumpy, the way it feels when I have to ride on the school bus with somebody. Aldo finished cleaning and ate his supper but I was so upset, I wasn't even interested in the carrot he offered me.

Aldo got up and pushed his trolley towards the door. 'Lights out, guys. Got to save that energy.'

After he left and the room was dark again, I squeaked to Og, 'Thanks for trying to warn me, Oggy. Next time, I'll pay more attention.'

'BOING-BOING,' he replied.

'I've got to get over to Mrs Brisbane's desk and throw that note away,' I told him. He twanged in agreement.

I went right to work on unbending the paperclip. I used my paws, my teeth (ouch) and even my tiny pencil. I wiggled it, jiggled it, pushed it and pulled it. But by the time the sun came up, I was still locked in.

I'd failed Golden-Miranda, a person who would never do anything to harm me (the same does not apply to her dog, however).

No wonder Mrs Brisbane didn't give me a real job. As a classroom hamster, I deserved an F for Forgetting-To-Pay-Attention-To-Everything-I-Was-Supposed-To-Do!

EMPLOYMENT PICTURE BRIGHT FOR HUMPHREYVILLE!

Students start a variety of jobs today.

The Humphreyville Herald

5

Miranda in Trouble

My paws were practically raw and my teeth ached from trying to remove that paperclip from my cage when I heard the doorknob turn, saw the lights come on and watched Mrs Brisbane enter.

'Morning, fellows,' she called out to us. She took off her scarf, her coat, her hat and her gloves and walked towards her desk.

Aldo's note sat squarely in the centre of her desktop. It might as well have been screaming, 'Read me! Read me!' I held my breath while she combed her hair, checked her make-up in a mirror and locked her handbag in a drawer. Then, she sat down at her desk. My whiskers drooped and my heart sank as she picked up Aldo's note and began to read.

'Oh!' she said out loud. 'Oh dear!' She studied the note for a while before walking over to my cage.

'So, Humphrey, I hear you had an adventure last night.'

'Not really,' I squeaked weakly.

'Squeaking will get you nowhere.' She bent down and examined the lock on my cage. She tested the paperclip. 'I see Aldo didn't want to take any chances.'

She turned towards Og. 'I suppose you witnessed the whole thing.'

Og stayed motionless. Good. He wasn't going to squeal – or rather croak – on me. A true friend!

Mrs Brisbane was staring down at my cage when Garth and A.J. arrived (they took the same bus and always arrived together), with Sayeh and Tabitha right behind them.

Mrs Brisbane went to the door to greet the students as they bustled in and headed for the cloakroom.

Kirk came in, then Seth, then Heidi and Gail (Heidi always waited outside until Gail got to school because they were best friends).

Next Miranda came through the door, a practically perfect person who never did anything wrong on purpose and who was about to get into BIG-BIG-BIG trouble all because of me!

I wished Ms Mac had taken me to Brazil with her.

Mrs Brisbane went about the morning routine.

First we studied the planets.

I wished I was on the planet Mars instead of in Room 26.

The teacher wrote out the words for our next spelling test. I almost fainted when she wrote the first one: TROUBLE. Trouble was something I could spell. Trouble was what I was in. Trouble was what I had caused. My paw was shaking and I wasn't able to write all the words down. I wasn't worried about next week's spelling test. I had bigger things to worry about.

I was so concerned about my troubles, I hardly noticed Paul when he came in and sat down for maths. My classmates didn't either. I did notice him when maths was over. He paused at the door and stared at the list of jobs on the board before quietly leaving the room.

The morning was almost over and Mrs Brisbane had still not mentioned the incident from the night before. Maybe she didn't believe Aldo's note. But that couldn't be, because everybody trusted Aldo and knew he wouldn't lie.

'Og, aren't you worried about Miranda?' I squeaked when the classroom was empty at break.

'BOING!' was his clear and obvious answer.

Of course he was worried.

I wished I was a frog in a glass house instead of a hamster in a cage with a stupid lock-that-doesn't-lock.

After break came the moment of truth. Except it wasn't the truth. It was all a big mistake.

Mrs Brisbane said, 'Citizens of Humphreyville, please come to order.' She spoke in her most serious and important voice.

'It is time to review the status of our community and the jobs you are all doing. As far as I can see, you all performed your duties as required yesterday, except for one of you. I'm afraid one of you neglected your responsibility and there could have been a disastrous outcome.'

My classmates were clearly surprised. I glanced at Miranda's face – so totally innocent. I had to look away.

I wondered if I could go back to live at Pet-O-Rama where I came from.

'Miranda, you were in charge of Humphrey and Og yesterday.' Suddenly, nice Mrs Brisbane turned into the unsmiling Mrs Brisbane, the way she was when I first met her.

'Yes,' Miranda answered.

'Last night, Mr Amato, the caretaker, found Humphrey out of his cage. Luckily, he hadn't fallen off the table and broken his neck and Aldo put him back in the cage and locked it. It's obvious that you weren't careful when you locked his cage yesterday.'

Miranda looked as sick as I felt.

'But I *did* lock the cage,' said Miranda. 'I remember.'

'Then how do you think Humphrey got out? Do you think someone else in this class unlocked the cage?'

Miranda looked confused. 'No, of course not.'

'It was your responsibility. In the end, you are the one who is accountable.'

Miranda was blinking hard. 'I remember locking the cage,' she said softly.

'YES SHE DID!' I squeaked loudly, desperately wishing someone could understand me just this once.

'BOING!' Og chimed in.

Mrs Brisbane ignored us. 'I want you to think about how serious this is. Humphrey might have ended up stuck behind a cabinet or even got out into the corridor. We may never have found him again. He might even have starved to death.'

My whiskers quivered and my body shivered until I remembered that I'd been out of my cage many times and none of those things had happened. In fact, I'd performed some pretty brave acts, if I do say so myself.

'In a real community, a person who doesn't do

his or her job well gets fired. I'm afraid I'm going to have to fire you, Miranda.'

'Oh no!'

Mandy's hand shot up in the air and Mrs Brisbane called on her. 'You can get fired even if you're good at your job. Like if your company closes down.'

'That's true, Mandy. That's different. Miranda is losing her job because she didn't fulfil her responsibilities,' said the teacher. 'Now, Kirk, I'll make you the animal keeper.'

Kirk made a great roaring noise, like a lion. A few kids giggled.

Mrs Brisbane did not giggle. She frowned at Kirk and continued. 'Art, you can be the door monitor. Miranda, you will get no points for this job but I will give you another chance. You can take Art's job as energy monitor. However, there will be consequences to your carelessness,' said the teacher.

I knew Mrs Brisbane wasn't a bad person. She was a good person but she was doing a bad thing.

Miranda covered her face with her hands and we could all hear her crying.

'What am I supposed to do?' asked Art.

'Pay-Attention-Art,' said Mrs Brisbane, who by now was in a very bad mood. 'You will be in charge of opening and closing the door at break, lunch and the end of the day,' she said. 'Miranda, you may go to the toilet and wash your face.'

Miranda raced out of the room, sobbing.

My heart was aching. I was afraid it was breaking. Because of me, Miranda was crying. Because of me, her mark had gone down.

I was nothing but Trouble.

Usually while my classmates eat lunch, I take a good nap. Today, I paced back and forth in my cage until Mrs Brisbane came over. 'Humphrey, let me check this lock.' Thank goodness, she unfastened the paperclip, unlocked my cage, then closed it again. She tested the door to make sure that the lock was securely fastened. As usual, it seemed to be locked.

Mrs Brisbane sighed. 'I was hoping I was wrong. I was hoping the lock was broken. It's not like Miranda to forget.'

'You are making an unsqueakable mistake!' I yelled.

The teacher chuckled. 'Obviously you agree.'

I did not!

Just then, Miranda returned. Her eyes were red from crying.

'Mrs Brisbane, I'd like to apologize,' she said.

'Thank you, Miranda. But I still have to switch

your job.'

'I know. I'd just like to say I'm sorry to you and to Humphrey. If anything ever happened to Humphrey . . .' Her eyes filled with tears again.

'Everybody makes mistakes. Let's move on from here, okay? You go on to lunch.'

Miranda nodded and went to get her lunch bag. When she returned from the cloakroom, she stopped by my cage and whispered, 'I'm so sorry, Humphrey.'

What Mrs Brisbane said was true: everybody makes mistakes. Only in this case, it was the teacher making the mistake, not Miranda. All because of ME-ME-ME.

Somehow we got through the rest of the day, although it was hard to look at Miranda with her red eyes and her shiny nose. I saw Mandy staring at her. When it was time for afternoon break, she hurried over to Miranda's table.

'I know that losing your job feels really bad. I'm sorry about it,' she told Miranda. 'Want to play tetherball with me?'

Miranda seemed surprised. She and Mandy had never been close friends, but by the time they had their coats on and were heading out of the door, they were chattering away.

Art stayed in during break to retake his spelling test. I'd been worrying about Miranda so much, I had forgotten about Art's problem. He hadn't done a good job as energy monitor, but Mrs Brisbane didn't know about that. I was worried that Art had forgotten to study for his test . . . again. I had to hide in my sleeping hut so I couldn't hear Mrs Brisbane read out the words for him. PLEASE-PLEASE-PLEASE, I thought. Please, let Art pass the test!

I couldn't hear Mrs Brisbane very well but I certainly did hear Og when he let out a long series of BOINGs. Four or five at least. I darted out in time to see Mrs Brisbane smile at Art. She was holding his test in her hands.

'A 95. Art, that's the best you've done all year. Now that I know what you're capable of doing, I expect this kind of mark from now on. Think you can do it?'

Art squinched up his face. 'I think so.'

'Just remember to study. And pay attention, okay?'

Art nodded and got out of the classroom as fast as he could.

Whew! 'Well, Og, he did it,' I told my neighbour. He took a deep and splashy dive into the water of his tank, which meant that he was feeling as happy about Art as I was.

Late that afternoon, Kirk took charge of Og and

me. In his usual clowning way, he pretended to eat a cricket before he gave it to Og, and he also made icky gagging noises when he cleaned up my poo. But he laughed, so I knew he really didn't mind.

When he was finished and the students were doing silent reading, Mrs Brisbane quietly slipped over to my cage and checked again to see that it was locked. It was . . . or at least it seemed to be.

At last, the long and difficult day was over. I was greatly relieved when Miranda waited until everyone had left the classroom and carefully turned off the lights.

They didn't come on again until Aldo arrived that night. 'Give a cheer, 'cause Aldo's here!' he said, but I wasn't feeling too cheery. I was a tiny bit cross at him for writing that note to Mrs Brisbane, although I know he meant well.

'Glad to see you back in your cage,' Aldo told me. 'It's a dangerous world out here, you know.'

After all my fur-raising adventures, I didn't need anyone to tell me that!

Aldo jiggled my cage door the way humans always do. 'Nice and snug tonight,' he said. 'I guess Mrs Brisbane got my note.'

She got his note all right.

I just hoped Miranda wasn't still crying.

The next morning, Miranda came bustling into the room with Sayeh and not only was she not crying, she was smiling! I suppose I still have a lot to learn about human behaviour. Seeing Miranda laugh made me feel a lot better. Later, though, when she passed by my cage, she looked serious again and stared at me for a few seconds.

'I'm SORRY-SORRY-SORRY!' I squeaked.

She blinked hard and turned away. For the rest of the day she didn't cry, but she was a quieter Miranda than usual.

However, my other friends were anything but quiet. They were so caught up in their jobs, it was hard for them to concentrate on anything else. In the middle of science, Heidi leaped up, grabbed a pencil out of Richie's hand and ran off to sharpen it. Mandy spent more time writing up 'Messy Table' notices than she did labelling the planets. Mrs Brisbane did her best to try to keep things under control.

When it was time for maths, Paul slipped into class as quietly as ever. Mrs Brisbane handed out homework papers and when he saw his mark, Art rolled his eyes and suddenly looked smaller than Paul. When Mrs Brisbane asked if there were any questions, Miranda's hand shot up.

'It's pretty sunny outside. I was thinking that we could probably turn off the lights for a while and save some energy.'

Usually, when somebody asks a question that's completely off the subject, Mrs Brisbane isn't too happy about it. This time she smiled. 'Well, I suppose we could do without lights for a little while. Thank you, Miranda. I'll add some extra points to your job evaluation for thinking of it.'

Miranda was more like her old golden self. That was good. But there was something else that was bad. At the end of the day, Art forgot to shut the door when he left. Mrs Brisbane called him back and told him she had to deduct two points off his job score. Art was pretty upset. 'Does this mean I don't get to take Humphrey home this weekend?'

Ah, so that's whose house I would be visiting on Friday night!

Mrs Brisbane sighed and thought it over. 'No, you can take Humphrey home *if* you remember to close the door every single time tomorrow.'

'Gee, thanks!' Art said, carefully closing the door behind him as he left.

That night, I tried to work out how I could fix things for Miranda. I was usually good at fixing things. I needed a Plan.

'Og, I have a brilliant idea!' I squeaked out loudly. 'I'll get out of my cage tonight so Mrs Brisbane will know that Miranda didn't make a mistake!'

'BOING!' said Og, then slid into the water and splashed wildly. I don't think he liked that idea. I thought it over some more.

'My gosh, you're right, Og! Kirk will get into trouble and I don't want that to happen. There've been enough kids in trouble this week.'

I stayed in my cage the whole night. Aldo came and went, cleaning, reading and eating. Everything seemed completely normal. Too bad it didn't feel that way.

HUMPHREYVILLE CITIZENS ARE REMINDED TO OBEY THE RULES

Consequences of not doing a job are highlighted.

The Humphreyville Herald

6 The Difficulty with Art

On Friday, Mrs Brisbane added up the points everyone had earned in their jobs during the first week. On the whole, my friends did well. Miranda had made up some of the points she'd lost, Heidi and Mandy lost a few points because they were over-enthusiastic about their jobs. In fact, several people weren't speaking to Mandy for handing out so many 'Messy table' notices, especially Tabitha, since all she had on her work space was a pile of sharpened pencils which Heidi had put there.

'It's not fair! I was only doing my job,' Mandy complained.

'A little too well,' said Mrs Brisbane in her grumpy voice.

A.J. got full points for handing out papers, Tabitha collected homework every single morning and Richie kept the plants watered, though there was an unfortunate puddle on the floor one day when he over-watered the plants.

'That plant needs a nappy,' Kirk joked.

Richie cleaned the water up right away and didn't lose any points.

Near the end of the day, Mrs Brisbane made job assignments for the next week. Seth would take care of Og and me. Heidi would erase the board while Gail would be the energy monitor. I could tell that Sayeh was GLAD-GLAD-GLAD to be named Mrs Brisbane's assistant and Miranda was our new table inspector. No matter what her job was, she was always thinking about me. I heard her tell Seth, 'Please be careful to check Humphrey's lock.'

Mandy grumbled when she was assigned to water the plants but I don't think anyone heard her except Og and me.

When class was over, Mrs Patel arrived to pick up Art and me. She's one of our classroom assistants and lends a hand whenever our class needs extra help . . . or cupcakes – yum yum!

'I was thinking of not letting Art take Humphrey home until after our big maths test next week,' Mrs Brisbane told her. 'Then I had an idea. Paul Fletcher has been coming into our room for maths every day, because he's so far ahead of his class.'

'Paul! He lives right across the street,' said Mrs Patel.

'I know. And I was thinking that maybe if the boys studied for the test together, it might help Art.'

'That's a great idea,' Mrs Patel answered. 'Paul hasn't been over for a long time. He and Art used to play together all the time.'

'Mum, he's a whole year younger than me,' Art protested. 'I don't play with little kids.'

'He's seven months younger than you. You used to like him a lot.'

Art stood there looking miserable. 'When I was a kid.'

'Art, you have to do something to improve your maths skills,' said Mrs Brisbane. 'I can recommend a tutor, if you like.'

'Absolutely, let's get Art some help. He's a clever boy, you know.' Mrs Patel messed up Art's hair and he made a face.

'I know,' said Mrs Brisbane. 'He's a nice boy, too.'

'You know what? I think we should invite Paul over,' said Mrs Patel. 'I bet he'd like to get to know Humphrey, too.'

YES-YES-YES, I squeaked. I wasn't exactly sure if Paul wanted to get to know me but I certainly wanted to get to know him better. And maybe, just maybe, Mrs Brisbane had a very good Plan. I like Plans a lot.

We had to climb up many, many steps to get to Art's front door. Mrs Patel wasn't much bigger than Art, so they each took one end of my cage and carried me up that way. They had trouble keeping my cage level, which meant I was sliding around like those ice skaters on Dobbs's Pond, except I'll bet they were more graceful than I was. I tried to grab onto something: my ladder, my wheel, the edge of my cage, but as soon as I reached out, the cage would tilt and I'd slide in the opposite direction.

'Hang on, Humphrey. We're almost there,' said Art.

I was too weak to squeak.

Somehow, we got into the house where I was put down on a table – more like banged down on a table – and Mrs Patel took the blanket off my cage. 'Sorry, Humphrey. We did our best.' She turned to Art. 'Why don't you straighten his cage out?'

Art bent down and laughed. 'It looks like a tornado hit it.'

Mrs Patel peered in at me with sympathetic eyes. She reminded me of Ms Mac for a second. 'Are you okay, Humphrey?'

She opened the cage door and gently took me out. This was a woman who knew how to handle hamsters. She stroked me gently with one finger while Art straightened out my bedding and put everything back where it belonged.

'I think I'll have to find a special treat for our guest,' said Art's mum. 'Then we'll call Paul.'

Art leaned down and glumly stared at me. 'Humphrey, I had a big surprise for you. We were going to have a lot of fun. Now I have to sit around and do maths with Know-It-All-Paul.'

'Who?' I squeaked.

'That's what some of the kids in the playground call him. Once, I think they made him cry. I suppose he can't help being clever but I wish he wouldn't ruin my weekend.'

Mrs Patel came back in with a big juicy strawberry for me. 'I called Paul's mum and she said he'd *love* to come over tomorrow.'

Art acted as if he'd just lost his best friend. He seemed so unhappy, I couldn't even eat my strawberry. I hid it in my shavings and saved it for later.

In the evening, Mr Patel came home from work. He was a kind man in a grey suit and he said I was a handsome gerbil. Art was paying attention for once and he told his father that I am a hamster. Mr Patel nodded and said, 'A handsome *hamster*. Do you know how to take proper care of him?'

Art showed him the guide that goes with my cage whenever I go home with students on weekends. Within minutes, Mr Patel was reading the booklet from cover to cover.

'Very interesting,' he said.

A few minutes and several pages later he added, 'We must plan some stimulating activities for Humphrey.'

Stimulating activities! I liked the sound of it. I jumped on my wheel and started spinning like crazy.

'He's certainly active for a nocturnal creature,' Art's dad commented.

'Can I take him to my room?'

'I don't think you should move that cage around too much.'

'I'll hold him.' Art opened the door to my cage.

'And you won't let him get away? I understand hamsters are quick and crafty creatures.' Art's dad was a pretty clever guy.

'I promise.' Art picked me up and held me with both hands – gently but firmly.

'Come on, Humphrey. Wait till I show you my surprise,' said Art, heading down a long hallway.

In some ways, Art's room was like most rooms I've seen. A bedroom is basically a square box with windows and a bed. Sometimes there's a desk or a dresser. Art's room had all those things. In another way, his room was unlike any room I ever imagined because just about every single inch was covered with tracks and bridges and houses and TRAINS-TRAINS-TRAINS! Not big trains but very small trains. There were open wagons and passenger carriages and carriages I don't even know about because I'd only seen trains in pictures.

There was a big circle of track in the middle of the room with a bridge going across it. In the centre of the circle was a town with houses and trees. On the edge of the town, there was a red-and-white tent and a big wheel.

'What do you think, Humphrey?' Art asked as he cupped me in his hands and let me look around.

'It's unsqueakably sensational!'

'See that lake?' Art pointed to a pool of actual water near the big wheel. 'That's Lake Patel.'

'Unsqueakably brilliant!' I shouted.

'Ever since I got the train set for my birthday, it's all I can think about. I'm going to have a town and an amusement park – see, there's a ferris wheel and I'm going to put in a roller-coaster and maybe a zoo. Isn't it great?'

'GREAT-GREAT-GREAT!' I squealed.

It *was* great. But now I knew why Art wasn't paying attention in class and why he was doodling all the time. *This* was what he was thinking about. I could see why. This world he'd created was Fun with a capital F.

Maybe this fun was also causing Art to fail?

Which didn't seem fair, because you should be able to have fun without failing.

Paul wasn't failing but he didn't act like he was having a lot of fun, either.

This was all very confusing for a small hamster. But when a human has a problem, I always try my best to help, especially if that human is a friend.

Later that night, I was back in my cage and Art was back in his room, probably working on his train layout. I was spinning on my wheel when I heard Art's parents talking.

'We have to do something. His marks are falling every day,' Art's mum said.

Art's dad thought for a while and replied. 'I don't understand it. He's always been a bright boy. What does his teacher say?'

'She suggested a tutor. I think it's a good idea, even though I'm not sure all the tutors in the world would make Art pay attention in class.'

'It's that train,' Art's dad said firmly. 'I think we'll have to take it away from him. Once he started with that, his marks went down.'

I stopped spinning. It made me SAD-SAD-SAD to think of Art losing the train set he loved so much.

Art's mum sighed. 'I hate to, but we may have to.'

The Patels sat in silence for a while. Then Art's mum said, 'Paul Fletcher is coming over tomorrow. Mrs Brisbane suggested he might help Art with his maths.'

'Paul? Isn't he a year below Art?'

'Sure is. I think he's a maths wizard. He comes into Art's class for maths every day.'

'I hope it helps,' said Art's dad. 'Those two were best friends when they were little. What happened?'

'I don't know. Art seems to think Paul's too young for him to play with. But he's only seven months younger!'

The Patels both chuckled about that. Soon, they went to bed and the house was quiet.

I had all night to think of a Plan. Somehow, I had to put two and two together to get Art back on track with his maths . . . and with his old friend, Paul.

'Look who's here,' Mrs Patel announced the next afternoon when the doorbell rang. Paul stood in the hallway, holding his maths book. 'Come on, Art!'

Mrs Patel took Paul's coat and hung it in the hall

cupboard, while she asked him how he was, how his parents were and how school was going. Finally, Art came into the room. He wasn't smiling.

'Hi, Paul.'

'Hi, Art.'

They stared at each other for a second. 'Come and say hi to our house guest,' said Mrs Patel, leading the boys towards my cage.

I jumped up on my ladder and squeaked, 'HI-HI-HI!'

'It's Humphrey,' said Paul. He was almost smiling, I think.

'That's right. I think you know him from coming into Room 26 for maths,' said Mrs Patel. 'And speaking of maths, why don't you boys settle in the kitchen to study? I'll make some hot chocolate.'

Neither of them moved.

'Art,' said Mrs Patel, 'take Paul to the kitchen.'

Art grudgingly led Paul to the kitchen and out of my sight.

I could hear Art's mum say, 'Here's your hot chocolate, guys. Now, you know how to study together?'

'I thought we could work out a few problems together,' Paul said.

Art didn't answer. I heard papers shuffling. I heard Paul mumbling and Art mumbling but it was pretty clear there wasn't all that much happening in the kitchen.

Mr and Mrs Patel were down in the basement. I heard her say something about 'organizing the boxes'.

I could hear occasional sounds from the kitchen. Once, when Paul made a suggestion to Art, I heard a piece of paper being crumpled up. 'I don't get it. I'm not like you – some kind of genius.'

Paul quietly said he wasn't a genius. He just liked maths.

'I hate numbers. They're just squiggles on paper. They don't mean anything!' Art burst out.

Then things were VERY, VERY, VERY quiet.

I had my Plan but it was risky. The last time I'd left my cage, I'd caused some Big Trouble, especially for my friend Miranda. Still, I felt I had to take a chance in order to help Art. After all, he was my friend, too.

So I opened my good old lock-that-doesn't-lock, grabbed onto the table leg and slid down to the nice soft carpeting. I quickly darted under the table to make sure that no one was around. I could hear the boys in the kitchen and I hadn't heard Art's parents since they went down into the basement.

I took a big huge breath and scampered across the living room, turned left at the hallway and ran straight back to Art's room. Thank goodness, the door was open or my Plan would have ended right then and there.

The maze of train tracks looked much different from a hamster's point of view. There were many tracks going this way and that way and a string of colourful carriages attached to a big, shiny engine.

My Plan was a simple one, as most good plans are. I thought the boys would eventually realize that I'd got out of my cage. They'd search for me and end up in Art's room. When Paul saw Art's amazing train layout, they'd start working on it together and remember how much they'd liked being friends a few years ago. Art would be willing to let Paul help him with maths and his marks would go up. We'd all live happily ever after! (Except Miranda, of course. I was still feeling guilty about getting her into trouble.)

Maybe it wasn't such a simple Plan after all.

It was taking the boys a long time to discover that I was missing. I realized it could take them hours. Or possibly, they'd never notice that I was missing at all. I yearned for my comfy cage that offered so many fun things to do, like spinning on my wheel, climbing my tree branch, swinging from my ladder or dozing in my sleeping hut.

I was feeling sleepy right then and I saw a bed that was exactly my size. It wasn't really a bed, just an open wagon on the train. I scurried over to it and was easily able to pull myself up the side and settle down inside. Yes, it fitted me perfectly and what a thrill it was for me to be sitting in a train for the first time in my life! Ahead of me was a tank wagon made of gleaming metal. Ahead of that was a passenger carriage with tiny plastic people looking out of the windows. And in front was the powerful engine with a whistle on top!

I was too excited to take a nap. Instead, I stretched my paws and, as I did, I hit some kind of switch or lever. I didn't have time to see what it was because when I touched it, the train lurched forward and began to move around the track.

Once I realized I was going on a train trip, I decided to sit back and enjoy it. I loved the way the train's wheels went clickety-clack on the track and the way it travelled in a wide curve past the general store and the tall pine trees. The train picked up speed and I could feel the breeze in my fur. Everything went dark – completely dark – for a long time (at least it seemed long). A tunnel! I hadn't seen that coming.

When I came out at the other end, the train veered left and began to climb UP-UP-UP. I could look straight down on the roof of the general store and the tops of the tall pine trees. That Art was certainly clever to be able to build a bridge.

The train stopped climbing and moved across

the straight centre of the bridge. The pine trees looked small from what felt like the top of the world. But straight ahead, what I saw was Trouble! As the train started down the incline on the other side of the bridge, the bright, shiny engine tumbled off the side, pulling the passenger carriage with its tiny people off the edge and then the shiny metal tank wagon. I was certain I was headed for a huge fall and as I glanced down, I saw that I was going to land right in the middle of Lake Patel!

HUMPHREY SPENDS WEEKEND WITH ART!

Classroom pet makes his first visit to Patel house.

The Humphreyville Herald

7

Test Distress

My whole (short) life flashed before me: my days at Pet-O-Rama, Ms Mac bringing me to Room 26, the days when Mrs Brisbane was out to get me, the day Og arrived and the faces of all the friends I'd helped since I'd come to Longfellow School.

'Help!' I squeaked.

I heard the muffled voices of Art and Paul.

'Maybe he's in here!'

'How'd he get out of his cage?'

'I don't know . . . he just did!'

'Hurry, please!' I squeaked, because I was hanging from the bridge by one paw and I was getting TIRED-TIRED-TIRED. The cool waters of Lake Patel would have seemed inviting to Og, but hamsters are not especially fond of swimming. In fact, we're desert creatures, a fact I never knew until Richie did a report on hamsters.

'I hear him!' Art shouted.

There were sounds of footsteps as Art and Paul rushed into the room.

'Oh no! The train fell off the bridge again,' Art exclaimed.

'There he is!' said Paul. He raced forward and I dropped into his hands as gently as falling into a nice warm pile of bedding.

I must admit, I was quivering and shivering a bit but I relaxed as Paul stroked me with his finger. 'It's okay, Humphrey. You're safe now.'

I looked up and saw Art staring at his train layout: the bridge, the lake, the carriages and wagons lying in a heap. 'I don't understand why it always falls off. And how'd he get the train going in the first place?'

'How'd he get out of his cage?' Paul asked.

These were not questions I was about to answer.

Holding me in his hands, Paul kneeled down to inspect the train layout. 'Wow, this is awesome! Did you do this all by yourself?'

'Yeah.' Art sounded proud. 'And I have lots more I want to do.'

'So that's what you're always doodling. It's really cool.'

'Thanks.'

'About that bridge . . .' said Paul, handing me to Art.

'It looks okay,' Art replied. 'But every time, the train tumbles off the edge. Gee, Humphrey could have been hurt. The fall could have killed him. Or he could have drowned!'

'He's safe now,' Paul reminded him.

'I'm a loser,' Art said quietly. 'I'm sorry, Humphrey.'

'No problem,' I squeaked softly. But it was a problem. I'd been one whisker away from plunging into – yikes – a lake! (Believe me, hamsters should NEVER-NEVER-NEVER get wet.)

Paul got down on his hands and knees, examining the bridge. 'I think I see the problem.'

'You do?' Art knelt down next to Paul.

'You don't have the same number of each sized support on each side. See? They look almost alike but they're slightly different sizes.'

Art did. 'That's weird. It looks even.'

'It's just enough to throw the train off. I'm pretty sure that's the problem if you measure them. Let's get Humphrey back in his cage and we can work on it.'

'You really think you can fix it?' said Art.

'*You* can fix it,' Paul replied. 'It's all a matter of measurement.'

'See, numbers are always my problem!' Art pretended to smack himself on the forehead.

'They aren't just squiggles on paper?'

'I get the point,' Art admitted. 'Can you stay a while longer?'

'Sure, I can stay.'

Luckily, when the boys put me back in my cage, they brought it into Art's room so I could watch what they were doing.

'I'll measure the supports and count them to make sure we have the same number of each.' Art got out a ruler and went to work.

'We'll need two of each size,' said Paul. 'And I think you have a problem with this curve over here.'

'I have accidents there all the time,' said Art.

'The turn is too sharp for the length of the engine. We'll need to extend it,' said Paul. 'I'll help you work out the angle.'

I crawled into my sleeping hut for a nice long doze. I woke up when I heard a train whistle. By the time I was out of my hut, the train was climbing towards the bridge. I gulped as it chugged along the top, remembering how high it was when I'd been riding in that wagon.

'Keep your fingers crossed,' said Paul as the train approached the downward slope of the bridge.

I must admit, though I've done some brave things in my short life, I closed my eyes. I couldn't stand the sight of that train plunging off the tracks again.

I waited for the crash but instead I heard the guys cheering. When I opened my eyes, Art and Paul were high-fiving one another. 'We did it!' said Art.

'Good job,' said Paul.

Mrs Patel appeared in the doorway, smiling. 'What's going on in here?' she asked.

'Paul helped me fix the train,' said Art.

'Art did all the work,' said Paul.

'That's great! But how about the maths?'

'We studied for a while,' Paul said.

'I don't quite get it yet. Could you – I mean, would you help me some more?' Art asked Paul.

'Sure,' Paul quickly replied.

'Tell you what. I'll call your mum and see if you can stay for supper,' Art's mum suggested. The boys thought it was a great idea.

'First, maybe you could clean up in here?' Mrs Patel suggested.

Soon, Art's train layout looked neat and the extra track was put away.

'We'd better take Humphrey back to the living room,' said Art, picking up my cage.

'Say, how'd he get out of that thing, anyway?' asked Paul.

'Maybe I wasn't paying attention when I closed it,' said Art. 'But it's not the first time. Miranda got into a lot of trouble when Humphrey got out the last time. Mrs Brisbane might not let her take him home again.'

Never, ever again? My whiskers wilted when I heard that news.

Paul seemed surprised. 'Miranda? That doesn't sound right. Let me check that lock.'

Art put the cage down and Paul bent down and checked my cage door. My whiskers quivered. I was nervous because Paul was a smart kid. He might actually uncover the secret of my lock-that-doesn't-lock.

'Looks fine to me,' he said and I breathed a sigh of relief.

But I only felt relieved for a while. After I was back in the living room and the boys were off studying, I wasn't thinking about trains or numbers or even the fact that I had narrowly escaped a disastrous accident.

I was thinking about Miranda and the trouble I'd caused her. Mrs Brisbane had said there would be 'consequences to her carelessness'. Miranda was suffering the consequences but the carelessness was all mine.

Paul ended up staying for supper *and* spending the night *and* studying with Art on Sunday. In the afternoon, Art's dad told them he thought they needed a break and the three of them went into Art's room to work on the train layout. They were in there a LONG-LONG-LONG time. Finally, they came out with big smiles on their faces.

'Humphrey, we have a surprise for you,' said Art. He opened the door to my cage.

Surprises are sometimes nice things, like birthday parties or an especially juicy strawberry. Surprises can also be scary things, like being snowed in and hungry, or strange things, like suddenly having a frog as a next-door neighbour. So, as Art carefully picked me up and took me out of my cage, I had a queasy, uneasy feeling all over.

With Mr Patel and Paul following him, Art carried me down the hallway to his room.

'It's all finished!' he said.

I peered over the edge of Art's hand. The train layout was amazing! The town now had streets and even street lights, along with the houses and trees. Between the red-and-white tent and the big wheel were an elephant and a clown. It looked like a real town, although I could have done without the lake or the dark tunnel.

'Everything's working now,' Art said. 'So we thought you'd like a real train ride.'

Sometimes humans imagine that they know what you're thinking. *I* was thinking I could skip riding a train ever again!

'We tested it with a weight to make sure that the car won't tip over with you in it,' said Paul.

'Maybe Humphrey doesn't want a ride. Did you think of that?' asked Mr Patel.

Art placed me in the open wagon. 'He's the one who had the idea in the first place.'

Paul pushed the switch and said, 'All aboard!'

I clenched my paws along the side of the wagon as the train started chug-chugging down the track and around the wide curve, past the town, the general store and the tall pine trees. The train picked up speed just as it entered the tunnel. It was dark but I didn't mind this time. In fact, I would have been happy to stay in the tunnel for ever, as long as I could avoid that bridge. All too soon, it was light again and the train began its climb.

As soon as it hit the straight bridge, it picked up speed again. I tried not to look down, but I couldn't help taking a peek. Lake Patel was right below me, looking dangerously wet. At least Paul and Art and Mr Patel were there to catch me – I hoped! All of a sudden, the train dropped and headed down the incline. I closed my eyes tightly. The speed of the train created a strong wind in my fur. I opened my eyes. The train had almost reached the bottom of the incline now and it hadn't tumbled off the tracks! I was safe.

The train veered around another curve, around

the back of Lake Patel. Whee! This was one fun ride! Suddenly, the train began to slow DOWN-DOWN-DOWN.

'Coming into the station,' Paul announced.

'Don't stop now!' I squeaked. 'Once more around!'

'I think he likes it,' said Art. Boy, he was really paying attention now! So around I went, not once, not twice, but three more times. It was thrilling, chilling and I was perfectly willing to keep going around for ever. Then Art's dad said it was time to stop or I might feel sick.

I must admit, when the train stopped I felt a little strange. Once I was back in my sleeping hut, my head stopping spinning and I began to write in my notebook, trying to find the words to describe my wild ride.

A train
Makes your brain
Click and clack
Around the track.
And even when the train is slowing,
Your brain just keeps on GO-GO-GOING.

My brain kept going round and round that track all night. The next morning, when we got back to school, I couldn't wait to tell Og about my exciting adventure. But as soon as I saw Miranda come into class, I was squeakless because of that hurt look in her eyes every time she glanced at my cage.

The look that had my brain hurting.

The look that made me remember the Trouble all over again.

*

My mind was a million miles away until it was time for maths and Paul came into the room. I realized that while Art and Paul had studied hard for the test, I had not.

The test was HARD-HARD-HARD! My friends wrote and stared at their papers and stared at the ceiling, erasing and sighing. Seth sat amazingly still, glancing over at my cage now and then. Miranda did more erasing than writing, which was strange for her. Paul wrote quickly while Art seemed to struggle. He kept running his fingers through his hair but his eyes were right on his paper.

Art was paying attention. But did he understand the maths?

At last, Mrs Brisbane called 'time' and collected the papers. When Paul got up to leave, he whispered something to Art. Art nodded his head.

'I will mark these during break,' said Mrs Brisbane. 'I know you're all anxious to know your marks.'

Soon, my friends raced outside to play.

I, on the other paw, stayed inside, watching our teacher mark the papers and feeling about as worried as a hamster can feel.

Mrs Brisbane worked quickly. Sometimes she smiled. Sometimes she frowned and made a lot of marks on the paper. Sometimes she shook her head.

I was gnawing my toes, wondering what marks my classmates were getting, especially Art.

The bell rang again. Break was over and the students burst in through the door, all red-cheeked and excited.

Once they were settled, Mrs Brisbane said, 'Class, I'm not quite finished. If you'll take out your social studies books and read the chapter on how communities are organized, starting on page 75, I'll keep on marking. All right with you?'

Mandy sighed loudly. Mrs Brisbane ignored her.

'How many more do you have to mark?' Heidi asked.

'Heidi . . . what are you supposed to do before you talk?'

Heidi raised her hand.

'Thank you. I think I'll be finished by the time you've all read Chapter Ten.'

I don't have a social studies book so I continued to watch Mrs Brisbane and nibble at my toes. Og dived into the water for a long, splashy swim. He was probably worried about the tests, too.

Just when I thought I'd have no toes left at all, Mrs Brisbane stood up.

'Class, I've finished marking the maths papers and I'm pleased to say that all around, I've seen improvement. In fact, most of your marks have gone up.'

She began to pass out the tests. One by one, I could tell what marks my friends had got from the expressions on their faces.

Sayeh – 100 per cent, of course.

Paul – 100 per cent, of course. Paul smiled, then glanced at Art, obviously worried about his friend.

Seth broke into a broad grin and made a V-for-victory sign with his fingers as he turned to Tabitha. She seemed happy, too.

For the most part, friends like A.J., Garth, Richie, Heidi and Gail looked relieved when they got their papers. I was holding my breath as Mrs Brisbane handed Art his test.

'Good work,' she said. 'I knew you could do it.'

How do I describe the look on Art's face? Glowing? Gleaming? Beaming? As happy as he looked when he viewed his beautiful train layout? All I can say he was HAPPY-HAPPY-HAPPY and when Paul saw him smile, he beamed, too.

For once, Art had paid attention and his attention had paid off.

The only person who was extremely unhappy was Mandy. She actually put her head down on her table.

'Mandy, we can talk during lunch break,' said Mrs Brisbane.

Soon the lunch bell rang and all my friends raced out of the door – except for Mandy.

Mrs Brisbane sat down next to her. 'I'm sorry, Mandy. Do you know what happened?'

Mandy lifted her head. She looked as miserable as Miranda did the day she got into trouble. 'I don't know. I studied. But –'

She flung her head back down on the table.

Mrs Brisbane looked sad, too. 'Would you like to retake the test? I could give you another chance later in the week.'

Slowly, Mandy raised her head. 'If I do better, can I take Humphrey home this weekend?' she asked.

'Yes, if you can get one of your parents to sign the form.'

Mandy let out a huge sigh. 'I'll take the test again. And I'll get that paper signed.'

'Good. Now, is there something about these problems you don't understand?'

Mandy slowly shook her head. 'I just had trouble concentrating.'

Mrs Brisbane dismissed her so she could go and eat her lunch.

I was too upset to eat. I hopped on my wheel and went for a spin.

MATHS TEST PROVES TO BE BIG
CHALLENGE FOR HUMPHREYVILLE

'With a few exceptions, most students did well,' Mrs Brisbane reports.

The Humphreyville Herald

8 Double Trouble

Trouble. Rhymes with Double. Believe me, I was thinking about Double Trouble that night.

Art's good mark in the maths test was cause for celebration.

Art becoming friends with Paul was cause for celebration.

Seth sitting still (or at least not popping up out of his chair every few seconds) was cause for celebration.

But I had not done one thing to help Miranda, whom I had got into trouble. And now Mandy clearly was having some kind of trouble I didn't understand.

Lately I'd been spinning more to keep my mind off my friends' troubles. I was spinning so much, I wasn't eating all the food I had stored away in various places in my cage (all hamsters know that it's a good idea to have some food stashed away in case of emergency).

'Og, being a classroom pet may not be an important job, but it's not an easy one either,' I squeaked to my neighbour. 'Because we've got to try and keep all our friends out of trouble.'

'BOING-BOING!' he twanged back at me.

He's a very wise frog.

'I'm worried about Miranda,' I breathlessly explained, without stopping my wheel.

'BOING!' Og did a giant leap.

'And I'm worried about Mandy,' I said.

'BOING-BOING!' Og jumped up and down twice. I knew he was worried about Mandy as well.

'And I can't think of one single thing to do that would help either one of them, can you?'

From Og: silence. This was not a good sign.

I got out my notebook and decided to make a Plan. To make a Plan, it helps to make a list. So I wrote:

PLAN TO HELP MIRANDA
1.

I stared at that '1' and I stared some more. No matter how hard I stared at it, I couldn't think of anything to write. The only way I could help Miranda would be to prove to Mrs Brisbane and the whole class that she didn't leave my door unlocked. And the only way I could prove that was to let everyone see that my lock-didn't-lock. Which meant that someone would put a new lock on my cage and I'd never be able to get out again. I wouldn't be able to have any more exciting adventures and more importantly, it would be a lot harder for me to help my friends.

I closed my notebook and went into my sleeping hut. I couldn't sleep because every time I closed my eyes, I saw Miranda's face in front of me.

I couldn't stand that for long, so I crawled out of my sleeping hut and went over to the side of the cage closest to Og.

'I tried to make a Plan, but I didn't get far.'

Og sat there like the lumpy, bumpy frog he is and blinked his eyes.

'That is, the only Plan I can think of would mean I'd be locked in my cage for ever.'

Og sat as motionless as the rock he was sitting on.

'Well, you must have some ideas!' I was practically pleading with him now.

He didn't even look at me. But I'd learned an interesting fact in science class. Frogs can see all around them without moving their heads because they have 360-degree vision. That's good because they don't have much in the way of necks.

'I know you can see me, Og. And I know you can hear me, even though you don't have any ears that I can see. Are you ignoring me?'

It appeared that he was.

'Are you trying to think of a Plan, too?'

Og jumped up and let out a very loud 'BOING!'

I was so startled, I jumped backwards and hit my head on my wheel.

Our strange conversation – which to humans would sound like a golden hamster squeaking and a green frog twanging – ended abruptly when the door handle rattled, the lights came on and Aldo pushed his trolley into the room.

'I'm baaaack,' Aldo said. His greeting didn't sound as warm and cheery as usual. In fact, he parked his trolley in front of my cage and let out a loud yawn.

'Sorry, fellows, I'm kind of tired tonight. I've been studying and writing papers and working and – aw, you don't want to hear about my problems, do you?'

'YES-YES-YES!' I squeaked. Because if your friends won't listen to your problems, who will?

Aldo pulled up a chair and took out his supper. He yawned again. 'I've been working and studying more than I'm sleeping, I suppose. I'm knocked out.'

After he chewed his sandwich in silence for a few

minutes, he opened his bag. 'Whoa, I must be tired. I almost forgot, Humphrey. Here's a tomato, thanks to Aldo Amato.'

It was a perfect plump cherry tomato, the kind that usually makes my whiskers wiggle with joy. But I'd been thinking so much about my problems, I didn't feel much like eating.

'Thanks,' I squeaked. Aldo didn't notice that I was unusually quiet because he was yawning again.

'You know, guys, I think I'll take a short nap. I'll work twice as fast if I can just rest my eyes for a few minutes, right?'

To my amazement, Aldo rolled up his jacket, sat in a chair and using the jacket as a pillow, put his head on the table and closed his eyes.

He was sound asleep in a matter of seconds. He really must have been tired!

It was quiet in Room 26 with only the TICK-TICK-TICK of the clock (which I couldn't hear in the daytime) counting off each second.

'Do you think he'll sleep for a long time?' I squeaked to Og. 'After all, he has work to do.'

Og dived into the water and went for a swim. Big help he was.

Aldo looked peaceful, dozing there. Still the hands of the clock kept moving round and round. Fifteen minutes, twenty minutes, thirty minutes. At one point, Aldo moved. Good! He was waking up! But instead, he rolled his head to the other side and kept on sleeping.

'Og, how many rooms do you think he has to clean?' I asked. After all, Aldo had a big responsibility, getting all the rooms in Longfellow School clean each night. Classrooms have a way of getting messy, with squashed crayons, crushed chalk and lots of scuff marks on the floor.

Og splashed again as he climbed back onto his rock. When I glanced over, I saw he was staring down at Aldo, too.

'I wouldn't want him to lose his job.' I knew how terrible Miranda felt when she lost her job.

Og let out a big twangy 'BOING!'

Aldo didn't move a muscle. He was really sound asleep.

I checked the clock. Aldo had been sleeping for one hour! At this rate, I wasn't sure he could get his job done, at least not as well as he usually did it.

'We'd better wake him,' I squeaked to Og.

I took my friend's silence to mean 'yes'.

'On the count of three, okay, Oggy? One . . . two . . . three!'

Og and I let loose with a series of SQUEAKS and BOINGS that was quite amazing . . . even alarming! Aldo remained fast asleep. How else could one small hamster and one small frog wake up their sleeping friend?

Then I remembered something that was BAD-BAD-BAD. However, in this case, it might turn out to be GOOD-GOOD-GOOD.

Once when I was riding on the bus home with Lower-Your-Voice-A.J, Mean Martin Bean, the bus bully, told him to be quiet. When A.J. kept talking, Martin took some paper, wadded it up into a little ball and put it in his mouth to wet it. Then he threw it and hit A.J. in the neck.

'Yuck!' A.J. had said, rubbing his neck.

That wad of wet paper had made an impression and I thought of a Plan.

I gathered together some of my bedding material, which is shredded paper, and tried to mould it into a ball. Being a clean and sanitary hamster, I wasn't going to put the stuff in my mouth. Instead, I went to my water bottle and tapped it so that a few drops trickled down onto the paper until I was able to shape it into a ball.

I worked it between my paws until it was as round and smooth as a ball. I went to the side of my cage and looked down at Aldo, who was sleeping peacefully.

Then I had a terrible thought. I was a small hamster, after all. How could I be sure I could throw the ball so it would hit Aldo on the neck and wake him up? I'd have to throw it with all my might. Even though I was strong from spinning on my wheel and climbing ladders and tree branches, I was tiny compared to Aldo.

Then I remembered GRAVITY. Mrs Brisbane had explained gravity to us in science (she is an excellent teacher). Gravity is a force that pulls things towards the ground. It's the reason we don't float above the ground all the time (which might be fun for a while but not all the time). I realized I would have the power of gravity on my side. The ball would naturally go down. And if I aimed it correctly and put my full force behind it, I should be able to wake Aldo up.

I stopped to think about what I was doing. It was wrong for Martin to throw that spitball at A.J. Could it be wrong to help Aldo keep his job?

I explained my mission to Og. 'I'm ready to fire on Aldo and wake him up. Do you think it's a good idea?'

'BOING-BOING-BOING-BOING-BOING!'

I think he was agreeing.

Making sure I could clear the bars on my cage, I concentrated on a small portion of Aldo's neck and let loose.

The ball slammed downwards, directly towards Aldo's neck. I crossed my paws, hoping this would work.

Bingo! That paper ball hit him square in the neck! His hand went up to rub the spot and best of all, his eyes opened.

'Hmmm?' he mumbled sleepily.

He sat up and glanced at the clock. '*Mamma mia*, I've been asleep for an hour!'

Aldo leaped to his feet and grabbed his broom. 'I thought I'd just nap for a few minutes. You guys should have woken me up! If I lose this job, I won't be able to afford to go to school.'

Sometimes humans don't give credit where credit is due. But all I cared about was Aldo keeping his job.

'Whew! I'm going to have to hustle to get all my work done. I do feel better now.'

Aldo pushed his broom around the room like an artist painting a masterpiece (we saw a great film showing a famous artist at work – I like seeing films in class). He missed the spitball on the floor but at least he didn't notice it. Whew! He finished cleaning the room in half his usual time.

'Got to run, guys. Catch you tomorrow night!' he said as he raced out of the door with his trolley.

Og and I sat in silence for a while, listening to the clock TICK-TICK-TICKing away.

'I'm really glad that worked,' I finally squeaked.

Og jumped so high, he hit the cover of his glass house and almost popped the top.

'BOING-BOING!' he twanged.

For once, I knew exactly what he meant. Even

though I'd kept Aldo out of trouble, I had a lot more work to do.

LONGFELLOW CARETAKER ATTENDS LOCAL COLLEGE!

Aldo Amato says the extra hours of studying will be well worth it once he becomes a teacher.

The Humphreyville Herald

9 Too Much Payne

While I'd been worrying about everybody's troubles, my classmates kept working on Humphreyville. One day, they all left to go on a field trip to the town hall. How Og and I would have loved to go along! When they came back, Tabitha, Seth and Richie made a model park with swings and a slide, a baseball field and lots of trees. Tabitha must have made dozens of paper leaves for those trees!

At the same time, Gail and A.J. built a court house with pillars made out of the cardboard tubes from the middle of paper towels (Mrs Brisbane always keeps plenty of paper towels near my cage).

Garth, Art and Heidi made a school out of plastic blocks. It had a playground, too! Humphreyville would certainly be a fun place to live, with two playgrounds in it.

I wasn't sure what Miranda and Sayeh were

working on, but they kept looking over at me and giggling. In fact, their giggling made me uncomfortable. The more they giggled, the more I wiggled and that made them laugh even more. I was glad to see that Miranda was feeling better.

I wished *I* felt better.

I felt especially bad when, on Tuesday, Mrs Brisbane suggested that Paul spend some time helping Mandy study for the maths test she was going to retake.

'Know-It-All-Paul?' she blurted out. 'He's just a baby!'

'Is not!!!' a voice called out.

Art had actually jumped out of his seat and his fists were clenched, though I don't think he was the type to hit anybody.

Paul looked as if someone had already punched him in the stomach.

Mrs Brisbane wasn't happy. 'Sit down, Art. Now, Mandy, that was cruel and uncalled for. I demand that you apologize right now.'

Mandy hung her head. 'I'm sorry,' she said. 'Paul's so clever, he makes me feel stupid.'

'You are not stupid, Mandy. No one in this class is stupid! Now, I want you and Paul to sit at the back of the room and go over your test together while the rest of us work on some other problems.'

This time, Mandy didn't complain. She and

Paul sat at the back of the room. He went over her paper and quietly talked to her about it. Sometimes she seemed puzzled. Sometimes she nodded her head. By the time the maths class was over, she and Paul both looked happier.

On Thursday, during morning break, Mandy took her maths test again. She worked HARD-HARD-HARD, sometimes tugging at her hair and sometimes sticking the tip of her tongue out a little (I do that, too, when I'm concentrating). She worked through the whole break period and then, with a loud sigh, handed her paper to Mrs Brisbane.

'I'll mark it right now if you like, Mandy.'

'Okay, but I probably didn't do any better.'

'You studied, didn't you?'

'Yes.'

'Do you want to stay while I mark it?' Mrs Brisbane asked.

'Yes please,' said Mandy.

Mrs Brisbane took the test to her desk. Og didn't move a muscle, but I nervously gnawed on my paws. The teacher's pencil made some marks on the first page and a few on the second page. On the third page, her pencil didn't even move.

Mandy sat with her head down on the table. She couldn't stand to watch Mrs Brisbane mark her test.

Finally, Mrs Brisbane stood up. 'You got 85 per cent, Mandy. That's a good solid B. Maybe even a

B plus. Congratulations!'

Mandy had a smile on her face that I'd never seen before. 'An 85!'

'Yes. You must have studied. And maybe Paul helped a little?'

'He did,' said Mandy. 'I'll thank him. And I have something else.' She reached into her pocket and pulled out a somewhat crumpled piece of paper. 'The permission slip to bring Humphrey home. My dad finally signed it.'

Mrs Brisbane walked over and took the paper and examined it carefully. 'Well, this is a good day for you, Mandy. Your maths mark went up and you'll be taking Humphrey home this weekend. Now, you have to promise me one thing.'

'What's that?' asked Mandy.

'That you'll never say you're stupid again. And that you won't ever call people names.'

'I promise,' said Mandy.

I felt so happy, I jumped on my wheel and spun like crazy. I heard a giant splash and knew that Og was taking a swim because he was GLAD-GLAD-GLAD too.

For a while, I'd forgotten the Trouble. I even chewed some Nutri-Nibbles and yoghurt drops I'd been saving. Yum!

That afternoon, Mrs Brisbane called Miranda and Sayeh up to the front of the room. 'Why don't you two tell the class about the surprise you've been working on?'

Sayeh and Miranda smiled at one another. Miranda had something wrapped in a cloth which she put on Mrs Brisbane's desk.

'In most communities, people honour whoever the town is named after by putting up a statue,' said Sayeh in her clear, soft voice.

'So we made a statue of our founder . . . Humphrey!' Miranda lifted the cloth and unveiled a statue of ME-ME-ME! It looked exactly like me except that they had painted it shiny gold.

All the students applauded and Og let out a loud 'BOING!'

Miranda and Sayeh placed the statue right in the middle of the park.

'I hope you like it, Humphrey,' said Miranda.

I liked it all right. Okay, I loved it. But I didn't like the feeling I was feeling inside. I think it's called 'guilt'. It's an awful feeling, like when someone does something nice to you but you do something rotten to her. I crawled into my sleeping hut. The guilt feeling came right along with me.

When Mandy's father arrived in Room 26 to pick us up after school on Friday, he also had a small boy by the hand. The boy had big brown eyes, like

Mandy, and a brown coat which was too big for him. Mrs Brisbane shook hands with Mr Payne and bent down to greet the boy.

'What's your name?'

'Bwian,' he said.

'Brian? How old are you?'

Bwian – or Brian – held up three fingers.

'Three! Well, in a few years, I hope I'll have you as a student in Room 26.'

'There'll be two more coming before him,' Mr Payne said in a gruff voice I didn't like.

Mrs Brisbane led Mr Payne over to my cage. 'And this is Humphrey.'

'I hope it doesn't eat a lot,' he said, eyeing me suspiciously.

Mrs Brisbane handed him a couple of plastic bags of food. 'This will take care of him. Humphrey likes vegetable treats, too. Mandy knows what to do – right?'

Mandy nodded and tugged at her father's jacket. 'Come on, Dad. Let's go now!'

'Stop rushing me.'

'You left the twins in the car?' asked Mandy.

'Had to.'

'Well, they'll murder each other. Come on!'

Mandy took Brian's hand and Mr Payne took my cage. He wasn't too gentle so I flipped and flopped around.

'Bye, Og. Wish me luck!' I squeaked to my friend. I usually feel sorry for Og. He doesn't go home with students unless it's a long weekend, because he doesn't have to eat every day.

Today, I envied him. Murder? In the car? In the car I was going to ride in?

'BOING!' Og twanged. I appreciated his concern.

It was a LONG-LONG-LONG ride to the Paynes' house, or maybe it just seemed that way because of the Payne family. In addition to Mandy and Brian, there were the twins: Pammy and Tammy. I'd guess they were around five years old. They may have been twins but they didn't look alike. Pammy had light-brown hair and red skin. Everything about her was round: round face, round eyes, round cheeks and a round body. Tammy was as thin as a stick of rock. Her hair, eyes and skin were very pale.

There was one thing they had in common: they both liked to complain as much as Mandy did.

'I get to sit next to Humphrey,' said Pammy.

'No, *I* get to sit next to Humphrey,' said Tammy.

'You're too rough,' said Pammy.

'You're too loud,' said Tammy.

'Pipe down!' Mandy shouted.

'You hurt my ears!' said Brian.

'You kids all drive me crazy!' yelled Mr Payne, glancing at the back seat.

'You're driving too fast!' said Mandy.

'He's driving too *slow*!' said Tammy.

'You hurt my ears!' said Brian again, covering his ears with his hands.

I wanted to squeak, 'PLEASE-PLEASE-PLEASE be quiet!' but no one would have heard me anyway.

Finally, we got to the house. I thought the Paynes wouldn't argue as much outside the car. I was wrong.

When Mr Payne plonked my cage down on a table in the living room, it felt like an earthquake. He helped Brian take off his coat and gloves, muttering, 'Hold still, Brian!'

Pammy, Tammy and Mandy threw their coats on a chair and rushed over to my cage.

'I want to hold him!' Pammy announced.

'Me first!' said Tammy.

'Later,' said Mandy. She peered in at me. 'Sorry about the commotion, Humphrey. I'll let you rest a while, okay?'

'Thank you, Mandy,' I squeaked loudly.

'Hear that? He said "You're welcome",' Mandy told her sisters.

'I heard him say, "You're ugly",' said Pammy, giggling.

'I heard him say, "I like Tammy better than Pammy",' said Tammy, poking her twin in the ribs.

Mr Payne slumped down in a beat-up old chair and rubbed his eyes. 'Let's get this show on the road,' he said. 'Mandy, why don't you make us some macaroni cheese for supper?'

'Again?' asked Mandy.

'You're the oldest.'

'I hate macaroni cheese,' said Pammy.

'I love macaroni cheese,' said Tammy.

Mandy stomped into the kitchen. Brian followed her, shouting, 'Bwian help! Bwian help!'

About that time, Mr Payne turned on the television. The twins immediately raced over to watch it.

'I want Channel 5!' said Pammy.

'Channel 11!' said Tammy.

'Stop your bellyaching. We're watching Channel 7 and that's that,' said Mr Payne in a voice I definitely wouldn't argue with.

For a while, the twins were silent. The TV was loud, as people were screeching – or maybe they were singing. The Paynes remained quiet until I heard Mandy say, 'Get out of the way, Brian. This is hot!'

Soon I heard Brian go 'Ow!' and Mandy said, 'I told you it was hot. Now sit down!'

Brian rushed back into the living room, rubbing his hand. Then he noticed me and started poking his fingers in my cage. Meanwhile, I could hear dishes banging around in the kitchen.

I really wished I could see what she was doing.

I'd been to a lot of houses and I'd never seen anyone as young as Mandy make supper. But that's what makes being a classroom hamster interesting: I'm always learning new things about humans.

Later, Mandy brought plates with macaroni cheese in and the family continued watching TV while they ate. When they were all finished, they argued over who would do the dishes.

'It's your turn,' said Mr Payne.

'It's always my turn.' I'd never seen Mandy so annoyed. Finally, she carried the dishes into the kitchen, muttering under her breath, 'I have to do everything around here. I'll soak 'em but I won't wash 'em.'

The Paynes carried on watching TV, arguing from time to time over which channel to watch. Brian fell asleep first. Pammy fell asleep next and soon after that, Tammy dozed off. Mr Payne carried them off to bed, one by one.

'Fun evening, eh, Humphrey?' said Mandy. She checked to make sure I had clean water and food and that my bedding was all nice and fluffy. She was really nice, although if she'd complained, I'd have understood.

'I'd like to keep you in our room, but it's too crowded,' she said. 'If you need anything, just squeak.'

I'm never shy about squeaking up for myself.

Mr Payne came back into the living room alone

to watch TV. He dozed off eventually but I was wide awake. Around midnight, I heard a scritch-scratching at the front door. Mr Payne didn't wake up and the scritch-scratching got louder. Someone was fiddling with the lock! Someone was trying to break into the house!

'Wake up, Mr Payne! Wake up!' I squeaked as loudly as a small hamster can. Before he opened his eyes, the front door swung open, a bright light was flicked on and I heard a heavy CLOMP-CLOMP-CLOMP across the floor. My eyes were adjusting to the light when a loud voice said, 'What is *this* doing here!'

I saw a very tall woman looking down at me (at least she seemed very tall to me at that moment – most humans are tall compared to me). 'How *dare* you bring this *rat* in here without asking me!'

It wasn't the first time I've been insulted, but I never like being called a rat or referred to as an 'it' or a 'that'.

The woman didn't stop there. 'If you think you're bringing another mouth to feed in this house . . . another mouth for me to support . . .'

'Pat, it's not like that.' At last, Mr Payne was up on his feet, rubbing his eyes. 'It's Mandy's class pet and it's her turn to bring it home for the weekend.'

'If the teacher wants a pet, why doesn't *she* take it home?' said Mrs Payne. I could see her better now. She was wearing a light-blue cotton top and matching trousers, with white shoes. Her hair was pulled back in a ponytail and she looked tired and unhappy.

'They sent food for it. Mandy was so happy. She'll do all the work.'

Mrs Payne looked a little less angry and a lot more tired. She sighed loudly. 'She'd better. Speaking of food, I'm starving.'

She disappeared into the kitchen, but I could soon hear her complaining again.

'*Thank you* for washing the dishes!' I was pretty sure she was being sarcastic because nobody actually *had* washed the dishes. 'You expect me to work these awful hours at an awful place with those awful old people and come home and do the dishes?'

She was back in the living room now, yelling at Mr Payne. 'And you sit around all day waiting for a job to fall into your lap?' she continued.

'It wasn't my fault the factory closed down. You know I've been trying to find a job for a year now. I've applied everywhere.'

'When was the last time you had an interview?'

Mr Payne had that look some of the kids get when their team loses a game. 'Jobs don't grow on trees. I'll do the dishes . . . *after* I make you a sandwich.'

Mrs Payne sat down in the shabby old chair. 'I

know it's not your fault that I hate this job. The pay isn't even enough to support us and at night, the old people get so restless and crabby, it's awful! It wasn't as bad on the day shift but I get paid more working at night . . . even if I hardly ever get to see my own kids.'

Mr Payne sighed. 'And I see too much of them, believe me.'

'I don't want to hear any complaints about the kids. They need their mother, that's all.'

'You think I'm not doing a good job taking care of them?' asked Mr Payne. His voice had an angry edge.

'You're doing an okay job. Not a great job.'

Mr Payne stomped towards the kitchen. 'I'll get that sandwich. Of course, it'll just be an *okay* sandwich since I can't do anything right.'

I thought Mandy's mum was about to cry. Suddenly, she noticed me again.

'What are you – a gerbil?'

'Golden hamster,' I squeaked. Not that she understood – or even cared.

Mr Payne brought his wife a sandwich and sat down on the sofa.

'More bad news,' Mrs Payne announced. 'Trudy's moving to day shift, which means she can't give me a lift any more. That means you'll have to pack up the kids in their pyjamas and put them in the car . . .'

'I know, I know. We'll have to pick you up late at night,' said Mr Payne.

'It's not *my* fault.' Mrs Payne took a big bite out of her sandwich.

'You're saying it's my fault? Look, we've been over this a million times,' he said. 'I need a job and you need a break and the kids need clothes and we need another car!'

'Never mind, Jerry. Let's drop the whole thing.'

Mrs Payne nibbled at her sandwich and turned the sound up on the TV. Mr. Payne went into the kitchen and ran a lot of water, so I guess he was doing the dishes. When he came back, Mrs Payne turned off the TV without saying a word and went to bed. Mr Payne followed her.

Finally I was able to piece together the trouble at Mandy's house. Her father had lost his job. His mother had a night job, apparently taking care of sick old people, and she didn't like it. The Paynes needed more money!

All weekend, I listened to the Paynes complain to one another. On Sunday afternoon, Mandy performed a superb cage-clean for me. First, she put on the disposable plastic gloves Mrs Brisbane made all the kids use. She took a plastic spoon and cleaned up my poo corner, fluffed up my bedding, changed my water dish, and while she did so, she talked to me. Now I was only too happy to listen.

'I'll bet the other houses you go to are happy and fun and everybody laughs all the time – right? We used to be like that. Well, kind of like that, till Dad lost his job. You understand?'

I squeaked as sympathetically as I could.

'I'm glad you can't talk. I wouldn't want you to tell my friends about my awful family.'

'They're not awful,' I had to squeak up. In truth, they were pretty awful but more than that, they were unhappy.

Just then, her Mum came into the room. It was Sunday, but she was dressed to go to work. 'What on earth are you doing?' she asked.

'Cleaning Humphrey's cage,' Mandy explained.

'That's disgusting! I can't believe your teacher makes you do that kind of stuff. It's worse than my job and you don't even get paid for it!'

'Really, it's okay,' said Mandy. 'I have gloves, see? I put everything in a plastic bag. I don't mind.'

'Well, I do.' Mrs Payne looked around the room. 'Where is your father?'

'How should I know?'

I wasn't sorry when Mrs Payne tramped out of the room. I *was* sorry she was so unhappy.

'Lucky you, Humphrey. You don't have to live here all the time,' said Mandy as she closed my cage and ripped off her gloves. She even jiggled the lock to make sure I couldn't get out.

'Got to go and wash my hands. Back in a flash.'

While Mandy was gone, I thought about all the students and their families I'd helped on my weekend visits. I'd managed to get Miranda and her stepsister to go from being enemies to being friends. I'd helped Mr Morales, the Most Important Person at Longfellow School, get his children under control. I'd even helped our teacher's husband, Mr Brisbane. Still, what could one small hamster do to help with such a BIG-BIG-BIG problem?

This family was in trouble and I didn't have any idea of how to help.

I knew one thing: compared with the Paynes, I had absolutely nothing to complain about.

HUMPHREY SPENDS WEEKEND WITH THE PAYNES

'I've dreamed of this for a long time,' says Mandy.

The Humphreyville Herald

10

My Payne-ful Problem

'Humphreyville is going to have some special visitors in two weeks,' Mrs Brisbane announced as soon as class began on Monday.

There was a buzz around the classroom. Who would these guests be?

'We're having a parents' night so that your families can see what a great town you've created. And I've invited one of our local councillors to come and talk about our own community.'

A local councillor sounded Very Important. Almost as Important as Mr Morales.

'We'll have to make sure that Humphreyville is in the best shape possible in the next two weeks.'

All my friends were excited. Mrs Brisbane gave out new job assignments for the week. When Gail was named animal keeper, I couldn't help noticing that Miranda stared down unhappily at her table.

How could one small hamster (namely me) have caused trouble for one nice human (namely Miranda)?

Suddenly, Mandy began to wave her hand. Mrs Brisbane called on her.

'I think it's unfair,' she said in her cranky voice.

'What is unfair?' asked the teacher.

'Paul doesn't have a job. He's part of our class, too, and he's helped us with our maths. Well, me at least. Why can't he have a job?'

For once, I agreed with Mandy's complaint and so did Art.

'He helped me, too,' he said. 'And he always checks that list of jobs.'

I had to speak up, too. 'They're RIGHT-RIGHT-RIGHT!'

'I agree!' Mrs Brisbane replied. 'I don't know why I didn't think of it. And I know the perfect job for him, too. He can be the class accountant and add up all these points you're earning.'

Mandy bounced up and down in her chair. 'Can I tell him?'

'No, let me!' Art protested.

Mrs Brisbane laughed and shook her head. 'You can *both* tell him.'

At the end of the maths class, they did.

Paul looked so tall when he left the room, he must have been walking on air.

That night I waited anxiously for Aldo to come in. I was prepared to do anything to keep him awake. In fact, Og and I decided to practise louder wake-up calls in case Aldo was sleepy again. I was SQUEAK-SQUEAK-SQUEAKing, Og was BOING-BOING-BOINGing and the crickets were chirping in the background when the caretaker entered.

'Whoa, fellows, why all the noise?'

Og and I quickly quietened down but the crickets kept singing away.

Aldo was his old lively self again as he wheeled in his trolley and spun it around. 'I feel like making a noise, too, because I'm not tired tonight. No sireee. I came armed with this!'

He reached down to a shelf of the trolley, next to his lunch bag, and held up a metal container. 'Maria made me a big thermos of coffee. It will keep me awake until I've finished cleaning.'

'GOOD-GOOD-GOOD,' I said, and when he opened the thermos, the coffee smelled yummy, even though it isn't something hamsters usually drink. I was glad I didn't have to launch another unsanitary spitball that night.

The next morning, it was pouring with rain. March was still coming in like a lion, just like Seth's grandma had said. When Mrs Brisbane took the register, no one answered when she called 'Mandy Payne' or 'Art Patel' or 'Heidi Hopper'. None of them had shown up for school!

From time to time, one of my fellow students missed a class or two because of the sniffles or a cough but on the whole, we had a healthy class and this was the first time three students were ill at the same time.

Mrs Brisbane made sure that the homework monitor, who was now A.J., wrote down all the assignments to send home to them.

I spent most of the morning watching the rain drip down the windows, making everything outside – the trees, the street, the passing cars – look blurry. It was too wet for my friends to go outside for break, so they stayed inside and worked on Humphreyville.

When lunchtime came, my friends raced out of class as usual. Mrs Brisbane was preparing to go to lunch herself when Mr Morales entered. He was wearing a tie that had all the letters of the alphabet on it in bright colours.

'Sue, can you talk for a minute?' he asked. Sue is Mrs Brisbane's first name. Most students don't even know their teachers have first names.

'Of course. Have a seat,' Mrs Brisbane told him.

'I don't want to take up too much of your time, but I have to tell you I've had a complaint from a parent.'

Mrs Brisbane was surprised. 'Who's that?'

'Mrs Payne. Apparently Mandy and her whole family are ill. Coughs, runny noses, watery eyes. And she blames it all on . . . Humphrey.'

Blames . . . me? I felt as if all the air was being sucked out of me.

Mrs Brisbane was as surprised as I was. 'Humphrey! Why on earth would she think that?'

'Well, he spent the weekend at their house and now they're all sick.'

'So are Art and Heidi . . . and the weather has been horrible. Goodness, I think I've had fewer absences this winter than usual.'

'I believe you, but she's pretty angry. She doesn't think the kids should have to clean out his dirty cage. She's rung some of the other parents. She even threatened to start a petition to get all classroom pets banned!'

Banned! My whiskers drooped and my heart was heavy.

'BOING!' Og burst out. I guess he realized he was a classroom pet, too.

'That's ridiculous. Just because her children have colds –'

'Mrs Payne says her children are never sick. She said she's going to the school governors and complain.'

Now Mrs Brisbane was getting angry. 'Paid by

whom . . . Humphrey? You've had him in your house. I've had him in my house. We didn't get ill.'

'I'm on your side, but I have to respond to her. I'll compare the attendance records from last year with this year to see if there's any difference. You could check to see if any of the other students have fallen sick after Humphrey's been at their house. And I'll talk to the other teachers who have classroom pets.'

'Yes, those guinea pigs in Room 14,' said Mrs Brisbane. 'And the frog in Angie Loomis's class. And there are rabbits in Mr Olinsky's class. Oh, but the children love to have Humphrey come home with them! The parents love him, too.'

'Except for the Paynes.'

Mrs Brisbane got very quiet. She was thinking of something. And I don't think it was something good.

'Art Patel is absent today and he had Humphrey at his house last weekend. I'll call his mother and see what's wrong with him.'

'Good idea. And for now –' Mr Morales stopped and glanced over at Og and me. 'Maybe you'd better keep Humphrey at your house. Og, too. Mrs Payne was pretty upset. She even said she might call a lawyer.'

A lawyer! Was I going to end up in court? Or in jail?

This wasn't just Trouble with a capital T.

This was Total Disaster with a capital everything!

•ö•

For the rest of the day, I stared through the bars of my cage and imagined myself looking through another set of bars: those on a jail cell. Would Og end up in there with me, too? After all, he was a classroom pet, although he didn't go home with students at the weekend.

At the end of the day, Mr Morales helped Mrs Brisbane to cover my cage and carry Og and me out to the car. Thank goodness, the rain had stopped. They brought along our food, including Og's icky, yucky crickets. Luckily it was cold, so they were quiet in the car.

'I'm really sorry about this, Sue,' the principal told Mrs Brisbane through the car window.

'My husband will be thrilled to have these two home with him. But I'm afraid my students will be very disappointed.'

VERY-VERY-VERY, I thought.

'I'll try to get this resolved as soon as possible,' Mr Morales promised.

Mrs Brisbane thanked him and rolled up the window. Soon, we were on our way to her house – but for how long?

Just as she'd said, Mr Brisbane was really glad to see us. Mrs Brisbane honked the horn and he came out to the driveway in his wheelchair to meet her, even though it was extremely cold.

'Put Humphrey's cage right here across the armrests,' he told his wife. 'I'll come back and get Og.'

'Okay. I'll bring in the food.'

Soon, Og and I were side by side on the Brisbanes' wide coffee table. It was warm and cosy in their house and before long, Mr Brisbane had everything in my cage and Og's house in tip-top shape. Mrs Brisbane came in with steaming cups of tea and the two of them sat and watched us as they drank it.

'This Payne family sounds like a nuisance,' said Mr Brisbane.

'I don't know much about them. Mandy complains a lot but she's a nice girl. I think it's a habit she's picked up.'

'Maybe she has a lot to complain about,' Mr Brisbane said.

'YES-YES-YES!' I said, hopping onto my wheel and spinning to get their attention.

'Whatever their problems are, they don't have to take them out on Humphrey, do they, buddy?' Mr Brisbane wiggled a finger through the bars of my cage.

Mrs Brisbane picked up the phone and rang Art's mother.

'I'm checking to see how Art is doing,' I heard her say. 'We missed him in school.'

I would have loved to hear what Mrs Patel was saying. Mrs Brisbane said 'Oh' and 'I'm sorry' and 'What did the doctor say?' She listened and then said, 'Did Art show any signs of illness right after Humphrey was there?'

I held my breath while she waited for Mrs Patel to answer.

'This is private, but since you're a classroom assistant, I'll tell you that a parent has complained that having Humphrey at her house made her whole family ill. He and Og are temporarily banned from the classroom.'

Art's mum answered so loudly, even I could hear her say, 'That's ridiculous!'

'I know, Mrs Patel, but we have to check this out. No, I can't tell you who it is. A number of students were absent today. I'll let you know. And I think you should keep Art home another day.'

After a polite goodbye, Mrs Brisbane hung up and turned to her husband.

'He has a bad cold. Her husband got it first. Everyone in his office has a bad cold.'

'Well, they didn't catch it from Humphrey,' Mr Brisbane said, setting his cup down hard.

'No. She was terribly upset. You can imagine how the children will feel. I'll ring the Hoppers.'

After a short talk with Heidi's mother, Mrs Brisbane told her husband that Heidi also had a bad cold, but that she had got soaked in the rain two days before.

'Humphrey had nothing to do with that. He hasn't even been to her house,' Mr Brisbane insisted.

'You know, I think I'll make another call . . . to the Paynes.'

'The Paynes! I wouldn't talk to that pack of troublemakers.'

'Now, Bert. You can catch more flies with honey than with vinegar, you know.'

Sometimes humans say the strangest things. Why was she ringing the Paynes about catching flies? Og might be interested, but not me!

'That is a silly expression, if you don't mind me saying so, dear,' said Mr Brisbane.

Mrs Brisbane laughed. 'You're right. I've never understood why anyone would want to catch flies.'

I didn't understand either, but before I could work it out, Mrs Brisbane decided to call the Paynes. I held my breath again while she waited for someone to pick up. 'Hello, is that Mr Payne? This is Mrs Brisbane, Mandy's teacher. How is Mandy feeling?'

She and Mr Payne had a long exchange about

Mandy's health and the health of Tammy, Pammy and Brian. Then she said, 'Well, I certainly hope Mandy will be back in the classroom soon. We all miss her.'

She paused to listen for a while longer. 'The animals are at home with me and we're looking into it. Please give Mandy my best. By the way, is Mrs Payne there? I'd like to talk to her.'

Mr Payne gave a short answer this time. 'I see. Well, please tell her I rang. Thank you. Goodbye.'

Mrs Brisbane hung up the phone and took a long sip of tea.

'What did he say?' Mr Brisbane was not a patient man. At that moment, I was not a very patient hamster.

'It sounds as if they all have colds. The same as Art. When I asked about Mrs Payne, I learned something new. Mrs Payne works nights.'

'That could be hard on the family,' said Mr Brisbane.

I had to squeak up. 'It IS-IS-IS! Especially since Mr Payne lost his job.'

Mr and Mrs Brisbane burst out laughing. 'I think Humphrey is trying to tell us something.'

Mrs Brisbane became more serious. 'I wish we could understand him. After all, he spent a whole weekend there. I'll bet he could tell us a lot.'

Boy, was she right! I could write a book about

the Paynes (if only I had room left in my notebook).

It was pleasant at the Brisbanes' house. They took me out of my cage and made a maze for me to run around in on the floor, but my heart wasn't in it. About the second time around, the phone rang and Mrs Brisbane answered.

'Aldo! Is everything all right?'

She listened for a few seconds, then replied, 'Sorry. I should have left a note for you. Of course you'd be worried. No, I have Humphrey and Og here for a while. Frankly, there was a complaint about Humphrey making one of the students sick, but please don't tell anyone, not even Richie's family. I don't know how long they'll be here.' She laughed. 'I will definitely give them your regards.'

Once she hung up, Mrs Brisbane told Og and me that Aldo missed us.

'How did he happen to have your number?' Mr Brisbane asked.

'I gave it to him when he was trying to decide whether to go back to college, in case he had any questions. He's going to make a great teacher.'

Yes, Aldo would make a great teacher unless he fell asleep on the job. And now I wasn't there to wake him up if he was tired. I hoped he had a lot of coffee with him.

When she was ready to go to bed, Mrs Brisbane brought me a slice of apple, but it didn't appeal to me.

'I'm not hungry, are you, Og?' I asked my friend a little later.

'BOING!' he answered.

For the rest of the night he was quiet. The crickets were quiet. I was quiet, too. My brain wasn't quiet, though, as I thought about the next day when I would be absent from class for the very first time.

It felt so strange to see Mrs Brisbane head off for school. I couldn't imagine Room 26 without me. I could imagine it without Og, since I was there before he came. But I'd never seen Room 26 without me in it. How could I?

As the day went on, I tried to picture my classmates having maths class, doing their school jobs, working on Humphreyville – named after me!

Mr Brisbane tried to keep my mind off school by giving my cage a terrifically good clean, though he did uncover a secret.

'Humphrey . . . I don't think you've been eating your food. You've just been hiding it!'

I hung my head because it was true. Ever since

Miranda got into trouble, I hadn't been hungry. My yummy treats didn't taste yummy any more.

'If you don't eat, you'll get ill,' said Mr Brisbane. 'Now, I'm going to give you some yoghurt drops right now and you're going to eat them.'

'Yes, sir,' I squeaked weakly.

Mr Brisbane headed his wheelchair for the kitchen, then abruptly stopped. 'Wait a second. Maybe you *are* sick! Why didn't I think of this sooner? You need to see a vet!'

Soon, Mr Brisbane whizzed back into the room and held out his hand, which held some crunchy, munchy yoghurt drops. 'Eat up, my boy. You have to keep your strength up. You can't give in to troubles. You have to fight back!'

Was that really what I was doing? Giving in to troubles like Mr Brisbane had done the first time I met him?

I reached down and took a yoghurt drop and ate it. It tasted good. I realized I was hungry so I took another one.

'That's a good fellow. You've got plenty of fight left in you, haven't you?'

A few more yoghurt drops and I felt a little fight coming back.

'I'll call the neighbours to get the name of their vet and I'll make you an appointment. You'll be back in the classroom before you know it.'

Mr Brisbane seemed determined, but Mrs Payne was determined, too.

Once Mr Brisbane went off to make his calls, I asked Og, 'Don't you miss school, old pal?'

The frog, who usually sat like a large green lump, began to jump up and down, twanging loudly. 'BOING-BOING-BOING-BOING-BOING!'

I took that to be a 'yes'.

HUMPHREY AND OG MISSING FROM ROOM 26

Mrs Brisbane says they are safe at her house; no explanation for their absence is given.

The Humphreyville Herald

11

The Difficulty with Dr Drew

Mr Brisbane was right. I hadn't been eating much lately, but it wasn't because I was ill. It was because I felt so guilty about Miranda. Could a veterinarian (Mr Brisbane called it a 'vet') work that out? I didn't think so.

It was quiet in the Brisbanes' house for most of the day. Mr Brisbane spent a lot of time in his workshop making things out of wood, like bird-boxes and picture frames. Og was unusually quiet, even for him. There were no giggling students or break bells or spelling tests to keep me awake. I finally crawled into my sleeping hut, but I didn't actually fall asleep. I kept picturing my friends hard at work on Humphreyville. Or since I was in so much trouble, maybe they'd changed the name. Somehow, 'Ogburg' didn't sound very good to me.

Time dragged on until Mrs Brisbane finally came home.

'How are the guys?' she asked her husband.

'Fine, fine, although Humphrey is quieter than usual. Did you get my message about the vet?'

'Yes. I telephoned Mrs Payne to tell her we're getting Humphrey examined this afternoon. In fact, I invited her to come along.'

Gulp. I was going to the vet's surgery that same afternoon? With Mrs Payne?

'What did she say?'

'She goes to work at four.' Mrs Brisbane checked her watch. 'Which reminds me, we'd better get going if we're going to make it there by four-thirty.'

Four-thirty? It was close to four-thirty already. I only had time to squeak 'Wish me luck' to Og before my cage was covered and I was whisked out of the door with the Brisbanes.

As long as I'd been in Room 26, I'd worried about the problems of my classmates.

Now I was in Big Trouble myself . . . and my friends didn't even know about it!

I was glad my cage was covered because the air was freezing cold. But travelling that way is like being blindfolded. By the time I could see what was going on around me, I was in the waiting room of the vet's surgery.

'Dr Drew will see Humphrey in a few minutes,' a man behind a desk told us.

I had a few minutes to look around and I was SHOCKED-SHOCKED-SHOCKED!

To the right of me was a large white dog with brown freckles and huge teeth, like Miranda's unfriendly dog Clem. He licked his chops. That meant he was hungry!

I quickly turned my head. To the left of me was a cage with a cat in it. The cat had black fur and white paws. Its dark-green eyes were staring right at me, a little *too hard* for my own comfort.

I decided to look straight ahead, where there was a huge tank with fish of every colour. Some had stripes and even polka dots, and they swam round and round a pink castle. I wished I could be behind glass instead of sitting so close to those two dangerous creatures. Those few minutes the man at the desk had mentioned seemed like a few hours to me.

Then something shocking happened. The door swung open and in walked Mr Payne, followed by Mandy, Pammy, Tammy and Bwian – I mean Brian.

Mrs Brisbane was as stunned as I was. 'Mandy! What are you doing here?'

Mandy looked as if she wanted to be anywhere

but in that surgery. Mrs Brisbane gained control of herself and put her hand out to Mr Payne. 'Hello, Mr Payne. This *is* a surprise.' She introduced the Paynes to Mr Brisbane and everyone said hello. I must say, Mr Payne didn't seem very happy to be there. Mandy seemed even unhappier (I didn't know if that was because of me or because of her red nose). Pammy and Tammy were too busy kicking each other to notice where they were, while Brian tore pages out of a magazine.

'The wife said I should come and see what the doc says.' Mr Payne was extremely glum. 'If that's okay with you.'

Mrs Brisbane politely said it was fine with her, but it didn't seem fine to me. Mandy's mum didn't trust Mrs Brisbane to tell her honestly what the vet said? *That* ruffled my fur a bit.

'Now see here, Mr Payne,' I squeaked, which wasn't such a good idea. When they heard me, the dog and the cat got excited, barking and snarling and growling and meowing in a very unnecessary way! I only hoped they wouldn't discover that my cage had a lock-that-doesn't-lock.

Just as I was about to escape into my sleeping hut for safety, a woman dressed all in pale green entered. She had dark skin, dark hair and big, dark eyes, like Ms Mac, my first teacher.

'Hi, I'm Dr Melissa Drew. Is Humphrey all set?'

I was all set to get out of that waiting room, I can tell you that!

Mrs Brisbane stepped forward and introduced everyone to the vet. It was decided that Mandy and her sisters and brother would stay in the waiting room while the adults came into the examination room with me.

It was nice and warm inside, so why was I quivering and shivering?

Dr Drew put my cage on a padded table and smiled at me. 'Now, Humphrey, is this your first exam?'

'YES-YES-YES!' I squeaked loudly, which made Dr Drew smile even more.

'He certainly sounds healthy,' she said as she opened my cage and reached in and took me out. 'Don't worry, Humphrey. This won't hurt a bit.'

Dr Drew spoke to the humans. 'This isn't any different from the kind of examinations you get. Now, has Humphrey had any problems lately?'

'He's pretty lively but he hasn't been eating as much as usual,' said Mr Brisbane.

'Made all my kids sick,' said Mr Payne.

Dr Drew was surprised. 'Really?'

'Yeah. He spent the weekend at our house and all my kids got sick. Some of the other kids at school, too. Right?' He turned to Mrs Brisbane.

'Everyone who's been ill seems to have a cold, even children who didn't take Humphrey home,' Mrs Brisbane said firmly.

'It's highly unusual for humans to fall ill from handling a hamster. It's more common for a hamster to pick up a disease from a human or another animal. But let's check him out.'

Dr Drew's touch was so gentle, I relaxed. She put one hand underneath me and held her other hand above my head, making a little tent for me. VERY-VERY-VERY nice.

'We'll check the eyes first, because that's where we usually see signs of infection or disease in hamsters.' Cupping me in one hand, she shone a tiny light directly into one eye. Whoa – that's a wake-up call. Next, she checked my other eye.

'Looking good,' she said. 'No discharge or inflammation. Now, I'll listen to his heartbeat.'

Dr Drew picked up a stethoscope (a word I do NOT want to see on a spelling test). It had a plug for each of her ears and a teeny piece that she held against my chest. First, she listened. Then she smiled. 'Excellent. A very healthy heart, Humphrey. Now, let's check out that weight.'

She put me on a scale that was flat and square. She also put a few chunks of Nutri-Nibbles on the scale. 'Those will keep him there for a second.' She let go of me and while I picked up a treat she said, 'Well, even if he's not been eating well, his weight is completely normal.'

While I nibbled away, Dr Drew and Mrs Brisbane discussed what I ate.

'He usually eats everything: vegetables, fruit, hamster food, yoghurt drops,' Mrs Brisbane said.

'Excellent,' said the vet. 'Lots of variety. That's what hamsters like – right, Humphrey?'

'You bet!' I squeaked and the doctor chuckled.

'But I just found some old food hidden in his cage and realized he's not been eating as much as before.'

Dr Drew bit her lip for a second, then asked, 'Has there been any change in his environment lately?'

Mrs Brisbane nodded. 'Well, I had to take him out of the classroom because of the complaint.'

I noticed Mr Payne was staring at his shoes.

'So I suppose things are a little upset for him,' my teacher added.

'That could be it,' said Dr Drew. 'Some hamsters are very sensitive to even small changes.'

She was right about that. I am a very sensitive hamster. And Dr Drew was a very good vet.

'Sometimes hamsters get infections in their cheek pouches because they store food there. So, open wide, Humphrey.' She picked me up and gently pulled my mouth open, using the small light to look inside my mouth. 'Clean as a whistle,' she said. 'Fur is nice and shiny. I'll take a sample of some stool, if there's any in there.'

I was confused, but it turns out that stool is poo, and I have a corner of my cage where I make my poo. She took some with tweezers and put it in a tube.

'It's nice and firm, which is a good sign.'

What a surprise! Usually when my classmates clean my cage they go 'Ewwww' or 'Yuck', when they get to the poo part. But it didn't bother the doctor at all. She even had a nice name for it: stool.

The vet held me up to her eye level and said, 'Humphrey, we need to get you back to your old environment but in the meantime, you are one healthy, handsome hamster.'

I remember when Ms Mac picked me out at Pet-O-Rama and told Carl, the shop assistant, 'He's obviously the most intelligent and handsome hamster you have.' I really missed Ms Mac, but she sent me postcards so I knew she still cared. Dr Drew cared, too. She may not have been able to work out that I felt guilty about Miranda, but she had worked out that I wasn't sick.

'Try varying his food even more. And just to make sure he perks up, I'm giving you some yummy vitamin chews. I guarantee Humphrey will like them.'

I liked them already. In fact, I felt so happy, I was a little hungry.

She gently put me back in my cage. 'Humphrey, I have a friend here today you might like to meet.' She went to the door and called out, 'Judy? Could you bring Winky in here?'

Then she turned to Mr Payne. 'Tell me, what did the doctor say about your children's illnesses?'

Mr Payne looked down at the tips of his toes and squirmed like Sit-Still-Seth.

'Didn't take them. It's hard to get the kids all bundled up and in the car –'

'I see,' said the vet. 'But they're better now.'

'Yes. They had runny noses and coughs and a temperature for a few days. Just about drove me crazy. I take care of them now that I –' He stopped. Mr Payne really had a hard time finishing sentences.

'Well, I don't think it was from Humphrey,' said the vet.

'The wife's convinced it is.'

There was silence until Mrs Brisbane said, 'Dr Drew, could you write a report or a letter and send it to Mrs Payne? That would probably put her mind at ease. In fact, I could pass it on to the head and the other parents.'

Dr Drew smiled. 'Okay! I'd be glad to.'

Just then, the door opened and a blonde woman wearing a pink smock with pictures of teddy bears all over it came in carrying a small cage. 'Here's Winky,' she said.

Dr Drew introduced everyone to Judy and said, 'Judy rescues hamsters. Sometimes she has more than twenty of them in her house.'

'Rescues them from where?' asked Mr Brisbane. It was exactly the question I wanted to ask. I was picturing hamsters on top of burning buildings . . . floating down on rafts in a flood . . . trapped by the weight of an avalanche!

'Sometimes people decide that taking care of a hamster is too much work. That's something to think about when you get a pet,' said Judy. 'Mostly I get them from Pet-O-Rama. They're rejects, like Winky here.'

'Reject hamsters?' asked Mr Brisbane.

'Yes, if they're not perfect, people won't buy them.' She put Winky's cage on the table next to mine. I could easily see how he got his name because he was winking at me. I winked back.

'For some reason, Winky was born with one eye and he doesn't have any teeth. Neither of those things bothers him. He's able to eat a variety of foods and he only needs one good eye.'

'He does look like he's winking,' said Mrs Brisbane. 'He's very cute.'

He was not as handsome as I am, but I have to admit, he looked like a nice fellow.

'Hi, Winky. You look fine to me,' I squeaked.

And was I surprised when he squeaked back, 'Thanks, friend. I was kind of worried when Pet-O-Rama rejected me. Luckily, Judy came around and rescued me.'

He understood me and I understood him. This was a first!

'Pet-O-Rama! That's where I came from!' I told him.

'Remember Carl? He just got made assistant manager,' Winky squeaked at me.

'Imagine that!'

'They had a big party to celebrate,' he added.

'You don't say. Hey, did they ever sell that chinchilla?' I asked.

'Yeah. A real nice family took him,' he told me. 'Oh, and just before I left, they got in a big shipment of new hamster cages. One of them is four levels high.'

'No kidding!'

Suddenly all the humans, even Mr Payne, were laughing.

'Sounds like these two have a lot in common,' said Mrs Brisbane.

'Let's get them a little closer.' Dr Drew took me

out of the cage again. Judy took Winky out of his cage.

'Now, you shouldn't put hamsters together in the same cage unless they've been raised together. But they can sniff each other.'

Judy held Winky up close to me and we stared at each other, eye to eye. I took a big sniff. Yeah, he was a hamster all right.

'Where do you live now?' he asked.

'In a school room with lots of kids,' I said.

'Sounds like fun,' Winky replied.

'It is. But it's work, too.'

Winky definitely winked at me. 'Nice work if you can get it, pal.'

With that, we were whisked back into our cages.

'If you know anyone who wants a special winking, happy hamster, give me a call,' said Judy. I only had time to squeak 'Good luck' before Winky was gone.

'Any other questions?' asked the vet.

No one had any, so my cage was closed up and we were ready to go. Before we got to the door, Dr Drew said, 'Oh, by the way, if you know anyone searching for a job, we have an opening for a veterinary assistant.'

Mr Payne stopped in his tracks. 'What's that?'

'Someone to feed the animals, give them water, take them for walks, clean their cages, give them medicine. The person has to be able to lift heavy bags of food, interact with animals, that sort of thing. We'll train them.'

Mr Payne had a strange look in his eyes. 'And the hours?'

'There's some flexibility there. Do you have someone in mind?'

Mr Payne hesitated. I decided to squeak up for him.

'He needs a job! Hire Mr Payne! PLEASE-PLEASE-PLEASE!'

Dr Drew turned towards me. 'Humphrey, do *you* have someone in mind?'

'MR PAYNE!' I had never squeaked so loudly in my whole life.

'I know you're trying to tell us something.'

Mr Payne cleared his throat. 'I might be interested. I mean, I don't know if I'm right for the job.'

The vet turned to him and smiled. 'How do you feel about taking care of animals?'

'Good,' Mr Payne said. 'I had a nice dog when I was a kid. Name was Lady. And I learned a lot from watching this examination. I'm strong. I'm a good worker.'

'Why don't you fill in an application now and come in and talk to my partners and me tomorrow morning? You can bring the children if you need to.'

I saw something new in Mr Payne's eyes. They came to life for a few seconds.

'Okay,' he said.

Soon we were out in the waiting room. Mandy was holding a funny dog on her lap. He had short legs and a long body. Tammy, Pammy and Brian stood around her, staring at the odd animal.

'See, Dad? It's a sausage dog!' she cried out.

The lady sitting next to Mandy, who obviously owned the dog, smiled. 'A dachshund, actually. His name is Fritz.'

Fritz did look like a sausage. Or a hot dog.

'Do you like dogs, Mandy?' asked Mrs Brisbane.

'Yes. And cats, too. But what I'd really like is a hamster.'

Smart girl, that Mandy.

Dr Drew took Fritz and his owner into the office.

'Kids, I've got to fill in some papers,' said Mr Payne. 'Please be quiet and let me concentrate.'

'Okay. We'll watch the fish,' said Mandy. 'How's Humphrey?'

'Humphrey?' said Mrs Brisbane. 'Humphrey is just perfect.'

It was nice to hear that I was perfect even though I knew I was not.

HUMPHREY EXAMINED BY VET

Students anxiously await classroom hamster's medical report.

The Humphreyville Herald

12

The Domino Decision

I was hoping to get back to school the next day, but Mrs Brisbane said she wanted to present the doctor's report to Mr Morales and Mrs Payne and the classroom assistants, so that everyone would agree that it was all right for me to go back into the classroom. That was disappointing, of course. For one thing, my friends were putting the finishing touches to Humphreyville. For another thing, Og was able to go back to Room 26 – since nobody accused him of making humans ill – and I was all alone at the Brisbanes' house. The house was nice and the Brisbanes were nice, but my job was to help my classmates and it was pretty hard to do that without being there.

I wasn't sure what anyone else's job was any more. Did Miranda have a job she liked? Was Art paying attention in class? Did Paul look happier now? I had no way of knowing, sitting in my cage at the Brisbanes' house.

Mr Brisbane tried to entertain me during the day, but it seemed QUIET-QUIET-QUIET compared to Room 26. For one thing, he was out in his workshop a lot, making things out of wood. Or he was at the Senior Citizens' Centre, where he taught other people to make things out of wood. Some evenings, he went out and taught woodwork at the Youth Centre while Mrs Brisbane quietly marked papers.

I had plenty of time to think. Mostly, I thought about Miranda.

And I thought about what a rat I was. I've noticed that humans sometimes called bad people 'rats' (I'd like to tell them that the pet rats they sold at Pet-O-Rama were perfectly decent and upstanding rodents). I knew I was a 'rat' because I'd let Miranda take the blame for something I'd done. And I hadn't helped her because I wanted to keep my freedom, so that I could come and go as I pleased.

The way I'd been looking at it, I needed my freedom to help my friends as I'd done so many times before. I knew that if I let Mrs Brisbane know that my lock didn't lock, she'd get me a new cage with a lock that did lock. So I'd let Miranda suffer. I'd let her get into trouble and stay in trouble.

No wonder I'd had trouble eating and sleeping. However, the vitamin chews were just as yummy as Dr Drew had said.

When Mrs Brisbane came home, she was full of news about Room 26. She told her husband and me that Mandy, Art and Heidi were all back in school but that Richie and Sayeh were now off sick. Obviously, there was 'something' going around . . . and that 'something' was not me (thank goodness)!

She also told us that instead of having their homes sitting around on tables, the students had actually put Humphreyville together like a real town. 'I think I'd like to move there myself,' she told me. 'And your statue looks great.'

'You must be proud, Humphrey,' said Mr Brisbane. 'Not many hamsters have statues built in their honour.'

He didn't realize that it was the statue of a rat.

Mrs Brisbane said that Mr Morales had given permission for me to come back into the classroom. All the parents had been contacted and everyone wanted me back. Of course, she said the kids always did want me back.

'Here's the best news of all. Mandy's mother called and said that she'd read Dr Drew's report and that she was sorry she blamed you for making her kids sick. She said that they probably just had bad colds. Then, she told me something else.'

Mrs Brisbane paused.

'What?' Mr Brisbane asked.

'WHAT?' I squeaked.

'She said that in the end, it was a good thing Humphrey went to the vet because her husband ended up getting the job at the veterinary clinic. I guess he'd been out of work for quite a while. She told me to thank him.' She turned to me. 'Thank you, Humphrey.'

I was happy! I was ecstatic (which is a long word that means REALLY-REALLY-REALLY happy). Ordinarily, I would have jumped on my wheel and spun for joy. But for some reason, the more good news Mrs Brisbane had, the worse I felt. All the nice feelings just made me feel more and more like a rat.

It's not easy being a rat. It's easier to make a decision. And even a rat like me can make the right decision. Of course, I'd always known what was the right thing to do. Deciding to do it was another thing.

Later that evening, after their supper, the Brisbanes sat near my cage and played a game of dominoes. It seemed like an interesting game with lots of dots on rectangular tiles. They moved the dominoes around making long rows which crisscrossed around the table. Occasionally, one of them would shout out 'Good one!' or 'Oh, no!'

I took a deep breath and, as I had done so many times before, I reached out, jiggled my lock-that-doesn't-lock and opened the door to my cage. I darted out onto the table and danced across the dominoes, figuring I might as well enjoy my last bit of freedom as much as possible.

Mrs Brisbane gasped, 'Humphrey!'

Just then, I lost my footing on the slippery tiles and skidded across a row of dominoes, sending them scattering in different directions.

'Hey! I was winning,' said Mr Brisbane. He scooped me up in his hand and stroked my fur. 'Calm down, calm down.'

'How on earth did he get out?' Mrs Brisbane leaned over to inspect the door of my cage. 'I guess I didn't close it all the way.'

'I guess not.' Mr Brisbane gently put me back in my cage and closed the door. He tested it from the outside. 'Now it's closed tightly. Want to try another game?'

'Okay.' Mrs Brisbane turned all the dominoes face down so I couldn't see any of the dots. She mixed them all up and she and her husband each drew seven tiles – which they called 'bones'. Mr Brisbane drew one tile and put it in the centre of the table and the game began.

I stopped to catch my breath. Mrs Brisbane was convinced that she hadn't closed the door properly. I still had a chance to keep my freedom (and keep being a rat). But I'd made up my mind and there was no turning back.

I waited until there were rows of dominoes going in all directions. Picturing Miranda's face, I pushed my lock-that-doesn't-lock and the door to my cage swung open. I scurried across the table, leaped onto the dominoes and squeaked, 'Don't you get it? Miranda didn't leave my cage door unlocked!'

I knew it sounded like 'SQUEAK-SQUEAK-SQUEAK' to the humans but I had to get my point across.

The Brisbanes looked more than surprised. They looked stunned.

'How did he do that?' Mr Brisbane asked after a few seconds of silence. 'I know that door was locked.'

Mrs Brisbane picked me up. 'Humphrey, what are you trying to tell us?'

Mr Brisbane went over to my cage and fiddled around with the door again. 'I don't get it. I just don't get it,' he muttered.

He closed the door and joggled it. 'It certainly seems like it's locked tightly. Hey, I have an idea.' He grabbed a pencil from the table and pushed it through the bars of my cage, pushing it against the inside of the lock.

This was one clever man.

He pushed it and nothing happened until he twisted it from the inside, the way I do. Of course, the door swung right open.

'That's it! It looks as if it's locked on the outside, but Humphrey can open it. I wonder how many times he's done that?'

If they only knew!

'I always knew Humphrey was smart,' said Mrs Brisbane.

Mr Brisbane kept fiddling around with the lock. 'It's clearly defective. I suppose we'll have to get a new cage.'

'Or a new hamster,' said his wife. 'Just kidding, Humphrey.'

She put me back in the cage and Mr Brisbane closed the door. He wheeled out of the room for a minute and came back with a big piece of wire. 'I'll keep it closed for now. The wire will work, but it might be hard for your students to use. And who knows if Humphrey can undo it, too?'

I hoped I could.

Mrs Brisbane suddenly stood up with a look of horror on her face. 'Miranda!' she said with a gasp. 'I punished her for not locking the cage and she was sure she did.'

'She probably did,' Mr Brisbane agreed.

'Oh, I feel terrible, Bert. She even cried.'

So Mrs Brisbane felt as badly about Miranda as I did.

'Well, nothing's done that can't be undone,' Mr Brisbane said.

He was wrong. There was something done that could never be undone. My freedom and the chance to get out to help my friends were over.

Mrs Brisbane decided to keep me at home another day so her husband could get me a new cage. I was SAD-SAD-SAD to see my cage all wired up. But I went into my sleeping hut and slept soundly most of the day because I had a clear conscience for the first time in a long time.

I was no longer a rat.

The new cage looked a lot like the old one, especially after Mr Brisbane transferred all my belongings: my seesaw, my tree branch, my climbing ladder, my bridge ladder, my wheel (of course), my water bottle and my mirror – even the cage extension. I held my breath when he took that mirror out of my old cage. After all, I keep the secret notebook and pencil that Ms Mac gave me behind it. Luckily, I had planned ahead. The previous night, while the Brisbanes were sleeping, I spent a long time pushing the notebook and pencil against the back of the mirror. They fitted perfectly into the little notch behind it. When Mr Brisbane pulled the mirror out, he didn't even notice the notebook and pencil. He hung the mirror on the side of my new cage. Whew! I might have lost my freedom but at least I had my notebook and pencil to keep me busy.

Unfortunately, it was Friday, which meant that there was no school the next day, and nowhere to spend the weekend except with the Brisbanes.

It was a nice weekend, mostly quiet except when Bert Brisbane took me out of my cage and set up an amazing maze for me to run. The exercise felt good and I ate some more afterwards.

I guess I was healthy after all.

On Monday morning, Mrs Brisbane covered my cage with a blanket and took me back to school.

Room 26 was strange and yet familiar. For one thing, I'd been away for almost a whole week. For another thing, the houses of Humphreyville had been arranged on tables along the side of the room so that it really looked like a town.

Everybody seemed glad to have me back.

'Hiya, Humphrey Dumpty,' said A.J.

'I missed you, Humphrey,' Sayeh said softly.

'It was lonely here without you,' Miranda told me.

'It was hard to sit still without you here,' Seth whispered. 'But I did a pretty good job.'

'BOING-BOING!' Og greeted me. Even the crickets chirped.

The bell rang and my friends settled down in their chairs.

'Boys and girls, before we do anything else today, I have something important to say.'

The room was very quiet after those words. 'Something important' could mean a surprise quiz, a special guest, or someone getting into trouble.

'I'm a teacher but I'm also a human being. And all human beings make mistakes. I want to tell you about a mistake I made.'

There was one small giggle, probably from Gail. Then the room became even quieter.

'A few weeks ago, I accused Miranda of leaving Humphrey's cage open. Because I felt that Humphrey could have been seriously injured, I had to lower her mark. That was my mistake.'

I glanced over at Miranda – and so did a number of my friends. She stared at Mrs Brisbane, her eyes wide with surprise.

'It turns out there was something wrong with the lock on Humphrey's cage. It appeared to be locked, but he was able to open it from the inside.

He did the same thing to me that he did to Miranda.'

Now all eyes were not on Miranda. They were on me.

'Humphrey has a new cage now with a lock that works. Miranda, I am restoring your good mark.'

All eyes turned back to Miranda. She was smiling.

'Most importantly, class, I want to publicly apologize to Miranda for wrongly accusing her and for not believing what she said was true. She is an honest person and I hope she will accept my apology. Will you, Miranda?'

'Of course, Mrs Brisbane. I was never sure –'

'*I* am sure,' said the teacher. 'Now, please take out a piece of paper for our spelling test.'

Spelling test! I'd been gone all week and I didn't even know what the words were. I went into my sleeping hut for a nap and slept quite comfortably knowing how happy Miranda was and how happy the whole class was for her.

Miranda – being Golden-Miranda and practically perfect – came over to my cage at the end of the day. 'I'm sorry that you're stuck in your cage, Humphrey. You know I'd never do anything to hurt you.'

I did know that. That's why I did what I had to do.

'YES-YES-YES!' I squeaked out.

'I love you, Humphrey.'

Even being locked up in a cage didn't seem so bad after all.

HUMPHREYVILLE REJOICES AS HAMSTER RETURNS TO ROOM 26!

Mrs Brisbane apologizes to Miranda Golden.

The Humphreyville Herald

In a Tight Spot

That afternoon, feeling rested and raring to go, I crawled out of my sleeping hut because Mrs Brisbane was going to read to us. She was an excellent reader and was starting a new book that had something to do with pirates and buried treasure. That was interesting to me because I like to bury my treasures (like nuts and other tasty nibbles) in my bedding.

Mrs Brisbane sat down with the book but she never did read.

'My glasses!' she said. 'Where are my glasses?'

She looked for them on her desk, *in* her desk, in her handbag. Once before when Mrs Brisbane lost her glasses, they were actually sitting on top of her head. This time, they weren't there, either.

'Let's do a search,' she told the class. My friends ran around the classroom, checking every nook and cranny. It was like a treasure hunt, but they never found the glasses. And believe me, they looked everywhere!

'Sorry, class. I guess I won't be reading today.'

My classmates were as disappointed as I was, so Mrs Brisbane asked Tabitha to read a few pages, followed by Kirk. They are good readers but not quite as good as Mrs Brisbane.

Once school was over and the class was empty, Mrs Brisbane checked the entire room again. 'They have to be here, Humphrey,' she said. 'You haven't seen them, have you, Og?'

Og splashed in his water and I tried to tell her that I hadn't seen them. Since I couldn't get out of my new cage, I wouldn't be able to help her.

Mrs Brisbane finally put on her coat and left, muttering under her breath as she did.

When I was sure she was gone, I went to the side of my cage closest to Og.

'Og, I have something to tell you. Are you listening?'

'BOING-BOING!' Og answered.

'Good. I'm glad that Miranda is out of trouble but now I'm the one in trouble. This new cage they bought me has a lock that I can't open. Mr Brisbane tested it and made sure of that.'

'BOING-BOING-BOING!' Og repeated. He sounded truly alarmed.

'Now I won't be able to come over and have chats with you. And I won't be able to get out and help my friends. Og, my job as a classroom hamster won't be so much fun any more.'

Og dived into the water, splashing furiously. I suppose he had heard enough.

'It wasn't right for Miranda to take the blame,' I said, talking to myself. 'Not right at all.'

Og stopped splashing. Everything was silent until I heard the RATTLE-RATTLE-RATTLE of Aldo's trolley. He hurried over to my cage. 'Welcome back, Humphrey!' he said. 'Your pal Og really missed his buddy. Come to think of it, so did I!'

'I missed you, too!' I squeaked loudly.

Aldo pulled up a chair and took out his lunch bag. 'We've got some catching up to do. I hear you went to the vet! Richie told me.' Repeat-It-Please-Richie is Aldo's nephew. 'He said you were as healthy as a horse.'

Although I wasn't sure I liked being compared to a horse, I knew Aldo meant well.

'Guess what? I went to the doctor, too. And you know how I was tired all the time? Seems like I was low on some vitamins and I was drinking far too much coffee. I'd get a burst of energy and then be even more tired than before! Now I cut back on the coffee, make sure I eat better and I feel like my old self again. Maria and I even went bowling this weekend.'

I was glad. Aldo really likes bowling.

'Speaking of vitamins, here's something for you.' He took a juicy orange slice out of his bag and pushed it through the bars of my cage.

'I see you got a new cage, too. Looks pretty much like your old cage, but at least you can't get out any more.'

Thanks for reminding me, I thought. Still, Aldo meant well and the orange was extremely tasty.

'You know, a guy like you could get hurt out here in the classroom. You could fall and break something or get caught in a drawer and not have any air. You could be stepped on or sat on or eat something that would make you ill.'

Aldo was making me nervous. On the one paw, I'd been out of my cage many times and nothing bad had happened to me. On the other paw, maybe I'd just been lucky!

'Anyway, pal, glad you're safe and sound and back with Og.' Aldo folded up his lunch bag and went to work cleaning the room. He worked fast – no napping tonight – which made me GLAD-GLAD-GLAD.

Before he left, Aldo opened the blinds so I'd have light coming from the outside street lamp. He said goodnight, turned off the lights and left.

The full moon that night gave the room a soft, silvery glow. I sighed and stared longingly through the bars of my cage. Never again would I slide down the table leg to get to the floor. Never again would I scramble under someone's table to nibble at a peanut dropped on the floor or to perform one of my extraordinary deeds to help a friend.

As I gazed around the room, I saw something sparkling under Mrs Brisbane's desk. 'Og, look! It's a diamond! Maybe it's pirate treasure!'

Og splished and splashed.

I stared at the twinkling object. Aldo had probably missed it with his broom. The more I thought about it, the more I realized that there probably hadn't been many pirates around lately. So what was it?

I kept my eyes on the glittering thing under the desk and as it started to get light early in the morning, I finally saw what the treasure was: Mrs Brisbane's glasses!

She had missed them, my classmates had missed them, Aldo had missed them. I hadn't missed them, but now I had no way to recover them and no way to tell anyone where they were.

'Og! Og, wake up!' I said. It's hard to tell when a frog is sleeping because he does it with his eyes open. 'I found Mrs Brisbane's glasses! They're under her desk.'

'BOING?'

'If only I had my lock-that-doesn't-lock!'

'BOING-BOING-BOING-BOING!' Og twanged loudly, bouncing up and down. What on earth was my green and lumpy friend trying to tell me?

'BOING-BOING-BOING-BOING!' Og actually hit the top of his glass house.

'Are you trying to get out? What are you saying?' I squeaked.

'BOING-BOING-BOING-BOING-BOING!' Og was going to get a sore throat from all that croaking. Obviously, he wanted me to get Mrs Brisbane's glasses, but how?

'Okay, okay, I'll try,' I squeaked, hoping to stop the racket for a while.

I'd already watched Mr Brisbane test the cage door, but I decided to try again. I jiggled it, just as I had on my good old lock-that-doesn't-lock. It didn't budge. I pushed up. I pushed down. I pushed with all my might.

The door stayed shut.

'BOING-BOING-BOING-BOING!' Og started up again. I gazed at him through the bars of my cage. He was bouncing higher and higher with each leap and he was twisting and turning in a very un-froglike way. Gail had demonstrated an old dance like that for the class one day. She called it the Twist.

'BOING-A-BOING-A-BOING-A-SCREEEE!'

Again Og twisted himself from side to side. Maybe he needed to see the vet.

Or . . . maybe he wanted me to *twist* the door handle?

I twisted it to the left and I twisted it to the right. I jiggled it and I joggled it. At least Og couldn't say I hadn't tried.

I was getting discouraged – and out of breath – when I had a new idea. I crouched down and got underneath the lock. Then I pushed up with my back and twisted it to the right.

The door flew open so fast I tumbled out onto the table and did a double somersault.

I'd opened the door! Just as I did, Og leaped so high he popped the top off his tank. He splashed around in the water with glee. I was a little dazed, but once I got my bearings, I thought about what I had to do. I didn't want to get crushed or trapped or crunched or smashed. As always, I had to have a Plan.

I went over the route in my head for a few seconds.

TICK-TICK-TICK. I checked the clock and realized that school would start soon. I glanced out of the window and it was already getting light. It was time for action.

'Wish me luck, Oggy!' I said as I leaned over the side of the table, grabbed onto the top of the table leg and slid to the ground.

The floor was really slippery – Aldo must have polished it while I was gone – so instead of running across the floor, I skated as if I were on old Dobbs's Pond with Dot. Right paws – slide. Left paws – slide. Right paws – whoa! I spun around in a circle. I slowed down and managed to slide my way to Mrs Brisbane's desk.

There's just the tiniest space between her desk and the floor. No wonder Aldo had missed seeing the glasses. Only a hamster could fit into such a tiny space. Being a small hamster often comes in quite handy.

I never realized that a pair of glasses could be so large and heavy – at least compared to me. I tried pulling them but that didn't work. Instead, I moved behind them and PUSHED-PUSHED-PUSHED until they were out on the floor, out in the open. But how was I going to get them back on the desk?

Og was going BOING-BOING-BOING again. I checked the clock. Oops! It was getting dangerously close to school time. Sometimes Mrs Brisbane came in early and I couldn't risk getting caught again. I decided to leave the glasses on the floor, cross my paws that no one would step on them and get back to my cage. Try as I could, I wasn't getting anywhere *until* I remembered watching kids on sledges after the big snowstorm in January. I threw myself on the floor and slid all the way across on my stomach. You know what? It was fun!

I got back to my table safely. Now came the tricky part. I'd done it before and I could do it again. I had to take a deep breath, grab the long cord hanging down from the blind and start swinging. I pushed to start the cord swinging. Hanging on tightly, I pushed harder and harder so each swing carried me higher. I tried to ignore that churning in my tummy. There was no time to waste!

At last, I was level with the side of the table. I closed my eyes, took a dive and slid across the table, straight to my cage. Panting, I raced inside and shut the door behind me.

'BOING-BOING-BOING!' said Og.

'Thanks,' I squeaked.

At that exact moment, the classroom door opened and the lights came on. Mrs Brisbane had arrived.

'Good morning,' she said. 'You fellows are certainly talkative this morning.'

She took off her coat and walked towards her desk. All I could think was: PLEASE-PLEASE-PLEASE let her see those glasses!

She walked straight towards them. In fact, it looked as if she was going to walk right over them.

'STOP! LOOK! LISTEN!' I squeaked.

'BOING-BOING-BOING-BOING-BOING!' Og chimed in.

Mrs Brisbane turned to Og and me. 'What on earth are you trying to say?'

Realizing there was nothing to say that she would understand, Og and I became quiet.

Then – oh joy – Mrs Brisbane looked down. 'My glasses!'

She had a big smile on her face as she picked them up. 'Why, I spent last evening tearing up my house looking for these. How did I miss them yesterday?'

She stared down at the glasses. 'Aldo might have found them but he wouldn't have left them on the floor.'

Mrs Brisbane swung around and walked towards Og and me. 'Were you trying to tell me about these? Anything is possible with the two of you. I only wish you could tell me how they got there.'

'Me too,' I squeaked weakly.

Og dived into the water and splashed around.

'Well, all I can say is thank you. And I hope you understand what I'm saying,' said Mrs Brisbane.

She turned and headed back to her desk. 'I must be losing my mind. I'm talking to a hamster and a frog,' she said softly under her breath.

But I knew she wasn't losing her mind. I was just happy that she'd found her glasses.

MRS BRISBANE'S SPECTACLES MYSTERIOUSLY DISAPPEAR!

Just as mysteriously, they reappear the next day.

The Humphreyville Herald

14

Home Sweet Humphreyville

CLANG-CLANG-CLANG!

'Hear ye, hear ye! The town of Humphreyville welcomes you!' That was A.J., ringing a bell and wearing a funny three-cornered hat. I guess Mrs Brisbane picked him to be the town crier because he had the loudest voice in the class.

'It's seven o'clock and all is well. Your tour guides will now show you around the town.'

After two weeks of excitement and lots of hurried, scurried hard work, Parents' Night had finally arrived.

I'm so used to being alone in the quiet classroom with Og on weekday nights – with a visit from Aldo – that it was strange but wonderful to see the whole room filled with my classmates' families. I knew most of them from my visits to their houses. There were A.J. and all the Thomases; the Tugwells; Heidi and Gail and their families; the Rinaldis, the Patels, all the Golden family (except the dog Clem, thank goodness), including her mom, dad, stepmum, brother Ben and stepsister Abby.

Even Paul and his mum were there. The class had voted to make him a full citizen of Humphreyville.

Each student got to be a tour guide, showing his or her own family the houses, streets, park and yes, the statue of ME! There was a pleasant hubbub as the families admired the houses. Funny, all the parents thought the very best houses were made by *their* own kids!

'Hiya, Humphrey,' a familiar voice said. It was Seth's grandmother Dot Larrabee. She was all dressed up and had bright red lips and fingernails. I hardly recognized her. 'Still the daring young man on the flying trapeze?'

I flung myself at my climbing ladder to prove that I was!

After a half an hour of oohing and aahing over Humphreyville, A.J. rang his bell again. CLANG-CLANG-CLANG.

'Hear ye, hear ye!' CLANG-CLANG-CLANG. 'The town meeting will now come to order.'

A.J. certainly liked ringing that bell. He rang it a few more times until Mrs Brisbane told him that was enough. She asked the parents to take their seats. Mostly, they sat in the kid-sized chairs (though they looked a bit silly). Aldo brought in some folding chairs, too. The students stood so that their parents could sit down.

'Mind if I stick around?' Aldo asked.

'I'd be disappointed if you didn't,' Mrs Brisbane told him.

The entire Payne family arrived a little late: Mr and Mrs Payne, Mandy, Pammy, Tammy and Bwian (Brian, of course). I thought Mrs Payne worked at night!

CLANG-CLANG-CLANG! A.J. certainly knew how to get people's attention.

'Hear ye, hear ye! Presenting Mrs Brisbane.'

The parents clapped and Mrs Brisbane came to the front of the room. 'It's great to have such a big turnout tonight. I know it's hard to get here after a long day but I wanted to share with you all the work your children have put into building their own community from scratch. I think they did a wonderful job, don't you?'

The families clapped even louder. A.J clapped too, and dropped his bell with a large CLANG!!!

'BOING-BOING!' said Og. Maybe he thought the bell was another frog.

Anyway, everybody laughed. Mrs Brisbane said it was time to introduce our special guest, Mr Dudley Dalton, a member of our own town council.

A tall, very thin man with large round glasses and a skinny moustache came to the front of the room. When the clapping stopped, he cleared his throat and pulled a piece of paper out of his jacket pocket.

'Thank you, uh, Mrs Brisbane,' he said. 'I am honoured to be here to share this evening with these, uh, wonderful young people of Longfellow School. Truly, they are a, uh, credit to our community.'

He smiled slightly, as if smiling hurt his face.

'Since we've had a look at Humpfeeville – I mean Humphreyville – tonight, I'd like to share with you some background about our, uh, own town and how it's grown over the years.'

Mr Dudley Dalton unfolded the paper and began to read. And read. And READ-READ-READ. Instead of reading something like a story, he read facts and figures, dates and something he called 'statistics' which were harder to understand than the hardest vocabulary word we've ever had.

All the parents and students tried hard to concentrate on what Mr Dalton was saying, but as he went on and on, it was harder to pay attention. If only he could have made the reading of his statistics as interesting as Mrs Brisbane makes her stories sound! Soon, I saw Seth start to fidget. His sister Lucinda gave him a hard jab in the ribs with her elbow and he settled down again.

Mr and Mrs Payne looked a little drowsy and when I glanced at my friend Dot, I saw that her eyes were closed and her chin was dropping. Didn't Mr Dudley Dalton notice that he was putting his audience to sleep? I suppose not, since he never looked up from his paper, not once.

Everyone tried hard to pay attention until Mr Dalton got stuck on the word 'economics'. It's a hard word, I'll admit, but when he said 'eek-o-momics', Gail started giggling. And what's worse, Gail's mum started giggling, too.

Mr Dalton corrected himself: 'Economics.'

'And that pretty much sums up the growth of this wonderful community that we all call home.'

He folded up his paper and everyone applauded, probably because they were relieved that he had finished. When everyone clapped, Dot's eyes opened wide, her head jerked up and she said 'Oh!' rather loudly. The applause had stopped, so Mrs Brisbane asked her if she had a question.

Dot stood up. 'Not a question, just a comment. Facts and figures are fine, but what makes up a community is people. And I've known some pretty interesting people in my lifetime here.'

'*Mother*,' Mrs Stevenson whispered. '*Sit down*.'

'*Grandma*,' Lucinda whispered. '*Please*!'

But Mrs Brisbane smiled. 'I couldn't agree more.'

That encouraged Dot to keep going. I was hoping she'd tell the story of the dancing bear.

'For example, when I was growing up here –'

Lucinda groaned loudly and Seth squirmed in his chair, but that didn't stop Dot.

'I grew up in a yellow house with white trim, down on Alder Street. They were nice houses down there with big trees around them and a shop on the corner. Even though it wasn't as big as this room, you could find anything you'd want in that shop.'

'Where Pet-O-Rama is now!' I squeaked. I hadn't planned on saying anything. It just slipped out. Gail and her mum started giggling again. That didn't stop Dot, either.

'You kids like the shopping centre, but did you know there used to be a roller skating rink there with an amusement park next door? Had a merry-go-round and a ferris wheel. Oh, and there were pony rides, too!'

Boy, I have to say, Dot had everyone's attention now. Mr Dudley Dalton nervously folded and refolded his paper while she talked.

'When you talk about history, you have to know the facts and figures, of course. You also have to know how people lived. What they did, how they thought, what they did for fun.' Dot was running out of steam or else she was getting tired of Lucinda tugging on her skirt, trying to get her to sit down. 'Anyway, that's my opinion.' She sat down. Lucinda, Mrs Stevenson and Seth all seemed pretty nervous, but then, a nice thing happened.

People began to applaud. Not for Mr Dudley Dalton of the town council, but for Dot. Mrs Brisbane clapped, too. When the applause died down, Mrs Brisbane said, 'Class, I think we've found our next social studies project. I think we should get out and interview people like Mrs Larrabee and find out what life used to be like in this town. You can talk to your parents, your grandparents, your neighbours. Mr Brisbane works down at the Senior Citizens' Centre. I think that would also be a good place to meet people. What do you think, Mr Dalton?'

'A fine idea,' he said, running a handkerchief across his forehead. 'People are our, uh, finest resource.'

Mrs Brisbane did a good job of wrapping things up so that people could go home. Instead of leaving, parents and their children gathered around Dot, asking her questions about the amusement park and Alder Street and saying they'd like to get together. Dot's skin was rosy and she was smiling a lot more than when I'd stayed at the house.

'I think Grandma's a star,' I heard Seth's mother tell her children.

'*Great*,' said Lucinda, rolling her eyes dramatically.

It turns out that Dot wasn't the only one drawing a crowd. The entire Payne family gathered around my cage. For the first time since I'd known them, they were all smiling at once!

'Here's our boy,' said Mrs Payne.

'Yessir. Humphrey, we owe you our thanks. I'm sorry you had to go to the vet's. But if you hadn't, I never would have got that job at the veterinary surgery. A good job, too. Nice people and nice animals,' said Mr Payne.

YIPPEE! He not only got the job but he liked it!

'I think I'm going to take some classes so that I can get promoted,' he added.

YIPPEE-YIPPEE-YIPPEE!

'Without you, I wouldn't have been able to go back on the day shift and spend more time with the kids,' said Mrs Payne.

'And I wouldn't have got my very own hamster,' said Mandy. 'You know . . . Winky. He's the cutest hamster I've ever seen. Next to you, of course.'

Winky the toothless, one-eyed hamster had a real home!

'Thanks, Humphrey. You can come to our house any time,' said Mrs Payne.

'Next time *I* get to hold him,' said Pammy.

'No, *I* get to hold him,' said Tammy.

'Me too, me too!' said Brian.

Some things never change, I suppose. Winky had his paws full, living at the Paynes' house. Somehow, I knew he could handle it.

Later that night, after Aldo had taken away the folding chairs, it was quiet in Room 26, except for the TICK-TICK-TICK of the clock.

I spent some time writing about the evening's events in my notebook. The moon was full and bright. Even in the moonlight, I could see buds of green on the trees outside. The evening was warm. March was almost over and just as Dot had predicted, it was going out like a lamb.

'Og?' I finally squeaked. 'Og, are you awake?'

I heard some gentle splashing so I knew he couldn't be sleeping.

'Room 26 is a pretty special place, don't you agree?'

Og replied with a friendly, agreeable 'BOING.'

I glanced across the room. There was the town of Humphreyville spread across several tables. In the moonlight, it looked even more like a real town than during the day. It would all be over soon, of course. Mrs Brisbane was going to let my friends take their houses home with them. The room would go back to the way it used to be.

I crouched down and pushed up on the lock with all my might. The door swung open.

'It's a lovely night for a stroll,' I told Og. 'Sorry you can't join me.'

'BOING!' Og started bouncing so high, he might as well have been on a trampoline. What was he trying to tell me now?

'BOING-BOING-BOING-BOING-SCREEE!' My old pal did it again. He popped the top of his tank, leaped out and landed on the bag of Nutri-Nibbles nearby.

I must admit, I was worried when I saw him there. It took a lot of effort for him to bounce up high enough to get out of his tank. But how on earth was he going to bounce back in? And if he was out of the water for too long, he could be in big trouble. But he was already out of his cage and there wasn't a thing I could do about it except enjoy his company.

'It's a lovely night for a stroll,' I repeated. 'And I'm so glad you can join me!'

Og and I scurried along our table until we reached Humphreyville. The table it was on was quite a bit lower than ours. I remembered what Aldo had said about broken bones, so instead of jumping, I lowered myself by my paws and dangled there for a second, then gently dropped down. I landed pretty hard and even did a somersault, but we hamsters are good acrobats. Og had no problem making the big leap.

There we were, on the main street of Humphreyville: Taco Boulevard. For the first time, I realized that the houses were just the right size for a hamster like me or for a frog like Og. We strolled past A.J.'s house of blocks, which was next door to Miranda's purple castle. Across the street was a long drawing of shops, a cinema, a bowling alley – even a pet shop – which all my friends had worked on.

We turned down Basketball Avenue, past Garth's log cabin, which was next door to a small house with a large basketball court. That was Tabitha's house, naturally. She loved sport more than anything. On Soccer Street, we saw Seth's rocket-ship house. Sayeh's block of flats stood across from Art's amazing merry-go-round house with the slide coming down and the train tracks going through it. Across the street was a smaller version of Art's house. It was Paul's place, of course.

Video Game Way crossed at the corner and there was Gail's bright-yellow house with a picket fence around it and flowers painted on it. Pizza Place had a pizza parlour as well as the court house, with its cardboard pillars and a clock up on top. On this clock, it was always twelve o'clock. That meant it was either noon or midnight. Next to the court house was the school and playground.

We turned down Break Lane, which led to the large park and the playground and a baseball diamond. The grassy Og the Frog nature reserve had been moved to one side of the park.

'Nice sign,' I said. Og twanged in agreement.

We stopped in the centre of the park and stared up at the tall statue. There I was larger than life – and golden! Even a golden hamster was never that golden before. On the base of the statue it said: 'To Humphrey. A friend in need is a friend indeed.'

It's a funny kind of saying, but I thought about it and realized it's true. March had roared in like a lion, blowing in a whole lot of trouble for the students in Room 26. Seth's jitteriness, Art's failing marks, Mandy's unhappy family, and especially Miranda being wrongly accused of something she didn't do. These were my friends and I did my best to help them. Now March was ending and all those troubles had blown away with the blustery winds.

Tomorrow, Humphreyville would be gone. But my friends would still be there and Mrs Brisbane, Aldo and Og as well.

We walked back through the town and headed back to our table. I was relieved to see that Og had no trouble hopping up onto the table. He then leaped to the Nutri-Nibbles bag, bounced his way up to the top and then, with one enormous leap, jumped back into the tank where he landed with a very impressive splash!

'Well done, Oggy!' I complimented him. Of course tomorrow, Mrs Brisbane would find the top off his tank and wonder about it, but somehow I wasn't worried.

Once I was back in the safety of my cage, I felt unsqueakably happy.

'You know what, Og? We turned out to have the BEST-BEST-BEST jobs of all! The classroom pets of Room 26!'

'BOING-BOING-BOING-BOING!' Og agreed.

I'm absolutely positive that he was saying 'Yes'.

FAMILIES PROCLAIM HUMPHREYVILLE TO BE THE PERFECT COMMUNITY!

Students say they'll always think of Humphreyville as their home town.

The Humphreyville Herald

Humphrey's tips for staying (and getting) out of trouble

1. If you make a mistake and get into trouble, it's always a good idea to admit you're wrong and say you're sorry.
2. Sometimes you get into trouble for something you didn't do. Try and stay calm but squeak up for yourself and explain what really happened. (This doesn't always work but you can TRY-TRY-TRY.)
3. If you get into trouble and lie about it, you'll only get into more trouble – so always squeak the truth!
4. When a good friend (like Miranda) gets into trouble, sometimes you feel as bad as your friend does. That's what friends are for.
5. When a good friend (like Seth or Art) gets into trouble, a good friend (like Paul or me) can sometimes lend an ear – or a paw – and help out.
6. When a friend (like Og) warns you

that you're about to get into trouble – listen!

7 If people do something mean, like get you into trouble or even get you banished from your classroom, remember: they may have an even *bigger* problem than you do.

8 If you think you have troubles, think of someone worse off than you are, like my friend Winky, the reject hamster (whose troubles are happily now over).

9 A famous writer named Sophocles once said, 'Trouble brings trouble upon trouble'. I'm having trouble figuring that one out!

10 Another famous writer named George Herbert said, 'He that seeks trouble never misses.' Now *that* I understand! So don't go looking for trouble – please!

And remember: everyone gets into trouble at some time, even classroom hamsters and teachers. So if trouble comes your way, don't worry. You're in good company!

Join me for more
FUN-FUN-FUN
adventures . . .

Dear Friends,

I love my life as the classroom hamster in Room 26 of Longfellow School because it's always full of surprises. This time, there are fire alarms ringing, whistles blowing, Wacky Wednesday, an exciting new hamster ball, and a close encounter with an unsqueakably unfriendly cat. Eek! Even more surprising, an alien from outer space takes over Aldo's job! How can one little hamster keep up with it all? You'll find out in my latest book of adventures, so READ-READ-READ!

Humphrey

Available Now!

Ahoy, maties!

As the classroom hamster in Room 26 of Longfellow School, I've had many exciting adventures. But I really outdid myself when I set sail in a tiny boat and almost ended up at the bottom of Potter's Pond. And that was before I met up with a band of SCARY-SCARY-SCARY pirates! My paw was still shaking when I first scribbled the tale in my notebook, and I left out a few details. Now that I'm rested up, I've written out the whole story, including my mysterious midnight trips to the library, why Stop-Giggling-Gail actually stopped giggling, and the unsqueakably wonderful surprise at the end.

Your adventurous pal,

Humphrey

Available Now!

Dear friends,

I was unsqueakably worried when I learned that the end of school was near! I couldn't imagine life without Longfellow School and what I would do once I lost my job as classroom pet.

It turned out that summer was wilder than school could ever be. I saw new sights, made new friends and had FUN-FUN-FUN. But I also had to deal with strange new creatures, Og's mysterious disappearance and the scary-sounding Howler!

It wasn't the most relaxing holiday but it turned out to be my greatest adventure yet – and now you can read all about it!

Your pal forever,

Humphrey

Out February 2010!

Humphrey's Book of Fun-fun-Fun

Dear friends,

I LOVE-LOVE-LOVE being the classroom hamster in Room 26, Longfellow School. I've learned a lot about reading, writing, maths and making friends . . . and I've had amazing adventures, too. But I also love solving puzzles and riddles in the tiny notebook I keep hidden in my cage. They're not always easy but if I wiggle my whiskers and scratch my furry head for a while, I usually can solve them.

I'm sharing some of my favourites in this fun-filled book so you can find out if you're as smart as a hamster! (I'll bet you are.)

Your puzzle-loving pal,

Humphrey

What's more fun than a computer mouse? A computer hamster – that's me! You can have FUN-FUN-FUN with me online at my website:

www.funwithhumphrey.com